The Tree of Heaven

The tormented branches of the lofty Tree of Heaven cast their shadow about the house in Mornington Gardens where Mark Dolmen lived. In some ways this fine and uncommon tree is a symbol of events in Mr. Raymond's story. Its long roots, more than a century old, threaten to strike at the foundations of his home.

As the story opens, Mark, a distinguished surgeon, is about to become the first Labour mayor in the Borough of Keys. His home, with its pretentious Victorian façade, stands out, newly decorated, from all the others in a grey decaying street. He has refused to leave the home of his childhood, and in it he lives with his schoolboy son, while next door, in the twin house, also his property, live a well-loved niece and her mother—soon to be his mayoress.

His life has been fairly happy and successful so far, its one great sorrow the death long ago of his young wife. He has remained faithful to her memory, except once when he brought home for the night Desiderata, an Italian prostitute. And now, a year later, he meets her again and, as before, brings her home.

This starts the chain of disaster—an unexpected death, a guilty burial, the appearance of a sinister figure who knows enough to blackmail, a murder—and thereafter the enduring remorse, the hidden attempts at reparation, the fear.

Two years, three years, pass; all seems safe; fear is forgotten—when a shattering threat falls from the most unexpected quarter, his own Borough Council of which he is still the mayor. The nature of this threat and its issue are the climax of the story.

BOOKS BY ERNEST RAYMOND

NOVELS
A London Gallery *comprising:*

We, the Accused
The Marsh
Gentle Greaves
The Witness of Canon Welcome
A Chorus Ending
The Kilburn Tale
Child of Norman's End
For Them That Trespass
A Georgian Love Story

Was There Love Once?
The Corporal of the Guard
A Song of the Tide
The Chalice and the Sword
To the Wood No More
The Lord of Wensley
The Old June Weather
The City and the Dream
Our Late Member

Miryam's Guest House

Other Novels

The Bethany Road
The Mountain Farm
One of Our Brethren
Late in the Day
Mr. Olim
The Chatelaine
The Visit of Brother Ives
The Quiet Shore
The Nameless Places
Tell England
A Family that Was
A Jesting Army

Mary Leith
Morris in the Dance
The Old Tree Blossomed
Don John's Mountain Home
The Five Sons of Le Faber
The Last to Rest
Newtimber Lane
The Miracle of Brean
Rossenal
Damascus Gate
Wanderlight
Daphne Bruno I

Daphne Bruno II

BIOGRAPHIES, ETC.
The Story of My Days (Autobiography I)
Please You Draw Near (Autobiography II)
Good Morning, Good People (Autobiography III)
Paris, City of Enchantment
Two Gentlemen of Rome (The Story of Keats and Shelley)
In the Steps of St. Francis
In the Steps of the Brontës

ESSAYS, ETC.
Through Literature to Life
The Shout of the King
Back to Humanity (with Patrick Raymond)

PLAYS
The Berg
The Multabello Road

The Tree of Heaven

by

ERNEST RAYMOND

CASSELL · LONDON

CASSELL & COMPANY LTD
35 Red Lion Square, London WC1R 4SG
Sydney, Auckland
Toronto, Johannesburg

First edition June 1965
First edition, second impression January 1974

ISBN: 0 304 29276 1

Printed in Great Britain by
Fletcher & Son Ltd, Norwich
873

To the good memory

of

NEWMAN FLOWER

my publisher, counsellor and friend

of forty years

Author's Note

The Borough of Keys has no existence outside the covers of this story. It is conceived as a twenty-ninth metropolitan borough lying on the extreme west of the true twenty-eight which filled the metropolitan area round the City of London until they all disappeared as independent authorities in the great mergings of 1965.

The period of the story can be understood as beginning some six or seven years before this general merger.

E. R.

Contents

1. The Count

It happened in the Borough of Keys. Keys lies to the west of the old metropolitan boroughs of London, so far west that its postal district is numbered West 24. That its charter as a borough should date back to 1901 is, on the face of it, surprising since so much of it is red-brick villas, street after street of them; and this suggests a dormitory suburb for daily travellers to London. But, islanded in the heart of Keys, there are high old grey Victorian houses, ornate and pompous once, but mostly worn, decayed and crumbling now. They speak of a prosperous Keys a hundred years ago; and it is with one of these old time-deserted houses, as it stood till yesterday, that we shall have to deal.

The Town Hall of the borough looks only recent. Built just before the Second Great War as a successor to the old Vestry Hall, it is a square steel-framed pile faced with white stone and ornamented with Doric columns along its stylobate. This imposing temple—I had almost called it this big white mausoleum —fronts the Keys High Road where the traffic roars all day towards or homeward from London.

A morning in May, only a few years ago, in a long avenue by the side of the Town Hall the cars stood parked, bumper to bumper, under a march of municipal trees as far as eyes could see. It was as if a mayoral levee or ball was taking place in the Town Hall, but ten in the morning was hardly the hour for a party. None the less, people on the pavements, hurrying about their morning business, heard a blend of many voices up there in the Assembly Hall on the first floor. A serious occasion it seemed, because young men stood in the vestibule, checking passes and resisting frivolous entry. And not only this: most oddly, and with the aid of a large, benevolent policeman, they were resisting any exit from the building.

There were, in fact, a great many people in the Assembly Hall upstairs, and many of them were seated at long parallel tables, just as at a banquet, while others sat at a 'Head Table' crossing the tops of these parallel tables. Others were walking along the lanes between the tables and peering over the shoulders of those seated there. Yet others sat on chairs along the walls, under colourful portraits of honoured but forgotten mayors. One is tempted to say that the great room this morning was a flower-garden because nearly all the people sitting along the walls or walking between the tables were wearing rosettes, green, red, and blue rosettes; and not small rosettes, either; most were as big as dahlias or chrysanthemums; and some of the more enthusiastic rivalled the sunflowers.

This was not a party; it was a Count. Yesterday saw the polling for a new Borough Council; today they were counting the votes. Those at the long parallel tables were the 'counting assistants', sitting in teams with their captains in the midst of them, all bowed over the ballot papers; those along the top table were the Town Clerk, presiding as Returning Officer, with his deputy and other departmental officers left and right of him. The people behind their rosettes, whether walking about or seated like wallflowers, were the candidates for the borough's six wards, their 'spouses' (whom the Law allows in on such occasions), their agents, and their party executives. Blue rosettes embellished the Tories, red the Socialists, green the Liberals; and blue, red and green went floating behind the counting tables as their wearers studied how the count was going: who was ahead, who lagged, who'd 'got it in the bag' and who 'hadn't a hope'.

Of all these scrutineers none was more conspicuous than Mark Dolmen, a Labour member of the old council, seeking re-election. Sixty next year, tall, of round and comfortable rather than corpulent shape, scrupulously dressed in the black jacket and striped trousers of an eminent surgeon, he looked less like a

2

Socialist councillor than (as the wags of Keys liked to say) 'one of our most senior clergy, a suffragan bishop at least'—though what round bishop or portly dean would wear, every day of the year as Mark Dolmen did, a red carnation in his button-hole, except in June and July when he usually wore a pink rose? Perhaps this episcopal appearance was in part suggested by the gold-rimmed 'quizzing glass' which hung always on black silk cord down the front of his breast. Since the neat little gold-rimmed eye-glass had a gold handle, it was not too unlike a pectoral cross; and in fact Councillor Dolmen sometimes called it his pectoral cross. At this moment, bending over one of the counters, he had lifted it close to his right eye to study the present position of a candidate. A red Labour rosette (instead of a carnation) on a breast so prosperous-looking was perhaps something of a surprise even in these days. One would have supposed a capitalist and high Tory here.

By his side walked another big man, a square-shouldered heavy-built, loosely dressed man, to whom anyone might have applied the term 'burly', while no one would have thought of applying it to the elegant Mark Dolmen. The large red rosette sat much more fittingly on his untidy breast, and, in fact, Councillor Arthur Lammas was the leader of the Labour minority group in the late council. If Councillor Dolmen's features, under his close-cut silver hair, were finely cut and suggested distinction, those of Councillor Lammas were brief and blunt and rude—as brief and blunt and rude as some of his remarks in council.

The counting table behind which these two large figures moved was the one where they were counting the votes in the Brides Ward. Because, *if* the Brides Ward fell to Labour this time, as many expected, then control of the Council would pass from the Tories to the Socialists for the first time in the history of Keys. No wonder blue rosettes drifted behind the reds of Mark Dolmen and Arthur Lammas, and their wearers peered down at the counters' sheets.

If the Brides Ward fell . . .

'Good enough so far,' said Arthur Lammas to Mark. 'Mary and Humph are well ahead. Even if only they and Mossy and Bill get in, we shall have our majority. A majority of one.'

3

'Yes, but we could do with all eight seats,' said Mark, 'if we're to sit comfortably in control.'

'*And* we're going to get 'em.' Arthur Lammas dropped his voice because of a blue rosette behind. 'God, what a jar for the bloody Tories. Keys a Socialist borough! Gor! And likewise Blimey!'

'Bill Hutch is romping ahead.'

'Yes, yes. The Brides are in the bag, I think; all eight of 'em. Gawd's Love!'

'Arthur, can you believe that those who built the Brides Ward houses ever foresaw the day when their tenants would vote Labour?'

'No, because they never foresaw that their fine houses'd turn into over-crowded and slummy tenements—if you'll forgive me saying so, Mark, dear boy, being as how you live in one of 'em.'

'Go ahead, Arthur. Say what you like.'

'Well, yours may be properly looked after, but it's the only one that is. It always beats me how a blasted plutocrat like you can live in an antediluvian place like that.'

'It was my father's house before me, I was born in it, I've lived fifty-nine years in it, and I intend to die in it.'

'Your old man built it, didn't he?'

'Lord, no. He was only just born when those houses were built. He bought it in the eighties when he really began to make money.'

'Wonder what he'd have said if he'd lived to see you a Labour councillor.'

'He'd have survived. It was my mòther who'd have turned her face to the wall and died.'

'I suppose she had heaps of servants to run that awful great place.' Arthur, sprung from poor parents and a pinched home, could still be fascinated by thoughts of wealth.

'She had three.'

'How paid?'

'Twenty pounds the cook, twelve the housemaid, six the tweeny.'

'Christ!' said this Labour leader. And then, 'Gawd!'

And Mark endorsed, 'I agree.'

As they talked of these things Mark was seeing the house and

4

the long street in which it stood: Mornington Gardens, a straight wide road of massive, grey-brick, large-windowed, stucco-dressed houses, representing the first advance of money-making London into the green fields around the little western village of Keys. Proud homes then, pompous and pretentious, but old and moribund now. They had a certain loneliness in Keys because they had long since been caught up and surrounded by the red-brick homes which were lower in roof and got smaller and smaller as the decades passed, wealth went farther afield, and the pools of household servants drained away. In the long drear stretch of Mornington Gardens, Mark was seeing only one house well painted and dressed, his own, No. 21, where it stood in startling contrast to all its neighbours at the corner of Menworthy Rise. All these old mansions, so grey and melancholy now, stood in the Brides Ward, a polling district carrying this name because the Seven Brides Road ran through it, and some sixty acres of it were known as the Seven Brides Estate. Why 'Seven Brides' no one knew any more. There were theories to account for the strange, haunting words, but no local scholar would swear by any of them. Some lost legend lay buried for ever in the name.

'Mossy and Bill are well home.' Arthur, looking down on a counter's sheet, dispersed this vision of Mornington Gardens. 'Hurray. God bless the Brides.'

Mark put up his quizzing glass and looked down on the same sheet. 'That's four. If four are home and dry it means the other four'll come too.'

'It does. And it'll mean we shall have a majority of seven. Eight if a Lib. wins in Park Ward, and George Colls looks like doing it.' Arthur slammed a huge broad palm on Mark's back. 'End of Tory rule in Keys, old cock.'

'Thanks to the Brides Ward. And chiefly, I'd say, to the Mornington Gardens area where I have the honour to live. We've swamped the red-brick area which is Tory to a man. Arthur, we've been trying to seduce the Tories' brides for a dozen years, and we've debauched them at last.'

Arthur gave little heed to this witticism. Still looking down on the figures, his only answer was, 'Yes, poor bloody Tories.'

A great stirring in the room. Everyone reporting to everyone else that the Brides Ward had fallen. Red rosettes hurrying with the news, 'We've won it.' Blue rosettes deploring to one another, 'The Brides has gone.' Mark looked around at Tory councillors to see how they were taking it.

There walked Major Roper, leader of the Tories, another big heavy man but very different from Arthur Lammas. He had a small beaked nose which dipped towards a small crisp military moustache and the tight straight mouth of a disciplinarian. Strange in an old soldier, but he was a waddling man; under the accumulating weight of sixty-three years, he went waddling now from side to side on large bandy legs in wide billowing trousers. 'The heavy father', Mark called him.

There, long and thin, and standing alone, was Merlin Evans. 'Evans the Echo' was Mark's name for Merlin because, while he never rose in council to offer a speech, he never ceased to murmur endorsements from his seat, one or two every minute, such as 'Yes, yes' and 'I agree with that' and 'Hear, hear' and 'No, of course not; no, no.' Sometimes he even finished the last words of a speaker before the orator could encompass them himself, so remarkable an echo was he, able to repeat sounds even before they occurred.

And there, wandering around was James O'Donoghue, a little Irish dandy, in a pale brown neat-waisted suit, with a pale brown bow-tie, shirt, handkerchief and socks—all pale brown to accompany his sandy hair. Mark usually addressed him as 'Shamus' rather than 'James', holding that so decorative a little person deserved the more decorative and exotic name. Not a doubt about *his* election as one of the eight councillors for the North Ward. Put up a tailor's dummy as Tory candidate in the well-to-do North Ward and it'd be elected with a handsome majority. At least, so said the Opposition.

Seated under the picture of Sir Torrens Hawkhurst, famous and now forgotten mayor, was Mrs. Pearl Runciman, the Rector's wife and another candidate for the North Ward. 'Our Pearl,' Mark used to say, 'is a very large pearl indeed and a damned vigorous one. Pearl sees no reason at all why she shouldn't fight strenuously for the Conservatives and so guide the souls of her husband's cure into the ways of truth. Father Runciman sees several reasons why she shouldn't, but they don't impress her. With our Pearl a duty is a duty.' Most of the other

6

Tories seemed merry enough, probably because they'd come into the hall fearing the loss of the Brides Ward and partly resigned to it. Only Pearl Runciman sat disconsolate and indrawn, her mouth tight, as if she were angry that so many of her husband's flock should have scampered away from her shepherding.

Half-past eleven. 'Park's finished,' said Arthur. 'One Lib. in. George Colls. First time in history. He's kicked out Tom Houser.'

'How's Old Common going? Am I being kicked out?'

'Don't be daft, Mark. Old Common's never kicked out a Labour boy yet. You're safe as houses, Mr. Mayor.'

'*What* did you say then?'

'I said you're quite safe, Mr. Mayor.'

'For God's sake don't start calling me Mr. Mayor before I'm even elected. It's as unlucky as to call a girl Mrs. Smith before she's married Smith.'

'That's bilge. You've got Smith in your pocket. The borough's yours. What's it feel like, Mr. Mayor?'

'What I'm chiefly feeling is that *you* ought to be mayor.'

'No, no, Mark, old boy. We've all decided who's going to be the first Labour mayor of Keys. No arguing.'

'But you've been on the Council far longer than any of us.'

'Thirty-odd years.'

'Just so.'

'Just so, and cut it out. We're not fools and we know we're lucky to have you for mayor. You're a great scholar—'

'On the contrary, a very small one.'

'Well, anyhow, you're a famous surgeon, known all over the country—'

'And that's another gross exaggeration—'

'—while I'm only a thoroughly mediocre chap. Just a common craftsman—'

'So'm I—'

'Before I started up on my own in the jobbing builder's line— and my first office, I may tell you, was my little parlour in Hobman Street—I was just a carpenter, joiner, plumber, gasfitter and drain-layer, all rolled into one.'

'Which is an excellent description of a surgeon.'

'Oh, wash it out, Mark. We want you for the window. *You're* going to make the headlines. Nobody'd want to write a line about me. We reckon it's good for the Party all over the country that people should see we've plenty of distinguished and out-and-out gentlemen on our side.'

'Out-and-out gentlemen! It's only the other day that surgeons were hack assistants to the local barber. And hack's probably the right word.'

'I'm not talking about the other day. I'm talking about Now. You're a big name. And, what's more, you're far and away our best and wittiest speaker. God, I always envy the superb ease with which you speak. For my part I can only sit and gape at it.'

Ease. Superb ease. So little our best friends know of us, thought Mark. Who in the Council knew that this apparent ease and fluency and impromptu phrasing, this instant readiness with the aptest word, were all an act; who knew that his major speeches were written out word for word at home, then learned by heart, and rehearsed night after night, or that sometimes they were delivered with every grace of pause and pitch and tempo, but with a nervous heart thumping in its private place; who knew that after this hidden distress he had to comfort himself with memories of Lister who was nervous on public platforms till the end? A little of this he might admit to some, but only a little of it, and even that little to only a few, so precious a possession was his fame as a speaker. Let him alone know that his art, fine as it might be, was the art of an actor, not of an orator.

'I'd much rather you were mayor, Arthur. Or Ronnie Scott.' (And what liars we all are. Here am I, acting a modest recoil from the honour, and all the time I'm tingling with pleasure at the thought of being the first Labour mayor of a Tory citadel, and having my name published abroad—which will be a nice comfortable advertisement for Mark Dolmen, the well-known surgeon in Queen Anne Street. Yea, all men are certainly liars, as the sparks fly upward.) 'I've a horrible feeling I shall make every kind of blunder in the job.' (But did one really mean this? One did not.)

'Well, we're all allowed a few mistakes in our jobs.'

'Yes, but when surgeons make a bad mistake, it's quickly put under ground, and it's relatives put an ornamental stone over it. I take it there's no such easy disposal of a mayoral blunder. And, my God, Arthur, a first Labour mayor ought to shine, not blunder.'

'Shine you will, cock. That's a cert.'

'Permit me to doubt.' He left Arthur's side, ostensibly to go and talk with Elsie Faber sitting wearily by the wall after making sure of her failure in a Tory ward; but really with a view to leaving her quickly and visiting the table where they were counting the Old Common votes. 'Well, Elsie, where are you going to be?' he asked.

'Somewhere at the bottom of the poll, Mark.'

'Well, never mind, my dear. You've flown the flag for us. We all owe a lot to you who fight without a hope. For us in Old Common it's just a walk-over. We have all the luck.'

'The Brides did well.'

'Yes . . . yes. . . .' And so to the Old Common table. Here, looking through his little gold-rimmed glass over a counter's shoulder, he saw that the votes after his name were lagging behind those given to Jack Freece and Sarah Bonnell. This was a stab of disappointment, a secret humiliation, not that there was any chance of his being thrown out, but that in the last two elections he had topped the poll whereas now he looked like lying third. A sick fall of the heart. Hide it. Go and sit quietly by Sarah. 'You're doing well, Sarah dear.' 'You too, Mark.' 'Not too bad, Sarah. Enough. Enough. It will serve.'

He did not sit long with Sarah, for a rustling everywhere, and a gravitation of many towards the Town Clerk's seat, showed that the counting was completed, the full results in. The Town Clerk, after a discussion with the candidates' agents, would rise and proclaim the results. Silence gathered around him, and at last he rose. A small man with humour about his eyes and lips, he kept the crucial Brides result till the end. In the other five wards the situation was as before, except for the election of George Colls, a sole Liberal, which was greeted with clapping and cheering, some really joyous, most merely humorous.

But now the Brides Ward. Last election two seats had fallen to Labour. This time?

All eight seats.

A roar of triumph from the red rosettes, a clapping that

9

endured a whole minute and then rose even louder for a second spell; a slapping of the backs of all eight winners; Ronnie Scott coming excitedly to Mark's side. 'Don't we sing the Red Flag, Mark?' 'God's pity, no! Got to use some tact now. Arthur, get going. This is your moment. Be pleasant to them all, and especially the Tories. It's definitely not their hour. Go on, Leader of the majority party.'

'Okay, Mr. Mayor.' And Arthur Lammas raised a hand to stem the applause, a gesture which only stirred up more applause for him. When he could speak he expressed, as custom demanded, his thanks to the Returning Officer, to all the counting assistants who had counted so excellently, to his opponents who'd served the borough for such long years and earned (he hoped) an equally long rest, and lastly—as duty did *not* demand —to the voters who had voted so sensibly.

Major Roper, the Tories' heavy father perhaps, but a good loser, and a sportsman whose tight, grim, military lips could smile at once grimly and pleasingly, waddled bear-like up to Arthur's side and followed him with a generous speech. 'I'm sure that the Labour group in the Council, now that they will have to bear the burden of control will, under the able leadership of our friend, Councillor Lammas, learn wisdom and display a sense of responsibility which perhaps has not been too evident in the past—' laughing *'Grrr, g'rrr's . . . !'* from the Labour group—'and I'm confident that Councillor Dolmen will make a very fine mayor for the short time he will occupy that office.'

'Hear, *hear!*' and 'Not so short, cock' from Arthur.

George Colls, the single Liberal, got an amused, satiric, but friendly cheer as he declared he was the first swallow of a Liberal summer, a dove to the ark, and various other things that foreshadowed a Liberal salvation for Keys.

Speeches done, Mark walked to the telephone in a neighbouring room that he might tell his sister the result. He walked with a studied slowness because he was feeling more pleasure than he cared to show. Mayor. . . . First citizen. . . . But the telephone was in the enthusiastic control of Stanley Mace, the Chief Reporter of the *Keys and Hadleigh News*, who was briskly reporting a sensation to the Exchange Telegraph, the Press Association and the London evening papers. 'Copy. . . . Wait for the copy, typist. . . .

Mace of Keys. . . . Keys election. Catch line "Labour Landslide". Labour wins Keys Tory stronghold for fifty years, comma . . . Keys Council dramatically swings over to Labour in borough election stop. Tories lose nine seats all told par [paragraph]. In his speech Councillor Arthur Lammas leader of the Labour party said quotes This is a great day for us we have been gaining ground in the last three elections and now at last we have brought the mighty Tory party to its knees close quotes. It is thought that Councillor Mark Dolmen, the well-known surgeon of Harley Street—mistake—not Harley Street Queen Anne Street—Councillor Dolmen is here at my side—it is thought he will be the first Labour mayor in the history of Keys.'

2. The House

Councillor Mark Dolmen walked homeward with little Jamie O'Donoghue ('Shamus') at his side. Jamie as he walked swung between two fingers an ivory-topped malacca cane whose coffee-brown sheen matched happily with his pale-brown suit and with his curly-brimmed brown bowler hat, which now crowned all. Mark, whose black Homburg hat was at least eight inches above little Jamie's bowler, carried his rolled umbrella on his shoulder, like a gun at the slope. This had lately become a habit of his, unconscious at first, but often conscious now. Nowadays when he realized it was upon his shoulder he might leave it there because he was not unwilling to have a faint reputation for eccentricity in Keys. To have one's little eccentricities spoken of with laughter was half-way to being loved. One loved those that amused one. So, walking with Jamie now, he left the umbrella at the slope.

Mayor-elect. Such was the secret glow in his heart that it almost prevented him from hearing Jamie's chatter. But he said 'Yes' and 'No' and 'Yes, I agree'—rather like Evans the Echo in council—because he was fond of Jamie and couldn't hurt him. 'Who could feel other than friendly,' he would ask, 'to anything so small and ornamental as Shamus?'

Now they were entering the first streets of the Seven Brides Estate, and Mark looked up at windows as they went by. 'Neither your constituents or mine, Shamus, but God bless them all, even those who still voted for your boys and girls.'

'Anyone could guess, Mark, that your Mornington Gardens area'd go Labour at last. The whole district's gone to pieces. But will you tell me again,' demanded Jamie, swinging between ringed fingers the fine malacca cane, which suggested his need of elegant surroundings, 'how you still manage to live there.'

'Home of my childhood, Shamus. Laden with memories.'

'Yes, but Mornington Gardens is surely the dreariest road in the borough.'

'Undoubtedly.'

'My father always says'—Jamie still lived with his parents at forty—'that the whole Mornington area is like one of the shabbiest parts of North Kensington which has somehow got lost out here.'

'Admirable description. But I can assure you it was mighty respectable some sixty years ago when I woke up in it. And here we come, Shamus, into the celebrated street.'

Mornington Gardens stretched before them: wide pavements, flagged and black-greased with recent mud; broad carriageway tarred and dark; tall grey houses not terraced but in pairs, each pair of twins a big square box under grey slates; narrow gardens in front of the semi-basements; long walled gardens behind, shadowed by trees now grown old and huge—it was mid-Victorian London indeed. And Mornington *Gardens*. What hope, long dismissed or forgotten, had conjured up this name? The trees along the pavement kerbs were but few: a sad small ash or two; a lean disheartened sycamore; and, strangely, two Lombardy poplars, side by side, and tall as twin church steeples. Perhaps the fine old trees, shadowing the back gardens but hidden by the high houses, were the true relics of that old hope.

In the whole long road one's eye caught but one bright house, its smoke-darkened London bricks new-pointed, its pillared and pompous portico new-painted; its front-garden privets and hollies lately trimmed. 21 Mornington Gardens, Mark's home; with 23, his sister's, beside it.

'Your house at least shows what they looked like once.'

'Yes, and I must really spruce up Belle's, my sister's, too.'

'She'll be your mayoress, I suppose?"

'No one's mayor or mayoress yet, Shamus.'

As he said this they were passing one house which had been

empty and derelict for years and which, accordingly, was reputed by the small boys of Keys to be haunted. Its shallow front
garden was a jungle of forgotten shrubs, self-sown tree shoots and
crowding weeds among which Mark could detect the rising
willow-herb, soon to blossom into mauve-pink rosebay, the very
flower of the London wastes. This tangle of brush hid the basement windows, barred against intruders like all the others in the
road by iron bars, spiked or spear-headed. The windows of
ground floor and first floor were smashed by the stones of boys,
either because there's always joy in sending stones through
grimed and uncurtained glass or because they were engaged in
psychical research and hoping for some spectral phenomenon.

A hundred yards and they were abreast of the twin houses that
were Belle's and his own. They hardly seemed twins now for
Belle's was still, in appearance, as haggard and dejected as
others in the road, its stucco cracked or flaking, its brickwork
mildewed and furred. Mark felt a need to apologize for it. 'It'll
be done up soon, Shamus. Don't worry about it. But I could only
afford one at a time.'

'Yes, but you must posh it up now for a mayoress.'

'Now leave that, Shamus.'

'And what's more, you'll have to buy her a whole trousseau of
suitable dresses. I've noticed that all new mayoresses insist on
that.'

'Good lord! Will I? I don't know that I can afford to decorate
her and the house too.'

'Oh yes! You must certainly do both,' said Jamie, swinging
the stick.

Mark didn't feel guilty about the outside of Belle's home. He
had bought the house for her and Bronwen, her twelve-year-old
daughter, only a year or two ago, after Dewi Hamps, her husband, had deserted them. As it was the house next door to the
one in which he and she had shared a childhood, he had
delighted in making its interior beautiful for her from top to
bottom; and since its Victorian rooms, like his own, were
spacious and lofty and plastered with ornament, the cost had
been high, but he had met it with a delight that stayed with him
still. There had been moments when he wondered whether to
take Belle into his home but—'Oh no! God help us! Not quite

14

that'; because Belle was everywhere described as 'highly vivacious', and high female vivacity was something of a hair-shirt at times. So he had done the next best thing and done it unsparingly.

'Well, good-bye, Shamus. See you at the Annual Statutory Meeting—but on the wrong side of the council chamber for a change, dear boy.'

'Yes, Mr. Mayor. And I'm looking forward to seeing you in all your glory, robed and enthroned.'

'Well . . . all that remains to be seen. Meanwhile . . .'

Raising a hand in farewell, he passed through the shrubs of his front garden to the steps of his house. Eight stone steps climbed to the heavy columned portico and to the wide front door with its two panels of coloured glass. He let himself into, and shut himself in, the big empty house.

That people should comment on his continuing to live in the home of his childhood though the whole neighbourhood had fallen into decay around it did not disturb him; if anything, it pleased him; it added its little to that reputation for a mild eccentricity.

The house was empty because he had told Mrs. Pelly, one of his two 'daily women', that she need prepare no lunch for him even though he would be in Keys all day. There was no knowing, he had said, how long the count would last. It was lunch time now but he could feel no hunger when replete with a secret gratification: Mayor of Keys . . . the story of it in the evening papers . . . interest and excitement in his hospitals. Who wanted food? He preferred to go along the passage to his study at the back and there to stand at its window, hands joined behind him, while he gazed out at his tree-shadowed garden.

It was the most shadowed of all these leafy back-gardens because the trees along both its side walls were old and full and far-spreading. He loved his tall trees, loved them better than flowers or turf, and would never let them be lopped or pollarded. No one could order him to lop them. This being a corner house, those along his southern wall spread their branches over Menworthy Rise, the side road that mounted gently to Hadleigh Hill. And those along the opposite wall overhung Belle's garden next door, his own property.

Three great trees along that southern wall, the ash, the ailanthus and the black poplar; and of these three his love was the ailanthus. Though was love the word for the spell this strange tree cast on him? He was fascinated by its air of difference and mystery as it stood between the light-leaved feathery ash and the huge black poplar whose leaves were never still, ever twisting and scintillating in the wind. He looked at it now; at the rounded bole with its crumpled hide of elephant grey, the thick tormented branches outflung like writhen arms, and the dark green, divided leaves that threw dappled patterns on his thinning grass and on the pavement of Menworthy Rise. Grown strong in London's clay, indifferent to London's smoke or fouled air, it had raised its crown higher than the house itself. Its topmost spread must be seventy or eighty feet in the sky.

Men called the ailanthus the Tree of Heaven because it grew quickly towards the sky. But even now it was not as tall as the black poplar. An import from China, it always seemed to Mark like a gigantic enlargement of one of those miniature Oriental trees in a toy model of a Japanese or Chinese garden.

While he was looking at it and thinking this he heard a shrill laughing voice in Belle's garden. 'Nineteen, twenty, twenty-one —oh hell!' His heart swelled with pleasure because here was one with whom it would be good to share the day's news; and instantly, because the trees along Belle's wall—a magnificent beech, a dense holly and a dark ilex—blinded his view of her garden, he ran up the stairs to the big guest-room above his study. This commanded broad peeps into the garden.

If the outside of Belle's house looked neglected and haggard, this was not at all the complexion of her garden, which was as cared-for and flowery as his was shadowed and worn and largely unworked. In her beds today were violas and daffodils, scarlet tulips and blue-grape hyacinths, iris, thrift, honesty, and polyanthus of every colour; in her rockeries the Alpine flox, the blue-eyed mary and the white iberis. Belle's many-flowered garden, he thought, was a very fair picture of that famous vivacity.

But he hardly heeded the flowers now for there on the trim lawn was Bronwen, home for her dinner hour from Keys High School. Bronwen in her uniform of blue gym tunic, white blouse, and red-and-yellow school tie. Twelve years old, she was at play with racquet and ball, trying to keep the ball in the air for a hundred hits and yelling her score to Mrs. Warman in the kitchen.

'Twenty-nine, thirty, thirty-one, thirty-two, thirt—— damn and blast.'

'Really, Miss Bronwen!' came the voice from the kitchen.

And Mark flung up his window and called out too, 'Really, Miss Bronwen!'

She looked up, saw his face, yelled 'Uncle, Uncle, Uncle!' and tossing down the racquet to deteriorate on the grass, came running by the tradesman's path at the side of her house to the front of his.

He in his turn hurried to his front door. He opened the door and there she was on the threshold, jigging up and down on her toes so that the bob of her brown hair shook. 'Oh, *darling* Uncle. Mummy's told me. Mummy's told me. Your Labour boys have won control and you'll be Mayor. I think I'm a Conservative— we mostly are at my silly school, except a few awful cocky types who pretend to be Labour, just to show off—but I did want you to win and be mayor. You'll be a fabulous mayor. Mayn't I be mayoress? Why must Mummy be?'

'Who ever said she was to be mayoress? I didn't.'

'No, but others did. And *she* did.'

'Very wrong.'

'Yes, and no one mentioned me. Why shouldn't I be? It's the age of youth. You're always saying so in your speeches.'

'Yes, but I don't mean it. Certainly not.'

'Oh, yes you do. Of course you do. Oh isn't it all terrific?' At this point she flung her arms around him. 'Oh, darling, I'm so happy about it. I think I'll be Labour.'

He lifted her right off the ground, kissing her on her brow and then on the parting in her hair before he put her down. That kiss on the crown of her head he had allowed to stay a little, because it expressed something deep in his heart.

Mark's love for this affectionate and effusive child had taken on a special quality after the early death of Lorelei, his loved young wife. He had dreamed that Lorelei, after the birth of their son, would give him a daughter like herself, but she had died all too soon and suddenly, with the dream still unfulfilled. And

Mark had somehow contrived to vest Bronwen—was she not, to his joy, very well worthy of it?—with the robe of full love he had designed for a daughter.

'Is your mother there, pet?'

'Yes, she's writing that piece for the paper about this old election. She was thrilled to bits when you telephoned her.'

'Could you fetch her, darling? I want to ask her something.'

'Yes, but look: there's one thing I'm rather worried about if she's to be mayoress. Or if I were to be, for that matter.'

'What is that?'

'It's our name.'

'What *do* you mean, child?'

'Hamps. Can you have a mayoress with a name like Mrs. Hamps? Belle's all right, and Bronwen's delightful, but *Hamps*! Why on earth did Mummy marry a Hamps? Or why didn't she do something about it after she'd done it? She ought to have, if only for my sake. I suffer agonies at school with it.'

'Oh, darling . . . oh dear. . . . I never thought of that.'

'Well, never mind. I stick it out. Do I go and get Mrs. Hamps now? Yes? . . . Okay.'

He opened the door for her and watched her running down his eight steps and so to the front of her house and her eight steps. She disappeared under the portico and banged one disgraceful bang on the door. A minute later she reappeared, bringing her mother along by her fingers, hurriedly, as if to an important meeting.

Belle was a very small, spare, bony woman, as small as he was big, as thin as he was well fleshed. Her narrow back was rounded and her shoulders heightened by her sixty years. Just now she was wearing an astonishing high-peaked hat like a pixie's. Its pointing top and the up-pointed shoulders of her street coat sorted well with her thin, pointed, witch-like nose. That she was still in this hat, though she'd been writing something upstairs, was a fruit, perhaps, of the vivacity. But who could understand a woman's dress, thought Mark. So high-peaked a hat made her look yet smaller than she was. It was like a black candle-extinguisher on top of a half-burned candle.

Older by a year than Mark, she had lost her first child while still an infant, and no other had come till, in her own words, 'I was well stricken in years, whereupon Bronwen chose to announce her arrival and in due course came barging in among us. So like Bronwen.'

Together these two approached at speed, Bronwen because twelve-and-a-half hurries towards most things (if not towards school or on an errand to shops), and Belle because she was usually impatient of any quiet interval between one business and the next.

'Here's Belle Hamps,' said Bronwen, bringing her up the steps.

'Marcus, my precious,' said Belle, while still three steps from the top. 'This is all wonderful. I'm thrilled.'

'Then come into the study for a proposition I have to lay before you.'

'You hear that, Bron? He has a proposition he wishes to lay before me. You will stay outside.'

'I won't. I know what it is. I'm sure I do. He and I've been discussing it together.'

'Bronwen may be allowed in,' said Mark. 'For this once.'

So all went into the study and stood around, Bronwen with her lips parted in an eagerness to hear the proposition stated.

'It seems pretty certain, Belle, that they want me to be Mayor.'

'But of course.'

'I don't know about "of course"—'

'*I* do. You're the obvious choice.'

'Of course,' agreed Bronwen.

'—and I can't see that I can do anything but accept.'

'Who wants to see anything else?' demanded Belle. 'I've known for ages they were going to make you Mayor.'

'You couldn't have known before eleven-forty-five this morning. It was only then we knew we'd be the majority party.'

'Oh, don't be so pernickety, Marcus; you know what I mean. Who else could they have but you? Not Arthur Lammas, that rude old thing.'

'They could very well have him.'

'No, no, no. He's too rude to the Tories.'

'And the ruder he is, the better they like him—or nearly always. With some exceptions sometimes. Arthur's the bang opposite of me. I'm always worried to death lest I've said the wrong thing or a rude thing—'

'Oh, and me too,' said Bronwen. 'Tortures.'

'—but Arthur doesn't care a damn whether he's liked or not, with the result that they all love him—with intermissions.'

'Maybe, but he has hair coming out of his ears. I never trust any man who has hair in his ears.'

'May we come to the point? My point is that I shall invite you to be Mayoress.'

'But of course.'

'Could all these "of courses" be omitted?'

'But who else could you have—'

'There's Bronwen,' came Bronwen's voice. It was unheeded.

'I've been wondering when you were going to ask me. Others suggested it ages ago but I didn't like to mention it before you did. Bronwen and I, of course, have been discussing it for ages.'

'Not, I hope, with many people. Belle dear. Bronwen. Women are awful.'

'Oh, yes,' said Bronwen. 'I agree.'

'They haven't a scruple among them. Well, Belle, will you act?'

'Of course she will.' From Bronwen. 'She's simply dying to. Naturally.'

'Will I? It sounds rather terrifying now you ask me. Mayoress. And surely I'm not really a Socialist, or am I? I never voted at all until you stood for the Council—and then only to support the family. . . . But yes, I'll be Mayoress, if only to spite that shocking old Tory bull-dozer, Mother Pearl Runciman. I should think our Pearl's feeling a trifle sour, just now, isn't she? I hope so.' Here the clock on his mantel struck one. 'Goodness gracious, it's lunch time. What are you doing for lunch, Marcus? Where's Pelly?'

'I told Pelly not to stay as I didn't expect to be back.'

'But, heavens above, what are you going to do for food?'

'Do nothing.'

'Don't be ridiculous. You're coming to lunch with Bronwen and I—'

'Bronwen and *me*. . . . *Me*. If you're going to speak as Mayoress you must speak grammar. No one can come to lunch with I.'

'Oh, I'm not going to do any speaking. I couldn't. It's you'll have to do that.' (At these easy words, his heart missed a beat or two; nothing *she* knew of his day-long qualms before a big public speech.) 'Bronwen and me, is it? I never knew any grammar. Well, bring him along, Bron. Uncle's coming to lunch with us.'

'Oh, hallelujah!' said Bronwen.

And she picked up the end of his fingers to lead him into her home. When they were come to the eight stone steps she held the fingers carefully and cautiously, her feet one step below his. This he found touching but alarming. Never had he felt healthier or stronger, but this was all too like solicitous youth helping age; confident and kindly feminine youth, remembering the dangers of the sixties and the onsets of decrepitude.

3. Councillor Dolmen at the Window

At five o'clock Jasper was home. He was out of the house from eight in the morning till five in the evening, his prep school being four miles away in West London. Jasper, little older than Bronwen, was the other love of his father's life. A buried seed of it was the straight beauty of this slim boy's features and their almost perfect reproduction of Lorelei's. Only in the promise of a tall figure one day did Jasper show any resemblance to his father; every feature of his narrow face was Lorelei's.

Lorelei's real name had been Laura. It was Mark's teasing love of her which had altered these unworthy syllables into Lorelei. Was not Lorelei a siren of the Rhine who sat combing her hair by the river's side and luring men to their ruin? He had married Lorelei when he was forty-one and she but twenty, and only six years after Jasper's birth she had lain ill for three brief days and died on the fourth.

That day of bright sunlight, nearly seven years ago, when she had died beneath his eyes, he in a gasping agony of grief; he falling to his knees by her bed and burying his face in his arms. . . . Lorelei . . . Lorelei. How, rushing from that room, alone and desperate, he had wandered through room after room of this house, and aimlessly up its stairs and down again—then to a back window to stare out at the garden where he and she had played with Jasper; thence to a front window to look along the stretch of Mornington Gardens and remember how he would watch for her if she was not yet home when he had returned; back again to the stairs and up them as far as the top landing and its skylight, only to come down them again, past closed doors—past the door that was closed on her. At last a mad rush to the big dining-room, a slamming of its door, and a falling on his knees by the long mahogany table, that the anguish of tears might break all bounds and spend itself. Hands clasped behind his head; heart repeating a hundred times through wide-parted lips, though lower than any whisper, 'Lorelei, Lorelei, Lorelei, Lorelei . . .'

Rising at last to walk up and down by the table's side, he had longed to die too. He had dreamed of inducing his death. Easy enough for him, a surgeon with easy access to lethal drugs. 'I shall record,' the coroner would say, 'that he took a dangerously large dose of this powerful drug in a desperate effort to get some sleep after his wife's tragic and untimely death'—that was the way all coroners talked. Strange and sad, however, that even in that torment of grief, walking up and down, he had thought with pleasure how the sentimental would admire him and say, 'He died within a few hours of his lovely young wife. He just lay down and died too.' But . . . no, he must live for Jasper's sake. Lorelei, dead in that room, cried to him to do this. And on the stairs outside, for he was wandering up and down them again, he had answered, 'My dear . . . my darling . . . I will.' Thereafter a long year of solitude and stoicism, with work, work, fine work, his only analgesic, and a weak one at that; a long year in which he often lay sleepless but repeating that name rhythmically, helplessly, hopelessly, even mechanically and forgetfully, 'Lorelei, Lorelei'—till at last he emerged out of the desert of grief into the happiness of this love for Jasper.

So here, on this day of the Count, he sat at dinner with Jasper only, at the end of that same long dining-table, telling him with laughter of the day's events and making their customary fun out of Auntie Belle's words and behaviour. After a time he told him that they had asked him to be Mayor.

'Gosh!' said Jasper, to whom he had not spoken of this before. 'How super. Can I tell them all at school?'

'Better wait till it's a fact rather than an idea.'

'Oh, but look, they'd like to know. And I think they ought to know. They'd treat me with more respect. Spencer, F. E., that frightful ass, was blowing off today about his old man being an M.P. A mayor's as good as an old M.P. any day. And I'd like to tell old Wobbles.'

'Wobbles?'

'Yes, our Mr. Collison, who takes us in maths.'

'But why Wobbles?'

'Colly-wobbles.'

'Oh, I see. Yes, that's obvious. Continue.'

'He was not at all polite to me this morning about my jometry. Have you told Bron about this mayoral how-d'ye-do?'

'Yes.'

'What did she say?'

'She was up in the air about it. Literally. Bouncing up and down like a ball.'

'Gosh, she's a silly kid, isn't she?'

'Not at all. A most loyal, loving and attractive child, who has the sense to be devoted to her old uncle. If you've finished, ring for Pelly. I mean Capes.'

Mrs. Pelly and Mrs. Capes, their daily women, were a fertile field of humour for father and son. Pelly was long and gaunt, with spindly, wiry legs, while Capes was shorter and rounder—not fat, but fat enough for Mark to call them Don Quixote and Sancho Panza. Pelly, who came in the body of the day, was a nervously rapid worker, and it was Jasper who called her their daily express. Pleased that this jest had been a success with his father, he promptly carried it farther by calling Capes, who came in the evening and was a congenital gossip, their daily news. Sometimes he called Capes, who arrived in the kitchen about six, 'our evening standard', or he revised the thirtieth psalm (he had a relish for words and liked to make parodies of everything) saying, 'Capes may endure for a night, but Pelly cometh in the morning.'

After dinner that night Mark sat at the boy's side, an arm along his shoulder, and helped him with his homework, a Greek exercise and a Latin 'unseen'. He was always glad when Jasper begged his help, both because it was flattering and because he liked to display such Latin and Greek as he remembered. 'Maths I was never any good at, but I was always pretty good at Classics.'

24

'I think you're rather wizard at it,' said Jasper when Mark had translated the unseen with hardly a halt. 'I mean—after all these years.'

'It's less than a hundred years since I was at Cambridge.'

'Yes . . . but still . . .' objected Jasper, to whom forty past years were an epoch in history. 'Even so . . . to do an unseen right away like that is—what you might call—pretty whoreson clever.' (They'd just been doing Shakespeare at school.)

Work finished, and nine o'clock: Jasper rose from the table to go to bed. Though nearly thirteen and beginning to be tall, he still kissed his father good night and was kissed by him in return. Mark was always made happy by the boy's kiss and would feel sad at times when he thought that it would soon be a thing of the past. Jasper climbed the many stairs to his room on the top floor, not a small room, for no room in this house was small. On the top floor there was this large room in the front, a cistern room like a windowless cupboard, and another large room at the back which long ago had been bedchamber for housemaid, tweeny, and cook. As soon as Jasper must be in his bed Mark went up to him for the last good-night-and-sleep-well. He laid a kiss again on his forehead.

Then, coming downstairs, full of thought, he wandered into the drawing-room, the room which still bore so much of Lorelei, and stood at one of its windows. Their curtains were undrawn and he could gaze along Mornington Gardens even as earlier he had gazed, broodingly, from his study at his trees. Straight, wide, and unvisited, the road ran as far as he could see, between lamp-posts deviating from kerb to kerb. Fitly in a street of old Victorian houses those marching lamp-posts, though now lit by electric bulbs, were the old gas standards of a lost age, their cast-iron shafts upholding four-sided lanterns topped with coronas. Under one of them, against the kerb, he saw one of his borough's grit bins, with borough notices pasted on its sides.

To stand at this window was to remember how as a boy of Jasper's age or younger, and as soon as it was six in the evening, he would slip guiltily into this room if it was empty and watch and watch for his 'bad old father's' homecoming. That loved figure would turn the corner of Welbon Rise because this was the way he came from the station. Mark's heart rejoiced when he saw that figure, for when his father was in the house all was peace. He did not love his mother; had he told himself the truth he would have said he hated her. Lady Clara Dolmen—she had this title as the daughter of an impoverished earl—believed in beatings for children, and believed in them fervidly enough to speak of them often on public platforms, a symptom about which her son, when a medical man, would sometimes speculate. And not beatings only for Mark but snubbings and humiliations if he tried to display knowledge or to brag.

The contrast was complete between mother and father. Never once was he beaten or snubbed by his 'bad old father', to whom he was never anything but 'Marco Polo', the loved and teased. 'Marco Polo, the intellectual giant'—after winning a third prize at school. 'Marco Polo, the great traveller'—after visiting a school friend in Loughborough. 'Marco Polo, the best-dressed man in London'—after a new Eton suit. To this day Mark thought of him lovingly as his 'bad old father' because bad he was with many women other than his Lady Clara at home. Fifty when Mark was born, he was still all too gay in his sixties—and seventies. But to Mark he was nothing but 'good', the best thing in his life, loving and teasing and lavishly generous. Therefore all the love of which a boy was capable poured towards this man and sent him secretly to windows to watch for him. And all was peace when that big figure in the silk hat came round the distant corner, for his mother, as the boy had noticed, never scolded or snubbed him, and certainly never beat him, if his father was in the house.

His mother might beat Belle sometimes but less often than Mark; it was to Belle that she gave her affection, possibly because her husband gave so much of his to Mark, and the boy so clearly gave all of his back to him.

At the window now, looking past the lamp-posts to that corner, Mark was telling himself that he'd never beaten Jasper because he knew so well that it was his mother's beatings which had turned him into (his own private words) 'that horrid little boy of a hundred deceits'.

Such ingenious deceits, and admirable of their kind. That evening when, idling about the house, he fiddled with the hand-mirror on his mother's dressing-table and, dreaming, let it fall.

26

Cracked. What to do? He laid it face-downwards on the carpet with some of the lace doilies from the table here and there around it; then opened the window wide so that it would seem that a rushing mighty wind had blown all these articles to the floor. An Act of God, in fact—and out of the room quickly.

Or that evening when he upset the inkpot on the big dining-table as he did his homework, and the ink, running, dripped on to the carpet, and on to a ribbed stocking beneath his knicker-bockers. What a cleaning of table and carpet. Rubbing, scrubbing, behind a closed door. What a rearranging of furniture so that the big dining-table could hide, or at least shadow, the stains of a crime. A change of the ribbed stocking for a new one upstairs, and a hiding of the blemished one till he could put it in his satchel tomorrow for casting away on that rubbish-dump near his school. Then to arrange the rubbish over it till it was hidden. Hidden deep.

Or that important letter which his mother had given him to post and which he found, crumpled and messy, in a pocket of his Norfolk jacket five days later. Nothing but the Keys Canal to receive that letter; from a bridge's parapet he watched it drift away on the sullen water, its inked address melting and spreading, and the limp envelope striving to sink. Worst of all, that morning in the prep school playground (Jasper's school today) when he saw a boy sitting on a rail and mischievously pushed him from behind so that he swung, fell, and broke an arm. What an acting then of innocence and compassionate interest. A rush to help a fallen friend. Calling others to help. Declaring, truthfully enough, that he had not seen anyone push him. Perjuries to the headmaster when the inquisition began (one hated to be caned). Fluent, picturesque lies at home. 'Johnson major says it's going to cost a lot of money. Billy Bridges says he'll be in hospital some time with it. What I can't understand is what became of the chap who did it. I suppose he's afraid to own up.'

Shame and guilt as he spoke, but also the pride of an artist in these ingenuities.

Well, perhaps fifty years later, one could forgive that frightened boy. But the child lived still. Even now, though nearly sixty, he could be tempted many times a day to some deceit if thereby he eluded blame. Within his big, comfortable,

27

well-favoured, well-dressed body that little boy of a hundred ingenious deceits lived still, desiring praise and dodging blame.

Heavens, he must have been dreaming here at the window for an hour. A tiring day with its excitement and its disturbing promise. He would go up to bed. He went down to the dining-room, mixed himself a whisky nightcap, and went up to the one-time servant's bedroom next to Jasper's. He had made this his bedroom, perceiving that the boy was apt to be nervous at night, up there on the top floor, just as he himself used to be, unless someone slept near. There were strange noises in the cistern cupboard and always the thought of that creaking sky-light as a means of sinister entry or of that long flight of stairs between oneself and the floor below. To him, as a small boy, the house, from basement to roof, always seemed to enlarge for the emptiness, the silence, the darkness and the ghostly sounds of midnight. How far this was so for Jasper he could not say, but he perceived enough to know that the boy would sleep more easily if his father slept near him in the night.

4. Mr. Luddermore and the Trees

Mark was home early from a long session at one of his hospitals. After doing the major operations on his list from half-past one till five he had left the minor ones to the registrar, paid a dutiful visit to the Sullivan Ward to hearten a patient on tomorrow's list, looked in on a private patient in the St. Mary Wing, and then flung himself into his car and driven wearily home.

The car was a Rolls-Royce, but an old model which, bought at third hand, had not cost him too much. When he was home in his house the long black car was a familiar sight to all who passed in Menworthy Rise, for it usually stood parked near his garden wall under the out-flung branches of his Tree of Heaven and their 'half-weeping' leaves.

Now, standing behind the narrow glazed door of his study which opened on to an ornamental iron stairway leading down into the garden, he was watching Jasper and Bronwen playing French Cricket on the grass and old Mr. Luddermore lifting the last sad tulips from a shadowed and languishing bed. He was listening with a bemused love to Bronwen's voice as she shouted, 'Oh, stinks!' because Jasper had tricked her into lifting her racquet and exposing her feet to the touch of the ball. 'A dirty trick, and it's not fair,' she declared with a pout as she surrendered the racquet to him. 'Take the beastly bat.'

Old Mr. Luddermore came for but one evening a week, apart from an occasional Saturday or Sunday in summer when the grass was long. At other times there was little enough to do beneath these old, exacting, wide-ranging trees. Seventy and a retired gardener from London Landscapes, Ltd., he now did odd jobbing in these long back-gardens of Victorian Keys. With his sparse white hair blowing in wisps when his sweat-soiled hat lay on the grass, and with his long white moustache weeping (like a willow, said Mark) over his mouth, he looked ten years older than his age. New to this garden, he abounded with despairing strictures on it, most of which he would repeat, visit after visit, without varying the words. These strictures he adorned with small but shining specimens of his horticultural knowledge, and these specimens appeared again and again too, and shone, word for word. Sometimes when the white moustache wept more than usual he looked like an old and worn Prince Bismarck, so that Mark would sometimes refer to him as 'Old Bismarck'; but out of respect for the white hairs he never addressed him as other than 'Mr. Luddermore' or suffered the children to use any other title in his hearing. With the last of the tulips in his trug he picked up a daisy-grubber to root out sadly the plantains and the dandelions from this coarsened and cankered lawn.

Opening the door, Mark went down the iron stairway into the garden. 'Not out!' he called in triumph as Bronwen, holding the racquet again, dashed the ball from her feet at the last second. 'Most definitely not out. But go easy, Bron dear. Mind poor Mr. Luddermore.'

Hearing him, she looked up, threw down the racquet, deserted the game and ran to leap up at him. '*Darling* Uncle!' she cried as her arms went round him. 'Have you finished with all your silly hospitals? Then come and play French Cricket with us. That'd be a nice change for you.'

He returned her kiss, and jovially smacked her on the bottom.

'Come along,' she commanded, taking his fingers to lead him to the area of play. 'You can go in first. I was in, but I'll let you be in instead.'

'No, no,' he protested. 'I've had a tiring day. They work me too hard at that hospital.'

'Oh, what a dirty shame. It's wicked, isn't it? It's just not fair.'

'Not fair in the least. And it's left me much too weak for the ardours of French Cricket. Besides I haven't come out here to talk with you; I've come to drink of Mr. Luddermore's wisdom.'

'Mr. Luddermore's what?'

'I want to hear all about the terrible defects of this garden. He has a very poor opinion of it. Why he comes to work in such a desperate place I'm not quite sure—nor, come to that, how he manages to do any work with you and Jasper around.'

'He likes it. He likes to have us here, don't you, Mr. Luddermore?'

'Don't mind.' A grunt, but accompanied by a half-smile under the weeping white moustache. 'It don't interfere with me all that much.'

'You see? He loves it. When are they going to do this hallowing of you as mayor? I'm dying to see it. I'm coming, aren't I?'

'Hallowing? What on earth do you mean?'

'Your hallowing as Mayor. Isn't that what it is?'

'What it certainly isn't. Qualifying is the word. Electing and qualifying.'

'Well, Mummy called it your hallowing.'

'She would.'

'She said they sort of enthroned and robed you. She said you'd look smashing in your robes.'

'I'm sure she didn't say smashing.'

'Well, anyhow, she said you were ever so handsome and a marvellous sixty.'

'I'm not sixty.'

Here came a call to Bronwen from Jasper who'd heard some of this from a distance. 'Are we playing French Cricket, or are you having a feminine gossip with that man?'

'Oh, you shut up,' Bronwen advised, and she went with Mark, holding his fingers as he walked to the side of Mr. Luddermore.

'He's in his sixtieth year,' Jasper explained the matter enthusiastically and, left to himself, he stood swinging the racquet, or tossing it up and catching it, while he spouted a new parody, 'It was a summer evening, Old Jasper's work was done, And he within his garden walls Was playing in the sun.'

Mark, aware that the best way to deal with strictures was to agree with them, even, if possible, stating them first, said, 'Not much of a lawn, Mr. Luddermore.'

'Shocking,' said Mr. Luddermore, but only after he'd grubbed up another daisy and put it in his trug.

'Can't we do anything for it?'

'No.' Or rather '*Nah*,' the final negative, the ultimate despair. 'Can't expect grass to grow under them trees.'

'Quite a lot does.'

'Some, but not to be any good. Grass needs two things, light and food. And the branches of them there trees take all the one, while their roots take all the other. Worst of all is that there Tree of 'Evan.'

'But, Mr. Luddermore! That's my favourite tree.'

'I dunno about that, but if you'll par'n me saying so, it never ought to be there at all, to my thinking. You'd agree with me, I reckon, if you could see what its roots is doing underground. Never known why they call it the Tree of 'Evan.'

'Because they say it's tall enough to reach the skies.'

'And that's just plain daft. An ash or an elm or a good old London plane'll beat it any day, given 'alf a chahn'st. And look at that there black poplar. Beats it 'oller. Tree of 'Evan! Tree of 'Ell's more to the point if you ars't me.'

'This one's as high as the ash.'

Mr. Luddermore looked up at the ash's crown. 'Well—yur, it is. It's a quick-growing tree, I give you that, but skinny in the trunk like all quick-growing things. And it's a dull tree'—his nostrils dilated with distaste—'dull, dismal, compared with the ash.'

'Dull? No, no, Mr. Luddermore. A handsome, beautiful tree.'

'Not to my thinking. Look at its gloomy leaves—all dark and heavy compared with them there dainty leaves of the ash—the *fraxinus*.' This Latin name was the first of the ornaments hung on to an expert's talk; more would come later. 'Gi' me the good old ash any day. Grows in any soil we got 'ere. Your Tree of 'Evan never looks like an English tree to me.'

'Well, it's not necessarily the worse for that.'

This point seemed one which Mr. Luddermore had not considered before and was not ready to consider now. So he continued in his present line of thought. 'I never know what it makes me think of. Something un-English and unnatural—see what I mean? An *ailanto*, some fellows call it, and they say its leaves are good for silkworms.'

32

'Could well be, since it comes from China.'

Now it was plain that this was a piece of knowledge new to Mr. Luddermore and that he didn't wish to admit it. A moment of empty silence and he veered away from it, saying, 'Yur— China—I suppose *ailanto*'s Chinese—but what's it doing underground, that's what you got to ars't yerself. What about its roots, eh? What about them?'

'Well, what about them?'

'Just that they'll be getting at the roots of your 'ouse one day.' Annoyed that he, the expert gardener, should have been told an unknown fact by a mere amateur, he countered by making *his* piece of information as alarming as possible. 'Its roots travel deep down and 'orizontally and, before you know where you are, they're messing about with the foundations of your 'ouse. And quite likely playing 'ell with them. Look at that there brick wall under your tree. Bending over into the street and bulging out like it was three-months-gone—if you'll par'n me putting it like that. You'll have it tumbling on to the pavement one day. I wonder the Council isn't after you about it.'

Mark felt like saying. 'I am the Council. *Le Conseil, c'est moi*,' but decided that Mr. Luddermore was not the right audience for this allusion. So he just said, '*That's* hardly likely. It's almost the borough's most famous tree. Often mentioned in local articles and farther afield. How deep are its roots?'

'Could be all of five feet down and pretty long by now. That there tree's sixty years old.'

'More. Much more. It was there when I was a child, and it was forty years old then.'

Mr. Luddermore didn't like to be so badly wrong. He hedged quickly, 'Well, then its roots are big pah'ful fellers by now. They'll be man enough to be up to any sort of games. Wait till one of 'em throws up a sucker outside your kitchen window. Then you'll know a thing or two.'

At this point Jasper was heard demanding, 'Am I to conclude that we've finished with cricket? I would wish to know where we stand.' Deserted by Bronwen, he was killing the interval by 'keeping the ball in the air' with the racquet, as she liked to do. 'If no one's interested in me I'll go indoors and get on with my foul homework.'

'Oh, you go and shoot yourself,' said Bronwen. 'Uncle and I are talking to Mr. Luddermore.'

So Jasper just exclaimed, 'Women!' and continued his solitary juggling with the ball.

Meanwhile Mark, discounting most of Mr. Luddermore's words as the talk of one who, by nature, preferred glóomy prognostications to comforting ones, turned from the offending tree to the lawn. 'You say there's nothing we can do about the lawn?'

'Mighty little. Might try to drain it a bit. But where's there an outlet? There ain't one, so drain-tiles'd be no good. We'd have to dig a sump-'ole about six foot deep. That might work, but I dunno: this 'ere London clay drains badly in wet weather and cakes badly in dry.'

'We could lighten the soil, I imagine?'

'Might try something like that, but it wouldn't pay to do too much of it, or the grass'd get done in by drought.'

'Yes, yes, but we could hit the happy mean.'

'The 'appy mean. Yur—the 'appy mean. But 'ow're we to know what the 'appy mean is unless we know what them roots is doing? Could be they're doing a devil of a lot of draining their-selves.'

'I see. Well, there's no hope for the lawn apparently. Unless we dig up half of it. What about the paths? Where they're not green they're black. Anything we can do about them?'

'Not much.' Mr. Luddermore scratched his head over this difficult and depressing question, and smoothed back the dis-ordered white hairs. 'It's the lay of yer land, yer see. No outlet. The rainwater comes down that rise and lays in any dip or 'oller. There's an 'oller under your tree there, you see, don't you? One could try a sump-pit again, say five or six foot deep, and drain into it, but these paths are 'oggin, and there's a lot of sand in 'oggin. It comes washing down into drains and blocks 'em. I could mix cement with the 'oggin to 'arden it, I s'pose, but then you'd prob'ly get a pool instead of a swamp.'

'I see. Doesn't seem much we can make of this garden.'

'Not reely; not with them trees.'

'No. I see.' And, weary of these truths about his garden, Mark

34

was about to turn away, but Mr. Luddermore hadn't finished. 'It must be a reg'lar breeding ground for pests—thrips and slugs and weevils and such like. I'll lay there are plenty of wireworms getting at your roots—yur—*agriotes*, wireworm.' The learned name to shine again. '*Agriotes*. One could spray the 'ole place with insecticide, I s'pose, but you'd 'ave to keep at it. It's the devil getting shut of pests, I don't mind telling you.'

'Well, there are precious few flowers in the garden and I don't imagine the wireworm can do much damage to the trees. I back the trees to win; they're rather bigger. So let's not worry.' And he turned away towards Jasper. Mr. Luddermore went on grubbing up his weeds and tossing them sadly, even despairingly, into his trug.

Bronwen and Jasper were in the garden today because Bronwen was to have dinner with Mark and Jasper, her mother having gone to a theatre. After a lively dinner, made merry by Mark's teasing and illumined by much heavy (often poly-syllabic) prep-school humour from Jasper, the two children sat at the same dining-table to do their homework, with Mark sitting between them to help now one and now the other. Sometimes his arm was around the boy's shoulder and sometimes around Bronwen's.

Bronwen did not easily keep her thoughts on her work; she preferred to talk about other things. Social things. And at one point she looked up at him, her forehead still creased by some taxing arithmetic, and asked, '*Re* that hallowing? They're going to let me come, I hope? I mean, it'll be a dirty shame if they don't; I'm giving them my uncle as mayor and my mum as mayoress.'

'To hell!' Jasper interposed. '*I'm* providing the mayor. You're only providing a mayoress? What's a mayoress? Merely an appendage.' He pronounced it *appen*-didge. 'What you might call a mere concomitant to the mayor.'

'I'm not sure,' Mark teased, 'that they'll let either of you in. I mean, mere children! Mere whippersnappers. You're both irresponsible infants, in the eyes of the law.'

'But I've never heard such abject nonsense,' protested Bronwen. 'I'm most certainly coming.'

'So'm I,' said Jasper. 'But what about these scholastic studies?'

'And I'm not at all sure that I'm not bringing half my school with me,' was Bronwen's last word.

At nine o'clock and bedtime Bronwen returned to her house next door. There was no difficulty about this because Belle had let the basement rooms of the big, unmanageable house to a young working couple, Mr. and Mrs. Warman, with a girl of Bronwen's age, and this girl slept by arrangement in one of the top rooms (the equivalent of Mark's at Jasper's side). It was only Mark who said he couldn't stomach the thought of tenants in his house whether high up or down below.

So Bronwen ran home soon after nine, and Jasper climbed unwillingly to his own high bedroom. He went spouting a rhyme which he'd lately composed for use whenever his father rebuked him for a fault or insisted on his going to bed. 'It must be allowed'—so he spouted on the first steps of the stairs—'it must be confessed, That Jasper's far From popu-lar In Mornington Gardens, West.' It was from a friend at school that he'd acquired this taste for private rhymes and parodies. Only yesterday morning he had been bellowing from the bathroom, 'Come into the bathroom, Maud, I'm here in the bath alone, And the clouds of steam are wafted abroad, And the scent of the soap is blown.' Mark came to the bathroom door to rebuke him for indecency, as a father should, but stayed to proffer a quick rhyme of his own. He knocked a knuckle on the door and said, 'Come down to your breakfast, Maud, I'll be there at my place alone, And the scent of the bacon is wafted abroad, And the Pelly's beginning to groan.'

'Super!' acknowledged Jasper in appreciation of this rapid addition to *his* little effort.

Tonight, after Mark had seen him comfortably into bed and adjusted his bedclothes and the curtains of his high room, he came downstairs again and stood by the window of the dining-room. There for a while he remained in thought. Before his eyes lay the long stretch of Mornington Gardens, wide and quiet and empty. So often it was empty between nine and ten, an hour when people were neither setting out to their entertainments nor returning home. Now and then a pedestrian passed as he stood there or a speeding taxi rent the silence and the emptiness.

But here at last came two lovers. Locked together they went

slowly by, their feet moving in step because they were holding one another so tightly. They went beyond the shrubs of Belle's garden and out of view. He forgot them till, to his surprise, he saw them on the other side of the road, not enlaced now or walking, but standing shoulder to shoulder, with the boy's fingers holding the girl's against his thigh. He was glancing cautiously up the long road and down it. To see if they were watched? Yes, surely, for at a safe moment, and unaware of a lonely householder at a distant window, he drew the girl quickly through the gate of the house. It was an empty house, up for sale, but becoming derelict. So why draw the girl in there at such an hour? Ah, one could guess. The night was warm beneath a rising moon, and the house's back-garden, long-walled like one's own and curtained by trees, was out of the world's sight.

Mark smiled to himself. 'What can part young limbs and lechery?'

Which set him thinking of Desiderata and Half Moon Street.

5. Desiderata

One might be fifty-nine and the hungers of youth be quietened (he thought at the window) so that they mounted only seldom, but they could leap capriciously still. It was six years since Lorelei died, and for three of them he had stayed celibate, his thoughts absorbed by work that he did well or by activities that would promote his fame. Ambition had always seemed stronger in him than the need of women. He had not married till he was forty-one, and his sexual adventures during that long bachelor-hood had been far rarer than most men's. In marriage he had desired none but Lorelei; and in the years of mourning after her death, if temptation assailed him, he found the strength to overcome it and forget it. The memory of Lorelei helped him to forget it.

But that night last year. Then the body's clamour for justice had mounted till it was hardly to be borne. The hour was after midnight, and ever and again, as he restlessly paced the study, his mind was seeing the big guest-chamber above this room, with its large and handsome bed, his mother's and father's bed, splendid with flowered walnut panels at head and foot. Temptation was heated higher by the simple memory that the bed was made up and sheeted, ready for a guest. Tom Brooker had occupied it for two nights; and this morning, Pelly, unsure whether the gentleman was coming back, had made it up again. Strange chance, and what invitation it offered! When a chance like this again? Take it. Take it. Long after midnight, and by the side of his house in Menworthy Rise stood his old-fashioned car, parked against the kerb, under the spread of his ailanthus tree. He hurried out to it, got in, and closed the door as softly as might be. Nothing but the sides of big houses, and the trees of walled back-gardens, looked down upon Menworthy Rise, but even so, if anyone had seen him from a staircase window, he or she would surmise that Mr. Dolmen, the famous surgeon (as always, his neighbours exaggerated their neighbour's fame), was hurrying to a midnight emergency.

He drove at speed towards likely places in the West End, and all the way shame sat with him, but the bigger part of the shame was, not that he was offending God, but that he had betrayed Jasper by leaving him alone in a large frightening house, with no father near him. Oh God, let him not wake. Let him not wake.

Furtively he drove on, thinking, 'Fifty-eight, and still that little boy of a hundred deceits lives in me, though I'm not deceiving a harsh mother now but a trusting son whom I love. Jasper, don't wake. I won't be long.'

As he drove on, he tried to justify himself a little in what he was doing. It was the truth that a passionate, angry loyalty to the memory of Lorelei had held him back from thoughts of re-marriage or a mistress; truth that scruples had made him always turn away from any obvious encouragement in the eyes of a friend's or a neighbour's wife; but true too—and surely this drained away some of the merit—that, preoccupied with en-grossing work and secret ambition, he had seldom, strangely seldom, craved this manner of release.

Hyde Park Corner being the gateway to the likely places, he slowed down the car that he might look from its side windows. The pavements of Piccadilly were almost as quiet now as those of Mornington Gardens. The few people in sight walked quickly; the occasional taxi ripped by. But at the corner of Half Moon Street he saw a woman standing. As he slowed yet more, her eyes looked straight into his through the car window, and she smiled her invitation. His heart clamoured, and after driving a few yards farther he turned it about and brought it into Half Moon Street. Stopping it and getting out, he saw the woman wandering from her corner towards him and bringing her smile with her. She was a tall girl, hatless, with black hair parted in the middle and falling in abundance to her shoulders. Her face was pale, and all the paler for that rich black hair. It had something of the Orient about it, he thought, the eyes set wide apart and the small nose set close to the face. She was perhaps twenty-seven or eight and, however flawed in the daylight, beautiful enough in the night to trouble heart and throat and breathing.

'You take me?' she said.

The words were unusual, and the accent that of a foreigner speaking English. Always courteous, Mark returned her smile and said, 'I will take you anywhere you want to go.'

'I want to go with you,' she answered, her head trickily and coyly to one side.

'Well, jump in and be comfortable,' he said, pretending ease, though the hand that held the door wide for her, as for the most gracious of ladies, was shaking.

'You take me somewhere, no?' she asked, leaning lovingly against him when he was in the driver's seat.

'We'll see.' Swinging the car out of Half Moon Street he turned its head towards the West and after a silence said, 'I take you home with me, no?' imitating her idiom so as to introduce some merriment.

'Oh, yes,' she said, and deliberately snuggled up closer. 'I go home with you. That will be vary nice.'

Quickly home. An uneasy player in this London street game he was afraid of going into one of these women's lairs, lest she had a 'protector', a 'bully', a 'bloke' there, or lest the shame of her room disabled him; but more than all this his conscience was still stabbing him for his desertion of Jasper. It was wholly unlikely that the boy would have wakened and called for him, but he felt no less guilty for this. He longed to be back. He would take this girl softly into the guest-room on the floor below Jasper's bedroom, where at least he would be near the boy again.

While his hand shook on the wheel his heart was a theatre of conflicting emotions: this longing to be home with Jasper; a craving for the cover of his house's four walls because of this stranger nestling warmly against him; excitement at what he was about to enjoy; and a sick distaste of all that he was doing.

'You are not English, my dear, are you?'

'Italian.' And, as if emphasizing this, she smiled and pressed yet closer.

'Italian, are you? Well, what is your name?'

'Desiderata.'

'Beautiful name. And your surname?'

'Ah . . . never mind that. Who wants to know that?'

Remembering some shreds of Italian, he displayed one for her. '*Saprebbe lei che ora è?* Long after midnight.'

'Ah!' she exclaimed. '*Sa parlar italiano?*'

'No, no,' he laughed. 'I have been in Italy often, but I forget most of the Italian I once knew. I know *Buon giorno* and *Buona notte*. Not much more. You are young.'

'Twenty-two.'

A trade lie. Having her closer now, he could see she might be thirty. But for her comfort he accepted the lie and, again for some words that would ease a disturbing encounter, said with a rather foolish laugh, 'Dear me, that makes me feel very old.'

'But you are nice. Vary nice. I like you.'

They said little more as he drove. Once, perceiving that she was looking up at his eyes, he dipped his head and kissed her.

In Menworthy Rise he stopped the car at its usual parking place beside his garden wall. 'Stop. Stay there,' he ordered her; and getting out of it alone, he opened the side door at the foot of the garden by the tool shed. Looking everywhere and satisfied that no eyes were awake anywhere, he summoned her to come. Three seconds, and she was within the garden and the door shut behind her. No fears for him in this garden with its brick walls nearly six foot high and its full-leaved branching trees, so he left her at the foot of the iron stairway that mounted to his study, and walking easily to the front of the house (a surgeon come home) let himself in. In the study, without putting on any lights, he opened the glass door for her.

She came with an odd dignity up the iron steps, though bringing the smile which her trade required. A shy smile, and he, now really noticing the grace and poise of her tall figure, picked up her fingers gently and without another word led her up the dark staircase to the big guest-room above. Here, where it was safe to put on the lights, he first held her by both hands to study her; to smile at the pale slightly Oriental face and the black hair mass-

41

ing on her shoulders; then gathered her for a long embrace. It was sweet, this long embrace, for he had known nothing like it for years. When it was over he laughed and said, 'Thank you, darling,' for which courtesy she flung her arms round him again. Oh, yes, she was expert at this game of one-night wifehood, and he was now well at ease with her. Again holding both her hands, he said, 'You are tall for an Italian girl.'

'*Sì*,' she said, and undoing his fingers, walked round the room. 'Such a lovely room! *Bella!*' Then suddenly she hastened to look at the large picture of the Capitol which hung on the chimney breast. 'Ah! But our Rome! Our Rome!'

'Yes. Your Rome. The Capitol.'

'I been in Rome,' she said proudly; and the Cockney 'I been' surprised him. 'The Piazza del Campidoglio,' she explained still looking at the picture. 'I been there.'

'*Bello?*' he asked, trying to copy her.

'*Ma sì*,' she answered. '*Sì, sì*. I been in Rome.'

When she lay naked in the bed, he saw hanging between her breasts on a thin gold chain a medal of the Madonna, and marvelled at the way Latin people could stay good Catholics and practise mortal sin. For him, at any rate, it would be impossible to rest upon her with this lying between them. It was too like a drawn sword. He removed it to the bedside table while she only smiled.

Rather than reveal any weariness or shame when his lust was sated and his body emptied, he continued to caress her in his arms, hoping that desire might rise again; and to laugh and talk with her. The reading-lamp above the bed was still on, and by its light he saw how the blue eye-shadow made her face seem even paler. Together with the red-painted lips, now smeared, it made the skin look like yellowing ivory. One could but love a little after what had happened, and he asked tenderly, 'Now tell me all about yourself, Desiderata,' kissing her as he spoke the beautiful name. 'How do you come to be in England?'

'I come over to work for an English family, it is three years now. But last year I stop. I choose to live in my own way.'

So it was only a year she'd been plying this trade. If true. If not the trading lie. Dared one ask more about the trade? 'You live alone now?'

42

'Oh, but yes. I have a room of my own.'

'Where?'

'I think I do not tell.'

'Why, you silly child?'

'Because I do not care to.'

'Very well, my dear.' Should one continue? 'You're not married?'

'No, no; no, no, no.'

'No lover?'

'No, no.' More doubtfully. 'I want no lover. . . . I hate men and despise them. They're all brutes.'

'Oh, not all, my dear, surely?'

'Not you. You are nice. Vary nice.'

'Talk softly, dear. My boy is sleeping just above. I've never known him wake and come downstairs, but he's a nervous boy just as his Old Man was, ages and ages ago. Are you not lonely, living alone? Probably you have women friends.'

'I have *not*!' Angrily. 'Or only one or two. Very few ever speak to me. An Italian girl taking their business. I want no friends. I live by myself and for myself.'

'Will you tell me something else?'

'Perhaps.'

'Are you saying it's a year you've been . . . living as you . . . as you do now? I mean . . .'

'You need not be afraid to say what you mean. I am not ashamed of nothing I do.' (The Cockney again.) 'My life is my own. I make money for a year, two years perhaps, and then I go back to Italy. I have my mother there in Catanzaro—'

'Where's that?'

'In Calabria. In Southern Italy. She is very poor because Father was killed in the war and my brothers too. I am going to take back money to her. I come here to make money. It's no money I make working for your English families. But now I spend little on myself and shall have much to take home.'

'But Desiderata, dear, you are a Catholic?'

Naked, she shrugged within his arms. 'I am born a Catholic but what is that to me? There is no God. God? That is nonsense.'

'Oh, I think I believe in God,' he said, with her in his arms.

43

'I do not. Nor would you if you could see some of the diseases among our people and some of the deformities of the poor little bambini. I sometimes think of him as rather more cruel than the worst of our *mafiosi*. And even worse than that. So why should I worship him or obey his laws? Why in hell when I think him a monster? He seems as happy making hideous, beastly things as making beautiful ones. Whatever I may be I reckon I'm a sight better than what he is.'

('Reckon a sight better.' This odd blending of Cockney with the careful English of a foreigner.)

'But what about your Madonna?' he asked, glancing over her head at the medal where it now lay on the bedside table.

'Oh, she is perhaps different—I don't know. But she is a woman. She has pity, I am sure. It could not be otherwise.'

Extraordinary answer, with which it would be unkind to argue. He stayed silent till she asked surprisingly, 'How long is it since your wife died?'

'My wife? A long time ago. . . .' And he offered no more. He didn't want Lorelei mentioned here tonight.

That was an October night, and the sun did not rise till after six. He slept hardly at all, but she after a time lay sleeping at his side with the black hair thrown about the pillow. At three minutes past five, by the luminous dial of his bedside clock, he awoke her. 'Desiderata. . . .'

Her eyes opened to the low voice; her brow creased till she recognized him; then she smiled, as her business required.

'*Buon giorno*, Desiderata,' he laughed, adding gently, 'I think you'd better leave while it is still dark, darling.' The endearment had slipped out, but after the night he didn't feel it was insincere.

'Yes,' she agreed. 'Of course. Dark . . . I understand. *Che ora*— what time is it, dear?'

'Past five.'

'*Davvero!* Past five.' She sat up, stretched her long bare arms, yawned, and slipped from the bed. He rose too and put on the light. To consider the weather she peered through the window curtains. He too. They saw a sky brilliant with stars above the dark garden, the black poplar, and the ailanthus tree.

'*Fa bel tempo*,' she said to herself.

44

'Yes, and now look: you go from the garden, dear. The gate is unlocked. Slip out, will you, while it's still dark.'

'Of course I will. I understand.'

She dressed quickly and while she was combing her hair at his dressing-table, throwing her head back to let the comb pass through, he went to his pocket case that lay with his loose money on the mantel. Unobserved by her, he took out all the notes in it and put back only two. Then he said, 'I'd like to take you home but I can't, my dear. My young man is sleeping upstairs and I mustn't leave him. He's only twelve.'

'No, no. That is all right. You mustn't leave him, the poor bambino. I shall be all right. The trains start early.'

'Besides,' he chaffed her, 'you don't want me to know where your home is.'

'No, it is not in a good place. Not really a place for gentlemen like you. I'm glad you brought me here. Do you know, I don't yet know your name.'

He gave the first name that came into his head, the name of a Lord Chief Justice dead these twenty years. 'Hewart.' Why this name had jumped into his head who could say? Still it would serve. Picking up her hand, he crushed the pound notes into it. 'Thank you, dear.'

A look at the notes, and she cried, 'Oh!' in surprise and gratitude.

'Ten for you,' he said, 'and let's say ten for your mother.'

'Oh, *grazie*! *Mille grazie!*' Rising on her toes, she flung her arms around his neck to kiss him.

This was another long embrace, for with the morning his desire was astir again, but after much kissing he let her go. Together they went stealthily down the dark stairs, he leading her by the hand to bring her down in safety. In the dark study, softly, he opened the narrow garden door. She gave a wave on the first step of the iron stairway; he said '*Buon giorno*' again for fun; and watched her till she had passed into Menworthy Rise, closing the gate soundlessly.

October. May now. Eight months. Once in that eight months, on a night in February, a deliberate recollecting of her had kindled desire till, desperately yielding, he had gone out to the car and committed again that shameful crime of leaving the

45

house at midnight with the boy in it alone. In the absurd hope of finding her at the place where she had loitered before. Of course she was not there nor anywhere else near by. He saw other available women and was half tempted . . . but no, he now felt secure only with Desiderata, and one day he would find her again. He swung the car round, more glad than sorry that his search was a failure; that he could get back to Jasper and be quit of guilt.

Yet once again, when Jasper was staying with a school-friend for the night of a party, and the house was empty and silént, he had driven the car to the West End, untroubled by thoughts of Jasper alone, and finding no Desiderata, had gone at last in desperation with another street-corner woman to a musty top room in Gerard Street. There he had spent fifty minutes with her in a waste of shame.

This night, recalling these things by the dining-room window, remembering the prolonged embrace when he first saw her in the lighted room, remembering her skilled smiles in the great bed beside him, remembering, perhaps most of all, the exuberant black hair spread wildly over the pillow, he felt the old foolish desire mounting to go and seek her again; it even drove him into the study where he could look at his Tree of Heaven beneath which his car waited in the quiet of Menworthy Rise. Though it was May now, the tree was only beginning to bud, and its tormented branches, empty of leaf, stretched out crooked, clutching fingers, upturned towards the sky. He even put his hand on the latch of the door that led down into the garden— but no; he brought the hand away, pulled the curtain, and went straight to some tasks on his desk. These defeated the desire gradually but finally, and this success made him happy. It was a happy thing, after an hour or two, to go faithfully up to the room at Jasper's side.

6. The Hallowing

'Now, children, listen.' Belle held the paper in her hand. It was after dinner in Mark's house and they were in the big drawing-room on the first floor; Belle and Mark with coffee and brandy before them on a low table; Jasper distributed sideways over a corpulent easy-chair, his legs dangling from an arm; and Bronwen on the carpet, her legs drawn under her. Mark never sat in this daintily furnished room without thoughts of Lorelei; it bore her signature everywhere. Across the dark landing was the guest-room to which he had once brought Desiderata and to which, a few nights ago, he had longed to bring her again; but its door was shut on all these memories and its bed shrouded in a green counterpane. 'This, dear children, is how they set about hallowing your father—and your uncle—as Mayor.'

'Darling Uncle,' said Bronwen, gratuitously, from the floor.

'I wish you'd drop that nonsensical word "hallowing",' said Mark.

'Oh, never mind all that,' Bronwen urged. 'Go on, Mum.'

'You are hereby summoned,' Belle read, 'to attend the Statutory Annual Meeting of the Council at the Town Hall, High Road, Keys—yes, we know by this time where it is—at half-past six in the evening precisely—note that "precisely", Bron—'

'Heavens, I shall be there long before that—'

'—for the following purposes, one, to elect a Mayor for the

47

ensuing year, two, to qualify the Mayor-elect—what in mercy's name does that mean? Surely, Marcus, you've been qualified for the last twenty years to make a nice mayor.'

'It means, my dear Belle, that Councillor Dolmen will solemnly declare that, having been elected to the office of mayor, he will duly and faithfully fulfil the duties thereof.'

'But of course he will. Who ever supposed anything else? And what about the Mayoress? Don't I have to swear something?'

'No. All that happens is that people say nice things about you.'

'Oh, well, that should be pleasant. Where do I sit?' This was the eve of the Statutory Meeting and Mark had assembled the family for a briefing.

'They will provide a special seat for you. Somewhere not too conspicuous.'

'I see. I'm nobody much really. Just an appendage, as Jasper says.'

'That's right.'

'That's right,' Jasper agreed. 'Just what you might call an ornamental adjunct.' He said this even as Bronwen was demanding, 'Where shall *I* be?'

'You two'll be up in the public gallery. You're not held to be of any importance at all.'

'Oh, heck!' Jasper complained.

'Well, can we get into the front row?' Bronwen asked.

'Easily. The architects of the Town Hall had far too large an idea of the number of burgesses who'd care to come and look at their councillors. One or two interested persons may come in and three or four unemployed who've nothing else to do. And perhaps a few old women who've come in out of the rain.'

'It may not be raining,' Jasper supplied unhelpfully.

'Then perhaps there'll be no one. Just tier upon tier upon tier of empty seats.'

'Gosh,' said Jasper. 'How madly gay.'

'Oh no, there're going to be heaps of people,' Bronwen insisted. 'I've told all the girls at school and they're coming in crowds. Some of them know you by sight and think you're smashing. And Pelly and Capes are coming. *I've* seen to that. I've told them all about it—Capes is telling everybody else, you bet. You know what Capes is.'

'The daily news,' said Jasper.

'She's told Mr. Capes, and he says he's half a mind to come.'

'*Mr.* Capes too, oh dear!' The Mayor-elect would have to make a graceful speech of thanks and promise, and a touch of the old nervousness troubled Mark's heart; he who would like his speech to be 'one of the best the Council had heard' and one that would impress the children and his servants and Bronwen's school-friends. As always he hid the nervousness behind apparently casual words. 'I trust, Jasper, that you're bringing no deputation from *your* academy.'

'Lord, no!' said Jasper. 'Old Hassell who takes us in English History, talking yesterday about the old moot courts or some such nonsense, must needs go and say—trying to be funny, "There's Dolmen's father, for instance. I see he's going to be mayor of his village," and Heavens! Did I feel a fool?'

Bronwen, uninterested in Mr. Hassell, turned to feminine concerns. 'Aren't you longing to get into those robes, Uncle?'

'Yes, my dear. I intend to look smashing.'

'And he will, Bron,' said Belle. 'Your uncle's far and away the most impressive figure in the Council. I've been there and had a look round, and I must say, a less distinguished-looking lot I—'

'Oh, come!' Mark objected. 'What about old Major Roper, Leader of the Tories? He's a fine big boy.'

'He's not unimpressive, but he waddles. I could never take seriously a man who waddles. Handsome old face but his legs are obviously bandy in those enormous trousers of his. That's why he keeps them enormous, I expect. To hide his shame.'

'Shamus O'Donoghue?'

'Pooh, a little fopdoodle, like that dandified creature in *Hamlet*—Osric, wasn't he? Can't stand fops. How long do you think you'll be mayor?'

'Who knows? The Tory mayors have usually served for two terms. But there's nothing to prevent a mayor being elected again and again.'

'Which is what Arthur Lammas wants you to be. He's a nice devoted creature, even if uncivilized. Give me a little more coffee, there's a dear. He said to me, "When we've got a first-class mayor, I guess we'll keep him. What the hell does it matter what the bloody Tories do?"'

49

'*Ssh*, Belle! Not before the children.'

'Lots of girls at school say "bloody",' Bronwen provided.

'So do we,' said Jasper, not to be outdone.

'Well, I'm sorry to hear it. So they'll keep you as mayor, Marcus, for three or four years?'

'Good-*ee*!' cried Bronwen. 'In four years I shall be seventeen—'

'You *won't*,' Jasper denied indignantly.

'Well, as good as seventeen. Sixteen and a lot. So can't I be Mayoress then?'

'Don't be absolutely daft, Bron,' Jasper requested.

'Win Melville says daughters of seventeen are often mayoresses and I'm almost Uncle's daughter.'

A leap of happy love because these were words that sat well with an old dream, but all he said aloud was, 'I very much doubt if I shall need a mayoress in four years' time. Either they'll have had enough of me or I shall have had enough of the whole business. It may prove too expensive in time and money. I'm a poor man, and I have my own work to do, if we're not all to starve.'

'Rubbish, Marcus. You could well afford to go on as long as you like. And I think it'd be quite nice for Bron one day to be a mayoress. Certainly a little hallowing of her wouldn't do any harm.'

'*Do* stop using that frightful word. To hallow is to consecrate something for a religious purpose.'

'Well, isn't that more or less what they're going to do to you?'

'It isn't.' Mark was now warming again his balloon brandy glass with the palms of both hands. 'The word might perhaps fit the Mayor's civic service.'

'Especially if you have it, as you suggest, at All Hallows,' said Belle.

'Oh, what's a civic service?' cried Bronwen.

Mark explained that the Mayor with all his Council and the Borough's principal officers went in procession to church to be prayed for and preached at—'in the hope,' he added, 'that they may pray for themselves. At least, that's the idea.'

'But does a Labour Council do that sort of thing?' asked Belle, surprised.

'Surely. Why not?'

'I thought all Labour people were either heathen or went to weird non-conformist chapels. We know the Anglican Church is the Tory Party at prayer, but I thought the Labour Party hardly prayed at all.'

'You're going to learn a lot, Madame Mayoress. On occasions like these, whether they're churchgoers or not, tradition takes over from Theology. In the North they've been known to close the streets and proceed from Town Hall to church in top hats, with bands playing.'

'Golly!' murmured Bronwen. 'Will *you* have a procession?'

'Certainly.'

'With Mummy in it too?'

'Perhaps.'

'I say! Isn't it all going to be rather fab?'

Jasper and Bronwen looked down from the front row of the public gallery. Behind them, too shy to sit in a front row, sat Pelly and Capes—and, as Bronwen had foretold, Mr. Capes. After Bronwen had explained at some length to Pelly and Capes that they could come, Mr. Capes had assured his wife that Miss Bronwen was right. 'Why, of course you can go, Mother, if you want to,' he had said, surprised at the political ignorance of women. 'It's your right. It's your civic right. I never been meself, but I might come too, being as how it's Mr. Dolmen being elected.' Mr. Capes was taller than, and almost as thin as, Mrs. Pelly so that the plump little Mrs. Capes sat tonight like a Sancho Panza by the side of two long Quixotes.

It was not yet fifteen minutes past six but some of the councillors were already standing here and there to chatter in groups, or were wandering with their papers towards their seats. The seats for the forty-eight councillors were in a three-tiered horse-shoe about the Press table in the pit of this fine new Council Chamber. Behind and above them the public gallery swept in another horse-shoe like the dress-circle of a theatre. Before the councillors' seats was a platform on two levels, the lower for the Town Clerk and the principal officers, the higher for the eight aldermen, with the Mayor's uplifted throne in their midst.

The Chamber was crowned by a domed glass roof from the

51

centre of which depended a magnificent rock-crystal chandelier (gift of a former mayor). Though it was daylight outside, the lamps of the chandelier were alight, for the lofty windows were all of stained glass; they pictured episodes in the ancient history of Keys. Between these windows hung portraits of past mayors in their robes and chains of office.

Jasper and Bronwen, looking for Mark, were surprised when he strolled in and went, not to any remarkable place but to his usual councillor's seat. Both children were still excited at having been stopped on the steps of the Town Hall by a posse of photographers who wanted to take a picture of them together. One of them had noted down their names for the caption. 'Miss Bronwen Hamps and Master Jasper Dolmen, the children of our new Mayor and Mayoress, on the steps of the Town Hall.'

'I tried to smile,' Bronwen was saying to Jasper now, 'but I didn't think it was a success.'

'Nor did I,' said Jasper.

'Still, all the girls at school will see it. Everyone takes the *Keys and Had*.' (The *Keys and Hadleigh News*.) 'But "Hamps". Oh, dear, "Hamps" is a pity.'

'Won't they rag you about being pictured in a paper?'

'Oh, yes. Rather! That's what I'm looking forward to.'

'Good Lord.' And Jasper was left meditating on the difference between girls' schools and boys' schools. Evidently ragging by schoolgirls was less brutal an affair than that of prep school boys, or girls were less shy and sensitive about it.

But now everyone was suddenly standing. The red-robed aldermen were going to their seats; the dark-clad councillors were all in theirs; and only the Mayor's high throne stood empty. The clock above it lacked a minute from the half hour. The monkey-house chatter of fifty voices had stopped. Silence, a waiting silence, filled the great room.

A door opened. The tall mace-bearer appeared in his gown of black and gold with the mace on his shoulder. With him came the little Town Clerk in gown, bands and wig, and then the retiring Mayor, equally small, in scarlet robe, white lace and gold chain. Bronwen had been bending down to recover a hairslide, and Jasper had to kick her with his heel to draw her attention to what was happening.

'Lordy!' she said, as she saw this colourful procession.

The Mayor, now standing in his high place, bowed to the aldermen on his right, who bowed back; to those on his left, who bowed back; and then to all the councillors in the body of the chamber. They all, as one man, bowed to him, and Bronwen, fearful of being remiss again, produced a quick little bow too, only to be told by Jasper, 'Don't be an ass. He's not interested in you.'

'The little Town Clerk is rather sweet,' was all she said by way of answer to this, as she and all the company sat down.

The Mayor now called for a nomination—or nominations— for the position of mayor in the ensuing year, and Arthur Lammas rose. Broad-faced, blunt-featured, heavy as an ex-pugilist who had put on some fat, he attempted no grace or skilful timing in his speech, preferring a rapid level-toned utter-ance, as if to say, 'Let's get this business over quickly and have no truck with oratory.' Unlike Mark, who never wanted anyone to think him dependent on notes, Arthur held a small sheet of notes before him. Looking at these rather than at the Mayor, he began with a mistake. 'Mr. Chairman—I mean Mr. Mayor—I propose Mr. Councillor Dolmen be elected mayor for the coming year. He will be the first Labour mayor, and thank God for that—'

Loud laughter from the Tory benches, rising laughter—and Arthur, perceiving that his words could be interpreted in two ways, and never a man not to hit back if laughed at, said, look-ing at the enemy now instead of at the notes, 'I mean, thank God we shall have a Labour mayor at last after sixty years of reactionary rule by comfortable Tory gentlemen who know less than nothing about how the poor live—'

'Bosh!' muttered a Tory gentleman across the room.

Hearing which, Arthur, forgetting it was his duty to address his remarks to the Mayor, addressed one to this councillor. 'You shut up, chum,' he said.

The interrupter grinned, so Arthur gave him a little more. 'You belong to the so-called gentlemanly party, don't you, dear boy, and I've always heard that gentlemen learned at their expensive and privileged schools to take a hiding without losing their temper.'

53

'My temper's excellent,' said the Tory.

'Well, shut up, then,' recommended Arthur, and gave his eyes back to his notes. The day was uncommonly warm, Arthur wore no waistcoat, and since his unoccupied hand was in his trouser pocket, pushing back his dark jacket, this unveiled a broad expanse of white shirt and a powerful brown-leather belt, which, however, did not seem powerful enough, for lack of a waist, to hold his trousers in the exact place of truth. In addition to the trousers this belt seemed to carry and display his past as a foreman builder. Having found his place, he continued, 'I'm sure, Mr. Mayor, the Council will agree that there is no more suitable person on our side of the house, or indeed in the whole chamber, to occupy that chair which you, sir, in the last two years have filled with such distinction.' Arthur could be generous to an opponent as well as insulting. 'Councillor Dolmen has served our Council for nearly twenty years—longer, I think, than any other member except me and most of those picturesque fixtures up there on the aldermanic bench. He was born in our borough and has lived there all his life—born, actually, in the Brides Ward which behaved so splendidly in the recent election. Councillor Dolmen, as you know, represents the Old Common Ward, which as a workers' area has had the wisdom always to return a full flush of Labour members—'

'Stick to the point,' suggested a Tory voice.

Arthur removed his eyes from his notes to this interrupter. He waited a moment; then said, 'I know, cock, that you don't want to hear any mention of the Old Common or Brides Wards, and I'm not surprised. Sorry if it 'urts you, mister, but—'

'Doesn't hurt me. I'm quite untroubled.' Said with a happy grin.

'All right then. You leave the chatting to me for the present. . . . Okay, honey? . . . Fine. . . . I was about to say—I was about to say—what?' He sought the answer in his notes. 'I was about to say that I'm glad the Brides, having followed Old Common's excellent example, will be rewarded by having one of its residents as mayor. I'm sure all will agree that he will be an ornament to our Council, not only as a man of distinction in his profession—I'm told he cuts up people in the kindest and most competent way—but because he is a gentleman with a great social conscience, indefatigable in service to our borough—and this at no inconsiderable loss to himself (as I happen to know) because these surgeons can make a helluva packet if they really go to it. Mark gives up much too much of his time to us and is prepared to give up still more as mayor. You will agree that he is a man of great charm and humour, and I've no doubt he will conduct our proceedings, sir, with the fairness and the courtesy that you have always shown us. It's a proud day for me, Mr. Mayor, to stand here and propose Mark—I mean, Mr. Councillor Dolmen as our first Labour mayor.'

Bronwen, looking at Mark whose eyes were on the ground as if in discomfort at so much praise, guessed nevertheless that his pleasure outweighed the embarrassment. She whispered to Jasper, 'I suppose Uncle's enjoying this, but he doesn't look as though he was. He looks rather as if they were sentencing him to death.'

'The old man hates being praised in public,' Jasper explained.

'I bet he does, and I bet he loves it all the same,' said Bronwen. 'I should. I should simply adore it.'

'That I conceive to be the truth,' said Jasper in his finest manner.

'Well, so would you love it,' she pouted.

'It is possible,' he allowed. 'But in the excellent words of Mr. Councillor Arthur Lammas, *shut* up! Listen to the lady. She's talking about your Mum. It's conceivable she may talk about us.'

'Crikey! Will she? Oh, *lord*!'

Councillor Miss Goodall, another Labour member, had risen to second the nomination, and she was devoting most of her words to the lady who would be mayoress. She reminded them that, like her brother, Mrs. Hamps had lived and spent her childhood in the Brides Ward and after leaving it for a short period, had come back to it as quite the best place to live in; since when she had been known in Keys as a voluntary worker in any number of good causes. 'We know her as a woman of the liveliest wit and the most gracious manner, and are confident that in Mrs. Hamps we shall have a Mayoress as outstanding as her brother, the Mayor.'

Bronwen murmured, 'Gosh, the family's doing well.'

Major Roper, Leader of the Tories, ruddy-faced, beak-nosed, army-moustached, and not only as big as Arthur Lammas but clad in a billowing jacket and trousers which suggested he might require room to enlarge yet further, now rose slowly and baggily from his party's front bench.

Since 'Evans the Echo' was also a Tory, there were frequent echoes, in a low bass, of the Major's speech, from Councillor Evans's place among the back-bench members. A quarter-smile crumpled the Major's lips as he began, 'We have decided, Mr. Mayor, to offer no candidate in opposition to Councillor Dolmen, and I have therefore little to say now. What I do say will, I feel, be somewhat displeasing to my good friend, Councillor Lammas, so may I assure him, with all respect, and ask him to believe without any reservations, that this is fully intended. I wish only to say that Councillor Dolmen will receive from our party all the respect and support which we have always accorded to the occupant of your chair. We may differ from him in politics but one and all of us know him to be a man of unfailing courtesy—which, alas, is more than I can say of a certain other member of his party.' ('Exactly. Hear, hear. Ha, ha,' from Councillor Evans's bench.) 'We know him also as a man of the highest integrity and a devoted servant of our common Borough—' ('Oh, yes. Agreed,' from the same point.)—'and I am happy to add that I can also say this much at least about the councillor who proposed his election, however I may deplore his manner of doing so.' ('That much, yes. Certainly.') 'Let me therefore conclude, on behalf of us all, by wishing him a happy time during his brief occupation of your chair. We do not know how many terms he may serve but it is safe to call the occupation brief since it is unthinkable that Keys in the next election will not return to its ancient loyalty.' ('Yes, yes. Of course. Ha, ha.') And with a small contorted smile for all, a pleased smile, Major Roper relapsed baggily but comfortably into his seat.

George Colls, the sole Liberal, rose to say that 'speaking for the Liberal Party, which for the moment is me' he would wish to endorse everything everyone had said about Councillor Dolmen and about the readiness of all parties in the Chamber, 'including this one', to give him their support.

The retiring Mayor then put the nomination to the vote and,

there being no dissentients, declared Councillor Dolmen duly elected.

All stood again as the procession of mace-bearer, Town Clerk and retiring Mayor went from the chamber, Mark following. A few minutes, and the procession returned, with Mark as Mayor, in all the majesty of furred scarlet gown, spreading lace jabot, spotless white gloves and heavy gold chain and mayoral badge.

For once Bronwen was struck almost speechless by the splendour of his appearance (for Mark was a much bigger and handsomer man, a far more formidable figure, than the little retiring Mayor). All that she managed to mumble was, 'I *ask* you! Oh! . . . How inexpressibly glam.'

But the thoughts of Mark were not flippant as he stepped on to a high throne majestically carved with the arms of the Borough of Keys. Two thoughts lay paired within his mind, the one a good thought of which he need not be ashamed, the other, though not wholly ignoble, one that he could hardly tell to his dearest friend. As he remembered the long dynasty of mayors before him, all of them esteemed civic fathers in their day but most of them forgotten now, names and no more, his first thought was that he would like to do this task in his brief hour as dutifully, ably, and successfully as possible; his second that he would like his mayoralty to be a famous and long-remembered one, nothing less than the most celebrated of all, till the time came for it to be forgotten.

One of the first steps of the first Labour mayor was to break with tradition and have his civic service, not in the ancient Parish Church of Keys, but in the church of All Hallows in the Seven Brides Estate. This had been the church of his family and his childhood.

The Parish Church, St. Peter's, dated back to the fifteenth century and was the lineal descendant of an old chapel which had been in the fields before the Normans came. The little shrine had been known as the Chapel of St. Peter's Keys and had given its name to the village that slowly gathered around it. The church of All Hallows, on the other hand, had no such glamour

57

of age and history. Built in the 1860's to meet the ever-swelling overspill from West London, it belonged, in modern eyes, to the Victorian Gothic Revival at its most corrupt. It was faced with stucco from its bases to its meaningless battlements; its long rectangular shape, for it had no transepts, ended with a square pinnacled tower which rose, strangely enough, behind the chancel instead of over the west doors. Within doors its plastered arches were a stock imitation of the Late Decorated style. Steep galleries hung over the aisles and the west end, darkening them. The builders in the religious exuberance of the mid-Victorian era had made ready a church for a thousand people, but in these faithless days, a hundred years later, it seldom had more than seventy or eighty for Matins and twenty for Evensong. Like too many of its sisters, it was a huge church with a heart beating weakly.

Mark's stern mother had been a regular attendant at this, her local church; his 'bad old father' a much less regular one, though a generous subscriber to its funds. Mark and Belle had attended regularly too in those days, having no option to do anything else, with such a mother. Belle still reproduced the faith and loyalty of her mother, but Mark in his adulthood became his father over again—rarely seen among the deserted pews, but always ready with a handsome cheque. Bronwen went regularly with her mother, lodging an objection only seldom; Mark never forced Jasper to go; and Jasper didn't go—unless he accompanied his father on some state occasion.

It was not only for these family reasons, but partly to help an ailing church, and because he had an amused and pitying affection for its old and failing vicar, the Rev. Simeon Craik, that Mark had decided his mayoral service should be at All Hallows. 'Let's give poor old Craikie a lift,' he had said to Belle and the children. 'A mayoral service should be a shot in the arm for his church. Besides Mother Pearl Runciman, the Rector's wife, won't approve at all. That settles it.'

Yet another reason for a sensational step, but one which remained only among his hidden thoughts, was his usual faint pleasure in being styled by the people of Keys as 'somewhat eccentric'.

'Poor old Craikie,' as Mark always called him, was pleased

that Mark had chosen his church for the municipal service but much tasked by the thought of how such a service should run. Though he was the Vicar, and had been a priest for nearly fifty years, he came on a most anxious visit to the Mayor for instruction and help. In his anxiety he arrived at Mornington Gardens many minutes earlier than the appointed time, which was ten o'clock on a Saturday morning. Craikie was a little grey man with moist, red-rimmed eyes and thin disordered grey hair. His chin this morning could hardly be called clean-shaven, for too many silver bristles glistened in the bright June daylight. On his lips, and indeed on his black clerical stock, lay some of the egg which he'd boiled for his recent, lonely, and hurried breakfast. From his breath came the odour of some gulp of whisky which he'd taken for his encouragement, though it was not yet ten in the morning.

Like Mark, Craikie had lost a loved wife all too soon, and this added to Mark's affection for him. His two daughters had been only sixteen and fourteen when his wife died, but they had long since left him, one to a husband, and the other to a teaching job in the North and an early death. In his loneliness and increasing age he had sought much help from the whisky bottle and, he would admit, from stimulant drugs. 'It's the only way I can get through my work.'

In a single word of Mark's, poor old Craikie was a 'mess'.

'Do you really think he'll be able to manage a municipal service?' Belle had asked.

'No, I don't.'

'Won't it be a series of disasters?'

'Quite likely, but let's give the old boy his chance. He'll do his best.'

And here he was, in Mark's study, asking, 'What do you want me to do? Do tell me exactly,' as he sat with elbows on knees, a large hymn-book open in both hands, and prayer books on the floor. 'What do I do?'

'You pray. For us. For me.'

'Yes, yes, yes—don't be silly—this is serious. What hymns, for instance? Mark, what hymns?'

'*I* don't know. The only hymn I can ever think of is "Onward, Christian Soldiers".'

'I've brought a hymn-book. Do choose what hymns you fancy.'

'Oh, heavens! Must I?' Mark took the book and after turning the pages and finding no help, consulted the index. The index provided him mainly with opportunities for teasing Craikie. Thinking of himself with the Town Clerk, the Deputy Mayor, the mace-bearer and the aldermen, all in their robes, he said, 'I suggest 598.'

'What hymn's that?'

'One for a Flower Service.'

'No, come now, Mark. Don't be absurd. Choose something sensible.'

'Well . . . Commemoration of Saints—no, that's not very appropriate. Oh, here we are. Here's the very thing. All three parties will be represented, so here it is, Craikie. "Fight the good fight".'

'No, do, please, Mark—'

'You don't think that'll do? No, perhaps the irreverent would laugh. What's wrong with 268?'

'What's 268?'

'Ye servants of the Lord, Each in his office wait. . . . Most of the borough officers come along. Good for 'em to be told to gird up their loins in his sight. Yes, And let their lamps be bright.'

'I don't think anyone knows that hymn. Shouldn't we have something they can sing?'

Mark's finger slid down the index of first lines. '"Weary of earth and laden with my sin . . ." that's all right for me—fits me like a glove—but I wonder if it'd suit old Major Roper. Do you think he feels weary of earth and laden with his sin? *I* don't. "Out of the deep I call. . . ." That sounds right for a hopelessly bewildered mayor. Let's look at it. "Out of the deep I cry, the woeful deep of sin, Of evil done in days gone by, Of evil now within." That's me exactly, Craikie. Let's have that.'

'No, please, *please*, Mark, you're just joking.'

'Well, it's a problem. Some of the councillors are Jew boys, but they come along nobly. We must find something they can sing without too much embarrassment. Others are plain heathens but we want 'em to enjoy themselves too. What can we have that all our Jews, Turks, and infidels can sing?'

The two of them arrived at last at the Old Hundredth, as the one least likely to trouble anyone. Other 'safe' hymns they chose were 'O God, our help in ages past' and 'Be thou my guardian and my guide'. But Mark insisted they must have 'Onward, Christian soldiers' to finish up with. 'Nobody can resist that tune, whatever its words say. So let's all really enjoy ourselves with it. Let's fairly go to town with it.'

Sunday morning, the Sunday of the service, and a noise of many voices filled the vestibule of the Lauder Road School. Mayor, Deputy Mayor, aldermen and Town Clerk were robing, while the councillors, borough officers, and co-opted members in subfusc suits stood around talking, till such time as the Mayor's Secretary and a committee clerk, acting as ushers, should marshal them into a column for the procession through the streets.

Outside the school the church bells, near and far, were telling the world that it was Sunday morning and nearly the hour for Divine Service; but the world in the streets seemed to be giving them little heed. Within the school, at ten minutes to the hour, the marshals began to walk around and say 'Gentlemen, will you take your places, please. . . . Ladies, would you . . . *please!*' and the gentlemen promptly, the ladies gradually, stopped their talking and took up their correct positions. The least important went to the head of the column, the most important, the robed figures, to the rear, and the climax of all was the Mayor. With a crooked finger the Mayor's Secretary summoned the column to march and, following him, it went out into the street where a few policemen waited to shepherd it through the traffic of a fine June morning. The unecclesiastical pedestrians halted on the pavements, or just turned their heads, to watch it pass.

Mark, behind all the others, was amused and touched to see the Tories in good strength marching ahead of him. Many of them had been aggrieved by his desertion of the Parish Church, but there they were, marching along, because Tories were nothing if not men with a high sense of duty and a desire to do the right honours to their mayor, even if he was a misguided Socialist. There on his bandy legs in his over-full trousers

61

waddled Major Roper, and Mark could guess the thoughts in his head or his words to the Tory at his side. 'A municipal service should be in the municipal church. Why the hell we're being made to pray in the old Brides' wedding cake—' his name for the stuccoed and crenellated church of All Hallows—'just because it's Dolmen's church, God alone knows. But pray there, of course, I will, though under protest. We've got to pray somewhere for Keys now that we've got Socialists in control.' There went little Shamus O'Donoghue, Sunday-neat in a well-waisted black jacket and shepherd's-plaid trousers, a curly-brimmed bowler standing small and high on his head, and his rolled umbrella swinging like a pendulum between two fingers. There behind the Major was Evans the Echo—after all, was it not the business of an echo to follow close behind his principal? Perhaps more noteworthy than any of these were two of the Jewish Tories, Councillors Woolfe and Raphael, marching along to an Anglican church. And Arthur too; perhaps he deserved even more credit than these excellent Jews because while his Jewish colleagues believed, one in the Pentateuch, and the other in modern Liberal Judaism, Arthur believed in nothing. Like Craikie he had come anxiously to Mark's study for instruction and help. 'It'll be the first time I've come along, Mark, I don't know anything about church, but, by golly, I'm coming along to *your* service. *Our* service really, isn't it? What do I do?'

'You pray.'

'I can't pray. I don't know anything about praying. Shouldn't know what to say.'

'Well, let the Vicar, the Reverend Mr. Craik, do the praying, and you just say Amen when he stops.'

'Amen. Yes?'

'And then the old boy'll announce some hymns.'

'Yes?' as if not much wiser.

'Well then you have the words in front of you, and you sing them heartily. You make a joyful noise before the Lord.'

'Oh, my God, no. No, Mark, don't ask me to do anything like that. I'll just stand there and wish you well.'

From this point the new Mayor, walking in his fine robes alone, began to dream. He lost himself in memories of long winter Sundays fifty years ago; of All Hallows, as it had been in his childhood, crowded to the walls; even of times in his youth when religion had seized and obsessed him for a while, so that he'd had thoughts of becoming a friar in a coarse brown habit and knotted white cord rather than a mayor in a scarlet robe and golden chain.

But now they were in sight of the church, and he saw a crowd about its gates awaiting this Local Mayor's Show as they might await a wedding. Drawing nearer, he saw that old Craikie stood vested in the west doors with an old retired parson who sometimes helped him on Sundays at his side. Behind him was a young crucifer with the processional cross; in front of him the two churchwardens (one a plump lady) with their wands. In the high church tower a harsh-tongued bell was clanging monotonously, its repeated notes so slow as to be almost a tolling. One felt that the bell-ringer below had small heart for his task and was tiring.

As the head of the column met the Vicar, he turned about; the crucifer did the same; and now processional cross, parsons, and wardens led the long column into the church. Meanwhile the church bell clanged on. All eyes, first in the churchyard and then in the church, fixed on Mark, the new Mayor, as they might on a bride; and his own eyes, fixed ahead, hid from all the pleasure this temporary interest gave him. When they were out of the summer daylight and in the dimness of a church darkened by leaded windows London-grimed, he was disappointed to see how small was the congregation even for such a service as this. There were perhaps forty more persons than usual scattered among the dark-brown pews. The long aisles were as empty as the steep galleries above them. Only the sunlight, fragmented by the stained windows into many colours, visited the empty south aisle. Unable to find men or boys for his choir Craikie had only women in the choir stalls, women in black gowns and square Tudor caps. Always some women were faithful.

While all the congregation stood in honour of the new Mayor, the wardens ushered Mark into the front pew of all on the right-hand side, where Belle, his Mayoress, awaited him. There was some amusement these days among the citizens of Keys about their big mayor and little mayoress, for Belle came barely up to her brother's shoulder and presented a figure as spare and thin as his was large and ample. When they walked side by side she always seemed—so some declared—to be moving much faster than he, while only keeping abreast. And from the back view in church, they said, the two might be father and daughter. Jasper and Bronwen, standing in the other front pew, turned their faces unashamedly to watch Mark being installed and his sergeant laying the golden mace on a special bracket in front of him. Mark felt a great love going out to the two of them standing there. The mace in position, its bearer withdrew modestly to a neighbouring pew in the south aisle and for the rest of the service was the only figure in the dusk of that long empty avenue.

The bell stopped.

Since Mark had provided service sheets at his own cost there was no need for Craikie to announce a hymn, so organist and organ (perhaps the only two competent servants of this church) burst proudly into the familiar notes of the Old Hundredth, 'All people that on earth do dwell'; the congregation, such as it was, sang cheerfully; and Mark went into his brooding thoughts again.

Those close-packed congregations of his boyhood! But, even then, how few of the working classes sat among the well-dressed throngs. Once upon a time they had been in the little chapel of St. Peter's Keys, and later on they had knelt at mass in the stone church which succeeded it; but where were they now? How had the Church lost them, some to chapels, more to the free and open air? The Tory members of the Council behind him would be familiar with this service of historic chants and stately prayers, but what of his Labour colleagues? Those whose world was the working-class world. What would this service seem to them? Arthur—what was Arthur thinking?

But now, suddenly, these drifting questions were arrested by a remarkable discovery. There in that other front pew across the nave, and on the far side of Jasper and Bronwen, were two feminine figures surely familiar, one tall and lean, the other short, broad and fat. Yes, they were none other than Pelly and Capes, the expeditious Pelly and the chatty Capes, daily express and daily news. The children must have secretly engineered their attendance here this morning and their places in this honour-

64

able pew. Doubtless they had instructed them to tell any interfering sidesman that they belonged to the Mayor, and were entitled to the most prominent position in the church. Thinking this and grinning, Mark leaned back a little, half expecting to see old Mr. Luddermore on the farther side of Capes. But no; either the children had not attempted the difficult ramparts of Mr. Luddermore or the assault had not met with success.

Nor was Mr. Capes there, and Mark was now surprisingly disappointed by this. He, Mr. Capes, had been ready to come in the evening to the Town Hall to see the 'goings-on' there, but had probably declined to abandon his Sunday paper and his chair (or his bed) for hymns and prayers at eleven o'clock on a Sunday morning.

Mark paid but little attention to the service as it ambled along through canticles, lessons, psalms and prayers; he listened to the lessons but dreamed during the prayers; he who had instructed Arthur to pray didn't pray himself—until Craikie was stumbling up the pulpit stairs, when he began to pray speedily and almost desperately, lest his old friend should fail. It was on the third step that Craikie stumbled as he was pushing back his glasses on to his nose, and that Mark found himself at ardent prayer— or at least repeating fervently, 'Oh God, help him. . . . Help the old boy. . . . Help him. . . . Help him to do well.'

The old boy got himself into the pulpit without further floundering, and Mark told himself with relief, 'He's made it. He's made it safely.'

At the pulpit's lectern Craikie pushed home the loose spectacles again and arranged his notes.

All seated, he lifted his eyes from the notes and in a good full voice—relic of a once fine organ—he delivered his text into the waiting silence.

'Except the Lord build the house their labour is but lost that build it. Except the Lord keep the city the watchman waketh but in vain.'

The words, splendidly appropriate, were a shaft of pleasure in Mark's heart. It seemed as if Craikie might not fail. He had opened well.

After letting the splendid words sink in to that silence, Craikie said, 'Let me just give you the next verse too, because I shall come to it later. It runs, "It is but lost labour that ye haste to rise up early and so late take rest and eat the bread of carefulness, for so he giveth his beloved sleep."'

Wonderful how beautiful words, Mark thought, if spoken by a man who was really feeling their beauty, could for a moment light up his face and transfigure him. There was a faded light in Craikie's age-moist eyes. And if the old man's voice was hoarse and phlegmy, the splintered wreck of a once fine one, his manner in the pulpit, his use of words and his uttering of them suggested at times that he must have been something of an orator in his younger days, before things went amiss and his life drifted towards the rocks. There were relics in that drifting vessel of fine intelligence and taste. Mark, listening, was touched by the thought that Craikie must have laboured long on this sermon so as not to fail the occasion. One could picture him at his untidy desk with his forehead cupped in one hand, his pencil twisting in the other, and half his old College books around him. And possibly a strong whisky at his side or one of his stimulant drugs at its work within him.

He began, 'This is a happy day for us, Mr. Mayor, when we receive you and your Lady Mayoress—'

Yes, he *would* get that wrong, Mark thought.

'—as our borough's chief citizens into your own church and the church of your dear parents before you. Your good father and your good mother were pillars of this church before my time'—here he smiled down at the Mayor—'but throughout your childhood and youth.'

Well, yes, Mother was a firm pillar, but father, 'my good father'? Hmm . . . the dear and bad old man was rather a cracked pillar I should say.

'We feel it an honour to have been given the duty of—may I say?—consecrating you in your high office and your newly elected councillors in their places of great responsibility. I think "consecration" is not too large a word—'

It'll suit Belle all right.

'—for when a governing body like a town council comes formally and officially into God's temple, what is it but to acknowledge that one and all, mayor and councillors and officers, must endeavour to be servants of God. It is a demon-

66

stration before the world, is it not, that just as State and Church are partners in the country's government, so they should be in our cities and boroughs. It should all amount to a solemn declaration that the watchmen of a city wake but in vain unless the Lord is captain of the watch.'

Another splendid phrase. Where did the old boy get it from?

'This noble psalm must have been sung in Jerusalem's temple a thousand years and more before Christ came and stood in that temple, and its truth remains the same today three thousand years later. It is a very happy thing, I feel, that, as the Mayor tells me, men of all parties, and indeed of different religions, are present here today to acknowledge a truth that must be basic to one and all creeds. About other affirmations they may differ but on this they must all agree.

'I would wish to explain the strange, unexpected close to that second verse. "It is but lost labour that ye haste to rise up early and so late take rest, and eat the bread of carefulness, for so he giveth his beloved sleep." It means, we are told, that his faithful servants can take their natural rest with perfect confidence in his care, knowing that the ceaseless toil, in which those weary themselves who do not trust in God's help, is quite unnecessary to his beloved. If you are forwarding God's work in the day-time he will be prospering it and continuing it, even when you are taking your ease and slumbering—"as if a man should cast seed into the ground and should sleep, and rise night and day, and the seed should spring up and grow, he knoweth not how".'

Well . . . good old Craikie! It was a sermon most apt and interesting which he had put together, and Mark was in no way disappointed when his task was fulfilled and all rose for the last hymn. But—while all were singing, 'Onward, Christian soldiers' —there did come upon him suddenly the thought that, however apt, well phrased and delivered, however beautiful its Biblical quotations, its substance was commonplace. Pleasing but commonplace.

What was there in it to reach the ultimate bewilderments in every individual soul, whether mayor or councillor or burgess? What was there in it to ease the warring complexities in every human heart? Where was there anything in it to touch the nerve of all that was so dark and defeating in every secret human life?

67

A nice, well-meant comfortable sermon, but even as they sang, 'At the sign of triumph Satan's host doth flee, On then, Christian soldiers, On to victory,' he was visited and possessed by a certainty that, if religion was to mean anything again to men in this present darkened and threatened, even horrifying, world, with the atom bombs ticking, its sermons could not afford to be pleasing and satisfying, but should be disturbing, troubling, challenging, overturning; they should be charges of dynamite to every man's complacency, and yet the promise of a blinding hope.

The strange feeling was like a moment of vision.

'Like a mighty army Moves the Church of God; Brothers, we are treading Where the Saints have trod . . .' but were we? Who was? Who in this church really was? A good woman or two, perhaps, here and there. But never mind. Sing the lively, complacent words. Sing them joyously to their irresistible tune. By the Devil's mercy these moments of vision were but instantaneous things, lost as soon as seen, and comfortably left behind.

7. The Daily Work

June and the trees in the garden, now full of leaf, and neither lopped nor thinned, so darkened his study that on a clouded day he had to write with a reading-lamp, even at noon. July and all the young leaves themselves had darkened with the drooping of summer and the soots in the London air. One evening in the garden Mr. Luddermore, who had been mowing the patchy grass, paused on the handles of his machine and said to Mark who'd come down the iron stairway for a joke or two, 'Them trees.'

'Yes?' inquired Mark. 'What about them?'

'That there black poplar.'

'Yes. The black poplar. What about it?'

'Getting too big for its boots, a'n't it? I reckon its height's coming up a 'undred feet or more, wouldn't you say? Them lower branches that grow straight out, they over'ang the road far too much for my liking. I reckon you've a spread there of thirty foot.'

'Oh, no. Twenty. Twenty-five.'

'Well, any'ow it overshadders the pavement and part of the road. Even more than that there dismal Tree of 'Evan does—'

'It's not a dismal tree, Mr. Luddermore. It's a beautiful tree.'

'Well, I grant you its upper branches are not as 'igh and don't look as dangerous to me as them black poplar's. If you look up at *them* you'll see that they may grow upward instead of outward but, even so, they're pretty well across the 'ole road. A year or so and they'll be looking like my birch broom trying to brush some muck off the sky!' So Mr. Luddermore had his poetry! 'I'm thinking you'll 'ave the Council after you for darkening that there Menworthy Rise. Or for letting your poplar be a danger to the public. Them long branches crack easy and could fall on someone's napper. And that'd 'urt.'

Mark did on this occasion say, 'Mr. Luddermore, *I* am the Council,' and with more justice, now that he was Mayor, than on the last occasion when Mr. Luddermore threatened him with conciliar action.

'Well, yurse, I suppose you are, kind of, but that won't pay your damages when someone gets the law on you for a cracked head. Or what about if your Tree of 'Evan drops one of its branches on your car standing out there?'

'They don't look like falling to me,' said Mark, looking up at the tree's stout arms writhing out arthritically over Menworthy Rise, with their long slender ends weeping.

'Well, it's for you to say,' Mr. Luddermore accepted, with a shrug, and plain disapproval in his shoulders as he resumed his mowing. 'But, to me, there always seems something uncanny, like, about that there tree.'

Mark had been worried how far the many mayoral tasks would interfere with his professional work and diminish his income. 'I'm but a poor piece-worker,' he had said once to Arthur Lammas. 'Everybody thinks that surgeons earn fantastic sums but it's never been true of me. A few of our top boys do well enough but I doubt if there's one who puts into his pocket anything like the booty popular opinion imagines. And as for your present mayor, Mr. Lammas, he does fairly comfortably, but no more.'

'Wish I earned half as much,' was Arthur's reply.

Mark's words were true enough. He had never made the bigger money because his major interest was not money. From the first it had been ambition, an ambition hidden from the sight of all: the desire for an ever-widening reputation and perhaps— yes, perhaps—a knighthood one day. It was partly in the service of this ambition that he had given so much time to Labour and the Council, and had now taken the mayoralty. Labour would be the Government one day. . . . This striving ambition, however, had not so far got him up among the top men; there had been too many others, as skilled as he, climbing the same hill and meeting more luck on their way.

There had been other motives to limit his profits, less selfish and therefore less secret. He would say aloud and truly that he could have made a larger income if he'd treated surgery solely as a money-making trade and devoted most of his time to his private practice, instead of treating it as an enthralling art, with the result that he spent so much of his week in his hospitals. Of one less selfish motive he never spoke to anyone except perhaps to Belle; this was the keen happiness he got from operations done for the young and poor, or the old and poor, without fee.

Still, his income was comfortable enough, and Arthur might justly say, 'I only wish I could make half as much,' but it had never yet been enough to thrust all anxieties from his mind. Was he not getting older; might not brain, hands and eyes lose their skills; say he made a bad mistake and they sued him in court; reputation and career might be mortally hurt; say, even, that he made no mistake but someone sued him unsuccessfully; the mud might stick, the reputation which he'd been slowly assembling over the years be undone and his earning power lessened. It was partly this ever-reviving if unjustified anxiety which kept him in this great old-fashioned house since it was his own and not very saleable. It explained also the fine but long-outdated Rolls-Royce in Menworthy Rise.

A brilliant colleague who had achieved a resounding knighthood and was devoted to Mark, said once to a common friend in their club when both were well wined, but his words were not wholly astray, 'You know, an artist in any medium may be far from a saint; he may be a scamp for part of the day, and likewise at night, *tu comprends*, but when he's lost in his art he reproduces for a while the characteristics of a saint. Nothing less, old boy. That's to say, he gives the whole of himself, body, mind and spirit, to a perfection outside himself, a perfection which has all his worship. To watch our Mark doing his stuff is

71

to watch a consecrated soul at work just as surely as if you were watching Leonardo painting the smile of Mona Lisa or the face of St. Anne.' And he went on, 'There are too many surgeons like Mark who are as good as the most famous, and perhaps better, but are insufficiently known to the public. What's happened is that the limelight's too narrow to cover more than a few, and nowadays it often falls, not on fine surgeons because there are too many of them, but on some new wonder-working drug, which is a solitary thing. I suppose it's true of any art that when it gets crowded only a few can get near the turnstile into fame, but I'm pretty sure that all the chaps as good as our Mark, if they'd been practising in the past when there were few, would have left their names in medical history. Oh, yes.'

Some financial loss the mayoralty was certainly causing, but it was less than he had feared, because most of the Mayor's engagements were in the evening. The 'Mayor's Secretary', Noel Fowler, 'my Secretary of State', came in the morning with all letters and queries and, greatly efficient, got the answers down in half an hour or so, returning with them to the Town Hall. The evening engagements might be three or four a week, but he had always arranged for any emergency call to be telephoned to whatsoever place he was presiding in, banqueting in, speaking in, or visiting as the honoured representative of Keys. These 'calls to the phone' always rather pleased the self-showman in Mark; they declared dramatically to large audiences that he was a surgeon in demand. If by accident the call went to his home, Jasper would put it through with a lively delight; or Bronwen, if they were doing their homework together, sometimes begged to be allowed to do this. Usually he was able to ask a colleague to deal with an emergency, or he left it to the registrar, but he never failed to hurry to the hospital if the case was serious or if the registrar pleaded with him to come.

If the mayoral duties allowed it Mark's old Rolls-Royce might arrive in the courts of a hospital soon after nine in the morning and be parked on a site marked with his name. 'Mr. Dolmen.' In the entrance hall, after an amiable hand-lift to the porter, he might see his registrar waiting for him in the long corridor, ready to discuss his list for the day. If it was a day for a teaching round he would find his students waiting too, and he would set off for the wards with what he called his 'kite's tail' tagged on behind, this comprising the registrar, the house surgeon, a ward sister, a chain of students and lastly, to close the procession, an examination trolley with equipment, X-rays and notes.

But no: if the ward sister was there, she usually headed the procession because Mark, always delighting in courtesy, would indicate with a gesture of his hand that it was for her to lead. The ward was *her* kingdom, and he but a visitor.

Taking this muster from one bed to the next he would sometimes, if he saw fear in the face of a patient, use the assembly as a means of comfort for a man in his weakness. He would say, 'This mob of students, you know, is really a fine insurance for you, my dear chap. Believe me, I daren't make any mistakes with a bunch like this looking on. There's probably nothing they'd like better than to catch the old man out, even in a very small blunder.'

If his operation session was an afternoon one he would begin it at about two. These sessions were supposed to last three and a half hours, but as often as not they worked out much longer than this. He would go to the theatre corridor, where a stern red line crossed the floor to arrest those who were still in un-sterile clothes and carried the soilings of the street on their shoes. This side of the red line was the changing-room, and here he stripped down to a vest because of the probable warmth in the theatre. He got into green cotton trousers, green gown, green mask to cover mouth and nose, a white cap, and white rubber shoes. Anything green was sterile.

The operating theatre awaits him, probably a high-arched, white-tiled room, with a black rubber floor; in its midst is its heart, the operating table with a great white-domed light above it to flood the operating area, and perhaps other spotlights standing by. Here, waiting around the flooded area, either to aid him or to watch, are registrar, house surgeon, 'sister taking the case', students, theatre porters, and an extremely pretty little nurse ungallantly styled 'the dirty nurse', because she will carry away the bloodied swabs and mops. All are gowned, capped and masked, so that each individual is but a pair of interested eyes, naked or spectacled, between cap and mask.

73

Mark's entry is greeted with silence because he is one of those who dislike any talking in the theatre, except for their own soft orders or questions. Even when he is 'scrubbing up' to the elbows in one of the bowls at the far side of the room, there is only this waiting silence.

The patient is wheeled in, anaesthetized. Statuesquely still, like a stone figure on an altar tomb in the cathedral aisle, he is lifted by the porters, with two long poles, from trolley to flood-lit table under the lamp. He is now completely covered with green clothes except for the small area of the operation. All close around him. Ever preferring the old-fashioned courtesies, Mark turns first to the 'sister taking the case': 'Are you ready, Sister?' Then to the anaesthetist: 'May I start, Dr. Neave?' Both signify assent.

And Mark Dolmen, beginning to operate, is transformed, not only from the merry companion of the corridors outside, but also from the man of secret diffidences, deceits, and ex-hibitionist desires, into a cold silent machine of exquisite accur-acies. Most forgotten of all is the man who finds pleasure in a reputation for eccentricity. In a word, his ease is absolute once his fingers are active in this art. It is not only that he is absorbed in his work, but that he knows his coolness must be truly untroubled, so as to be untroubling to the others. If something is difficult and worrying let not the difficulty and worry be seen or felt by any but himself. Keep the casual, almost indifferent, look. No visible impatience; no hurry; no attention to time—and the result is an appearance of lazy leisure, which actually covers speed. All watch him fascinated, and not the students only, but his assistants, the nurses, the anaesthetist, and maybe some expert visitor as skilled as he. All are impressed by the supreme unfailing gentleness in his un-hurrying fingers. And because of his casual ease all his assistants support his movements in the same deft, unhurrying way. All look casual too.

A stranger might think those yellow thin-gloved fingers the parts of an inhuman machine, but the measure of their apparent inhumanity is the measure of their humaneness. Mark is but a poor believer in Craikie's religion, but sometimes, when the case beneath his hands is perilous, he will find himself praying

74

for his patient, 'God be good to him,' or 'God help me.'
Privately praying to some God to guide his fingers.

Once he delivered a lecture to the Medical College, a verbatim report of which can be found in contemporary medical
journals. To these lectures he gave the same pains as to his
speeches in the Council Chamber, writing them out in full,
getting quick pleasure when his gift of words flung up a fine
phrase, learning them by heart, and then delivering them as if
they were almost extempore. On the platform he generally stood
with carnation or rose in his buttonhole, one hand in a trouser
pocket, and the other holding the gold-rimmed 'quizzer', either
to glance through it at his notes or to wave it as he stressed a
point. 'Good surgery,' he said on this occasion, 'can never be
anything but gentle surgery. Have no doubt of this, my dear
fellows: in the heart of surgery there must always be compassion. Think of it like this: the surgeon is often said to be the
king of the operating theatre, but really the patient on the table
is the king, and we but his court. He may be silent and still but
he is the chief actor in the drama, because the whole story
amounts to his dialogue with death. Remember, he only, of all
the persons in that brightly lit room, is quite alone. And he, in
that hour, is all that matters to *him*. Surely his trust in you, his
hope in you, his surgeon, is a touching thing that should inspire
in you nothing less than a love for him, at least while the knife
is in your hand. . . . In sum,' he offered in conclusion, as he
folded up his notes with that studied but graceful platform
manner of which he was now a master, 'remember always how a
great surgeon expressed it, three hundred years ago, "We
surgeons need a lion's heart and an eagle's eye, but, most of all,
a lady's hand."'

8. A Silent House

September, and on the nineteenth of that month he must take Jasper to his new school. This would be a wrench for himself, and he saw with an upswell of sympathy and love that it was going to provide its painful hours for the boy. So to invest the occasion with both gaiety and distinction, and to stress without speaking the love and support that ever awaited the boy, he suggested a 'banquet' for his last night at home, with Bronwen and Belle as his guests. The menu to be entirely chosen by Jasper himself.

'Oh, whacko!' exclaimed Jasper, for he was keeping up a show of jollity. 'Anything I fancy. . . . Well, now, let us think. This is serious. This requires thought. Melon . . . clearly melon with ginger and all that. But please make it a largish melon, because I can see Bronwen going at it rather heartily and I wouldn't put it past Auntie Belle doing some good work on it.'

'Melon,' said Mark, pencilling it on his blotting pad. They were seated in his study.

'Then . . . let's see . . . oh yes, Vienna schnitzels with all the works: capers and slices of lemon and rolled anchovies with stuffed olives in them—like Auntie Belle does them. But please make them a decent size. Usually they're over too soon.'

'Wiener schnitzels.' Mark wrote it down. 'Large.'

'Then . . . it's difficult . . . oh, I know! TRIFLE.' The word certainly leapt forth in capital letters. 'Soaked in sherry and with buckets of cream. Bronwen'll probably be sick but it'll have been worth it. Then heaps of fruit. And will there be champers?'

'I beg your pardon. What did you say?'

'Champers. Champagne.'

'Oh, I hadn't thought of that, Champers? Well, it's your party, so, yes, perhaps a little champers for Belle and me.'

'Oh, heck, no!'

'Well, a bottle of—of what you called it—yes.'

'Oh, ta! Most infinitely ta.'

'Anything else?'

'But there's no room for anything else, is there?' asked Jasper almost sadly.

'I shouldn't think so.'

'No . . . perhaps not . . . but I may think of something later on.' Jasper did not wish to leave a handsome offer incompletely exploited.

Still masking his dreads of the morrow with shows of buffoonery, he greeted Bronwen, on her arrival, with ''Allo, mate. 'Ow art?'

And Bronwen answered, 'I art all right. But fancy your going off to boarding school tomorrow. Isn't it fantastic?'

'There's a rather fantastic meal,' said Jasper, quickly changing the subject. 'With intoxicating liquor. You'll probably get tight.'

'Oh, good-ee!' said Bronwen, whose local schoolgirl slang was several years behind his more metropolitan stuff.

At table Mark sat at the head with a child on either side, and Belle sat by Jasper because, as she said, the old family dining-table was so long that its foot always seemed in a different parish from its head, and she would like to spend this important evening in the same locality as Mark and the children.

All through the meal Jasper's persistent joking twisted his father's heart because he saw it for what it was: cover for a child's fears. Jasper, ever relishing strange words, would make play, not only with newly learned Shakespearean archaisms but with the resounding technical terms which he often overheard when his father was talking to colleagues. So now, when Bronwen, opposite him, was eating her melon vigorously, and not too nicely, he ventured, 'Bron isn't half putting it away, Dad.

77

Should she eat into the melon quite as deep as that? Won't it produce inflammation of her cervical oesophagus?'

'Jasper, that's no way to speak of your little guest. But it could be an intelligent suggestion, of course.'

'He's trying to be funny,' Bronwen explained, and after sucking her fingers, pursued her deep excavations into the melon.

'Yes,' Mark agreed, 'and his humour's a shade on the heavy side, don't we think?'

'If you can call it humour,' Bronwen objected. 'I never think it's funny.'

'It's not meant to be funny,' said Jasper. 'It's just that we've got to consider your pancreas.'

'My *what*? Oh, do tell him to shut up, Uncle Mark. He's just showing off.'

'Not at all. I'm not showing off. It's merely that I have your interests at heart. I don't want you'—and he enunciated his next words with a patent satisfaction—'to get chronic intestinal toxaemia.'

Even Bronwen emitted a small shriek at these remarkable syllables; and Jasper, regarding this as a success for him, drew her attention to another fact. 'And anyway, you're talking with your mouth full.'

'Am I?' said Bronwen, not greatly interested, and she asked, without amending the behaviour of her mouth, 'But what's a pancreas anyway?'

'A gland, chum,' Jasper explained. 'A gland that plays an important part in your digestive processes.'

'I thought it was a saint. With a station named after him.'

'Well, you thought wrong,' Jasper summed up, simply.

Mark listened to both children, smiling and feeling an uprush of love for both.

'If you've both got all you can out of your melon,' he said, covering up this love, even as the boy was covering up his fears, 'perhaps Jasper'll ring the bell. Unless, of course, you both contemplate eating the skin of the melon. If so, we'll wait.'

'Who's cooking downstairs?' Belle asked. 'Pelly or Capes?'

'Both, my dear. For once in a way, both. It's an occasion.'

'They're both here to say good-bye to me,' said Jasper, rising

78

to ring the bell. 'They have a heart, you see. They know I'm being evicted. They know I'm no longer wanted at 21 Mornington Gardens.'

Belle said, 'Don't be absurd, Jasper.'

'It's not absurd. It's quite true. I'm being sent away to an approved school.'

'To a very famous school. Benfield's one of the finest schools in the country, apart from being your father's old school. He distinguished himself there, and so will you. You'll probably get a great welcome there, as your father's son.'

'I'm afraid none of that'll wash, Auntie. The real truth is that Daddy needs a little peace. As I've had occasion to remark before, "Jasper is far From popu-lar In Mornington Gardens, West."'

'Crikey, he can be silly sometimes, can't he?' said Bronwen and, competing with him for unpopularity, she said, 'What about *me*?' and quoted one of his parodies which had pleased her, '"Nobody knows the trouble I've been. Nobody knows but Jesus."'

For which Belle chided her, 'Don't be a little beast, Bronwen, and don't be profane. Calling him silly the night before he goes to school, and you won't see him for months.'

'But that doesn't make him not silly,' Bronwen objected.

'He isn't silly. I think our Jasper's witty.'

'Good gosh, *do* you?'

'Yes, and I think you're just a rude little girl.'

'Well, anyhow,' said Bronwen, indifferent to this view of her, 'I jolly well wish I was going to a boarding school.'

'You *don't*,' Jasper denied incredulously. For the moment his joking had failed him, and this failure was a stab for Mark because he saw, hiding in the heart of a boy whose true habit was as shy and timid as his had once been, the fear lest something rough awaited him tomorrow. He saw the boy's thought: 'Girls' schools must be very different from boys' if she can really want to be a boarder at one.' Her words carried a small and absurd wound for him as well, with their readiness to leave him for so long. 'Why should you want to go to boarding school?' he felt driven to ask her.

'Well, everybody's heard of boys' schools. Eton and Harrow

and Benfield. Who's ever heard of Keys High School for Girls?
I want a nice old-school tie.'

'Girls don't need old-school ties,' said Mark, 'but I'm sorry to
say—as a good Labour mayor—that they can still be of help to
boys.' He was now justifying himself to himself, that he might
dispel the doubt. Had he really done the best thing for Jasper;
not just a proud thing, but the best? He must persuade himself
that he had. What else could he have done? Socialist he might
be, but he wasn't going to send Jasper to a local state school
where he'd be one in a class of perhaps forty or fifty boys.
Besides, his five years at a traditional prep school had prepared
him for nothing but a public school. And Benfield's fame was
standing high today.

'I think you know nothing about girls, Uncle darling,' said
Bronwen.

'The devil you do!'

'Yes, I know several girls who are extremely cocky about
having been to Roedean or Cheltenham. They blow off about
it. Besides, I should enjoy being a boarder.'

'Enjoy it?' exclaimed Jasper; and then propounded, 'Either
she's trying to be funny—without much success—or she's plain
nuts.'

'And Jasper'll enjoy it too,' Belle comforted, as Pelly came in
with the schnitzels. 'His father enjoyed it—didn't you, Marcus?'

So I pretended, thought Marcus, while he nodded, for Jasper's
comfort, and prayed that things were gentler at Benfield now
than in his day. It was true that he had enjoyed it in his last
terms.

'Well, at any rate,' said Jasper, 'I can tell all the boys that he's
a mayor; I don't suppose there are many chaps with fathers
who're mayors in this particular reformatory'; and the words,
with their undesigned pathos, were yet one more stab for
Mark.

Next day, abandoning all work, he took Jasper to Benfield in
the old Rolls. It was in a most modern, enviable study that
he presented the boy to his new headmaster, a man in an easy
grey suit and looking much too young for his high position—at
least in the eyes of Mark Dolmen, as he recalled the terrible old

man, Dr. Darvill, who'd been the Head in his day. That young, fresh face! That easy grey suit! Grey! No customary suit of solemn black. After a few merry exchanges with this surprisingly pleasant youth, he said, 'Well, Jasper. Good-bye, old boy. Work reasonably hard. You'll enjoy yourself more if you do. That may sound incredible but it's the way it works out in the end.' And he put forth a hand for the farewell.

Jasper took the hand nervously, and Mark saw that, by force of habit, he had taken one step forward to kiss his father good-bye—then stopped because of the headmaster standing there. He just shook the offered hand, and Mark saw a shine of tears in his eyes. Did the headmaster see this too, for he said promptly, laying a kind hand on the boy's shoulder, 'Oh, no. Good gracious! Go and see your father safely into his car.'

'Oh . . . I see . . . yes, sir,' said Jasper, nervously obedient, and together he and Mark left the headmaster's house and crossed the forecourt into the roadway where the Rolls stood against the kerb. Having opened its door, Mark turned and said, 'Well, good-bye again, old boy,' putting out the hand. But, as if driven by a sadness to do so, Jasper rose on his toes to kiss him in this empty street. Welcoming him into an embrace, Mark felt a kiss that was almost passionate. He patted the boy's back encouragingly but could not speak because a lump of sympathy had leapt into his throat.

'Good-bye, Dad.'

'Good-bye. . . . Home again soon. . . .'

'Yes. . . .'

Into the driving seat, slam the door, and wave as blithely as possible to the boy on the pavement. What else?

Then—what else?—drive on. On and away, thinking of that childish kiss. 'That will not happen again,' he told himself. 'Thirteen. And a public schoolboy now. It was the last kiss and the end of something. Well, there it is . . . oh God, be good to him, *please* be good to him, and make him happy there.'

Repeating this again and again, often unwittingly, he drove back to his empty house.

The air smelt stale as he entered his silent house. Strange how the silence and the tang of dust smote you as you entered, by reason of your knowledge that you'd be alone here for months. It was as a dust of old books. The house, always too big and spacious for one man and a boy, seemed emptier and larger than ever, and a little mustier, now that, in the silences of evening and night, it would lodge one man alone. And more and more depressing its emptiness became as days went by. Day-times were not too bad. Work dismissed anything but itself, and he was happy enough in his consulting room in Queen Anne Street or at one of his hospitals. It was after nightfall that the gloom gathered, when Capes had gone from the kitchen and all the big rooms above him were housing nothing but darkness. 'A suicidal business,' he told himself once, 'sitting alone in a big empty house with big empty rooms above you.'

One comfort, however, was that this heavy solitude proved he had not acted for his own sake in sending Jasper to Benfield. If he'd ministered to his own desires, he'd have kept the boy with him as a cure for loneliness. But now, without him, the eating of a meal was dull to dismal, and so were going to bed at night and getting up in the morning.

Sometimes in the loneliness of ten or eleven o'clock he would think of that car standing outside and of those likely places in the West End, but the memory of unhappy ventures there in the past kept him behind his study window, only looking out at the roof of the car beyond the garden wall. If only . . . if only, perhaps, the girl Desiderata could be found again and brought back to this house. With her alone, after the first discomforts, he had felt at ease. At ease and happy. And so easy now to have her in the house: often the large empty rooms, as he went up to bed, spoke her name. But it was nearly a year now, since she had been here, and possibly she had gone back to Italy. To Catanzaro in Calabria. How the name leapt in memory. 'In Catanzaro. My mother is very poor, because my father was killed in the war, and my brothers too. I take back money to her.'

True? Perhaps. Perhaps. He was inclined to believe it true. So it might well be that that she'd gone back home, rejoicing and taking her sheaves with her.

A late September night, and there was a dinner and dance at the Mayfair Hotel, to which Mark was invited, not as a mayor, but as an F.R.C.S. because it was in aid of a Cancer Appeal. Dancing would go on till three, but he had come without a partner and soon after midnight he wearied of loneliness and thought more and more of his bed in Keys. The drinks, many and good, had been stimulating at first but were somniferous now. He delayed some while longer and then, with an impatient 'Oh, hell!' got himself out of sight and went to the Rolls parked in Berkeley Square. Driving into Piccadilly, he was surprised to see that, though the streets were deserted, a few of their wandering ladies were still abroad. One was loitering at the corner of Stratton Street. Wine-drugged, he was interested and slowed his car just as she turned out of sight into the street. Coming to the mouth of the street, he saw her walking slowly, and as if disappointed, up the road towards Curzon Street. Curiosity, blent with prurience and a still unformulated desire, caused him to turn the car into the street so that he could look through its window at her. Driving slowly, he did so, and it was Desiderata. It was Desiderata, though at this moment, he'd had no thought of looking for her. Desiderata near her old beat, for Half Moon Street was but three roads away. This woman had not seemed tall enough for her, but he perceived, with an instant wild drumming of his heart, that it was certainly she—Desiderata hatless, with that black hair hanging at rest upon her shoulders.

He ran the car against the pavement beside her, and, startled, she halted. He got out and said smiling, '*Buon giorno, signorina.*' Then, remembering the inaptness of *giorno* in a midnight dark, he substituted, '*Buona sera*' which came conveniently into memory and was less absurd. '*Buona sera, signorina.*'

'Oh . . . !' and '*Dio mio!*' she exclaimed as she recognized him.

'*Come sta lei?*' he asked, attempting more of his phrase-book Italian.

'*Ben bene, grazie,*' she seemed to say, and '*Ma sono stata ammalata.*'

This, with thought, he translated into 'I've been ill'.

'Ill?' He spoke in his best bedside manner. 'Oh no, you mustn't be ill.'

'Ah, it wasn't nothing,' she said. She tapped her finger-tips against her breast. 'A little trouble here. But nothing . . . nothing.'

83

'Heart?'

'Something like that. Little pains in the heart. But nothing . . . nothing. All over now.'

'You look pale.' This was an exaggerated piece of sympathy since there was nothing but a street lamp on the other side of the road to suggest she was pale.

'I always look pale.' She said it coyly, head to one side.

'Desiderata. That was your name, wasn't it?'

'*Sì, signore.*'

'I have never forgotten it. Or you.'

'And I remember you well. You were so kind . . . so kind.'

Yes, that twenty pounds. 'Ten for you, and let's say ten for your mother.' Little doubt she would come again, and quickly, for more such kindness.

'Fancy you remembering my name.' Her head went to one side again. 'I'm afraid I've forgotten yours.'

(As well, since he couldn't remember what name he had given her.)

'You will come with me again, Desiderata?'

'I like to. I like to very much. You was the nicest and kindest. . . .'

(Of whom? Of how many?)

'Come then.' He opened the car door, and as she slipped in, he looked up and down the street in the guilty hope that no one had seen with a derisory smile this 'pick-up' by an elderly man in full evening dress. No one was in sight. Only a small black car stood in Curzon Street at the other end of the road, presumably parked there for the night, though it was a dilapidated little affair and looked comically out of place in these wealthy purlieus. His mind untroubled, he got in beside Desiderata and turned the car homeward.

He drove it to its usual place under his Tree of Heaven. Always safe to alight here since only the blank sides of houses, with small staircase windows, looked down on Menworthy Rise.

'Stay here a moment, my dear.' He got out of the car and repeated all the steps of a year before. He undid the gate in the garden wall. He left it open. He returned to the car and, ever quick with deceits, picked up from the back a small black bag

84

that he might look like a doctor returning from an emergency call. (Unlikely that any eye would be looking into the night from one of those small staircase windows at two in the morning, but . . . every care.) He said, 'Follow me quickly.'

His voice, weighted with guilt, had sunk to a whisper but she obeyed him, and he led her quickly into the cover of the garden. Safe here, he took her fingers and brought her over fallen leaves, copper and bronze and yellow, some dried and brittle, to the foot of the iron stairway that climbed to his dark study.

'Wait here, darling.'

'I remember all this so well.'

'Yes, yes,' he allowed, but impatiently. No time for reminiscences now. He had no key for the narrow study door, and he must hasten round the side of the house to its portico and front door. Seconds later he was opening the door above the stairway, and she came up it speedily, but never losing that grace of movement which belonged to her tall slim figure.

He took her first into the dining-room and at the big table offered to mix her a whisky and soda but she asked for gin instead. He mixed her a generous gin and vermouth, saying, '*Italiano*' as he pointed to the Martini and Rossi label.

'*Ma sì*,' she laughed.

Glasses filled, he lifted his and said, '*Alla vostra salute*' and she, lifting hers, responded with '*Ogni bene*' and a smile over the top of the glass.

When she had finished this drink he suggested, 'Another? Another small one?'

'*Ma no*,' she insisted, with her head to one side and a show of maidenly deprecation.

'*Ma sì*,' he corrected, and mixed her anything but a small one.

Then he led her up the unlit stairs, and not, as before, into the big guest-room on the first floor but up the further flight to his own bedroom above. Nothing to fear tonight from Jasper's room across the landing here; Jasper slept far away in a long school dormitory.

In this room she said laughingly, 'But not the lovely room downstairs? With that marvellous bed? I'd never been in

85

anything so beautiful before. And that there picture of our Capitol in Rome. You see how well I remember it.'

'I'm afraid that marvellous bed isn't made up, my dear.'

'Oh, well, this is very nice. This is where you usually sleep, yes? All alone? Ah, but you won't be alone tonight.' And straightaway, though he was still in his overcoat, she flung her arms about his neck, linking her fingers behind it and pulling down his face to begin the tricks of love. She pressed her lips on his mouth, twisting them there; opening her lips a little she pressed them so hard as she twisted them that he felt the firm wall of her teeth bruising his mouth; then came the wet touch of her tongue seeking to open his lips as hers were open. She parted his lips, and their tongues met, and her wet open mouth twisted again. It all heightened and heated his desire even though, beneath the mounting need, he was conscious of a distaste that she should know and do her part in the game so well.

When she released him, and he removed his overcoat, she cried 'Oh!' as she saw his silk-lapelled tail-coat, his white waistcoat, and his campaign medals. 'Oh!' She stepped back to enjoy the vision. 'But how beautiful! You have been to some great party, no? To Her Majesty the Queen's, perhaps? But you look like a king yourself—*signore*'; and she dropped him a curtsey with a humble bow, saying, 'Your Majesty.'

She seemed much livelier tonight than a year ago; perhaps the ample drinks downstairs were at work; so, to join in her humour (though a little uncomfortably), he said, 'Rise, dear lady,' and lifted her to her feet.

'Oh, let me kiss you again. You look that lovely.'

More of the twisting lips till the desire was hot in him and was trembling, it seemed, in her. Taking at last her lips away, she asked, 'There's no one in the house. Or do I speak low?'

'No one in the house tonight.'

'But there was "your young man", you said. I remember all things. A boy of twelve, you said. Isn't he here, please?'

He could wish Jasper had not been mentioned tonight, but he must answer. 'He is away at his school now. What a memory you have.'

'But why should I *not* remember? You was so good, so generous.'

It did not altogether please him that his twenty pounds, given in generosity, and somewhat desperately as one good deed in the midst of shameful ones, should so rattle in her memory. A weak effort at a decency in the heart of indecency, he would have liked it to remain tongueless.

In the bed far sooner than he, she lay looking up at him and smiling her mischievous invitation. Her black shoulder-long hair lay spread about the pillow, and he suspected she had passed her fingers through it like a comb to achieve this end. The hair, so thick and beautiful, was doubtless her pride.

This humiliation of male undressing, so he was thinking, would be over as soon as he was beneath those bedclothes and she in his arms. Probably she suffered no embarrassment, and he hid his own with a running talk. 'Still living alone, Desiderata?'

Her answer was delayed, as if this was a question she didn't want to be asked. When it came it was only, 'But of course.'

'What? No husband yet?'

'No, no. I haven't no husband.'

'No permanent boy-friend?' he teased.

'No, no.'

'Not even a nice girl companion?'

'No, no. I like to live alone in my own little room.'

'And you still refuse to tell me where it is?'

After a pause, and with the coy smile, she said, 'I think perhaps I rather not. Why should I, please?'

Standing and looking down on her, he put mischief into his own eyes. 'But, my dear good girl, consider. Supposing I wanted to get in touch with you again. It could be, you know. It could be.'

The smile went from her face; it was as if her thoughts had driven it away. That twenty pounds. Prospects such as this must encourage an answer. Little doubt she was thinking this because, after a time, with a new smile, she said archly, 'Perhaps I tell you before I go.'

'Yes, you tell me before you go. You said you had no friends. You have plenty now, I hope?'

'No, very few. But I don't want them. I go back to Italy soon. As soon as I can.'

'You hate all us English?'

'Oh no. Not your sort. Your sort are generally nice and kind with a girl. Real gentlemen. But I hate most of the fellows round about where we—where I live. Beasts and—'

'You said "where we". I thought you lived alone.'

'So I do. Yes, I do. Of course I live alone.'

'Desiderata.' His question was now disbelieving but kindly. 'Do you really live alone?'

'Please?'

He repeated the question.

Her eyes opened wide, as in wonder at this disbelief. 'But of course I do! Ain't I said so? "We"—by "we" I mean the people round about in our—in my horrid street. Most of the boys there are beasts and bullies. But so are a lot of our Italian boys. Savage brutes.'

'Yes . . . well . . . men are a pretty deplorable creation,' he laughed.

'Not all. Not those like you.'

In the bed with her, after a first long embrace he remembered her words about 'a little trouble in her heart', and the doctor in him took command, though he was careful to say nothing that would disclose his profession. 'Now then, darling, where's this pain you spoke of?' he asked, placing his gentle surgeon's hand on the flat of her waist and stroking it; then passing the hand beneath and between her breasts.

'Just where you are now,' she said. 'You have lovely hands. Go on stroking.'

'Is it bad when it comes?'

'Sometimes. But it doesn't last.'

'I don't think you need worry,' he said, still taking pleasure from this stroking of her young smooth skin. 'I've had pains like that sometimes, and my doctor assures me it's just nervous or quite likely caused by some focus of infection far away from the heart. It's almost certainly nothing to worry about at your young age. Do you smoke a lot?'

'Ah, yes.'

'Well, there you are. Maybe you've been over-smoking. That can poison the nerves near the heart a little. So cut down the smoking a bit . . . like a good girl.'

'That's just what Dr. Villani said, my doctor in . . . my doctor at home. Them were his words exactly.'

'Were they now? Well, that shows I could be quite a doctor if I tried.'

'I like you as my doctor.' And she pressed her body closer against him. 'Nice doctor.'

'Good; then be a good girl and do what your doctor tells you.'

'*Sisignore.*' With a smile and grateful kiss.

No talk after this, but the beginnings of reciprocal play. His left arm was under her waist while her left hand was stroking the length of his back. His right hand smoothed down the thick hair, then sought and stroked her breasts, her hip, her thigh. Her eyes now shut, her lips parted for pleasure, her breaths quickening with desire, she drew, almost dragged, him on to her. She welcomed him into her. They played their parts together, and suddenly, sooner than he expected, she loosed the familiar cry of an ecstasy past bearing, 'Oh, no, *no*!', a cry which delighted him so that he came to his ecstasy too—but, even as he did so, nay, even before he had done so, her back arched stiffly on his arm, her hand grasped his wrist so convulsively that the nails bit into its flesh; sweat broke out on her forehead; her breathing became strangled gasps, and, in horror, he saw between her open lips a moisture flecked with blood. The arched back fell on to his arm like a lifeless thing, and she lay still.

Her eyes were now open. They gazed up into his. And they were unseeing.

'God! Oh, God! *What*—'

Her heart? Neither his hand nor his ear could detect a beat. 'Oh, God!' No pulse at neck . . . at wrist. . . .

Dead?

'Oh, no, no, no, no!'

He had heard of sudden deaths during strain on playing fields or cinder tracks, and of older persons in sexual excitement, but these last were rare in the young. In all his years of experience he could recall only two cases when a young heart failed in the wild exultation, the ruthless racking, of sex.

But such a thing could be. In this terrible moment, he remembered a third case, a soldier in the war, passed fit for the roughest commando training, who had passed out on a brothel bed. Mark, as a surgeon, knew enough to complete his terror. He knew too much. Staring in panic at those sightless eyes, he knew that secondary diseases of the heart could lie undetected in the young. And could be a cause of . . . *this*.

But, in the name of mercy, in the name of fairness, why should *he* have been caught as victim of a disaster so rare? He who had given all the years since Lorelei died to his work rather than to women; he who, needing little, had indulged himself so little. This was only the second time in a life of sixty years that he had brought a woman into his home. What wicked trick of Chance or Fate or God was this?

But perhaps not dead. Yet to be saved. 'Oh, come back. Come back to life.' Distracted, had he said these words aloud? But now he said wildly, almost angrily, 'Desiderata, come back to life. Come *back*. Oh, God, in mercy, mercy, what?'

He leapt from the bed. As an expert, he knew that what could be done must be done quickly. Three minutes . . . four minutes, and, after this, too late. He knelt by the bed; he lifted her neck to force her head back and her mouth open; he opened wide his own mouth and with it enclosed the whole of hers; he breathed down into her lungs, breathed again and again, slow, firm breaths with pauses and deep inhalations between them; not easy to do, while his heart hammered in panic. With every breath of his her lungs expanded, her breast lifted and sank, and he went on and on with his labour, on and on, in hope, in despair, trying at the same time to massage her by rhythmic pressures on the breast. So different this mouthing about her mouth from that of an hour ago, so different this handiwork on her breast from the caresses of only minutes ago. 'You have lovely hands. Go on stroking.'

He tried masking her mouth with a hand and breathing into her nostrils, not without a flash of remembrance, 'God breathed into his nostrils the breath of life, and man became a living soul.' Back to her mouth again as the better way, the easier way—oh, make her a living soul . . . breathe, breathe, breathe . . . but it was five minutes now, and her heart was not beating—no, not at all—so that he heard himself moaning a feeble, hopeless, childish 'Oh, dear . . . oh, dear . . .' while he continued the hopeless work. Her breast still rose as he breathed, but her heart did not wake. And he prayed. He prayed for a miracle. 'God give her life again.' Even as he would sometimes find himself praying for his patient when the operation was perilous, so now. 'God help me give her life again.'

He dared not stop; dared not give in; unless she came alive again, what, *what* was he to do?

Still, one surrenders at last. One lifts one's head and surrenders. One rises from useless work. There was to be no miracle.

Over.

What to do? Habit drove him to the window where he drew the blind and looked out at the night. Moon down now, and clouds in total occupation of the sky. A beginning of rain. A wind swaying the higher branches of the black poplar and twisting all its remaining leaves, those leaves that never rested day or night, whatever was happening.

What? How could he admit to anyone this thing that had happened? A woman from the distant streets lying dead on his bed. A woman who had died beneath him while he . . . He the Mayor of Keys. A famous surgeon. Sixty. A magistrate. It would be published to the farthest corners of the land; placarded in every street; exploited for laughs in every club-room and saloon. *Jasper.* Jasper at school. Bronwen. No need to think of Council, borough officers, doctors and nurses in his hospitals, members of his two clubs, Athenaeum and Royal Vesalian; nor of Pelly and Capes and Luddermore; Jasper and Bronwen were enough to stop him telling anyone.

'I can't take it. I can't take it.'

Then what? Was ever man in such a position? He walked back and looked down on her. Dead, with the black hair disordered on the pillow. To the window again, away from that sight. And, as he stood there, thinking, many ingenious deceits, in the old way, came quickly, one after another, before him. Hide her. Hide her somewhere in the house till such time as he could get rid of her. And how 'get rid' of her? The words nauseated him. Bury her in this garden on to which he was now looking? Under the Tree of Heaven? He laughed at the notion, bitterly, miserably, as he imagined a privy one-man funeral, with a prayer, on a dark night under the tree. Besides, ever protecting his hands for delicate surgical work he had always refused to do heavy digging in the garden. He had got Luddermore to do this. And as he thought of Luddermore the ingenious deceits instantly recalled the old man's voice. 'That there tree, its roots travel deep down and 'orizontally and before you know where you are, they'll be getting at the foundations of your 'ouse.'

'How deep are they, Mr. Luddermore?'

'Could be five feet down and more. That there tree's sixty years old.'

'Five feet down.'

Get Mr. Luddermore to dig a hole five feet down, just to see what the roots were doing? Then, at night . . . ?

But impossible. All impossible. Carry her to the car standing there and drive her to some wooded place? Epping Forest or the Surrey Woods? A second emergency call tonight?

No, he could not bring himself to do this. He turned again to look at her. Hide that body in some underbrush, and leave it there to be ravished first by decay and then by a thousand crawling beasts? Compassion and guilt together could not endure the thought. 'No, not that. I won't do that.' There must be some kinder way. A way that would get her poor body into good hands and yet cause no suspicion to fall on him.

How? Sometimes he walked up and down with the question; sometimes stood at the window, fingers entangling behind him. The rain was now falling steadily. God, show me what to do. Not wrong to ask help of God; one had sinned, but if the punishment was total ruin, it was too much. It was unfair. Such hideous punishment for a sin so rarely committed. God of pity, show me a way. Quickly. The night is passing. Help me.

And whether it was from God or from the old deceits, a plan built itself in his mind.

A woman had collapsed in the street. Not an unknown thing. She would be found, and the doctors would discover the indirect heart disease or the aneurysm in the brain which had killed her. *I* did not kill her, God. He would lay her in the street for kind hands to find her. Where? It was here that the plan became cleverest. Lay her on the pavement in Menworthy Rise, against his own garden wall. That could be done in seconds, and it freed him from all suspicion, for what man responsible for a death would put the body of his victim against his home? And nowhere more quiet, more unespied, than Menworthy Rise. The rain falling steadily would help. Between three and four in the morning was the stillest hour of all, and with the rain helping, no one would be abroad in the length of Menworthy Rise. Fifteen feet from his garden gate to the poor shelter offered by the branches of his ailanthus tree. Between garden wall and the old Rolls, with the Tree of Heaven's outreaching arms spread over her—it was not an indecent resting place and some cover—though what cared she for rain now?

No one would know that she had come to this house. No one could have known which way she had gone, when he had brought her at speed all of six miles across London from Piccadilly to Keys.

It was with a hopeless ache of misery that he dressed her for the pavement—so fitting a couch for the death-bed of a street-walker. Finesse in deceit saw to it that the dressing was done well. First on her bare breast he rehung the Madonna on its golden chain; then redressed her, even to the high-heeled patent shoes, and the grey gloves on her hands. The lizard-skin hand-bag was ready to lie tumbled at her side.

Now he must prepare himself for the street and the rain. It mattered little what he wore, for he must be seen by none, or all was instantly at an end. He put only a long waterproof over his sleeping suit; the wet September night was warm. Or warm enough for one in despair.

Nearly four o'clock, and the rain heavy. She lay dressed. In a passion of guilt but incapable of tears he kissed her pale forehead, stroked her hair into place and, gathering her up, carried her down the dark stairs. He carried her through his study to that iron stairway up which she had come only an hour or two ago. Down that stair and across the garden to the gate— quickly. A peep through the gate—nothing but the rain anywhere and so, with the hateful speed of guilt and fear, to the pavement under the tree. Lay her as she might have fallen. Misery forced from him the futile words, 'Sorry, darling.

93

Someone will come for you. They will come.' Then back, shamefully back, into the refuge of a garden behind a wall.

Now up the dark stairs to that high room again, shamefully, saying, 'God forgive me, but what else, what else?' and yet pleased with the completion of a subtle work, since all completions had a quality of pleasure. No light, but take a chair to the window that he may sit in this high seat with only darkness behind him and watch through the night and learn what will befall. Pity would not suffer him to end this watch till he'd seen her into safe hands.

No one was likely to pass for a long while, unless a constable went by on his beat. But he had learned as a councillor that, owing to the shortage of constables, some beats were now covered by motor patrols. Was Menworthy Rise patrolled by constables or by cars? One private car sped through the night, observing nothing of that fallen figure behind the long body of the Rolls. It seemed hours that he sat by that dark window, looking down. Looking down at an impossible fact in Menworthy Rise—impossible, and yet *there*. There among the yellow light of street lamps. Some of the yellow light illuminated the aspen trembling of the black poplar's leaves, and occasionally one of its tricorne leaves went down the wind. The heavier leaves of the ailanthus were quite still but, fittingly enough, its outer branches leaned half-weeping over her. Was no one ever coming? Oh come, someone, come and take her. Among his thoughts as he watched were, 'Poor child, who came in hope from Italy,' and her words about where she lived in London, 'Perhaps I tell you before I go.' But she had left the house early tonight without telling him, and now he would never know.

The rain stopped and he was glad of this; those branches of the Tree of Heaven and their scant autumn foliage were but a hapless shelter for her. The clouds parted, and a few stars appeared. Yet another private car went blindly speeding by.

It was only when a grey of dawn, rose-tinted, paled the low eastern sky that an obvious police car, its wireless mast on its roof and its blue lamp flashing, came along the Rise with a slow dignity so that the officers inside could look left and right and learn that all on their beat was innocent.

It stopped abruptly. He heard its startled brake. They had

94

seen her. One policeman got out, followed by another. Their heads sank below the garden wall where, doubtless, they were kneeling to test for death or life. Their heads rose again and, strangely, both got into the car and sat there waiting. Was it that they were using that wireless? Did they wireless to the Yard, and the Yard telephone to Keys? He did not know, but it was only a few minutes, six or seven perhaps, before the white ambulance came. Gentle Samaritan work by the ambulance men; brief, low midnight voices; then the slam of their doors noisily since there was no fear of waking her; a slight grinding of gears; the motor's diminishing sigh; and Desiderata was gone.

9. A Stranger in the Rise

The days of trepidation linger and pass. Day follows day, and none differ in pattern from those when one was happy before the incredible, the impossible, thing happened. No dreaded word came from inquiring police—why should it? No word about a woman found dead in the street was spoken to him by anyone in Keys; it was not an event uncommon enough, and people had brisker things to talk about at assemblies honoured by the presence of the Mayor. Patients in Queen Anne Street, colleagues in the hospitals, friends in his clubs had heard nothing of a commonplace event so far away. Only a half-inch paragraph in the *Keys and Hadleigh News* drove a knife into his heart as he sat alone at breakfast, but it left no lasting pain because it was so small and lay at the bottom of a page. 'Found Dead. On Tuesday last an unknown woman was found by the police lying dead in Menworthy Rise against the wall of the Mayor's house—' these were the words that momentarily knifed him. 'So far the police have failed to identify her. They are satisfied that there is no question of foul play. The death has been established as due to natural causes.'

And there the end?

The days passed, one by one, each shearing away a little more of the first anxiety, but the nights did not lose their burden so soon. Never a night in this hazardous time but he woke at some small hour, and the apprehension was with him, as large as ever it had been so that he got little more sleep till it was daylight again. There were even nights when he asked himself if the room was now haunted because more than once he had been awakened—or thought he had—by a woman's voice; not a voice that he recognized but a young voice. No doubt it had sprung out of a troubled and recurring dream—but had it? In the deep of the night a man could believe anything.

In the day-times with their many activities, some unselfish, a few even quixotic, the fear might be often at his side, but it was a fast-fading fear. He did more and more quixotic things in these days, half hoping to please God and earn forgiveness. And in the end it looked as though God had understood all and withheld all punishment. Lunching one day at the Travellers' Club, which had welcomed as temporary guests the members of his own club during a brief closure, whom should he see, lunching alone at a distant table, but Lynn McLaurie, Coroner for the district which included the Borough of Keys. More and more he felt driven to speak with him before either left the club. This would not be difficult because he had met McLaurie before, once at his court and once at a civic reception. So later, in the long Morning Room where fifty members were chatting together over their coffee and cigarettes, he strolled past McLaurie, who sat alone. This first time he pretended not to recognize him.

Dr. Lynn McLaurie was a long narrow man with a spectre-thin face—a face admirably suited, so the wags said, to his throne in a court of death. But behind his cold, unsmiling eyes one could suspect the hidden twinkle, and in his flat voice, never raised, an austere humour that didn't believe in underlining with vocal tones any witticism or attempt thereat. His lean figure was always dressed for his court as a gentleman's should be—black jacket, spotless triangle of white handkerchief peeping from left breast-pocket, grey silk pearl-pinned tie—so that some of the wags went farther and said that if he played the part of Death in a fantastic drawing-room comedy, he would need no make-up. He could just walk in, and all would know who he was—Death, who, whatever else might be said of him, must surely be a distinguished-looking gentleman.

Mark came back, acted a recognition, and spoke, 'McLaurie,

97

isn't it? So you're a member here. You remember me. Dolmen. Mark Dolmen.'

'Do I not, *Mr. Mayor?*'

'I come from the Vesalian, which, by the way, should have you as a member. A doctor, a barrister, and an expert in forensic medicine, why, you're a natural for the Vesalian. We're your temporary guests.'

'Very welcome guests. Do sit down.'

Mark sat on a leather arm-chair beside him. 'I can't stay long, but it's remarkable to find you here because there's something I've had a mind to ask you for several days.'

'Then shoot now, my dear sir.'

'I was naturally interested in the case of that young woman who chose to die against my garden wall—you remember it? Well, what was the end of that story? I've seen nothing about an inquest. Maybe I missed it.'

'There was no inquest. Don't you smoke?' He proffered a gold cigarette case.

'Not before going to the hospital. No inquest, you say?'

'No. I ordered an autopsy by Freddy Relph—you know Relph, the pathologist?'

'I've heard of him. Who hasn't?'

'Well, he reported nothing serious. Just natural causes. No barbiturates. No arsenic.' For this last word he allowed the ghost of a smile. 'So all I decided to do was to report to the Registrar and leave it at that.'

'Oh, I see. Yes, I see. Well, who was the woman anyway?'

'They never found out. No one identified her or claimed her.'

Exhilarating the sense of relief; as exhilarating as shameful. 'What do the police do if—if they've no idea who a woman is?' He asked it nervously lest the answer marred this new peace.

'They distribute a message to all stations, and to the Press Bureau hoping for a note in the papers.'

'Extraordinary then that they learned nothing, isn't it?'

'Only in the sense that it's extraordinary the number of missing girls and women whose names stay for ever in the files of the police. Apparently there was some reason to think this girl was a foreigner. But there was no alien's certificate in her bag.

Probably one of those *au pair* girls come to do domestic work over here.'

'But then surely *someone* would miss her?'

'Unless she'd turned to a more profitable trade. The lady was no virgin. And her last fun and games were very recent.' A mercy McLaurie couldn't see the inward shiver at these words. 'They finger-printed her but got no help from that. If she was a lady of the town she was without convictions.'

'She could have been one of those, I suppose.'

'Or perhaps just one of those lonely women, of whom there are all too many in London.'

'Hardly likely, from what you've just told me.'

'I don't know about that. Who knows anyone's secret life?'

'Who indeed? Who indeed, McLaurie?'

'No one ever. That's a truth which probably comes home to us coroners more often than to anyone else. A few years in my daily employment, and you begin to suspect that everyone's mind is a pretty dark forest with all manner of little devils hiding in it somewhere. Have you had your coffee?'

'I don't take it. She was young, wasn't she? So I read.'

'Under thirty. But as *you* will very well know, heart trouble can be there at any age. Probably she was running up the hill, your "b.i.d."' McLaurie stubbed out his cigarette in the tray on his chair's arm, and looked at his fingernails.

'My *what*? What did you call her?'

'Your b.i.d.: "brought-in-dead". She was facing up the hill as she lay.'

'Was she? . . . . up the hill? . . . but Menworthy Rise is only a gentle slope.'

'It could be enough.'

'I suppose it could. Yes, it could. Poor child. . . . McLaurie, tell me: who buries a poor woman like that, if no one knows her or claims her?'

'The borough. *Your* borough.'

'The borough?'

'Yes, in a sense, *you* bury her, Mr. Mayor.' The ghost of a smile again.

'But in what sort of grave, McLaurie? I must be going soon.'

'Why, a common grave. You probably have an undertaker who contracts for pauper funerals.'

'I'm afraid I know nothing of these things. A pauper funeral. What does a pauper funeral imply? Any stone?'

'Oh, no. They sometimes bury five deep in a common grave. How can there be a stone? A registration in the cemetery office, that's all.'

'I see.' Five deep. Mark rose. 'Well, thank you. It's all very interesting. And I'm learning things I never knew till today. I must learn my job better.'

A smile, and he went.

Unidentified, unsought, no inquest, no stone—Mark came out of the Travellers' and into the clean autumn sunlight of Pall Mall, not happy, sick with shames, but almost at peace.

Since Menworthy Rise was a long side-road, he had been in no position, sitting in his study on the third evening after his desperate act, to see a small black Ford car, dented and scratched and rusted, standing at the beginning of the Rise where it came out of Seven Brides Road. Nor to take interest in a small square hatless man, with small black eyes between his untidy black hair and his blue ill-shaven chin, who had got out of the car and was now sauntering past the wall of Mark's garden. He was looking up from under his eyebrows (as one who does not wish people to see where he is looking) at the high side-wall of Mark's house. A rather swarthy little man: where his skin was not blue for want of the razor it was a sallow brown so that one guessed a foreigner: Spanish perhaps, or Greek or Italian; even a gipsy? The sallow skin was vilely associated today with a brilliant pink shirt, which, in its turn, was vilely associated with a red tie. He wore an overcoat too long for his figure; high-shouldered and un-buttoned, it hid his two hands thrust deep into its pockets.

Nor of course did Mark see him turn into Mornington Gardens and now look out of the side of his eyes at the eight front steps and portico of the house; nor know that after walking fifty yards along Mornington Gardens the little man stopped, enacted very skilfully (in case anyone was watching him in this long street of windows) a sudden memory that he had left some-thing behind and must return the way he had come. He turned about and walked again past the front of Mark's big grey house, slowing his steps that he might better consider its portico and double-windowed front door. Into Menworthy Rise again, addressing an averted eye at the mellow bricks of Mark's bulging garden wall; then half-way along the wall—indeed at the very point where Desiderata had lain under the tarnished autumn leaves—he stood and, rising on his toes, tried to see into the garden, but he was not tall enough. So? Ah well, he turned— and saw the Rolls-Royce behind him. Presumably he had not noticed it before, because now he nodded at the sight of it knowingly, pressing his lower teeth against his upper lip, while he meditated on that particular car.

Walking on, he came to the garden gate, and halted, not looking at the gate but enacting with a pinch of his upper lip a man suddenly visited by an important question. A hasty look up the Rise and down the Rise—and he tried the handle of the gate.

Now it was strange that, whereas no strolling policeman entered the Rise while Desiderata lay there, two at this very moment should turn out of Seven Brides Road and come along the opposite pavement. They were far off, and since they were chatting pleasantly together, each with both thumbs hooked in the breast pockets of his tunic, it seemed plain they had no professional interest just now in anything Menworthy Rise might hold; but they were tall, and the little man let go of that gate handle as if it had been white-hot and scorched his fingers. And never did a little man walk onward from a gate more innocently or pass two policemen more phlegmatically. Only when he reached the corner of Seven Brides Road did he turn his head— and even then not the whole way round—to learn if those two coppers were still in sight. They were not.

So after a visit (all quite natural) to that little black Ford and a pretence of getting something from its dashboard, and a further delay with his back to the road as if a new thought had struck him which compelled a stationary posture (though an acute eye might have read it as the delay of a man over-insuring against a suspicion) he turned his face again, saw the emptiness of Menworthy Rise, and came slowly back towards Mark's garden wall. A little man of great ingenuities.

Pretending an absent-mindedness, still looking straight ahead, not stopping, he trailed his fingers over the handle of the gate and, satisfied that no one was in the road, turned it. Locked, and on he came without stopping. At the same instant a girl-child in a school uniform, with a red-and-yellow school tie, came round the corner of Mornington Gardens. A child was not very important; none the less he put the inquisitive fingers between his lips, as if the simple fact had been that he was dreaming, and, when dreaming, one might put fingers anywhere. Walking on, he came opposite the child and with a smile, said, 'Excuse . . .'

Stopping, and looking startled, Bronwen stuttered, 'Y—yes?'

'Excuse . . . please . . . but can you tell who lives in this house?' He jerked a broken thumb-nail, black-edged, over his elbow towards Mark's garden. 'I—I am looking for a friend's house and, *Dio mio*, ha, ha! I've forgotten his number. Just forgotten it. Can you believe it?'

'What was your friend's name?' asked Bronwen, delighted to be a fount of information. 'Dolmen?'

For a moment it looked as if he had forgotten, not only the number of his friend's house, but his name. 'His name? Harvey. Yes. 'Arvey.'

'Well, it's not a Mr. Harvey who lives there. It's a Mr. Dolmen.'

'Please, missy?'

'Dolmen. He's my uncle.'

'Your uncle? No, *is* he now? Your uncle. Well, well!'

'Yes. Mummy and me live next door. I'm being sent out on an errand. Mummy says I ought to do one good deed a day, and this, alas, is today's. Our house belongs to Uncle too.'

'It does, does it? Well, well!'

'And he's Mayor,' Bronwen bragged. 'He's the Mayor of Keys. Mummy's the Mayoress.'

'Mayor! *Dio mio!* Mayor of What-did-you-say?'

'Keys. This is the Borough of Keys.'

'Is it now? A mayor, my dear! Really! Wealthy, I suppose?'

'And he's a rather famous surgeon too. Some people say he's one of the best in England.'

'A surgeon. So I suppose he makes a tidy bit of money, eh?

Many thousands a year, I bet. And this here's his car, a'nt it?'

'Yes, that's Percy. A Rolls-Royce,' she added, wanting the portrait of her uncle to sound as grand as possible.

'Please? Percy, my dear, did you say?'

'Yes, Percy. That's what we call it. Though Percy's getting a bit old now. He says he's going to get a new one, but we're all so fond of Percy. I must go on, I'm afraid. I'm doing this horrible shopping for Mummy, and she's in a towering hurry. She always is. I must go, truly.'

'Dolmen, did you say? Well, he obviously isn't my friend, Harper—'Arvey, I mean—Harper's another bloke. Quite another bloke. I also know a Mr. Herbert. They all begin with aitches, don't they? Yes, "'Erbert". Harvey hasn't a penny to jingle on a tombstone—and he only lives in a top room here. This Mr. Dolmen has all that big house to himself, I suppose?'

'Oh yes, and he owns our house too.'

'Go on! Oh, but so you said. Well, he clearly ain't my friend Mr. 'Arvey. You don't know where a Mr. 'Arvey lives, do you?'

'No, I'm sorry. I'm afraid I don't.'

'Never mind, missy. *Non importa*. I'll ask someone else. A copper, perhaps. Coppers know everything. He lives somewhere round here; I know *that*. Well, thank you, my dear.'

He smiled amicably, and Bronwen smiled too and said 'Good-bye,' since he seemed such a nice man; and they parted.

Unperturbed by anyone so naïve and unimportant as a child, he didn't walk away far. Rather, he stopped to look up again at the famous and wealthy surgeon's house; he looked at it from the top to the bottom; at the windows of Mark's bedroom where Desiderata had died; at those of the big guest-room below it to which she had first come; and at the just visible tops of the study windows behind which Mark was now sitting. This stranger's mouth, lips together, twisted to right and left as he dealt with one thought after another. And when he walked back towards the Ford, he had no need to enact a man deeply meditating; he was manifestly plunged into new thoughts: swimming round and round among them, and back and forth. At one point a small dog, a border terrier, appeared from somewhere and disturbed the thoughts by barking at his heels.

'*Via!*' he shouted irritably, but the terrier did not understand his language, so he aimed a savage kick at the animal's belly. This the dog understood. It eluded the full impact of a murderous kick, and ran away across the road yapping indignation and protest.

That was on the third evening after Desiderata died. Not till two evenings later, for he was obviously a cautious, hesitant, and calculating little man, did he bring the battered Ford into Mornington Gardens, park it at an uncompromising distance, and, returning from it, walk into the front garden and up the eight steps of No. 21.

Within the portico, he waited for courage to assemble, and when it was there he pressed the bell-push nervously and let fall the brass knocker so that its single stroke was less a bang than a courteous tap.

But that evening Mark was dining at his club, and neither Pelly nor Capes was in the kitchen. The bell rang and the knocker sounded in an emptiness.

After a few more rings, getting progressively less gentle and longer, and after a pushing open of the letter-box and a peering through it at the emptiness, he came away, a sour grimace at his mouth.

Three evenings later, in the hour before dinner, Mrs. Capes opened the study door where Mark sat with the evening paper by a glowing anthracite fire.

'There's a man come wants to speak to you, sir.'

'A man? What sort of a man?'

Mrs. Capes, a fat little woman with hands resting on a round stomach, lifted plump shoulders and spread open the hands as if to show she had no good answer.

'Could be a foreigner, by his accent, like. Not a gentleman, though I think he's dressed up for a visit. His accent's not only foreign, like, but common. Dreadfully common.'

'There's not much you miss, is there, Mrs. Capes?'

'Well, when you're as long in the tooth as I am, sir, you've got an eye for most things. That's about the only advantage of being old.'

'Old, Mrs. Capes! You're a mere chicken.'

'Well, if I'm a chicken, sir, I'm a pretty tough old boiler by now.'

'Nonsense. Wait till you're sixty, as I am.'

'I'm rising fifty,' she said proudly.

'Well, you don't look anything like it. Thirty-five perhaps.'

'I *feel* it. Feel a hundred sometimes. What with Mr. Capes, and all.'

'And Mr. Dolmen and all?'

'No, no, sir. You and Master Jasper are no great trouble to anyone.'

'Well, that's good news. Have you asked this man what his business is?'

'He said it was private, but you knew all about it. Yes, he said it was something you knew all about.'

On hearing this, Mark wondered if the visitor was some old patient of his; possibly one of the poor on whom he'd operated free. If so, as he always felt tender towards these people, he began to think he must let him in.

'Is he old or young, large or small, Mrs. Capes?'

'Rising forty, I'd say. Small and dark, like.'

'Well, shall we see him or send him away? It *is* our dinner time.'

'I don't know, sir. He's nicely spoken. *Very* nicely spoken. But—you know—common.'

'When they're *very* nicely spoken, it generally means they've come to beg. Would you like to go out and ask if he's come begging?'

'No, sir, I wouldn't.'

'Oh, well, show him in. Maybe he's an old patient. Mustn't hurt anyone's feelings.'

'Very good, sir.'

One heard his steps as he was brought along the hall, and as one was wondering who he could be, Capes pushed the study door further open for him. A little man entered, and his smile at the door was most ingratiating. Too ingratiating, Mark thought. It seemed associated somehow with his clothes because he was obviously dressed in garments that were designed to make a favourable impression. White shirt, stiff collar, bow-tie, and a Sunday suit of too pale and brilliant a blue. Mark did not trust the suit; and still less did he trust the little black smiling eyes. He thought them the least trustworthy he had ever seen.

As for the smile, surely it was the smirking cover for some trickery.

Though repelled by it, Mark rose in courtesy to a visitor, but left it to him to speak.

The visitor said, 'Good evening.'

'Good evening . . . ?'

With a new kind of smile, significant, knowing, almost as if he would share a little joke, the visitor added, '*Buon giorno.*'

Mark stared. He did not answer again. He could not because struck dumb by a sharp, uncertain terror.

Still smiling, quite genially, not at all sardonically, the little man went on, 'That's what you used to say to my Desiderata, wa'nt it? Speaking your Italian for her.'

Instantly a whole armour of defence (from head to foot—helm, breastplate, and solleret, so to say) had sprung into place around Mark. 'What I used to say to someone? I don't know what you mean.'

'May I sit down?' It was asked with a little swing of the dark head and the same smile, as of a man who wanted to keep everything on the friendliest footing.

Mark motioned to the easy-chair opposite him, not answering a word, because his mind was racing in search of the best lies.

'Desiderata told me all about her first visit to you 'ere. How good and kind you was to her. She told me all about it. Natch'ly.'

'Of whom are you speaking? Your wife?'

'Well. . . .' A disarming smile. 'In a manner of speaking, yes. Not quite my wife perhaps. But she live with me and we love each other. My wife in the sight of God, if I may so put it. Yes. I'm Italian too, you see, and we meet each other four year ago in Stepney—in Welcome Street, acksh'ly, where a lot of us Italians live.' So this explained the blended speech of this man and Desiderata, which seemed to belong both to Italy and to East London, some aspirates standing, some falling. 'My name is Tancredi. That's my name. . . . Yes. . . . Angelo Tancredi. You see, my father was a very religious man and insisted on calling me Angelo after that there Angelo Tancredi who was with St. Francis when he preached to them birds. I don't know much about St. Francis—I'm not religious, meself—but probably you know all about it.'

Mark did not know all about it, so he left the allusion unpursued and said coldly, 'I have very little time, Mr.—Tancredi, did you say?—so could you please tell me why you have come? I am totally at a loss.'

'Oh no, *signor dottore*.' A smile for this joke in Italian. 'You will understand very well.' (*Dottore?* How much did this terrifying person know?) 'It must'a been about a year ago you stopped your car and talked with Desiderata in—in Half Moon Street, acksh'ly, and brought her here in your car.'

'*I* did? What *are* you talking about?'

'No, no, *signore*. It's no use to pretend. I was so interested that night in your fine car that I follered you both all the way 'ome to this 'ere house. I was interested, you see.'

'You . . . followed . . . me?'

'*Sì, signore*. Follered. That's right. In my own little car. Not to be compared with yours, but she runs smoothly and kep' pace—though I'll say you forced the pace a bit that night, you did. I just watched you and Desiderata come into this very house by the garden gate, and then I went 'ome to bed, leaving you to it. But I was interested. Who wouldn't be?'

'I still don't know what you're talking about. You must have got something very badly wrong. But am I right so far: your wife is a prostitute and you watch from somewhere while she plies her trade? Watch from your car? Is that it?'

The smile was now that of one man-of-the-world in a wholly understanding, tolerant, uncensorious conversation with another. A shoulder rose and the head leaned towards it as if weighted with admirable tolerance and understanding. 'I love my Dizzy—'

'You love who?'

'Dizzy. My Desid.' He pronounced it D'sid. 'I love her. Or I did, guv, and my heart is just broken about that—but, you see, when I meet her—it was in Welcome Street, Stepney—she was already leading the life she wanted to lead, and why not? I say she live with me, and I just—*you* know—look after her. Not interfering with nothing she does. See? That was all right, wa'nt it? I say it's her business, not mine. It was of 'elp and no mistake'—he seemed to need to stress this point—'because she paid her share of things, natch'ly.'

Mark could not help submitting, though his heart was now an oscillating pulp of fear, 'You are aware, I suppose, that the police would take a very different view of what you describe. They would call it "living on immoral earnings". I don't know how much English you know, but the English have a word for the man who does that.'

'Oh, "ponce", yes.' He provided the word cheerfully, perhaps proud of his English, and at the same time glad to show that the word had no embarrassments for him. 'But I'm no ponce. I done nothing wrong. I just say let her earn what money she likes, and God damn the police. And sometimes I 'elp her to earn it. I take her in my little car to wherever she wants to be, and I wait a little so as to bring her home, poor kid, if she 'asn't found a fare.'

'And, if she has, you follow her wherever she goes?'

'No. That's not it, sir. I don't usually foller. Only now and then. It was only when I saw her getting into a bloody great Rolls that I got excited. Because, I mean, you were obviously some very rich gentleman. I followed out of curiosity, as you might say. You might put it like that. That I wanted to see what she was up to, because I wasn't never too sure. However, she tole me all when she come back.'

'Mr.—', but momentarily he had forgotten that second name and wasn't disposed to call him Angelo. 'I don't know how to deal with you. You have some mad idea that has nothing to do with me. You must have seen someone else.'

'Oh, no, mister—I mean, *signor dottore*—I see you and 'er get out of that car, just where it's standing now under that there tree. That was a year ago but one doesn't forget a big well-dressed gentleman like you—and, if I may say so, an oldish one. That's why I recognized you at once the other day, best part of a year later, when you and she got off again, like.'

Mark was almost trapped into saying, 'So you were watching again then?' but he snapped his lips tight on the words.

Mr. Angelo, however, seemed to have discerned them behind the lips. 'Yes, it just chanced that I was there again, all of a year later, and I'll tell you for why. She'd already been with a man that night, and he took it into his head to go home after he'd had his bit of fun. She comes home and tells me how he was the nervous kind, glad to escape, like, after he'd given her a quid. A *quid* only, in these days! So I say, "Well, there's time to try again, ducks," and that I'd take her back and wait a little, late though it was. And did she find someone? I'll say she did! And when I recognized you, did I foller again? I did. I don't mind confessing I was a bit suspicious, because Desid had taken to keeping a lot of things to herself lately. She was very close about the money she was earning. So I was determined to know what 'appened, and I see her walk into this house along of you. And that's the last I ever see of her. And wouldn't I natch'ly want to know what happened to her? You see that, don't you? It's my right to know. She was my wife . . . practically.'

'What are you saying? That she never came back to you?'

'She's dead, guv. Dead, and you know it.'

Mark waited, staring into this visitor's eyes, while he summoned all the powers of deceit that were in him; then spoke. '*Dead?*'

'Yeah . . . dead.'

'Well, I'm sorry for you, sir, but what has her death to do with me?'

'Quite a littie, I reckon.'

(God, what did he know?) 'Oh no, sir. Even if all you accused me of were true'—and he accorded this a small laugh as of ridicule—'her death in the street somewhere could have nothing to do with me.'

'It could have this, that you was the last person she was seen with, and that she must'a dropped dead just outside your 'ouse *There!*'

Yes, there: there before him a promise of exposure and ruin. Jasper. Bronwen. The Council. The whole of Keys. His patients. Since his name as mayor and well-known surgeon would make the front pages, his punishment would be far greater than other men's. And never would he accept it. Never permit it. *Jasper. . . .*

But what to do? The same blinded question as when he lifted his eyes and saw Desiderata lying dead beneath him.

What to do? Not such a fool as to believe he could maintain before this terrible visitor an all-embracing denial. Enough that the man was wrong about the *whole* truth; that he, like police, pathologist, and coroner, supposed her to have died in the street.

He rose from his chair. He lifted his shoulders and dropped them. Ingrained habit sent him walking to the window though nothing could be seen there, the curtains being drawn. He could, however, staring at the blinds, see one tiny gleam, a pin-light of hope. Returning to his chair, he stood by it, fingering the gold-rimmed quizzer at his breast.

Shrugging again, he said, 'Mr. Angelo—I forget your other name—if I admit that your mistress was here some days ago, what can *you* do? Or what can I do for you? I know only what you know. She came and she went.'

'You know she dropped dead outside your house.'

'I read about it, yes. With deep distress. But how that happened, and when, I have no idea.'

'So did I read about it. Some days ago I come to this 'ouse 'ere, but you was out. I still didn't know nothing then except that she'd been 'ere with you and 'adn't come back; and, natch'ly, I was fair mad to find everything out. I'd already found out all about you, that you was a mayor and a famous quack—doctor, I mean—oh, yes, I met a little girl in the street who says she's your niece, and she tells me all. Prah'd of you, she is.'

Bronwen! Then Bronwen, poor little Bronwen in the street, had primed this enemy's guns for him.

'So I goes straightway to a pub 'ere to get talking about you with the fellers there. And one feller says something about a woman lying dead outside your house, not in a suspicious way, like, but just because you'd been mentioned. Outside *your* 'ouse! You bet I jump. I kep' quiet, and when they said it was all in the local paper, I drank up and nipped out. I know all about public libraries because I'm a reader, I am. I'm a keen Socialist, you see, and I use our Stepney library a lot. So I nips in and sees this paper. And when I read the description I knew it was Desid. You bet I was excited. You can say I was real excited.'

'And you didn't go straight to the police and tell them anything you knew?'

'Well, no. . . . I didn't, exactly . . . no. . . . But neither did you.'

'Neither did I. What could I tell them? I knew nothing about her beyond her single name, Desiderata. She'd never tell me anything else—where she lived or anything. Probably you instructed her to keep quiet about all that. Many days afterwards I learned from the coroner that she wasn't found till long after she'd left me.'

'Yeah . . . but even if you 'ad known her name and address I don't reckon you'd've gone to the cops with 'em.'

Mark did not argue this. Instead, still fingering the gold-rimmed eyeglass, he fired the same shot into the enemy's country. 'And I imagine, Mr. Angelo, you have reasons for not being over-anxious to help the police with their inquiries.'

'Oh, I don't know about that. I wouldn't say that. I might 'elp in some cases.'

'I think not, Mr. Angelo. Not in this case. Keeping watch while she solicits. Following in your car to see her safely home.'

'Oh, I could tell a tale all right. I know how much to say to splits, and how little.'

'And suppose, Mr. Angelo, I was to tell a tale too. Say your whole story was a lie, invented because she was found outside my house. Which of us would they believe?'

'Yeah, I thought'a that. But will you tell me how, if she never been in your house, I could describe your fine bedroom upstairs? She said it was one of the flashiest bedrooms she'd ever been in. How about the green carpet and gold curtains? Desid had an eye for them things. How about the pick-sher of Rome? The Capitol in Rome, eh? And how about the boy sleeping upstairs?'

('Oh God, God, keep the boy out of this.')

But Mark, though shaken by these sharp questions, as by sword-thrusts through his guard, suddenly perceived his retort.

'Bah! You could get those facts out of anyone if you wanted to frame me.' Yes, but as he tossed forth this idea, he pictured this evil-laden pedlar talking at the door with Pelly or Capes, and his heart seemed to faint. 'You could have paid somebody for all that.'

''Oo, guv, 'oo? But, more'n that, I could tell 'em the very day and hour you pick her up, see? You was in evening dress, come from some party, and they could find out and put their twos and twos together. Oh, they'd believe me.'

III

'While you'd incriminate yourself.'

'*Sì* . . . yeah . . . maybe. . . . But it could be I'd incriminate myself rather than be diddled by you.'

Yes, it could be. There had been an ugly hard line in his dark eyes and along his squaring mouth as he said this. One must drive any such fancy out of his dreams. 'Yes, Mr. Angelo, and it could be that you'd get all of seven years.'

'Could be. *Sì. Ebbene* . . . and it could be I'd take it rather than be cheated by anyone.'

'Cheated, Mr. Angelo? Diddled? What do you mean by cheated and diddled? Cheated of what?'

Mr. Angelo's small eyes swung away; then came back. With one finger he rubbed the side of his nose. His mouth twisted up towards his nose and down again. Plainly he was wondering if he'd revealed the blackmailer too soon.

'Well, Mr. Angelo . . . ? How cheated?'

'Well, let's be frank. I don't want to be unreasonable with you, no. . . . *Ma.* . . .' A shrug. 'You'll understand, won't you, that I've suffered a great loss. Desid was my wife in the sight of God, and . . . if you see what I mean . . . a . . . a source of income.'

'Yes, I thought so. I thought this was coming.'

'What you mean, "coming"? Natch'ly it's coming. What I mean to say is—putting it frankly—what I mean is, what's my silence worth to you? That's putting it frankly. I reckon you'd be prepared to make it worth my while not to start inquiries.'

No answer, so he continued, 'You see? I'm putting my cards on the table.'

'Mr. Angelo, you interest me.' Mark had decided what was the only possible course for him. He must pretend an ease in it, and a faith in it. Pretence it would be, but, whatever in secret he might be feeling, he thought he saw how to play and hook this particular little devil-fish. 'What do *you* think your silence is worth, my friend?'

'Well, you're not a poor man, are you? What's wrong with a thousand?'

'A thousand what? Pence?'

'No. Pounds, o'course.'

'You're so simple. Here you reveal yourself to me as a ponce and a blackmailer—'

'Oh no, I don't—I just thought: a gen'lman's agreement between us. He's a gen'lman, I thought. I always reckon I know a gen'lman when I see one.'

'—and you seem to have delivered yourself into my hands—'

'I haven't.' A sudden extrusion of the underlip accompanied this, but there was doubt in his eyes.

Mark acted a laugh for him. 'The law being what it is, Mr. Angelo, I suggest it's for you to ask *me* not to start inquiries. Just understand. I shall deny everything you say, if you say anything, and I shall then prove that you are both ponce and blackmailer. As a magistrate, I know that the penalty for the first can be up to seven years, and for the other up to *life*. Now will you please get out of here. You're getting nothing from me. *Get out!*' Mark moved quickly to the door and held it open. '*Out!*'

Mr. Angelo stood up. His shoulders fell forward like a gorilla's before pouncing. The black hatred in his little eyes would have frightened a stronger heart than Mark's. Teeth barely parted, he said in a lowered voice, 'You don't know what's coming to you, mate. *Dio*, you don't! You a magistrate! *Dio mio!* I tell you one thing. I been in prison before, and, by God, I'll go again for you. I'll go for *years*, if I have to. It won't be no new thing for me. Yeah, and it could be I'd *swing* for you.'

'Get out!' (He's bluffing. Keep up *your* bluff.)

Fast as fury could take him, muttering some word like '*Maledetto*', the visitor dashed out of the room, along the passage, and out of the hall door which he slammed behind him.

To display tranquillity before Capes, though his heart was slamming too as if it might burst his body, Mark went to the top of the kitchen stairs. 'You can bring up the dinner now, Mrs. Capes. He *was* begging, after all.'

'He was properly displeased with me, Mrs. Capes, when I refused to give him any money. You heard how he banged the door.'

'Did I not, sir? It shook the whole house.' Capes laid dish and plate before him. 'He kep' you long enough, I must say. Everything was in danger of being spoiled.'

'I thought I'd never get rid of him. These fellows with their hard-luck stories do go on and on. I fear that at last I told him to go in terms barely polite.'

'Do him good. Well, now have something nice to eat. I'm sure you must be hungry. I don't think anything is really spoiled.'

'He's Italian, and his name is Angelo. An angel, if you please.'

'A fallen angel, if you ask me. It's being a mayor that you get these pests. Like parsons. They get them regular. If I'd known what he was, I'd never have let him in. I won't again.'

'I doubt if he'll come again, Mrs. Capes.'

So he said, sweeping away, as it were, from behind Mr. Angelo, his footprints in the hall. So he said, sick with doubt.

10. Nine Days

No, he would come again. Almost one hoped he would. Better this than that he should go to the police. But how could he go to the police, taking his tale of planting Desiderata on her beat, and so risking long years in prison? Oh, comfort: he could *not* go to the police. *But*—'I been in prison before'—in a mad fury the words had slipped out—'and, by God, I'll go again for you!' Previous convictions. Possibly a recidivist. Convictions as likely as not for living on immoral earnings and, possibly, for procuring as well. In a mad fury he might go to the police but he wouldn't be in a hurry to do so; being obviously a slow-moving little man. He would come again. Unwilling to accept defeat, he would come and threaten again.

Somewhere among these harrowing thoughts there was a sadness that Desiderata, who'd had some charm and sweetness for the romantic fool in a middle-aged man, should have been proved a liar; just an actress skilled in the tricks of her nightly performance. He still longed to think she was not wholly a liar. Was there any truth in the poor mother waiting for her in Catanzaro? Any truth in a father and brothers killed in the war? Any truth in anything she said?

That night in bed, just as his throat had resisted the meal brought by Capes, so his brain closed the avenues to sleep. But one could force the swallowing of food so as to appear tranquil; one could not force the doors of sleep. He did not toss much with his beating dreads; he rather lay with them through the night, often with eyes open to the dark. It was four in the morning when an idea came to him of something which he could do—something to *do*—and after that he lost consciousness for a while.

'Yes, he will come again,' he had been thinking. 'Come and threaten again. Therefore I must—' and the idea leapt. He would employ a private inquiry agent and find out all about the ex-prisoner, Angelo, so as to outbid him with threats. Or at least to take comfort in the thought that Angelo would never risk exposure to the police again. Intuition, sprung from that 'I been in prison before', suggested that Desiderata had not been the whole of his stock-in-trade. A private inquiry agent in the morning. At once . . . at once. . . .

'Oh, but Angelo *What*?' He had forgotten the surname. Helpless without the surname. 'Tan . . . Tan-something.' Follow 'Tan' with every letter in the alphabet. 'Tanb, Tanc, Tand, Tang . . .' no, the name would not come. Then, suddenly, he remembered one thing; hadn't the fellow said, 'My father was a very religious man and called me after that there brother who was with St. Francis when he preached to them birds'; and, instantly rising, he hurried down the dark stairs to his study and the Encyclopaedia on his shelves.

'Francis, Saint'—no help here. 'Franciscans'—but so long an article in this cold! Shivering, he ran his finger-nail down its long columns. Ah! 'Angelo *Tancredi*, a noble knight of Rieti renowned for his courtesy.'

'Tancredi.' Oh, thank God, the senior Mr. Tancredi was a religious man. And, like the courteous knight of Rieti, had done him the courtesy of providing his son's name. Simultaneously, a name breeding names, words recalling words, he remembered, 'In Welcome Street, Stepney, where a lot of us Italians live.' So great was his relief in recovering these names that, like a sedative, it put him to sleep.

Patients had to wait in the morning while Mr. Seph Siemen of Siemen's Detective Agencies, Ltd., responding to an urgent telephone call, came to Mark's consulting room in Queen Anne Street. And in that consulting room, with its rich carpet and the framed portraits of Lorelei and Jasper on the broad desk, instead of patients consulting him, he, secretly the patient for once, consulted the expert detective. And just as some of his patients left that room comforted, so was his anxiety eased by Mr. Seph Siemen's smooth words and his promise of 'one of my best agents to get busy' among the Italians in Welcome Street, Stepney.

This expert arrived by appointment at five that afternoon. He proved to be a Mr. Harry Gayne, a bulky, rosy ex-airman with wide 'handle-bar' moustaches that embraced his cheeks almost as far as his ears, where they enlarged themselves luxuriantly. He soon displayed a joviality not less expansive than the moustaches, and a hearty view of all 'Dagoes and Wops' as quite the slyest and slipperiest rogues in creation—a view which his daily recording of deceits and chicaneries among his own countrymen had never caused him to reconsider. In the patient's chair by the side of Mark's desk, seated bulkily and comfortably, and often passing a knuckle along the moustaches, he made it clear that there was no need for him to know why Mark sought information about a Wop in Welcome Street. 'Why our clients require information is never any business of ours, sir. Absolutely none. Mr. Siemen's very clear about that.'

'I can willingly give you my reasons if you'd like them,' Mark offered, well assured what the answer would be. 'There need be no secret about them.'

'No, sir. That's all right, sir. It's part of our tradition never to seek that particular enlightenment. And I'd sooner make no distinction between clients.' (Was this always their opening, for the comfort of blameworthy clients?) 'Mr Siemen prefers it that way'.

'All right, then; if you say so. But it can all be above board any time you need it,' said Mark, batting on this excellent pitch.

'No, sir. I prefer to keep to the usual custom.'

Mr. Gayne also made it clear, if less explicitly, that he was delighted at being commissioned to do some field-work among brothels, ponces and pimps. Indeed Mark got the impression that he had not for years been given a task he would enjoy so much. There was laughter between the detective and his client as he expounded some of his methods. It was his conviction that he could prise out any information from anybody, sooner or later, by a mixture of joviality and beer—'or whisky at a stretch, but I bear my clients' expenses in mind.' He used his joviality in pubs, it seemed, as a kind of solvent which, along with the unloosing charms of alcohol, melted in due time all cautions and discretions in the questioned and allowed their deepest secrets to come gushing into the air like a geyser. 'I love my work,' he said to Mark at one stage.

And everything that this happy warrior uncovered and reported to Mark gave him comfort and hope, if not complete release. Never that. Happily housed in the patient's chair, leaning back in it with his thick knees crossed, ever knuckling the wide moustaches which clearly meant much to him, he reported first that Mr. Angelo Tancredi lived no longer in Welcome Street but in Kelso Street, Stepney. He had served a long term in prison for his part in a vice ring. His father had come to London to start a little trattoria in Whitechapel High Street at the gates of the City. For a time Angelo had been a waiter in his father's restaurant, but after violently quarrelling with his 'Babbo' —'his old man, sir'—who apparently was a very religious old boy with but a poor opinion of his son, Angelo had shaken his heels at his home and gone off and become a waiter in a famous Soho trattoria. Famous it might be to its patrons, but filthy and slave-driving and stingy to its waiters, so that Angelo, after a wild shouting-match which saw the handy knives picked up, left it and soon discovered that it would be more profitable, and far more restful, to join the Brothers Comati, a firm of pimps in a big way. No friends in Kelso Street spoke well of him, because the only friends of ponces and pimps, even in unrighteous streets, were their brothers in the profession, and no great love passed hither and thither between these. His neighbours asserted, and Mr. Gayne had no doubt they were right, that, while he had only one girl living with him, he had several others 'on the bash'. They admitted that he was fairly good to them unless he was in a violent temper when he was capable of anything. (Here Mark's comfort changed back to fear.) Apparently the woman living with him, an Eye-tie like himself, had had as much of this violence as she could take, for she had recently slung her hook—

'Slung her hook?' Mark interrupted.

'Yes, sir. Made off one night and has never been heard of since.'

'What? Just disappeared? But hasn't he reported this to the police?'

'Don't make me laugh, sir. In Mr. Signor Angelo Poncio's circles we don't help the cops with their inquiries.'

'So I imagine'—and Mark duly laughed—'but—I mean—surely if you found this out, others must have heard about it?'

'Oh, yes. Some. Not many. One or two fellow ponces, perhaps. But it's not an common thing for these ladies to go missing. Disappearing for months is quite a game round there, and no one sees any need to grass to the splits about it. You see, it's a rule among these sensible people never to go near a nick unless they're helped there by the police. In which unhappy circumstances they've not much chance to do anything else.'

Mark nodded, and Mr. Gayne continued, 'Not that the pretty little skunk who gave me this chip of talk was any pal of our Mr. Angelo. I rather gathered that he was another ladies' bloke in some sort of competition with Mr. Angelo—possibly about who should work which beat. I thought he was glad this girl had done a guy. All he said was, "Good luck to the puss wherever she's got to. Hope it keeps fine for her."'

'Where do they suppose she's got to?' Mark asked after a pause.

'Who knows? Italy, perhaps. She always wanted to get back to Mum there, it seems. And she was believed to have put together a nice little packet of money.'

So there had been some truth in things she had said, and Mark felt somehow glad of this. 'What was her name?'

'I didn't get that. The nark I squared didn't know. But it didn't seem important.'

'No, of course not. You have done a very fine bit of work, Mr. Gayne; learned a wonderful lot.'

'Thank you, sir. But it's just my job. I'm just one of Mr. Siemen's spies.'

Here, leaving his dark worry aside for a moment, and wondering pitifully about Desiderata on her street corners, he sought from Mr. Gayne, before he passed out of his pay, something he'd always wished to know. Like the most innocent of men he asked,

'I've often wondered, what do these girls do, the Italian girl, for instance? Did she take her customers back to Mr. Angelo's brothel, or what?'

'No, sir. Usually they have what they call gaffs, and the poor mutt has to pay for the room as well as for the entertainment he gets in it. If they find one gaff occupied they taxi off to another. Of course some sensible fellows, if they are bachelors, just take them to their own homes.'

'Oh, I see,' said Mark, as if this were a new idea to him.

'Yes, it must come a lot less expensive that way, and you can at least be sure that the lady hasn't got a bully in the gaff.'

'Well, well, well,' said Mark the inexperienced, joining in the laughter.

Mark had drawn both comfort and anxiety from this interview: the comfort from Angelo's record with the police and his hazardous standing now; the anxiety from Gayne's words, 'when in a violent temper he's capable of anything', and 'a wild shouting-match which saw the knives picked up'. These sorted too well with Angelo's own words, 'I been in prison before, and, by God, I'll go again for you. I'll go for *years*.'

The strain of daily portraying serenity when terror at any moment could close its fist round your heart! The need for one's usual manner of comfort and encouragement in one's consulting room when the anxious patient took the desk-side chair where Mr. Gayne had sat so merrily, and when, perhaps, the patient's doctor had come with him and taken another chair. These family doctors who brought him patients mustn't detect any loss of the old assurance and ease.

The usual jesting manner with ward sister, students, patients on teaching rounds. From bedside to bedside with smile and comfort, though he might be thinking, 'What may they not learn any day now?'

Operations. Sessions of three and a half hours, and never must the scalpel shake, voice tremble, or manner show inattention, abstraction, misgivings. Fortunately the habit of years and one's pride in one's celebrity (How long? How long?) ensured that control did not visibly slip. But often there was sweat behind his cap and taped mask when the strain was over.

Then the Saturday evenings when Belle and Bronwen came to dinner. This family gathering had been arranged by him after Jasper left. He had joked, 'Belle and Bronwen, my dears, time is flying and I for one am getting older, whatever you two girls are doing. I could wish to see you more often before the End. Capes roasts me a joint every Saturday, and I think you'd better have it with me, now that Jasper isn't here to dispose of most of it.'

'Oh, but how absolutely adorable!' was Bronwen's instant acceptance. 'How scrumptious. Not to say super.'

'It won't be scrumptious at all. Nor super. Just a piece of beef and some potatoes. And salt.'

'Yes, but food always tastes so much nicer in someone else's house.'

'In a friend's house, yes. Not in a dreary old uncle's.'

'Yes, but we only have macaroni cheese or an egg or something; and look, Uncle darling: if we came to dinner with you, we could play games afterwards.'

'Oh, must we?' Mark petitioned with a grimace.

'Don't be absurd, Bron,' Belle chided. 'Your uncle is an important man and will probably have some mayoral duty.'

'No, he won't. Not on a Sat.'

'Well, you'll have your homework to do.'

'Oh, heck, no! Not on Sats. Couldn't we play Scrabble, Uncle darling?'

'Scrabble? Scrabble? Certainly not. There's too much skill in it, and you always beat me.'

'*What* a whopper! You beat Jasper and I once.'

'"Jasper and *me*", for God's sake, child. Grammar. Grammar. Who can beat "I"?'

'Oh, well, never mind that. We'll play whatever you like.'

'Rubbish, Bronwen,' Belle insisted. 'Your uncle has something better to do than play games with a silly little girl like you. Do you remember he's now the Burgomaster of Keys.' She had taken to calling him this ever since she had seen an amateur production of *The Burgomaster of Stilemonde* and wept abundantly at it.

Bronwen paid no attention to this, and Mark said, 'I'll play a game with her that's all chance. Then I can blame Fate when I lose.'

'Oh, *good*! *I* know.' Bronwen's enthusiasm lifted her up and down on her toes. 'Escalado! Jasper's Escalado. Oh . . . *yes*!'

This was a game of horse races. A green linen 'Race Course' was strained on elastics down the length of the long dining-room table, and a heptagonal wheel in a housing at its top caused the linen cloth to jerk rhythmically and force the five leaden horses forward at every jerk. There were white studs on the green cloth to represent fences and here a horse might fall to yells of dismay from whosoever's wager lay on it. Jasper and Bronwen would bellow and jump and lift excited arms to heaven as their horses came jerking towards the white 'winning line'. Mark had been known to roar too when his horse was leading, and to swear when it fell.

Accordingly Belle now declared, 'It's a thoroughly immoral game, Marcus, and you shouldn't encourage an innocent child to play it. Besides, there's your language to consider.'

'Oh, yes, he should, he should! And "innocent"! My hat! Besides, I love it when he swears.'

'Well, I disapprove strongly, but rather than your uncle should lose his fun, I might consent to join you two infants.'

'Oh, stuff, Muzz,' said Bronwen. 'You know you enjoy it as much as anybody. You get frightfully excited. And definitely noisy. Oh, what fun it's going to be, Uncle sweetest!' And after her fashion, she flung enthusiastic arms around him. 'Next Sat. Next Sat.'

He kissed her on brow and cheeks.

It was the Saturday nine days after Angelo's appearance, two after Mr. Gayne's report, and about eight minutes past eight; Capes had cleared the table for them; they had fixed the green race-course on it; Mark was turning the wheel and Bronwen's horse was leading while she yelled, 'Green! Green! Come on, *Green*'; Belle was wailing quite loudly because her yellow horse lagged behind; Mark was adjuring Red more quietly, '*Come* on, Red,' as he worked the wheel—when the hall-door bell rang.

'*Shop*,' called Bronwen, even in the midst of her excitement. This was an imitation of Jasper who in humorous mood would often issue this call for assistance if he heard the front-door bell.

Mark turned his ear to a noise of angered voices in the hall. Raised voices. Capes . . . and . . . Angelo?

'What the devil—' he began, still unwittingly turning the wheel.

At this point Bronwen's horse crossed the line, so that she triumphed, 'Me! Me! That's twopence you owe me now.'

'Wait, darling . . .' he urged.

Capes' voice. 'Will you please go. I've told you he's not at home.'

'Twopence, twopence, Uncle darling.'

'Stop, Bronwen,' he insisted, almost angrily. 'There's someone at the door. Let me hear.'

A move to the door. Silence around the green field of play. The voices outside.

'But 'e *is*. I been watching for hours. I see him come in, and he ain't come out. I been standing at the corner, and no one's come out of the house, back or front.'

'Well, what I meant was he's not at home to anybody. He's got visitors.'

'I know. I seen 'em come. From next door. Well, he's got another visitor now. I don't 'ang about any longer. Tell 'im to let me see him or I go straight to the police. See? Straight.'

'Marcus, what is it?'

'I'd better go and see. I think I know this particular pest.'

'Oh, damn!' complained Bronwen, and Belle rebuked her. 'Quiet, Bron.'

'Yes, but oh, hell! What rotten luck. Just as we were happy. Honestly, what a time to come visiting.' Sorrowfully, and yet with fun, she called after him, 'Don't forget you owe me twopence, Uncle darling.'

That 'darling' was a spear-thrust in his heart as he went towards the dark figure on his threshold. 'What is it, Mrs. Capes?' he asked carelessly, that she might suppose him unworried.

'It's this man, sir. I've told him—'

'And I've told 'er that I only leave your 'ouse to go to the police. You know about what. You know all right.'

'You'd better leave this to me, Mrs. Capes. I'll see to it. Tell my sister and Miss Bronwen to go on with the game. Come with me,' he said to Angelo.

Turning, he led the way to his study, with a feeling of death around his heart. Angelo came sourly behind—like death's messenger at his heels. Oh God, was everything at its end? All life as it had been? Work, fame, income—all sentenced to a death tomorrow?

The end?

In the study he remained standing. Angelo too, hands asleep in the pockets of the too-long overcoat. Mark had shut the door behind them. 'Say what you have to say.'

'I been thinking.'

'Yes?'

'*Sì*, and I give you fair warning that after what you done to me and to the woman who was my wife for all practical purposes, I—'

'What do you mean: "done to her"? Are you suggesting I murdered her?' He provided a contemptuous laugh.

'We'll come to that, guv. I give you fair warning that I'm ready to go back to jug for a couple'a stretch rather than let you get away with it. Perfectly ready. See? I don't believe I'd get anything like the seven stretch you threatened me with. More likely a few months. I've found out that two years is the max. And, by God, I'd take all *that*, if I had to.' (So! While Mark had been employing his inquiry agent, Angelo had been pursuing inquiries too.) 'Okay. It's going to be more than your f—ing life's worth, if you try turning me away again. You don't know *me*. You don't know how far I'd go with anyone who's tried to play me up like you done.' His lower jaw shot forward, and an incomplete row of yellow teeth pressed on his upper lip. 'You may not believe me. All right, don't. And don't know what's coming to you.'

'What's coming to me unless I give you a thousand pounds, is that it?' Asked scoffingly.

'Yeah. Yepp. That's it. I thought at one time perhaps I'd take five 'undred but I don't feel like that now, not after the way you treated me. You should'a treated me different. I was ready to be friendly.'

'You've been finding out a lot, it seems, Mr. Tancredi; have you found out what's the maximum for blackmail?'

'Come off that. I found out all about that. I give you it might be three stretch but probably nothing like so much. If anything at all. You said you'd deny ever having seen Desid. Okay. *Va bene.* I shall deny ever having tried what you call blackmail. Fair's fair. I shall say it's all your make-up. Where's your proof? There're no splits, I suppose, in that there cupboard? Or behind them there books? And any'ow, if you accuse me of the black you'll have to admit a tidy lot to the judge, eh? Won't you? 'Ow's that?'

'How's that? I should say it'd mean the maximum for you, with, possibly, Mr. Tancredi, an added sentence for procuring women and girls.'

'Ah! Ah! You been finding out all you can about me, have you? So's you can stop me, eh? Some nice tailing, *non è vero?* Not that I admit to procuring or any of that fanny. Well, I been going through things too. And I make it that, if I tell the cops, there'd be an inquest after all. But whether inquest or not, there'd be a hell of an inquiry somewhere with you as chief witness. Oh, yes. *Sì, sì, signore,*' he added with a laugh. 'And listen to this: I been making my medical inquiries. And my guess now is she might'a died while you was having her. I don't say for certain that's what happened, but I daresay that's about the strength of it. You're going to look pretty—you and yer mayors! —when it's suggested you 'ad a woman die under you while you was charving her. And that you then dumped her on the pavement outside yer 'ouse.'

'Are you *mad?*' This was all Mark could get past his lips. The man's words, his terrible guess, were an unforeseen shot that paralysed thought. Coherent cerebral thinking gave place to confusion, while he stared at Angelo, and only after a time stuttered, 'How can you suggest anything so *ridiculous?* Such things can't happen.'

'Oh, yes, they can.' He whipped a dirty piece of paper from a vest pocket and glanced at it. 'Myo—myocarditis, the gen'lman called it—and it can 'appen, he said, while people are at it. Any'ow it'll be up to you to prove that *that's* not what happened. She *was* found outside your garden walls after you two'd been at it.'

'What do I know about how she got there?'

'Yeah, that's what we'd all like to know. Any'ow I know what I can suggest to the cops.'

'Suggest what you like, you little fool, and make them laugh.' So he said, but merely for the sake of speaking. While he gained time. He knew this defiance rang false. Useless to think he could prevaricate and palter with this creature any more. His very confusion now, and his disabled tongue, were proofs that he had things to hide; not—*not* that she'd died under him and that he'd placed her where she was found. Nobody could ever prove that. But why, oh why had he not carried her farther along Menworthy Rise and laid her elsewhere than against his own wall? This had seemed so clever; now it seemed too clever by half, since it could offer lickerish ideas to the stupid, the scandal-lovers, and the evil-minded. After all, he had only put her poor body there in pity, under the spread of a tree, because it was raining. Or partly in pity. Because it was raining.

All these thoughts plunged and raced through the long silence in which he could not speak, but only stand gazing bewildered at his visitor. A silence that proved his guiltiness. He turned and walked to the window. And then perceived that this was a further suggestion of surrender. Gazing now at a blinded window, he thought, 'Nothing for it but to come to terms with the blackmailer.' Never, *never*, would he allow the real truth to come to light. 'Dumped her on the pavement after having her'—never, never. A thousand? This little fiend of hell mustn't know, but he'd give ten thousand, he'd give all the capital he'd got, to keep the truth from the light.

Terms. Terms were inevitable. But what terms?

Long minutes he stood there with his back to Angelo who must be standing behind him, aware that he'd won. He actually heard the man, tired by this standing, seat himself on the arm of the nearest easy-chair.

Oh, get it over. He turned about and said, 'I do not deny that she was with me that night. All the rest of your ludicrous nonsense I of course deny. How and when she died I have no idea, and it's nothing to do with me. I suppose I must give you something. Let's get this over quickly. How much do you want?'

'I've told you. A thousand.'

Mark flung back his head, as in disdain of such a demand. 'Pah!'

'But what the hell's a thousand to you? It won't break you.

You're a rich man. I'm not. And she's dead. She's not just hurt, she's dead. My wife for all practical purposes. Last seen alive with you before being picked up dead, and you've not told the cops a thing in three weeks.'

'A thousand is ridiculous,' Mark stammered.

'Not for you. There's that there purse of a thousand they tell me your Council gives you. They say you don't have to give no account for none of it. You could kind'a save on that.'

So. Did this little lump of rascality imagine that, even if one fell from purity now and again, one would devote part of an 'expenses' trust to the settlement of private debts? Waste of time to explain this to him. 'A thousand is quite ridiculous. I won't stand for that.'

'All right. *Va bene.* I go to the cops.'

(He has me on the run. What does one do on the run? What does one do?) 'Mr. Tancredi, you must give me time to see how far I can go—'

'A thousand is what I said. It's only fair. She earned good money for us both.'

'And the less you say about that the better. I'm not the rich man you think, and I'll certainly not give you a thousand.' Hesitation. Then : 'Half that, perhaps.'

Angelo pretended to sulk at this offer, but Mark guessed that he'd probably never expected to get the thousand—it had been a bargaining price—and he was sufficiently dazzled by the prospect of 'a cool five hundred'. Sitting on the chair's arm, he lifted both shoulders to imply a reluctant acceptance and said only, 'I don't want no cheques. And no five-nicker notes neither. Pound notes, please, and not too many new ones o' them – unless you can't help it.'

Evidently a little man fully experienced in the receiving of ill-gotten money. Expert, but reasonable withal.

'Well, it'll take time to raise such a large sum of money.' (Untrue, of course. I could cash a cheque for it tomorrow. But gain time. Gain time.) 'Will you give me till—say, this day fortnight?'

'No, I won't. Not that.'

The humiliation! He, Mayor, First Citizen, Magistrate, begging for time from a criminal. 'Well, say ten days ahead.'

'I'll give you ten days, yes. Tuesday week. That's fair enough.'

'Very well. And kindly come when my servants are gone. They might not be willing to let you in. Say nine o'clock.'

'That's all right by me.' One gathered that he'd be willing to come at midnight for money. 'Fair enough.'

'And if I hear in the meantime that you've said one word about this to anyone, you'll get nothing out of me. I'll leave you to do your worst. It won't pay you. Except with prison.'

'You can trust me.' (Trust! The comedy of it.) 'I ain't told a soul so far. Why should I?'

No, why should he? These words expressed a truth, Mark thought. Why should this furtive and slinking little felon put the evidence of his present activity into anyone's hand? Here surely was a little pick-purse who walked in the shade or the darkness. 'All right then. Let us end this.' Mark walked to the study door, flung it open and, leading Angelo to the front door, opened this for him.

Angelo, still saying nothing, went down the steps with his head a little to one side, his hands thrust deliberately into his overcoat pockets, and an occasional shiver of one shoulder—all signs of a man whose back was proclaiming that he'd nothing to be ashamed of. A darkening night absorbed him.

The dining-room was silent. Belle and Bronwen had gone home, abandoning a game that was no fun without Uncle Mark. Capes was long gone too. The house was empty of all but a man in an agony.

11. A Man to His Limit

Five days of the agony. Days of mental disturbance so great that he claimed a sickness with some fever and withdrew from work. Certainly he was in no state to deal with patients in his consulting room; still less to operate in theatres; but, for the rest, the old elaborate deceits had to come into full play; the sickness was mental only. He provided coughs for Pelly to hear in the kitchen; he spoke in a thin, weakened voice to Capes; he ate only a little of what was put before him, and went out to find more food unseen; he received Noel Fowler, the Mayor's Secretary, in the dressing-gown of an invalid, when he came in the mornings with borough business from the Town Hall.

Most of the day-time he sat in his study before a hot fire, or wandered up and down it, thinking, thinking. Thinking ever, How cruel the trick that Fate had worked on him, how brutally unfair the punishment for a man who had sinned so seldom in this common field. Countrywide disgrace, professional ruin, a lifetime of shame—if such was the penalty God had assessed for him, he would not take it. No, no. Never, never. 'Oh God, you know I didn't mean it. I meant no harm to her. I didn't mean it. I felt cheated. Snared. Oh God. . . . God. . . .'

Thinking, Perhaps he had averted the punishment by his promise of payment to Angelo—but had he? How could he be certain that, as long as this little messenger of darkness was in the world, he would not speak in the end? That he would not come extorting more and more money, as blackmailers did, and, even so, even if silenced with large payments again and again, would not divulge all one day? Was he not a moody little snake, liable to venomous frenzies? So that, even if the public shame was averted, a tormenting anxiety must remain for the rest of one's life.

Even now, what was Angelo doing? Would he, after all, in some wild resentment, go to the police? Difficult to believe he would abandon five hundred pounds and risk imprisonment for himself, but could one be sure? 'In violent tempers, capable of anything.' 'A shouting match with the knives out.' Or, after he'd taken his five hundred and spent it, what then? No peace. No assurance. No peace evermore. Every ring at the door, every knock, an alarm.

Lying in bed through the nights, nearly always awake, he would sometimes gasp aloud (there was no one in that big empty home to hear), 'I can't bear it. I can't bear it,' and, tossing over desperately, eyes opening to the dark, would think, 'Nearing sixty, and what is this but the same cry of that passionate child whom I remember in this house fifty years ago? "I'm not *going* to be whipped! I won't, I won't!"'

Sometimes, after he'd been awake for hours, and the world lay silent and still around the house, he would seek peace in one dreadful imagining. . . . In such times reality, normality, daylight reason faded away, and the dream with its comfort was everything. One imagined it fulfilled, and the peace that would follow. The exquisite peace.

Mark had a good friend in Dr. Morris Ringmer, a brilliant Jewish psychiatrist with whom he would enjoy many an argument, disputing his more astonishing claims. Morris Ringmer had once discussed with Mark what he called 'the equivalent phase' of brain activity which might result from a torment of stresses. In such states, Morris declared, the amount and the nature of a man's response was 'equivalent', whether he was hit by a pebble or by a bullet, whether he was contemplating the theft of a shilling or the committal of a murder. Mark, believing little of this contention, had long forgotten it, but it was no bad description of his state in these midnight hours when he lay with a dream like a drug.

* * *

On the fifth day came Jasper's letter, well weighted with his own brands of humour. Evidently they had been 'doing', as before, a Shakespeare play in his class at school. Mark, seated for a lonely breakfast at the long dining table, raised the gold-rimmed quizzer to his eye, and read:

'Dearest Daddy'—that 'dearest' might be only a convention soon to be outgrown, but sweet to a father while it lasted. Time must deprive him of it in any case, but what might not his enemy do to it tomorrow?—'how are things in Mornington Gardens West? This comes hoping it finds you as it leeves me at present in this reformatory working reesonably hard and aching for the hols. Quite well in all other respects except for a displeasing imposthume in one tooth but if it gets any worse I am going to the dentist who will do whatever they do to an imposthume. I shan't much mind going to the dentist because I can never understand why people think the drill part of it slightly sinister, I always think it's rather fun. Apart from this interesting fact I'm afraid I have little to report except too much work alas and alack and woe is me and an occasional game of rugger which can be rather dim and unnecessarily painful. I have made a very great friend Mag Cooke his silly name is Magnus did you ever but he's a whoreson nice fellow and we do everything together. He was Oxford but when he knew I was Cambridge because you had been at Cambridge he changed over and we have idears of going up to Cambridge together when weve finished with this comic acaddemy. We are wondering if he could come and stay with me not these hols but in the easter hols—' Easter—would the household be standing then?—'you see Mag is crazy about butterflies and moths and such like fenomena and I conceave they would be up and about at eastertime. Mag would be no trouble to you and Pelly and Capes because he wouldn't get in the way at all, being merely a bughunter and perfectly happy so long as bugs are around. I even conceave that Pelly and Capes would rather like him. He is very impressed by your being a mayor and so are some of the other chaps. I begin to think I may have blown off about it a bit too much but the reason is I like to be treated with respect in this comic place. Love to auntie Belle and her daughter and to Pelly and Capes. Your ever loving son Jasper Mark Jepherson Dolmen.'

And then a fine flourish under the signature like the curl of a coachman's whip.

Ever loving son. Heart swollen with love and inflated with fear, Mark swore that never, never, would he let this boy's home be ruined around him. He would suffer nothing to happen, *nothing*, that would cover Jasper with shame at school and make him an object of pity; nor anything that would shatter this naïve pride in his father and fill the old affection with •shames and pains. His father's disgrace, flung wide to the world, would be too like a spiritual death for Jasper—yes, and a death of the heart for Bronwen.

Anything, anything, the impossible, the unthinkable, rather than such things should be.

The only hope, the only certain comfort, lay in the thought that, *if* there was no other way, there was still that dark idea, weird and awful though it was, with which he drugged his thoughts during the long nights. He took it with him into his bed that night and lay with it for hours. Hours because its end was not easy to define. Always those who took this idea into their minds had to wrestle with one dreadful problem. The final problem, after action. How did one solve it *if* one acted thus? One was only *thinking*, of course . . . and wondering. Wondering through the night. And as he lay there, tossing, the old ingeniousness began its work. That boy of a hundred silent deceits lay in this bed again, finding, as in the old days, the only healing for fear in long brainwork upon the best preservatives against discovery. And soon, one after another, ingenious plans presented themselves. He was seeing his garden with the tall trees shadowing it. He heard Mr. Luddermore speaking. 'Never do much with this garden. It's the lay of yer land, yer see. No outlet. The rainwater comes down that rise and lays in any dip or 'oller. There's an 'oller under your tree, a'nt there? One could dig a sump-pit there, of course, say five or six feet deep, and drain into it.' Then he heard himself answering Mr. Luddermore, not as on that day, but as on the garden lawn tomorrow when Mr. Luddermore would be there. 'Why not dig a sump-pit partly under the path and partly under the grass? You're always saying that some kind of drainage is necessary in this heavy London clay and that if there's no outlet, the only thing is a sump.

Well, what's wrong with a trench, say about five feet long by five feet deep, with a few tile pipes leading into it; wouldn't that drain both lawn and path?' And out of the past came Mr. Luddermore's comment, its last words shiveringly apt. 'I suppose it could do something, but you'll never make much of this garden, not with all them trees around. It must be a regular breeding ground for pests, and it's the devil getting shut of pests.'

Shut of pests. Mark felt he could hardly wait till Mr. Luddermore came tomorrow to sweep up the October leaves and perhaps mow the lawn, for Mr. Luddermore mowed on through autumn and winter, holding, and all too repeatedly stating, that mowing refined coarse grass.

In the morning, unable to think of anything else, Mark went down into the garden to reconnoitre and prospect. As he descended the iron stairway from his study he heard Pelly washing up the breakfast plates in the scullery sink below. For the present he certainly had no resolve to act upon his drugging idea; only a need to ease the aching anxiety by considering it—or (as perhaps he might have put it) 'making preparations in case . . .' He walked to the slight depression by the garden wall where the hoggin path was a swampy black beneath the Tree of Heaven and the soured grass was thinned by the same overhanging canopy.

For a time he stood looking down and thinking; then came away, still of course with no certainty in mind except this determination—now a compulsive need—to 'prepare in case . . .' But then, wandering back to the study steps, he observed for the first time, because he'd not been in the garden for days, a sucker growing up from the grass near the area-wall before Mrs. Pelly's scullery. An unhealthy symptom it looked in an unhealthy garden. He gazed at it longer than at the dank depression beneath the tree.

He gazed at that sucker, and his lifelong inventiveness spoke.

A sucker undoubtedly from a travelling root of the Tree of Heaven. Mr. Luddermore speaking. 'What about them roots? They travel deep down and 'orizontally and before you know where you are they'll be messing about with the foundations of your house.' 'How deep down, Mr. Luddermore?' 'Could be all of five feet down, sir.'

Five feet down. One could excavate just to see what the roots were doing. Was it not almost obligatory to excavate and see? Soon? At once? Reasonable. Convincing. 'Danger to the foundations of one's house. . . .'

From this moment the day was little but a restless waiting for Luddermore's arrival in the evening.

Back in his study he came again and again to the window and looked out at the garden. The sun's disc stood bright above the house. A northerly wind was blowing, and brusquely too, so that the last leaves of the black poplar were taking to the air like birds. Those that still twinkled on the lower branches glittered like sequins in the sun. Leaves, yellow, crimson and bronze, lay over much of the grass, but on the central parts where, undiscouraged by over-arching trees, it was in fair heart, its green was the deepest of the year, after the autumn rains.

. Next time he came to the window the sky was veiled in grey and melancholy, and at times the yet brusquer wind sighed among the tree-tops, shorn of leaves.

Soon after four he heard a stirring in the garden. Once more he rose to look. Mr. Luddermore had arrived early because the veiled sun would be down in an hour's time, and the dusk be darkness by six. He was standing in the midst of the garden, and lifting his sweat-stained hat with his right hand that its fingers might scratch his head while he considered the scattered leaves. The white moustache weeping over his lips, and the white eyebrows bushing over his eyes, made him look more than ever like Prince Otto von Bismarck, if you could imagine that statesman untidily at work in a garden. He walked towards the tool-shed at the bottom of the garden, and Mark stood back from the window, leaving him a few minutes to rattle in the shed for birch-broom and rake. One must not appear worried or hurried.

Now Mr. Luddermore was sweeping, and Mark went down the steps. 'Good evening, Mr. Luddermore.'

' 'Evening, sir.'

'Leaves really falling now.'

'Only beginning to. A tidy lot more to come yet. Them trees,' he despaired.

'Yes, it's late in the year. Mr. Luddermore, what's the best time to sow grass?'

The thing in his mind might be impossible, unthinkable, but its opposites were all impossible too, and because of this he could not stop his questioning. Unthinkable, yes, but chiefly because the whole matter seemed to have advanced into some region beyond thought. In this empty region the questioning would go on of itself.

'Sow grass?' Surprised by this untimely question, Mr. Luddermore rested with hands about his broomstick. He meditated, throwing his lower lip to one side. 'Wurl . . . in the autumn, I always say, because there's never no danger of drought then.'

The word 'autumn' was what he wanted to hear. 'Yes, I thought so.'

'September would be the time.'

September was less pleasing. 'What? Not later than that?'

'Wurl . . . I suppose you could risk putting it off till October but'—he shook his head and began to sweep at a few leaves—'I doubt if it'd come to any good.'

'Oh, dear,' laughed Mark. 'It's already mid-October, and I was wondering if we couldn't sow some grass now. We'd have to be quick, of course.'

'You sure would, sir. I suppose, if you 'ad to, you could sow up to the end of October, but I wouldn't 'ave much 'opes. Better wait till April. Could put turf down, but doubt if it'd be worth it.'

'April! That's a long time away. I hoped we could do it in a day or two.'

'Where would you want to sow, sir?'

Mark turned about and faced the house. 'Have you seen that sucker?'

Mr. Luddermore turned too. 'Gum! I know where that's come from. From that there Tree of 'Evan. I warned you of it. If you'd taken my advice you'd have thrown that old tree long ago.'

'Rather an extreme measure, Mr. Luddermore. Sounds rather like killing an old gentleman to cure his corns. Besides, there's a preservation order on the tree.'

'Always get round that if a tree's dangering your house.'

'My idea is just to dig down and attend to this root.'

'Likely as not it's five feet down.'

'Is it? As much as that? Really?' But this was exactly what he wanted to hear. 'The Council's Superintendent told me that the root would travel in a direct line, so I'm thinking that if we were to dig a small trench half-way between the tree and the sucker, we'd serve a double purpose: we could expose the root and do whatever's necessary; then fill the trench with rubble and what-not before adding the top soil and so have a sump that'd help drain the lawn—which you always say needs it.'

'Some job if it's five foot down,' Mr. Luddermore despaired again.

'I could get someone in to help you.'

Here Mr. Luddermore brushed at more leaves while he thought. Mark guessed he didn't want a stranger in his garden. 'If you really want it done I could get my son to come on a Saturday afternoon. Or Sunday, if you've no objection. He works for London Landscapes, same as I done. Ground's soft now, and a couple of us should ought to do it in an hour or two.'

'That'd be fine, and it's Saturday tomorrow. We must do it quickly, if we're to fill it up and sow the grass.'

'Sow grass? But, law, you shouldn't ought to sow at once on newly turned earth. You want to let the seedbed lie fallow for months.'

Sharp disappointment again. 'Why?'

'To let it sink down to its natural level, of course.'

Yes. Always the same. Ignorant dreamers never foresaw the simplest obstacle. 'Oh . . . I see. But one could stamp it down, I suppose?' he suggested sadly.

'You'd have to—good and proper.'

Not to be beaten, unable to be beaten, Mark persisted. 'But . . . all the same . . . I imagine we could have a shot at sowing the grass.'

'You can 'ave a shot at anything, but I'm not saying you'd get anywhere.'

'Still, if it doesn't work, we could sow again in the spring—as you said.'

That 'as you said' was politic. Mr. Luddermore's despairs

always went into brief abeyance when someone approved of his advice. 'Yes, you could do that, o' course.'

'Well, let us act at once. When can you'—he hesitated—'dig the trench?'

'Dig it any time. Tomorrow afternoon if you like. Get my lad'—his lad was fifty—'to come and bring his tools along. He's a rare good gardener'—a father's pride in his lad—'and I reckon that between us we'll come at that root all right.'

'Fine. Let's do it. It'll at least be interesting.'

'Very good, sir.'

Mark went back up his steps, wondering if sanity was slipping from him. Shaken sanity protested again and again that the whole idea was wildly impossible. Yes, yes . . . still, let them dig . . . dig. . . . The other things were impossible too. But . . . surely the whole idea withered away at a breath of clear thought. Perhaps, perhaps. Still, let it wait out there. Let it be there. No more than preparation for the other terrible Perhaps.

Let it be there.

Four days after. The electric clock on his mantel had hardly struck the hour, the clock in the tower of All Hallows, Seven Brides (Craikie's church), had just echoed it, when there came the ring at the door and the single fall of the knocker. Angelo. Evidently he'd been waiting at the corner, or up the street, for his appointed hour. Possibly he had watched Capes leave the house ten minutes ago.

Heart unshaken because thought and feeling seemed paralysed, Mark went along the passage and opened the door. The little man stood there with his hands as usual deep in the pockets of his long and loosely open overcoat and a friendly but awkward smirk on his face. Though plainly nervous and ashamed, he was attempting the geniality which might suggest he saw nothing wrong in what he was doing. It was just a bit of business between two men-of-the-world. Two considerate gentlemen, as you might say. 'Well, here I am,' he said quite merrily. But since there came no answering geniality, he could find nothing more to say and was left silent. Mark only murmured, 'Come in, then,' and stood back to close the door behind him. He closed it very sharply.

Unwilling to speak, and even more unwilling to lay a finger on this man, he just pointed towards his study door. Angelo walked the way of the pointing finger. The effect of this was that Mark came along the passage two paces behind a visitor whose left shoulder kept jerking forward as if to express, '*I'm* not worried, cock. I'm perfectly at ease.' Following him, Mark was thinking, 'What's he walking to? *I* don't know. Maybe there's plenty for you to worry about, Mr. Angelo.' In the paralysis of feeling and reasoning, this query, 'What's he walking to?' was but a dull doubt.

Since Angelo passed into the study first and turned round while Mark shut the room's door, he now stood, hands still happily pocketed, between Mark and the window. The window curtains were drawn but Mark was seeing a cavity in the dark garden behind them, with hills of brown earth around it. The root of the tree had proved to be unusually far down and the cavity, to Mark's unhinged, unreasoning satisfaction, was nearly five feet deep. And now his tormentor stood before him with that little plague-pit waiting out there.

The spoil of brown earth around the pit had been increased by Mark in a dark and quiet hour after midnight when he had enlarged the Luddermores' cavity a little, he who had vowed never to damage his surgeon's hands by heavy work in the garden. But he had dug there in the silent and sombre dark, behind the cover of his trees, wondering as he plied his spade or paused for breath, if he was now a madman. Here, once again, he was moving cautiously in his garden, in a small-hour darkness, with never sound of leaf stirring or foot coming near, just as he'd had to do when, watchfully, he carried Desiderata away.

His extremes of ingenuity had decided that, *if* he could do the unspeakable thing, his victim must never be found in some distant pit or underbrush lest, as was just possible, a confederate knew he had come this way, a confederate who could explode the whole story to the police. 'The Mayor of Keys.' No, never found dead; merely a disappearance that might start a confederate wondering, speculating, shoulder-shrugging, but hardly set him taking any risks.

A long disappearance; a strange departure and a forgetting; an 'out of the way for ever'.

In the one place where no one could come upon him.

What else? Where else? Or are these the thoughts of a madman? God, am I now mad? Has he driven me mad? But where else?

Nowhere else.

He did not invite Angelo to sit down, and they stood facing each other. In the silence Angelo tossed his head as one who would say, 'I'm not going to talk. It's for you to start a chat, if you want to'; and in the same silence Mark looked at Angelo's chickeny throat while he rubbed the forefinger of his right hand back and forth on his thumb. The two fingers that would be his tools.

In case he couldn't do it, Mark had assembled the five hundred pounds. The clerk at the bank, without lifting an eyebrow, had handed him a sheaf of five wads of a hundred one-pound notes, and Mark had been perturbed to see how small was such a sheaf. It looked all too small to hold any blackmailer long from the door. This sheaf was now in the left-hand drawer of his writing-desk, and the choice at this moment was between these notes and *it—it*, the dreadful dream, the deed. Two men opposite each other, one small and uncomfortably simpering, the other large and strong, but with body trembling within its good clothes, and jaws actually chattering together in the turmoil of a choice.

And he found he couldn't do it. How had he ever thought he could do it? A wildly impossible plan. Impossible alike to the civilized man in him and the coward. His hand wouldn't leave his side; it would lift a few inches and no more. Nothing then but to accept the risk of shame inconceivable and an end of all things. What would happen must happen. Perhaps Angelo would never talk. But he couldn't really believe this. Putting this money into his hands was putting an end to all denials. It was putting himself into the hands of a capricious, evil, vindictive little man.

Still, nothing to do but to let Fate have its way, and he went towards the writing-desk.

He stopped. Oh, but could he, could he yet . . . ? No. He went to the drawer and took out the packet of notes. 'Here you are. Take it.'

Handing away all hope of escape?

Angelo cursorily examined the notes while Mark wanted to

scream, 'Take it and go!' The conflict between his palsied impotence to do the deed and his dreads of what still might happen if he left it undone, was so near unbearable that he said it at last, in a low rather than a loud voice. '*Take* it. *Take* it. And go. You've got what you wanted. Go.'

And go with him for ever the assurance of honour, love, livelihood, peace—the love of the children, the honour of his friends. Let it go. There are things one cannot do.

Angelo was ready to take this money but not this tone. 'I don't see you've any cause to speak to me like that.'

'Never mind "cause". Go.'

'I been generous, I reckon. Taken half of what I reckon was fair to me, being as how Desid was my wife, practically, and made good money.'

'Will . . . you . . . go! I know nothing about her death. It's no responsibility of mine—'

'So you say—'

'Will you go, or—' Some unspoken menace in Mark's stiletto glare, in a sudden forward inclination of his head, so frightened Angelo that he shifted towards the door. He opened it but had to show an unbroken front by declaring, 'I'm not the sort that takes talk from you. You're no one to talk to me. You're no better than what I am. Anyone can see that. You and Desiderata! No one knows yet what you done to her.'

'Go!' Mark took three steps towards him—to what end he hardly knew—and Angelo retreated several paces along the passage ignominiously. Standing there, Mark watched him. Angelo, looking back at his stationary figure, said '*Sacramento!* I—I—' but no more. Mark never knew what he was about to say. In a fury Angelo opened the hall door and went out, slamming it behind him.

But the business was only delayed. It was a Tuesday night when Angelo took the money. For three days Mark lived with the incomplete wish that he'd had the courage to do the thing— why not, why not, when Fate had cheated him, *cheated* him, when a chance in a million, in ten million, had spread disaster around him? Had he weakly, helplessly, he, Mark Dolmen, consented to be no more than a little insect in the hands of a mischievous, torturing Fate? Why should he consent to being cheated? Tricked.

Friday, and he was thinking something like this when punctually at half-past eight, after Capes had gone from the house, the door-bell rang again. The promptness of the hour, the single heavy fall of the knocker, and then the low shadows behind the twin coloured panes of the hall door confirmed that this was Angelo.

And Mark went to the door with a quick delight. The delight of relief.

Angelo had come back once too often. Opportunity was here again; the last opportunity. Luddermore might come tomorrow to sow the grass. The trees that would screen any midnight movements in the garden were losing their leaves. Open the door happily to this evening caller. Pulling back the door, Mark said, 'Now what? What the hell have you come back for?' not minding in what manner he spoke to him because this would have no importance soon.

'I been thinking.'

'About what?'

'I still reckon you've not treated me fair.'

'Oh, you do, do you?'

'Yes, and I'm not so sure that I propose to let you get away with it.'

'I see. Well, let's hear what you propose to do.'

'I been thinking it might be well worth having an inquiry into how Desid came to be found dead outside your house and all. I just don't believe, that even if I 'ad to admit to an aspect of things the Law don't hold with, though I never see what's wrong with it, I'd get more than about half a stretch at the outside. And, as I've told you, guv, I'm the sort that'd do my ten stretch rather than be done in the eye by anybody, least of all by a wealthy cove like you—'

'Ah, here we come to it.'

'—and one gen'lman who knows the Law tells me I might even get nothing if I turned what they call Queen's Evidence.'

'Come in.'

Angelo stepped into the hall while continuing to talk. 'So you got something to think about, you see.'

'Indeed I have,' Mark agreed, caring not at all whether his visitor discerned a double meaning. 'Go on. Get inside. I don't discuss matters like this on my doorstep.'

'All right, guv. Take it easy.'

'Get inside.'

So it happened again that Angelo went ahead of him into the study and there stood between him and the window—with the night and the garden outside, and in the heart of them an un-filled cavity waiting.

Face to face with him Mark said, 'I suppose you want that other five hundred? That's what you've really come for. And then perhaps when you've had that and spent it, you'll come again, eh?' It didn't matter what he said; any words would do while he studied, like a good surgeon, the area of the operation. A small exposed area between open collar and chin. 'Let's have it out. Another five hundred, eh?'

'Well, yes, that's about it. I reckon that'd be only fair. I reckon that I should never ought to have settled for that five hundred. I mean to say—'

Mark wasn't interested in what he meant to say. He was learning, at this second chance, how strongly he had wanted to do the thing, and why he was so glad that his pest had come back. One finger was rubbing on the tip of his thumb, round and round. 'Well, say I give you that five hundred, what assurance have I that you won't come back for more? And again and again? Tell me that.'

'I could promise not to, like. And I would too.'

'I'm sure you would.'

'Yeah, I would, and you'd just have to trust me.'

'And do you really suppose I'd do that?'

'Don't see what else you could do, guv.'

'You don't?' Then this little man feels, does he, that the whip-hand is his? We shall see.

Mark had no thoughts just now of his good and clever friend, Morris Ringmer, and no remembrance of warm arguments with him, when Morris would distinguish between his 'equiva-lent phase of brain action in a torment of stresses' and what he called 'the paradoxical phase'. In the paradoxical phase, said Morris, a man's emotional responses to strong stimuli were not just equivalent to his responses to weak ones but, paradoxically, of far less force, so that for instance the dislike of inflicting death and the fear of consequences that might result—arrest, trial, scaffold—could be, for a time, less powerful deterrents than the recoil from the performance or the consequences of some quite inconsiderable offence. To all this clever stuff Mark, who could swallow little of it, would just shake a doubtful head, spread unassenting hands, and say, 'Sounds deeply impressive, Morris, old man, but I'm not sure I believe a word of it.'

And yet, in his condition now, when there seemed little in his brain but a kind of white, empty, amoral light, his skilled and delicate fingers were playing on his thumb, eager for their work—a small and neat task for a surgeon. The trench waited in the dark garden without. When Desiderata had died he had dwelt for a little with the idea of burying her beneath the Tree of Heaven. This had been impossible then, but the same pattern was in his mind now, though he was designing a different tenant for the grave.

'You don't see what else I could do? You really suppose I'd trust you? And pray, why should I? All blackmailers are the same. They come again and again if you give into them.'

'I'm no blackmailer. I just want my rights.'

'They come again and again. But *you* don't, my friend. Did you really begin to think that I was going to deliver my life into the hands of someone like you?'

Angelo stepped back, for Mark seemed to be coming towards him. 'What you up to—?' he began.

'Did you really think that?' Mark repeated. '*Did* you?'

Angelo's hands lay in the pockets of his long loose overcoat, sleeping carelessly. Mark's were free, and the fingers and thumb of his right hand shot forth to their work. His teeth set together while his mind thought simply, 'Close the throat up; press on the trachea; he will be unconscious in a dozen seconds; dead in a few more. . . .'

It was exactly so; a neat piece of work. In less than a minute Angelo, after abortive struggles, hands thrusting madly, was dead, and Mark was placing his body, gently enough, in his own easy-chair with its back to the window. The Impossible was there before him again, as it had been when he looked down from his high window at his garden wall beyond which Desiderata lay in the night. The Impossible had bred the Impossible. Silence in the room because Angelo was not moving on that chair. Nor Mark moving at all, as he stood staring at the dreadful fact before him with his hands fingering each other behind his back, the hands which had achieved it. Outside that room the pulse of life went on, and some part of him heard it: footsteps passing in Menworthy Rise; a car sweeping by; voices somewhere; a clock chiming far away while, nearer, in the tower of All Hallows, Seven Brides, an hour struck.

He would have to do yet another Impossible in the darkness of the small hours. Nevertheless a vast peace was in him as though with a morphia needle he had made all pain to cease. He was thinking with an ecstatic relief now of Jasper . . . of Bronwen . . . of his patients and friends . . . of the Mayor of Keys.

12. Intermission

At first the peace remained, though it was tainted with a fear: did anyone know that Angelo had come to Mornington Gardens that night? It was not a great fear. Mark, thinking of himself as a reader of character, and sure that Angelo was a secret, wary, underground little man, found it hard to believe that he had made any neighbour in East London privy to his games 'out West'. And as day succeeded day with never a question from the police, the fear diminished, leaving the peace almost untroubled.

In these first days he was surprised to perceive how quickly men could adjust to disastrous limitations in their lives—to the loss of a limb, say, to a sudden arthritic disablement, to a crippling road accident, or even to such a memory as was his now. A memory that lay low in his heart even as Angelo lay low in his garden. One accepted the Impossibles. A violent death in this his daily study; a grave out there; one accepted them and at times even forgot them.

If at other times Conscience leapt like a tiger and tore at him, he struggled from its claws by thinking of the great and easy killers, Nero, Ivan the Terrible, Napoleon, Stalin, Hitler with his night of the long knives. 'You are but a small one.' Or he thought of those Sicilian *mafiosi* about whom Desiderata had spoken. In their vendettas they killed not just one of their enemies but tens or scores. At his study window, if his eyes strayed to that scar in the lawn, he might remember First War stories of a body hastily buried in a trench's parapet or parados—from which sometimes its finger or hand emerged. He thought also of men buried in the muddy shell-holes of no-man's-land where they had crawled to die. Somehow the memory of these strange burials eased him.

Mr. Luddermore, whose attendances were optional and irregular, did not come again for several days. But at four one evening Mark, returning from a hospital, saw him standing in the garden by the brown scar in the lawn with the surplus of unused earth around it. His sweat-soiled hat was pushed back on his grey head as if he needed the breeze while he considered these unexpected phenomena.

'I see you've filled it up and stamped it down,' he said, as Mark, having parked the Rolls, came into the garden.

'Yes, I thought that if we were going to sow grass we'd better do it quickly. Time was short, as you said.'

'*I'll* say it's short. End of October now.'

'Yes, but it's six days since I filled it up and raked it over. You didn't come so I bought some seed and put it down. There was this hurry, you said.'

'Wonder the birds haven't 'ad it all. 'Ope you got the top-soil on top. If you haven't, nothing much'll come up nowhere, not as late as this.'

'Yes, heavy clay at the bottom, top-soil on top.'

'Seems a lot o' clay still about. Thought you said you couldn't never do any gardening because it'd spoil your 'ands for operating and all.'

'True enough, but it's not difficult to shovel a little earth into a hole and stamp it down. I don't operate with my feet, you know.'

Mr. Luddermore didn't laugh. He only deplored, 'There's a tidy lot of soil that we'll have to disperse somehow.'

'There is, but that's because I did what you said. I found some rubbish to put at the bottom.' Quickly he added, 'You said put plenty of rubble and rubbish, cinders and clinkers and such-like, so as to help drain the lawn.'

Mr. Luddermore, mollified as ever by that 'what you said', went so far as to nod in reluctant agreement. 'Yes, well, it ought'a do that, certainly. But what about that there root and its suckers? That was what we were after.'

'I was fortunate in having the services of an expert from the Council's Open Spaces Department. He just sawed through the root and left the severed part to die.' None of this was the truth. In a casual chat with the Superintendent of Trees Mark had asked what a friend in Bloomsbury should do about an ailanthus and its sucker in his garden. 'Sever the root and let it die,' was all the Superintendent had said. 'Easy enough with a surface-rooting tree. Depends upon the soil, of course, but the roots are seldom far down.' Mark had told him nothing about a root in Keys nearly five feet down. He had come home and on that dark night when he enlarged the pit he had sawn through the root at two places and lifted out some four feet of it—to make more and deeper room. It was not Angelo's body that he had conveyed to Epping Forest on the other side of London and hidden in the underbrush; it was a four-foot log. 'He said there was no need to worry any further.'

'No need to worry!' This statement didn't please Mr. Luddermore, who had no use for 'experts from the Council' coming into one of his gardens to do a job he could do perfectly well himself, so he objected, 'But it's a quick-growing tree, the Tree of 'Evan; what about its other roots. Lord knows what they're doing.'

'Well, we'll wait till they misbehave.'

'All right, if you say so.' And there was nothing for Luddermore to do but to find out some other trouble. 'You'll have to protect that there seed if the birds are not to have it all. Probably 'ad about half of it already. Not that it's likely to come to anything much, anyhow.'

'All the same. Let's protect it, as you say. But how?'

'A network of threads stretched across it.' Reaching up to a weeping branch of the ailanthus tree, he snapped small twigs from it. 'These 'ere'll do if you can give me a reel of thread.'

'I've no reel,' Mark laughed. 'Don't know if Mrs. Pelly has.' He called through the semi-basement scullery window, 'Mrs. Pelly, have you a reel of thread? Don't see why you should, but have you?'

Mrs. Pelly appeared at the window, wiping her hands on a

cloth. She'd no thread, she said, but she'd nip round to Mrs. Hamps next door. 'But what colour, sir?'

'What colour, Mr. Luddermore?'

'Lord, don't matter what colour. Birds ain't particular. Black best, I suppose.'

'Black, Mrs. Pelly, please.'

'Very good, sir.' And in less than five minutes she was back, not only with the reel, but with Bronwen too, who called out as they entered the garden by the side path, 'Can I help? Do let me help, Uncle darling? I love gardening with Mr. Luddermore. You'd like me to help, wouldn't you, Mr. Luddermore? What have we got to do?'

Instantly Mark was horrified, sickened, by the thought of Bronwen helping to weave this counterpane for the sleeper below. 'No, go back. Go back at once,' he said, pretending to joke. 'You've got your homework to do. Nobody asked you to come along.'

'I haven't got any homework. It's Friday. So sucks, sucks! A thousand times sucks!' And joyously she gave him a punitive slap on his trouser seat. 'You'll let me help, won't you, Mr. Luddermore?'

'I've no objection, miss.' Mr. Luddermore was now squatting down and forcing his twigs into the soft earth around the seed-bed. 'Just give me the end of that there thread and pay it out to me as I need it.'

'Oh, yes!' And Bronwen squatted opposite Mr. Luddermore, who began alternating the thread from twig to twig across the narrow earthy patch.

After he'd done half of the network, threading this way and that and across, Bronwen appealed, 'Oh, may I do some of it? I can do that easily enough, just stretching the thread from peg to peg. Besides, it's woman's work, isn't it? Kind of tatting. Like making a doily.'

Even Mr. Luddermore managed a smile at this. 'Anything you like, missy. Well then, 'and me the reel and take this 'ere end.'

Mark saw no way of stopping this amicable co-operation, so Bronwen, squatting sometimes and kneeling at other times, made the other half of this cover for Angelo's bed. While Mark watched her. Bronwen, the restless, merrily discharging a last courtesy to his enemy whose approach she had unconsciously aided.

When the two of them had finished the network, Mr. Luddermore came upright again. 'Very nicely done, and thank you, miss. The birds shouldn't ought to get more than half of it now. Not that it's likely the rest'll come to anything much. Not as late as this, nah.' And he shook a despairing head.

Still the days passed, seven of them, ten, twelve, three weeks in all, with never a word from any quarter about a missing man.

Anxiety faded, even to vanishing. He did after a time send the hearty Mr. Harry Gayne to Kelso Street, Stepney, 'to get some more information about our Mr. Angelo', but he sent him in curiosity, not in fear. And Mr. Gayne's genial report was somewhat in this fashion: 'He's gone. Yes, sir, "gawn", as they say in those parts; done a fair old scarper. Scarper, sir? Means doing a bunk. Legging it. No, no one knows where he's got to, and as far as I can see, no one cares. General view is that he thought the busies were after him. One of his ladies disappeared recently, you may remember, and it could be he'd heard she'd grassed. Grassed? Told the tale. Some of 'em think he got wind of the fact that the 'tecs were after him, which of course was true enough about a 'tec by the name of Yours Truly. Seems he did a spot of blackmail sometimes and that's considered a dicey business in Kelso Street; but whether poncing or blacking, he's lying low somewhere now.' Mr. Gayne knocked the ash, ill-advisedly, from the cigar Mark had given him. 'Yes, lying low for the present, but of course he may turn up again some day.'

Inevitably the thought rushed across his hearer's mind, 'That can never happen, Mr. Gayne.'

But with the ending of anxiety full sanity returned. An afternoon in mid-November, as he stood at the study window looking out at the garden the sanity seized him, entered him, and occupied him like a devil in possession.

His trees were nearly bare now. Such leaves as the tall ash retained were a tired green; the few lonely ones on the sycamore were a pale and dying yellow; the black poplar, as always, twinkled its few tricorne leaves before sending them down the wind into Menworthy Rise. The noble copper beech in Belle's garden was still partly mantled in copper and bronze, even though it had showered hundreds of leaves, copper, bronze and rust, on to the floor of Mark's garden, overspreading it from wall to wall. Some of the leaves lay on Bronwen's network threads, hiding the scar of a crime.

It was from this day, when fear was gone and sanity home again, that, harking back always to 'those days when I was mad', he became, not suddenly but surely, the lonely prey of an endless, helpless, unforgiving pain. From now till death he must live with that garden. He must stay in this house keeping watch over that grave. He might live another twenty-five years, and must always work, sleep and eat within yards of it. After his death, say at eighty-five, others would take the house, but surely it was unlikely they would dig deep in the midst of a lawn. Jasper would then be forty, Mr. Luddermore would be dead.

But wait! There was Luddermore's son. Still . . . he would be seventy-five and likely dead. That class seldom survived till eighty. In any case, who would dig five feet down in a lawn?

No longer was the thought of the multiple killers, the Caligulas, the Stalins, the Hitlers with their nights of long knives, the *mafiosi*, of any help to him. His morality was not theirs; and he was seeing with merciless clarity that to save himself he had denied Angelo all chance of repentance and reclamation. Unlikely as such amendment might seem in a creeping little scorpion like Angelo, it was not for Mark or any man to shut him away from all hope of it.

Oh, cursed sanity! The sin was irreparable. Where was forgiveness? How could one ask forgiveness from God? Only after a confession before the world, and this was for ever impossible; it was far beyond anything of which he was capable. He must stay then unforgiven. Reprobate. Enduring till death unshriven, with a crime unpurged, uncompensated.

There came a day when this hopeless thought threw him to his knees by the side of the big easy-chair, and laid his face on its arm. It was the chair, though he was not thinking this at the time, in which he had laid the body of Angelo. He was thinking only that his prayer was the prayer of a reprobate.

'Oh God, show me what to do. I can never confess. That is certain. What else can I do? Give me some hope that, even though I can never confess, never make reparation, and must ever remain reprobate, I can do something—a little—to counter the evil I have done. I *was* cheated, snared, oh God, I *was*, and driven mad by all that followed; can I not then hope for a little forgiveness? Oh my God, give me a trust that this burden of sin, this longing for forgiveness, are proofs of your existence. Let me trust in you. Let me trust. I suppose there can be no full restoration for me, unless I confess, which I can never do, but grant me some partial healing. I have seen too many thousand healings in my work not to believe that there is a merciful and beneficent power in the world—' and as he said this he remembered the words of a great father of surgery, spoken four hundred years before, and actually quoted them to God, or before his face. '"*Je le pansay, Dieu le guarit.* I dress it, God heals it." You are the healer of all wounds, give me some healing, if you can, oh God. I will try to make *some* amends. All I can I will do, I will, I will.'

He rose from his knees, less unhappy, but with no hope of ever being happy again. As he rose, his eyes fell upon the two framed portraits of Lorelei and of Jasper which stood always on his desk here, as did two similar ones on his great table in Queen Anne Street. And at once he felt he couldn't bear that Lorelei's face should be looking into this room and at that chair. He picked her picture up to take it to his bedroom—only to remember that this was the room in which Desiderata had died, and . . . and the rest. The big guest-room below? No. There Desiderata had lain the first time. All three rooms were haunted. So he took the picture into the drawing-room; this had been, more than others, Lorelei's room; and there perhaps he could go and look at the picture sometimes.

Her picture remained on the consulting-room table, and often a patient, glancing at it, would ask. 'Your daughter, sir?' And he would answer quietly, 'No, my wife. . . . My late wife.' And leave the matter there.

One fruit of this now abiding pain was a new tenderness towards all, no matter whom: towards Belle and Bronwen,

Pelly and Capes, even towards Mr. Luddermore, and certainly towards his patients. Another fruit was a heightened dutifulness as mayor with a new smiling friendliness towards all he must meet (no matter what his inward thoughts)—so much so that men began calling him the most popular mayor Keys had ever had. He acquired a similar popularity in the Magistrates' Court, offenders like old Ernie Brewer, after a conditional discharge (which greatly surprised him) declaring, 'That old bastard's the best of the lot. He understands a bloke's position and if he can he gives him a chahn'st. He says to me, "I can't 'elp feeling there's some good in yer somewhere, so we're bloody well going to give you another chahn'st." That's what I call being a gentleman. O'course he went on, "Gawd 'elp yer, if you let us down; we'll fair blast the skin off yer if we see yer 'ere agyne," but that was only fair, wa'n't it? Pity there ain't more beaks like 'im.' These prisoners and prostitutes couldn't know that he must feel always now on the side of the accused in the dock. Every accused was himself; every prostitute Desiderata. He had uprushes of feeling, such as could be told to none, when his heart felt ready to embrace with its compassion all sinful Man.

No one at first knew that he walked all day with a helpless grief at his side—he was too good an actor, before children, councillors, patients, prisoners. He still joked with all, donning the motley when needed. Only one eye after a time pierced the disguise and discerned a permanent grief suffered in loneliness—Belle. By now he had joined Belle and Bronwen, those regular attendants at Craikie's church, accompanying them, not only on state occasions as in the past, but regularly to Matins on Sundays—never to Holy Communion from which he considered himself cast out. He liked to think that the Mayor's regular appearance among the sparse congregation in that dim church might be some help to poor struggling old Craikie. And that this would be one small item in the compensation to God—if God there were. In fact it was doubtful if the Mayor's attendance did a thing for the ailing church. On the contrary, it was the worn and disheartened Craikie, long written off by his brethren in Keys as their local failure, who stretched out help to the Mayor.

13. The Message of the Wilderness

A December Sunday, and Jasper, home from school, was with the three of them in their forward pew. He had demanded on hearing this new custom of his father's, 'Golly, do we go to church now? Is it compulsory chapel, Daddy? It is not? Well, never mind, I conceive it my duty to support the family'; and he had come along chatting merrily to Bronwen about his first term at Benfield and the ghastly chapel services there.

The December morning was dull and drained of colour; and the grey, unlovely Victorian church when they entered was dim, even though the lamps were lit in the nave. In the empty aisles there was a darker than twilight under the sloping galleries, and below the coloured but grimy windows. Close-locked throughout the week, the church retained a fusty smell of staled air on this Sunday morning. The grey arches of imitation Gothic were powerless to inspire; true Gothic of the medieval centuries could stir Mark to a silence of wonder; this ready-made Victorian stuff only depressed him. Still . . . all well and good if it helped old Craikie to have him there; perhaps one could win a little more merit by labouring against the grain.

Morning Prayer dragged slowly onward, the thin choir and sparse congregation unable to give it fervour or strength. After the 'hymn before the sermon' Craikie, starting from his stall two minutes too late, hurried across the chancel to the pulpit, dropping his notes with a clatter on the way. In the pulpit he put on his glasses, forced them back on his nose, pushed some of the wispy grey hairs off his brows, coughed to clear his throat, and gave out his text to a congregation which had been standing there since the hymn's Amen.

It was three words only: 'In the Wilderness.'

Something unexpected here. Why this incomplete sentence? Unusual for Craikie to do anything original, and yet these words, because of their loneliness, struck home.

And no less strangely the sermon that now came haltingly on a tremulous old-man's voice, hoarse and viscid, had a quality above anything Mark could have expected.

Was this sermon then an old one belonging to the days when Craikie was young and ardent, with vision undulled? Its subject, the Temptations in the Wilderness, was more suited to a Lenten than an Advent Sunday—had he then dug it out from some piled drawer, or had he, alone yesterday in a littered study, recovered something of himself when he was young? More and more the hoarse words were impressing Mark so that he stretched an arm along the pew's back to listen better; and more today than in the Civic Service five months ago he was asking himself whether his old friend Craikie was the wreck of something which ought to have been splendidly seaworthy.

That civic sermon he had pronounced well phrased but fairly commonplace. He was thinking very differently of this one. Not only were the words well chosen, unexpected, and therefore striking; to Mark who lived now with a lasting pain they were often sharp as a sword that pierced to joints and marrow.

'What'—Craikie coughed again since his voice was not yet in order—'do you understand by a wilderness? It is a place outside the Law. No whisper of law and order, no murmur of any orthodoxy, troubles the desert winds; there is nothing here but loneliness.' And his belief, or his suspicion, said Craikie, was that Christ, just before his ministry, went deliberately into a wilderness, into a place of total loneliness which acknowledged the words of no government at all, whether of state or church; and did he not do this in order to find—and to fix in his heart—a creed, a purpose, and a ministry that were utterly his own? They were not to be dictated to him by any other authority than the God within his own heart. When he had found them some might run with the established laws, and some might not, but, whatever they were, they would have sprung out of himself and have for ever the endorsement of his blood, his pulses, his heart and his head.

'And so it should be for all of us in this church. I may be a citizen of a state, a member of a church, but the code and creed by which I am to live I must draw out of myself and create for myself—create them with excitement and joy because they are my very own; not taking them carelessly or slavishly from the lips of Authority, because if I accept them only thus they will be little but an outward uniform which I may perhaps admire, or just be willing to wear, but which I can never love with passion like the creations of my own heart and brain. As with the Master these codes and creeds which we build for ourselves may tally more often than not with those that Authority seeks to enforce, but now they will be things newly and excitedly unearthed by ourselves. And on the other hand, as with the Master, we may return from our wilderness to the places where the Law runs, eager to challenge, resolute to resist, much of it.'

Was this really Craikie hoarsely reading and speaking? Mark stretched his arm farther along the pew's back. There was a surprised stillness among the few strewn people in the church.

Craikie again pushed back the spectacles which slipped always down his nose as he bent to his notes; and just now he had lost his way in the notes.

'Let us—yes—let us try to see what the Master brought away from his wilderness; what he found to be true to the loneliness of himself and which therefore never again needed any synagogue or elders, any church or clergy, to tell him so. It may well be that out of our own loneliness—indeed I'm sure it'll be so—we shall find the same truths as he found, and if so, what a joyous discovery for us. Joyous because it will mean one of two things: either that the seeds which Christ found in himself are in us too, or that there is something in the soil of us which craves them. So joyous is it sometimes that people, on discovering for themselves that these things are part of themselves for ever, feel an urge, a compulsion, to go out and share with others what they believe to be the message of the wilderness.'

155

'The message of the wilderness'—had Craikie merely stumbled on this phrase or were there, even today, the lees of poetry in him? With this phrase, whether wittingly or not, he wielded like a thaumaturge the magic of the word. The same idea, phrased in commonplace terms, would never have flown like an arrow into the outlawed heart of Mark Dolmen. Mark was now listening as he had never listened to a sermon before. Never before, of course, had he been broken ground, harrowed and tilled, for the seeds of a sermon. This he understood, but he noticed too that Jasper, at his side, had the eyes of a rapt listener fixed on Craikie, and it pleased him to think that this revealed the beginnings of vision in a son of thirteen. He knew in this moment the immemorial wonder and delight of a parent when he sees the first blossoming of something older and finer in his child. Oh never, never, must that brightening vision be blurred, even perhaps refracted, by knowledge of a father's crimes.

Craikie was dealing now with each of the Temptations. The first: 'You are very hungry and you have great powers. Command that these stones be made bread.' And its answer: 'Man shall not live by bread alone.' In other words, said Craikie, the material satisfactions of this world were not enough, not enough. To be satisfied with them was not to live to the full. It was to be less than fully human. And the most greedy, grasping, materially minded men knew this at those times when, despite their sole pursuit of worldly comfort, they *had* to honour deeds of goodness and self-sacrifice in others. Whence came this involuntary, this unavoidable worship of nobility, of courage and compassion and forgiveness, and, most of all, of self-sacrifice for others even unto death? Why did we all, the world over, *have* to worship these things?

Here Craikie, looking straight at the people, spoke eight words which from that moment became seeds in Mark's heart. They were, 'God or no God, we can no other.'

All this Craikie had been delivering with a self-forgetting enthusiasm, his eyes often adrift from his notes. With the result that he was now lost again. An uncomfortable silence followed while he searched among his papers for his place, pushing back his spectacles as they slipped down his nose.

'Our daily bread is not enough,' he repeated, to gain time

while he sought. 'Not enough. . . . Not enough if I'm to be fully human. . . . No, certainly not enough. . . .'

Ah! The second temptation. That the Master should prove his calling and God's power by casting himself down from the Temple and demanding to be held up.

From this Craikie deduced that we must never expect any sign from Heaven which would prove beyond doubt the existence and the love of God. And why this enduring deprivation? Because there could be no faith if there was any such sign, no continuing search into the unknown, no wrestling with the challenge of the unknown and therefore no growth into fuller manhood, into that state 'wherein it doth not yet appear what we shall be'—none of these grand things but a mere stale and static credulity; a dead end, not a beginning and a becoming and a growing. Rather than ask such a disabling sign we must trust in and ripen our rooted longings, promptings, intimations, glimpses. . . .

Mark felt as if something about which he had always wondered had just received its answer.

Pat on his thinking this, Craikie, as if aware of the thought, declared, 'No, never any certainty this side of death but there may often be—and I think there always are—strange occurrences, almost frightening coincidences, which suggest that God is helping you.'

So much did it all seem as if directed straight at him, Mark, that he was now impatient to know what Craikie would make of the third temptation. 'All the kingdoms of this world if you will just worship me,' said Satan. Mark thought the old boy was as good on this as on the others. He said that the Master chose not the kingdoms of this world but the kingdom that was within him—'and that, as I have shown you, is within us all. This kingdom is nothing less than everything I have been putting before you: faith, trust, courage, search, love, with their result, a slow growth into full manhood. The Master came out of his wilderness certain that this kingdom was in all men, and that his sole ministry in the world was to awake in all the sleeping king.'

Another fine phrase, thought Mark. Awake the sleeping king. For Christ the kingdom, in the end, proved to be the cross.

And here by a successful trick Craikie gave a new powerful thrust to an old too-familiar text. 'Though he slay me, yet will I trust in him,' said Job of God. Craikie suggested that as the nails of the cross went in Christ applied these words to Man rather than to God: 'Though he slay me, yet will I trust in him. This is not the truth of them; they know not what they do.'

Craikie paused. He was still enough of an orator to make his last sentences, his close, remarkable by a silence, a gazing at his audience, before he spoke them. Then he spoke them with a level voice, a faint smile, and a slight shaking of the head. 'If only, if only you and I could fulfil this one young man's faith in us.' Strange and strong the appeal of that single word 'young'. A small pause before adding, 'How happy we should be'; and then he tossed into the broken soil of Mark's mind yet a few more words that stayed there as rich seeds. Mark wondered if he had been thinking of his young wife, long dead, as he wrote them down.

'Because,' Craikie said, 'the simplest truth in all the world is just this: there is no happiness without love, try as you may to find it. And equally no love without happiness. The two march as equal partners, I think, side by side.'

He waited, still looking down on the people as if wondering whether his words had helped *anyone*; then, brushing fallen hairs from his forehead, and sliding home the loose spectacles, he turned towards the altar and mumbled the ascription.

As they left the church Mark, to hide untellable emotions, asked cheerfully, 'Well, what did you think of that?'

Jasper said promptly, 'Gee, I thought it a super sermon.' The words rang with sincerity, and Mark felt again that pleasure in the thought that a boy of thirteen could respond to what Craikie had said. And didn't it support the old man's argument that these longings, promptings and intimations were in all men? Bronwen's comment suggested rather less than this. It was, 'I think Craikie's quite appallingly sweet.'

Belle said, 'He's not a bad old thing, and he could have been a real preacher if only . . .' The rest of the sentence she shrugged away, since all would know what she meant.

'Well, I think he's earned a stiff whisky after that,' Jasper said; and Mark rebuked him, not wanting to hear Craikie laughed at just now.

It was half-past twelve when father and son entered 21 Mornington Gardens. Mark left the boy without a word, went straight to his study, and closed the door on himself. This was the most haunted of his rooms, but there was nothing he could very well do except keep it for his daily living space, his hermit-shell. He looked out at the garden.

While they were in church the sun had dispersed all mist and clouds and it was now shining with a pale brightness, but the blue shadows of the tree trunks were already long on the grass, though it was only midday. There was a strange December clarity and cleanness about everything, as in a photograph whose precision is perfect. No tree was anything but a skeleton now. The higher branches of the black poplar rose like arms towards the sky; the lower ones drooped sleepily over garden and road. Belle's copper beech had abandoned all its glad regalia of copper and gold for a season in grimly puritan grey. As for the ailanthus, his Tree of Heaven, its stouter branches with no leaves to veil them showed their twisted and arthritic elbows black against the sky, while twigs of the thin outer branches looked like the crooked fingers of old witches begging at church doors.

The paths. Usually green-stained and damp, they were powdered now with some of the morning's hoar frost which looked to have caked them hard. So did the lawn seem frozen hard.

To what depth?

For a hateful second his eyes sought the scar on the lawn. A few spires of grass had grown on it. Deliberately he pulled the swivel chair from his writing-desk, swung it towards the window, and sat in it with his face to the garden.

'Face it,' he commanded himself. 'Face it.'

Pelly had thrown out broken bread, far and wide, for the winter-hungry birds. And now waddling, nodding pigeons, hopping sparrows and one yellow-beaked blackbird were skirting round the scar where Luddermore's threads still lay in ruin to trap their feet. One pigeon waddled bravely into the danger after a piece of bread.

'Face it.' Mark was seeing all that was implied in Craikie's words. Was ever a man more surely in a wilderness outside the Law than this man sitting in his study and staring out at a garden? He did not know what he believed, if anything, about him whom Craikie had called 'The Master', but this much he could see: if that man's strength had sent him into a wilderness, it was Mark's terrifying and unknown weakness which had lodged him in his. Nevertheless much of what that man had learned in a great solitude Mark could learn too. The State's commands and the Church's conventional morality were little more than an ordnance map. This map announced much but one must prove its statements; one must climb this steep contour, go down into that valley, walk by this twisting river, work through that tangled wood, and know each of these places with one's feet and breath, one's fatigue and joy. Maybe one would learn that the statements on the map were accurate enough but only thus could one give to these two-dimensional things the joyous third dimension of experienced truth.

The world might not know it, but with his eyes on that garden he was really a naked man, even though sitting in a comfortable room, in fine Sunday clothes; in appearance the very figure of a large, successful man, in truth a beaten vagrant, lost in a wasteland.

Well, this at least meant that he was free, as Craikie had said, to create some code, some creed, for himself. With an elbow on the chair's rounded back and his chin cupped in his palm, he sat there attempting this. That scar to which his eyes so unwillingly returned—it was providing for him, gradually, a simple, certain, undeniable vision of truth. Quite simply, quite clearly, and most surely, the truth was this: he saw the utter futility, in the end, of all things that were not of goodness. The pitifulness, the total defeat, in the end, of those ambitions that had incarcerated a man, all his life through, in the thick-walled cell of his self! Nothing sweet, in the end, at the last, except things of goodness and self-giving.

If only he'd been forced to see this old fact before he became reprobate! But it was too late now. Too late because he could never do the one thing that would clear the field for him: confess. Impossible, this. Forever impossible. That scar there. . . .

He could perhaps—just perhaps—face the public disclosure

that a harlot fetched in from her haunts had died beneath him, but never that, having taken her body and used it, he had stealthily put it out, like refuse, into the midnight street.

Never that. Amends must be less than this.

What he would have liked to do if it had not been too late—or so he thought, sitting here this Sunday morning—would have been to go out and passionately proclaim what he was seeing. Had not Craikie said, 'Sometimes people feel an urge, a compulsion, to go out and share with others the joyous things they've learned in the wilderness—' or something like that? But he—

A sound of plates and dishes coming up the kitchen stairs. Pelly bringing up the Sunday meal. He had, then, but one minute before walking out into everyday life again. In this last minute, his door being shut, he dropped to his knees and with elbows on the window sill, face in his hands, prayed as before, 'Show me what I can still do even though I can never confess. I am trusting blindly in you—or in whatsoever or whosoever has sown these struggling seeds in me; suffer me to do *something* in the way of reparation even if it is not enough. Even if it's nothing like enough. If it can be no help to me, let me do it for others. Help me, oh God, help me . . . *please*. What can I do?' There came into his head Donne's great prayer, to whose fearful truth he had often thrilled, though of course doing nothing about it, 'O'erthrow me and bend Your force to break, blow, burn and make me new,' but he could not ask that. That surely implied the total surrender and the truth of his garden. No, no; there was Jasper, and even if he could speak the truth for his own sake, which he couldn't, he would take the everlasting punishment rather than have Jasper broken and burnt too. Since this was a certainty he could offer only a compromise to God. 'Show me what, if anything, is possible to—'

Steps. Mrs. Pelly approaching the door. Deceitfully he sprang to his feet. The door opened.

'Your dinner is in, sir,' said Pelly. 'Master Jasper is already sitting there and waiting.'

He smiled gently at her. 'I'll say he is. Thank you, Mrs. Pelly. Now hurry home to Ted who wants his dinner too, I'm sure. He's probably getting impatient. Jasper and I'll put all the things in the kitchen for Mrs. Capes.'

'Well, thank you, sir. I think I will nip away now, if you don't mind.'

After she was gone he walked along the passage to the dining-room from which issued a Sunday smell of roasted flesh and boiled green things. And so back (he was thinking with a shrug) to the daily trivia, the heavy-hearted activities, and the sham laughters of one who must ever live with that garden behind him and never really believe in his forgiveness by whatever God there were.

14. On the Other Side of a Party Wall

'But, Arthur, listen: was it ever heard,' demanded Belle, 'that a mayor became a lay reader?'

'Oh, yes,' Arthur conceded. 'Up North. Not down South. We're not really religious down South. In the North where the Methodists are strong one often hears of a councillor or a mayor being a local preacher.'

'Well, then, was it ever heard that a distinguished surgeon became a lay reader?'

'Never, I should say, but I wouldn't know about that. Thought most medical men were atheists. But so much the better. I'm all for something really out of the ordinary. Sensational. It'll get us a lot more votes. Going to be one in the eye for the Tories who expect to get nearly all the C. of E. votes. Show me a Tory councillor who's leading the services in church and preaching and bible-thumping and all. Can't see old Major Roper doing it. Law love us, that'd be a scream.' And Arthur slapped his big broad hands on his big broad thighs and rubbed them there, as he was apt to do when he'd cracked a joke.

'To be frank, Arthur,' said Belle, smiling at him, 'I can't see you doing it either.'

'And how right you are, my dear. *Most* unlikely in an old heathen like me. I should be an even bigger scream than old Roper. But this is going to be a rare old fourpenny one for Ma Pearl Runciman. As wife of the Rector of Keys she won't relish a Socialist preaching in an Anglican church. I'm very pleased about that.'

Arthur, Belle, and Bronwen were sitting in the 'small drawing-room' of Belle's house, the little ground-floor room at the back which was the twin sister of Mark's study. Its narrow french window above the similar iron stairway looked out on a much more formal garden than Mark's. Winter had emptied it of flowers, but the turf of the lawn, less overborne by trees, was richly green and patterned with well-shaped beds of fine tilth awaiting the manifold colours of spring and the pink and red roses of June. The only big tree was the noble copper beech against the wall between her garden and Mark's.

Unlike Mark's study with its heavy upholstered arm-chairs this room was a lady's chamber with elegant pieces of Boulle French furniture and only small graceful chairs. Arthur was actually sitting on a slender lyre-back chair with his rump and thighs overhanging the edges of it, so that its thin legs with their clawed feet looked as if they might splinter under his weight. Generous upholstery was not in the chair but in its occupant.

Arthur had come visiting the Mayoress to secure her help in persuading Mark to serve at least two more terms as Mayor. He would have liked him to serve yet a fourth term after the next borough election, but Mark was now talking of a retirement at the end of his first year. Unthinkable, said Arthur. All the Tory mayors had done their two terms, and he, confident of winning the next election, wanted his Labour mayor to double their score, just for the hell of it.

'In every way he's the best bloke we've got for the job. I'm proud of him as mayor. You'd never know, to look at him, that he was a ruddy Socialist. You'd think he was the Lord High Bishop of Somewhere. He's handsomer too than any other mayor round about, and they're all Tories. It does me good.'

Bronwen sat listening to them from a Directoire *chaise-longue*, her legs drawn up under her. Belle had told her to 'make herself scarce' since these were no matters for her, but she had pouted and said that, as a citizen, she was interested. She had also suggested that she could use her influence with darling Uncle Mark. 'He always listens to me,' she explained to Arthur, who replied, 'Yes, let her stay. Quite likely Mark'd be less ready to

refuse anything to her than to me. She's rather more attractive.'
Here Bronwen, to underline her influence over the Mayor,
explained to Arthur, 'He dotes on me,' and he said, 'I don't know
that I wonder at that, my dear. I fancy I'd find it difficult to
refuse you anything,' making her a graceful and most un-
characteristic bow, so that she now sat on the *chaise-longue* full of
an unforeseen but delectable love for Councillor Lammas.

'I tell you another thing, Mayoress,' Arthur continued. 'He's
easily the most popular mayor Keys has ever had. He's so polite
and pleasant to everybody.'

'Yes,' Belle agreed. 'I know what you mean. Mr. Councillor
Sunbeam.'

'Mr. Councillor *what*?'

'Sunbeam. That's what I call him when he's really doing the
attractive stuff. Sometimes I think he's rather over-eager to
please everybody. Probably it's because our mother was beastly
to him as a boy.'

'That so? Go *on*!'

'Yes, and it makes one over-eager to be loved for ever after,
and therefore over-charming to people, sometimes.'

'Well, I certainly think he's over-charming to the bloody
Tories . . . oh, I'm sorry, miss'—an apology to Bronwen, who
sat there rejoiced by this word.

'We all say "bloody" at school,' she promptly told him, as
was her habit when this point arose.

'Well, then you all shouldn't. You tell 'em so from me. Girls
should not only look beautiful but sound beautiful. That's what
they're for.' He turned again to Belle. 'How does he set about
this lay-reading lark?'

'He's going to try and get licensed to our church, All Hallows,
so as to help Mr. Craik. He's always been fond of him.'

'Well, I must say the Reverend Craik looks as though he
needed a spot of help. But just you tell your Mr. Craik and your
Mr. Dolmen that this business is not to take precedence over
his being mayor. I won't have that. Since when has he suddenly
got religion like this? I thought he only went to church as a
matter of duty, just to set us common fellows an example. Like
my C.O. in the war. Doubt if *he* believed anything except that
his men ought to go to church.'

'Yes, it's only the last few weeks he's taken to coming with us regularly. He has never told us why. He never says anything to anybody about his thoughts on religion. Who ever knows what's going on in anyone's heart?' Belle was thinking other thoughts than she cared to tell to Arthur.

'Just as well they don't know what's going on in mine, sometimes. How much does he have to do in this new caper?'

'Not a great deal. The work's mostly on Sundays.'

'Oh, well, I'll let him have his Sundays off. I'll lay he preaches a sight better than the Reverend Craik. If he preaches half as well as he speaks in Council, he could be worth hearing. I often think—the way he manages his voice and all—that he could have topped the bill as an actor.'

'Maybe he knows that one thing he can do magnificently is speaking in public, and thinks he can do something for our rather seedy church by preaching there sometimes. But lay readers are not encouraged to preach at first.'

'Got to play themselves in, have they?'

'Exactly. And do you realize, Arthur, he's sixty and he's got to read for exams on the Bible and Church Doctrine and the Prayer Book and all?'

'What the hell's that for? He's got heaps of degrees, hasn't he?'

'Only medical and surgical ones, and he says they instituted exams when they discovered that most enthusiastic lay preachers could proclaim six different heresies in their first six minutes. The more they were educated, the worse their heresies. All the same, old Craikie'll be jolly lucky to get an unpaid curate like Mark.'

'Unpaid! Don't he get paid?' Arthur's eyebrows went up in indignant surprise.

'No. Only his expenses when he helps away.'

'Well, of course he could work *them* up a bit.'

'No, he couldn't. Any guineas paid to him for services away are paid to some central Board.'

'Well, I never! Wonder anyone wants this job. How does one get it?'

'The Vicar writes to the Bishop, and the Bishop makes inquiries. He'll accept Mark all right.'

'*I'll* say he will! How dare a bishop make inquiries about our Mayor?'

'Then after he's passed the exams, there's a special service of Admission and Licensing. Like an ordination.'

'Oh, what fun!'—from Bronwen on her couch.

'He was annoyed when I used to call his election as mayor a "hallowing", but this really is a hallowing.'

'Blimey! I shall have to come along and see him through it, I suppose. But I'm not much cop at praying.'

'No, you come along when he starts preaching. Who knows: he might do you some good. Stop you being rude to old Major Roper.'

'Oh, no,' Arthur objected, as at a highly unwelcome prospect. 'No, no; that's asking too much, my dear. Drains to him.'

'But you ought to stop it, Arthur. Really. As your mayoress I ask you to.'

'But he's a bloody man,' Arthur explained.

'No, he isn't. He's quite a nice old thing.'

'Well, out of the Council, perhaps . . . yes . . . sometimes. But in the Council he's a very bloody man.'

'Oh, *I* think he's an absolute poppet,' Bronwen put in.

But, no one heeding her, Belle went on, 'Then there's my pretty little Shamie O'Donoghue. You've got to stop insulting him, poor little man.'

'That little perisher? Can't imagine why he wasn't drowned at birth.'

'Well, he wasn't, for one reason or another; so promise your mayoress you're now going to begin to behave.'

'No, I can't and I won't. There are important issues coming up before the Council, and I'm looking forward to some really rowdy times. But, Lord save us, Belle, this Mark business! Amazing what people'll get up to when they begin to take religion seriously. Look at the Salvation Army. Holy Moses, before we know where we are, we shall have Mark going out into the streets to shout aloud salvation and bellow about the blood of the Lamb and Hell-fire and all that dance. He's no end of a speaker and he'll be scaring the pants off half the electorate. That won't do the party any good. Or will it?' And he rubbed his fat thighs again in joy at this joke. 'Too much religion is the

167

last thing I'd have expected of Mark. Well, well, well'—he shrugged—'good-bye, Mayoress; hold him for us as our mayor, whatever happens, and in the meantime be a good girl. You too, Miss Bronwen. I begin to think someone ought to start keeping an eye on you.'

With that he went.

So Belle talked with Arthur, gaily. In the sprightliest fashion, for Belle was an actress too. Very differently she spoke in that little drawing-room to Craikie, her old familiar priest. One day when Craikie at her invitation was sitting on the same chair as Arthur's, the little lyre-back chair, and Bronwen had been carefully excluded, she poured forth all her perception of Mark's hidden pain, and all her anxiety. 'I don't know what's happened, Vicar. He keeps up a show of happiness before his gallery, as I call you all, but oh, dear, none of the stage-craft looks right to me. I am behind the scenes, as it were—his sister. Some great change came over him a month or two ago, and I don't believe—no, I simply *know*—he's never been happy since. At first I wondered if it was the loss of Jasper, but that hardly seemed a large enough thing, though the boy means a lot to him. Jasper is Lorelei's son, and I suppose she partly lives in him again, for Mark. There's nothing else I can think of. Nothing's happened in my sight, He goes to his work as ever—are you comfortable in that chair, Vicar?'

'Perfectly,' he said, though he looked less than comfortable leaning from the chair's rim to hear better.

'Well, your glass is empty. Have some more whisky.'

'No . . . well, thank you, Belle. . . . But only a little.'

She charged the tumbler generously with whisky and some soda, and he did not stop her while watching her handiwork, except for one hesitant and unconvincing movement of his own hand. 'Only just a little,' he repeated when there was already plenty in the glass, and she had stopped. 'Thank you, Belle.' To herself she gave no more, wanting only to talk. 'He goes to his work as ever and is as good at it as ever, and he does his endless Council duties perhaps even more conscientiously than before; but I can see that he's really suffering all the time. One aches to help him, but how? He never speaks, and who dare intrude? He just suffers it alone, whatever it is, day in, day out, and I can't bear it. All his life he's been reserved and reticent, whatever acts he puts on in company, but this . . . but this . . . Much of the time he doesn't seem aware that you're there. We usually spend our evenings with him in the drawing-room and when he's not thinking of us, I've seen him shudder to himself or give a gasp. He'll stand at the window, though there's no chance of seeing much through it because the room is light behind him and the night is dark outside. He can even start speaking aloud to himself, but that always reminds him that we're there, and he stops. Bronwen's not too young to notice these things and to ask if he's happy: she is a woman. Of course he always contrives a smile when he's spoken to, but . . . But I mustn't go on worrying you like this. Oh, one of the most pitiful things is his strange new tenderness to everyone—the children, his servants, his friends. He was always friendly with people, and gentle when necessary, but now there's a new quality in this tenderness. *I* see it if no one else does. And, as you know, he's started coming regularly with us to church. Not a word to anyone why. And then comes this new idea of trying to help you as your lay reader. What I'm wondering, Vicar, is, *couldn't* you perhaps talk to him and help him in your turn.'

'Me?' exclaimed Craikie, as if surprised that someone should think him still capable of any delicate pastoral care. Craikie sat on his slender chair with broad hands spread over his knees, their finger-nails broken and not too clean. His celluloid clerical collar was yellowing and cracked above his food-spotted clerical stock; farther down that sad hunched figure the coarse grey socks had scrambled downward to the black shoes, uncovering excerpts of bare leg. It was only three in the afternoon but at his first entry Belle had detected the whisky on his breath and lost some heart for her enterprise, but she pressed on.

'Yes, you, Vicar dear. There's no one he likes better. And— do you know?—he said to me once that it was you who had helped him more than anyone else.'

'*Me?*' Craikie stared at her as if staring at something in the distance that looked to offer a touch of happiness—happiness long lost and long forgotten.

Belle nodded. 'I don't know if you know, but after a sermon of yours before Christmas, which he thought splendid, he came and said to me, pretending to laugh in case I thought him mad, that he was thinking of asking you to use him as a lay reader. He didn't say your sermon had anything to do with this, but I know what I know, and I see what I see.'

'Sermon? What sermon?'

'About the wilderness.'

'Oh, that? Oh, yes. The wilderness. The only place one can really find ourselves and what we truly believe. I see it all sometimes.'

'Well, it helped us all, that sermon, somehow.'

'A sermon of *mine*?' Was it the moisture of age round his red-rimmed eyes, or tears? 'But it was an old, old sermon of my youth, Belle. I was lost for something to say, and I read it again—and it seemed true.'

'Very true.'

'Still, I can't believe that any words of mine could ever help a man like Mark.'

'You're a very fine preacher, sometimes, Vicar.' Belle leaned forward and laid comforting fingers on one of his hands spread over his knees—a parishioner, for once in a way, comforting the priest. The business of this interview had suddenly become less a solicitude for Mark than the strengthening of Craikie. 'You helped my brother. Thank you.'

Craikie's lips were trembling. He shut his teeth on the lower lip to dam back tears. 'It's rather wonderful to hear what you've just said, Belle. Sometimes I've thought I'd never be of help to anyone again.'

'Nonsense, my dear. I want you to help my brother now. If you can.'

'I'm afraid I've little courage to speak to anyone like Mark, but if I can . . . if I can . . . And, anyhow'—he rose to go—'I can pray for him, and I will.' The promise came on whisky-tainted breath but it sounded deeply felt and true, while the red-rimmed eyes endorsed it sadly. 'I will. I'll ask God to do anything I can't do. And he will. He will.'

'Bless you, Vicar.'

15. The Preacher

The inescapable guilt, the remaining dregs of a child's fear of God's wrath, an ever-urging drive to tell the world that all things failed which were not aimed at good, a simpler wish, at sixty, to do *some* good before the end—these it was that swelled Mark's resolve to give poor Craikie all the help he could as his lay reader. These were the better drives; a lesser one was his old readiness to play the eccentric before the world now and then.

He first discussed the idea with Jack Paytons, a diocesan lay reader of thirty years' experience. Jack was one of those long, weedy, over-earnest men who, unaware of a paucity in their humour, affect a back-slapping ease, a muscular Christianity, not cut to their measure at all. Mark said to him at one point, 'The only thing that hangs me up, Jack, is this: as with most men, I suppose, there are things in my life that it would be very difficult to disclose'; and he was shaken when Jack, with gazing serious eyes, though pretending a small laugh, said, 'Oh . . . but if they were really serious things, I feel . . . oh, yes, I feel you'd have to disclose them to the Bish.' The 'Bish' was his concession to Christian humour. 'One wants to go into this job with absolutely clean hands. Yes, you'd be happier, I feel sure, if you just mentioned any serious falls to the Vicar or the Bish.'

'Not me, old chap,' Mark answered at once. 'I couldn't do that. I'm simply not made that way.'

'But why, old boy? It'd all be under the seal of the confessional.'

Mark only shook his head and remained wordless, so Jack, with a hearty Christian smile, went on, 'But I can't believe there's anything sufficiently serious in your life to be a barrier. No, no.'

'You can't?'

'No. All I'm trying to say is that, in my view, no man fit to be a lay reader would allow himself to be licensed, knowing there were things in his past that ought to be disclosed.'

'I dare say you're right,' Mark said, also with a smile—the smile that brings an argument to an end.

He didn't agree with him. He couldn't think it'd be wrong to do what he was feeling driven, passionately driven, to do, even though he withheld his past from all but God. Driven daily, unsparingly, by a mute, unmarked secreted grave not ten yards from his window. How could anyone call wrong an attempt at amends, however small?

And only in these attempts at amends could he find occasional peace.

So he continued in this chosen path and felt a little happier in it. He sat side by side with men thirty years younger than he, some of them uneducated working men, at lectures on English Church History, the Old and New Testaments, Doctrine and Preaching; he submitted, like any schoolboy, essays on these subjects to the Tutorial Department of the Central Readers' Board; and in due time, like any undergraduate, he sat with these new friends, whom he now greatly liked, for the General Readers' Examination. There was no question about his passing —his papers were easily the best of an undistinguished bunch— and on a June Sunday in the parish church of Keys, while serving his second term as the borough's mayor, he was licensed with four others as Parochial Reader by the Suffragan Bishop of Hadleigh.

This was certainly a sensation for Keys. Stanley Mace, Chief Reporter of the *Keys and Hadleigh News*, had 'written up' this excellent story of a mayor's installation in a holy job; the Press Association and the Exchange Telegraph had followed him up by passing the story to the national Press, some of which used it; and the result of all this publicity was that the Admission Service filled to the doors the church of St. Peter's, Keys, which, being the ancient village church, was not large. From a humble seat at the back Arthur Lammas watched with much interest if few prayers. In the Rectory pew Councillor Mrs. Pearl Runciman watched with mingled opinions; in other parts of the crowded church other councillors ministered to their surprise or their curiosity; Mark's family were there, Belle, Jasper, and Bronwen; and, thanks to the children's ardent promotion, Pelly and Capes sat with them, together with, if it could be believed, Mr. Capes, his first time in church for twenty years, the last time having been the occasion of his marriage to Mrs. Capes at this same altar.

Mark, though his strange step was a serious attempt at amends, was not yet so amended himself that this local sensation did not please him. He might have been less pleased if he'd heard some of the comments at the pub counters or over the tea tables in Keys; in the smoking-rooms of his two London clubs and in the surgeons' rooms of his hospitals; such comments as 'Extraordinarily odd! But religion does get 'em like that sometimes.' 'You mean you think he's come a bit unscrewed? I must say I've half suspected he was coming apart for quite a time.' 'No, I wouldn't go as far as that. I'm not saying religion can drive a clever man daft, but just that it can send him a yard or two round the bend. Only a yard or two. No more. Mark is still a superb surgeon.' The reaction of one simple soul to whom religion in any degree was absurdity ran, 'Good lord, how much madder can he get?'

As a licensed reader Mark was able to take Matins and Evensong for Craikie, saving only that the Absolution must be pronounced by a priest or a prayer for absolution substituted. Holy Communion could be celebrated only by a priest, but the Bishop, on special occasions, could allow a lay reader to administer the chalice. Craikie suggested once that they should seek this favour for Mark, but he would not hear of it. His refusal was instant. It was even passionate. The hand that had gripped Angelo's neck, how could it grasp a chalice? 'No, no,' he stuttered. 'I—I don't feel I could do the thing properly.

'I'm sorry, Craikie, but you must just accept that I have a recoil from the very idea. I'm just not holy enough.' To accompany this firm assertion he provided the necessary laugh.

'What about me?' asked Craikie.

'Just this. You may not know it, old boy, but you're a better man that I am.'

'Don't be an idiot, Mark,' said Craikie. 'I'm the unprofitable servant. A beggar on the bounty of God.'

'A far better description of me, old boy, if you only knew. And I gravely fear that the bounty won't stretch to cover me. *I'm* for the outer darkness.'

Craikie laughed. And Mark ended the discussion, promising, 'No, no, I'll just content myself with helping you in Matins and Evensong, Craikie, and perhaps now and then preaching a little, if you'll let me . . . and if I can think of something to say.'

At his own request Mark did not preach till he'd been a reader for three months. His first sermon was announced for a September Sunday when he was taking the services single-handed so that Craikie could have a fortnight by the sea. It seemed likely that the church would be fairly full for this novel and now widely discussed event. Stanley Mace, a crypto-Socialist and devoted to Mark, had been at his games again, making a welcome song about 'The Mayor's First Sermon' in the gossip columns of the *Keys and Hadleigh News*. London papers, as before, had followed him (it was late August and a news-naked season) with paragraphs headed 'The Preaching Mayor'.

These trumpetings brought Arthur Lammas, like an old war horse, to Mornington Gardens. 'Hey, what are you going to talk about, Mark?'

'Haven't the faintest idea as yet.'

'I've read your public relations boy in the *Keys and Had*, and I've been wondering, shall I put out a three-line whip and make all the boys and girls come along. It'd help to swell your audience for you, and might even do 'em all a bit of good, though I doubt it.'

'For heaven's sake don't do anything of the sort. And don't come yourself. I shall be nervous enough without you there.'

'*You* nervous! Don't talk such tripe. Never known *you* nervous.'

'There's a lot you don't know, Arthur,' said Mark, though still not intending him to take this demurrer too seriously.

'Maybe, but quite apart from what you want or don't want, Mr. Mayor, *I* want to get you a big house so as to upset the Tories—with especial reference to Councillor Mrs. Rector Runciman. Are you expecting a capacity house?'

'Certainly not. The capacity of All Hallows is about twelve hundred.'

'But haven't the audiences been much bigger since you became the curate?'

'"Congregations" is the word, Arthur; not "audiences".'

'Well, aren't the congregations twice the size?''

'No. Why should they be?'

'If they aren't, it's probably because you haven't done any preaching yet. Wait till you start this preaching lark. I fancy we shall really see things happening then. Isn't it a scream? We always said you looked like a bishop and now you are one, practically.'

'Less than the dust, my dear boy, compared with a bishop.'

'Still, I think it's all rather jolly. And quite good for the Party if it comes off properly and your sermon's a wow. It's got to be a wow. I'll be bringing the troops along to hear you. A three-line whip for that day. Not half! So just you show the boys what you can do with *this* extraordinary caper.'

As Arthur said this, the old nervousness struck into Mark's heart, coupled with the old desire to shine as an orator, so that he found himself dreading a big audience at one minute and longing for it the next. And in the following days the self-regarding motives shared his heart with the self-hating ones, and with the dedicated desire to proclaim forcefully the few things he now so surely believed. All these motives were at work in him, now one, now another, when (as for speeches in council) he wrote the sermon verbatim, learned it by heart, and rehearsed it ever and again behind a shut door, with a view to delivering it, no matter what the deceit, as if it were largely impromptu.

Evening after evening, in that study which had seen Angelo lying dead on a chair, he sat in the opposite chair with his writing block on his knees. He still thought at times of shutting up this haunted room and making a study elsewhere in the house, but where could it be? Not the large guest-room above this study; there Desiderata had first come to him and that room was almost as haunted as this. And not his bedroom above the guest-room; there she had died; there she now haunted it; but it was the room next to Jasper's and he still wished to sleep there, knowing from his own childhood that a boy, though fourteen now, could yet, in secret, feel lonely and afraid. Also he had by now got used to having a haunted study around him, just as he had got used to having a black memory in his heart.

Each evening, pencilling his notes on the writing-pad, he struggled to keep uppermost the selfless motives. He would even pray as he wrote or meditated, 'Oh God, help me to do this right.' How express one's truths with passion? Why did the passion go dry directly the pencil was in one's fingers? Why did it refuse to pour through the pencil on to the pad? Why issue only in short jerks? Why must he ever get up and walk about the room till passion germinated again?

Sometimes, to revive the passion, he flung a hasty glance through the window at the garden where the matted grass was now a full autumn green and the long contorted boughs of the Tree of Heaven held a canopy of leaves, already touched with decay, and half-weeping, willow-wise, over the one patch he must see. This small patch was greener than all the rest because the soil had been disturbed to a depth beneath it and Mr. Luddermore had sown new seeds on it in the early April days.

When inspiration languished, that small flush of deep green, with perhaps the shadows of the tree dappling it, could usually quicken the impulses into zealous life again. By such means his creative power could be made to spurt, even gush, till at last, in the final rewriting of the sermon, it was in spate. He had a high faith in the sermon now, provided he could deliver it well, and he knew that, if only his nerves would allow him, he could do this like a veteran actor. On the Sunday morning, with all these motives alight in him, he was impatient to get to the church, to robe in the vestry, and, on emerging from it, to see what sort of congregation had gathered. Confidence and eagerness had almost dismissed any nervousness. None the less, before leaving his house, he fortified himself, as Craikie might have done, with a dram of whisky neat.

The church clock in the tower struck eleven, and as he came out of the vestry, behind the small, inadequate choir, in his cassock, surplice, coloured hood, and the long blue scarf now granted to readers, his sidelong glance saw that the nave was nearly full; it held five times, perhaps ten times, as many people as when the Vicar preached. The big grey-arched church *looked* crowded so long as you didn't glance at the pews in the shadowy side-aisles or up at the desolate galleries above them.

This fine and flattering congregation stirred up all the lower motives, leaving little but an eagerness to shine and be acclaimed. At the same time he could be distressed that, as he led the prayers for the people and listened to them singing the psalms and hymns, his own head should be filled with hope of a triumph.

Now he was in the pulpit and looking down on them as they sang the last verse of a hymn. They must not think he was seeking familiar faces among them, but he did manage to see Arthur near the back with his hymn-book open before him but his mouth unopened over it; and Shamus O'Donoghue nattily spruce in a light summer suit; and, surprisingly, Councillor Mrs. Runciman who must have deserted her own church to get a sight of these 'goings on' at All Hallows and to learn how the Mayor compared with her husband as a preacher. He saw also three Council officers, Deputy Borough Treasurer, Mayor's Secretary, and District Surveyor, this last (Mark thought up there in the pulpit) surveying something quite new in the district. Belle, Bronwen and Jasper were there, of course, and in the pew behind them the faithful Pelly and Capes—not Mr. Capes, however, not for a second visit to church so soon, and at eleven o'clock on a Sunday morning.

The hymn died, the people sank into the pews, and all eyes converged upwards on him, except Belle's, lowered perhaps in nervousness. He allowed a few seconds of dramatic silence, and then, liking always to be a little different from other men, said with a small, broken smile, 'There are really fifteen texts to this sermon, and each is made up of more than one verse, but I will content myself with only two verses to begin with. They are perhaps the most famous in this whole collection of fifteen exquisite little poems, embedded in the hundred and fifty psalms of the Psalter and sometimes known as the Songs of the Steps. My verses are from the eleventh of these little songs, the hundred and thirtieth psalm.' He paused again, so as to frame the words with silence. '"Out of the deep have I called unto thee. . . . If thou, Lord, wilt be extreme to mark what is done amiss, who may abide it?"'

A great silence. The people staring. In his search for a sermon that would be dredged from the deeps of his experience he had come inevitably to the *De profundis clamavi*.

His half-humorous opening about the fifteen texts he now explained to them. These fifteen psalms, the hundred and twentieth to the hundred and thirty-fourth, were really a little psalter of their own. There were two traditions about the lovely little collection of songs. One said they were sung by pilgrims as they came over the hills to Jerusalem; the other that they were fifteen hymns, one sung on each of the fifteen steps that led up to the Temple's great portal. '"Songs of the Steps", you see. If we are thinking of the first tradition then in the first of the songs the pilgrims sing how weary they are of dwelling among the heathen. "Woe is me, that I am constrained to dwell with Mesech, and to have my habitation among the tents of Kedar. . . . I am for peace. . . ." In the second song they are seeing for the first time the hills that girdle Jerusalem, "I will lift up mine eyes unto the hills," and so, at length they come to this famous eleventh song and are now in actual sight of the Temple, but only from the deep valley below. Humbled by the holiness of the shrine before them they yet long to make their last ascent up the steep of Mount Moriah on which it stands. "Out of the deep, O Lord . . . if thou wilt be extreme to mark what is done amiss, who may abide it?"

'But this morning I want to remember the second tradition, and, if so, we are on the eleventh step and halting there because the Inner Court of the Temple is now very close; almost too close; and we pause to sing of our need to be forgiven. "Out of the deep of sin have I called. . . ." Who shall abide God's anger? Who shall stand? Yes, *who*? Well, the next verse sings of the only hope. As the Bible version, rather than our Prayer Book version, renders it: "There is forgiveness with thee. . . . I wait for the Lord, My soul doth wait, and in his word do I hope. My soul waiteth for the Lord more than they that watch for the morning.'''

Thanks to the incomparable words, which he knew how to speak, he had no doubt that he was holding the people tethered to his voice as by a rope that strains. He saw Jasper staring up as if so interested that he had forgotten this was his father. Belle too, held by words, not by a man. And Bronwen at her side. No eyes anywhere that were not his.

'It is a remarkable and lovely fact that the next song, the song on the twelfth step, is like a hush of humility and reverence, so close are we now to the Temple. "Lord, I am not high-minded; I have no proud looks. I do not exercise myself in matters which are too high for me. But I refrain my soul and keep it low. . . ." So on and up to the fifteenth step and now we are at the great portal and enter singing "Lift up your hands in the sanctuary." And the following words, the last words of this song, and of the whole little hymnary, are just the blessing of the pilgrims as they arrive. "The Lord that made heaven and earth give the blessing out of Zion."''

All the rest of the sermon, after he had mounted for it these picturesque scenes, was an analysis, and a long one too, but delivered with a conviction, and a forgetfulness of self at last, so that the people never ceased to listen—an analysis of the slow stepping upward from the first weariness with sin and the first desire for goodness and peace to the final triumph of this last song with its 'blessing out of Zion'. But the eleventh step was always there, intervening with, as it were, a sudden and awful realization of the nearness now of God and of his righteousness compared with one's own sinfulness. Then it was that one cried 'out of the deep' and knew that no one living could abide the judgment of God. One could only ask mercy.

'But there is forgiveness with thee.' He repeated the words passionately for their sakes, even as he was doubting if there was forgiveness for him. How could he go up from that eleventh step with a crime unacknowledged and amends unmade; with the acknowledgement and the amends for ever impossible? Passionately, notwithstanding, he proclaimed his now certain belief that there was no real happiness to be found in this bewildering world except in the attitude of the old Quaker,

'I expect to pass through this world but once. Any good therefore that I can do, or any kindness that I can show to any fellow creature, let me do it now, let me not defer it or neglect it, for I shall not pass this way again.' This was the only way of living we could really honour. More, something in us was compelled to honour and worship it. 'As your good Vicar said once in this pulpit, "God or no God, we can no other." We are so built "we can no other". And I remember he followed this with some words that rang an instant bell in my heart as they must do in yours, I believe, whether you wish them to or not. He said, "There is no happiness without love. . . ." Which carried with it the sure corollary, "There is no love without happiness." The measure of the one, I think he told us, is inevitably the measure of the other.'

For the rest he enlarged upon the 'joy and peace in such believing', describing them with the impassioned longing of one who was without assurance that he would ever inherit them himself. The sermon over and the ascription said, he came slowly down the pulpit steps, thinking of his garden.

16. The Keeper of the Garden

As the people poured out into the noon sunlight, all who spoke at all were speaking approval. Voices said, 'We don't often get sermons like that,' and 'He ought to be a full-blown parson if he can preach like that,' and 'Yes, why not? In these days they'd allow him to be a surgeon all the week and a parson on Sundays.' Shamus O'Donoghue, swinging an exquisite umbrella, said to the District Surveyor, 'That was an intellectual treat, I thought,' which was hardly what the preacher would have wished his appeal to be called. Arthur Lammas, waiting by the porch for Belle, said when she appeared, 'Didn't I tell you he'd knock spots off all the padres in Keys? Old Ma Runciman has just gone past, looking in two minds as to whether a layman, and a Socialist at that, ought to preach better than her old man. That's been the best part of the whole morning for me.'

When Mark emerged from the emptied church to join his waiting family, Jasper said, 'A helluva sermon, Daddy,' and Mark was glad to observe again that there were seeds in the heart of Lorelei's son to which such a sermon could speak. Glad ... and afraid. Bronwen said nothing, but most deliberately came and put her hand in his. Belle said, 'Yes, the family's proud of you, Mark.'

Proud!

Mrs. Capes, their 'daily news', who'd been talking with another woman, as she did at any door, whether of shop, house,

or church, came up and said, 'Oh, that was lovely, sir. I did
so enjoy it,' while Mark wondered if 'enjoy' was the right
word. 'Mr. Capes did ought to have come, but he *will* have
his lay-in of a Sunday. I shall tell him he don't know what he
missed.'

After that first sermon Mark preached often; sometimes every
Sunday, sometimes on alternate Sundays. The rumour of his
novel and striking sermons spread over Keys and beyond, so
that the congregations were always large, if not crowded, when
his name was advertised. They were three, four, times as large
as when the Vicar's name was announced, and because of this
obvious fact Mark felt a pity for Craikie that amounted to a
vicarious pain. But Craikie only praised him generously, though
Mark could see that his feelings were mixed. 'You're drawing the
people in a way I haven't done for ages, Mark,' he said, 'though
I believe I had a bit of a reputation as a preacher once—when
I was younger. But I can't get going now as I used to, somehow.
Don't imagine I'm not glad you're doing better than I am.
I know a better man when I see one.'

Mark, detecting the sadness behind the humility, hastened to
say, 'Now look, Craikie. I'm not deceived by these congregations. It's just a temporary local sensation. Something out of
the ordinary. In a few months—'

'No, it's more than that, Mark. It's that you do it ever so
much better than I can. Better than I can—nowadays.'

'Just you wait. In two or three months when this has become
a commonplace, these congregations will be a thing of the past.'

'They won't be as low as they were before you came.'

'And, anyway, Craikie, you can't weigh the worth of sermons
by the audience they draw. That bit of measurement has to be
done intensively, not extensively. Have you forgotten that it
was a sermon of yours which started an old sinner like me on
this present unfamiliar path? There were not many people in
the church that morning.'

Craikie looked pleased and said, 'But, Mark, I'm not jealous.
I'm only too happy that you're doing my poor old All Hallows
a lot of good, and I'm quite content to be in practice your
curate. Why, even when *I'm* preaching now the congregations

are a bit bigger. You've raised the low-water mark that much higher.'

Mark couldn't help delighting in his new fame, though his mind was often a battleground between this self-centred satisfaction and his first dream of proclaiming to the world a vision of good and so attempting amends. He tried to think that perhaps there was little harm in this natural human pleasure, but immediately the thought leapt that he, so grave a debtor, had no right to such reward till his debt was undone. So he went on creating the sermons sadly, but not without the artist's joy in charging them with power and vesting them with a beauty of words and shape.

After one remarkable sermon Belle, coming from the church with him, said, 'Well, I never knew you were a born preacher. Fancy only discovering it at sixty. I was wondering as you preached what Father would have thought.'

'Yes, the bad old man. It was hardly in his line.'

'But he'd have been as pleased as twenty Punches about it. Little Marco Polo in the pulpit and a celebrated preacher! God, he'd have been proud. He'd have been bragging to everybody and sending them all along to hear you. And probably sitting himself somewhere at the back.'

'Yes, and doing nothing whatever about it afterwards. The bad old man.'

A few months of this and, though the congregations which came to hear him at All Hallows grew less, his reputation spread to larger fields around. There had been competition among vicars of other churches to get him to preach (which was not difficult for him since he could always preach a sermon for them that he'd already preached and proved at All Hallows) and one of these vicars, Canon Lawes, wrote to Craikie, 'Surely your Preaching Mayor, my dear Craik, ought to be made a Diocesan Reader. He's much too good to stay as a mere Parochial Reader. Several of us think you ought to write to the Bp. and get Dolmen licensed.' Craikie replied, 'He's absolutely my right hand now, but I quite see I mustn't monopolize him'; and he wrote to the Bishop. The Bishop, who'd heard plenty about the 'Preaching Mayor' in his diocese, granted the licence at once.

183

Then did Stanley Mace do his stuff again in the *Keys and Had*, and the London papers copy him. 'The Preaching Mayor' was a good cross-heading for the happy gossip columns. One popular daily, in a long paragraph somewhat over-dressed for the party, declared, 'Mr. Mark Dolmen, the Mayor of Keys, is certainly a remarkable man. Not only did he make history as the first Labour mayor of Keys in the borough's sixty years of history; not only does he now seem to be its permanent mayor, since he is soon to be elected for his third term and his party insist that, if they win the next election they will keep him in office indefinitely; but he has also chosen to be a humble lay reader in his local church, and, despite this lowly position, is in enormous demand, we understand, as a preacher throughout his diocese and far beyond its boundaries. He is probably, at the moment, London's most famous borough mayor.'

With the passing of the months Mark was fairly happy, though always feeling that he ought not to be. 'But there's nothing for it,' he would think. 'I suppose I must just go on like this till death. Living in this room, which is my sentry-box over a grave.'

The thought was temporarily disturbed when Belle became possessed by a desire to get out of 'my huge, gloomy, unworkable house'. This new craving she fired like a broadside at him one day when they were having an early supper before going to the Council (for Belle as Mayoress liked to attend the Council meetings, sitting in her inconspicuous chair by the wall).

'Nobody lives in houses like these now. Nobody but an incurable old Conservative like you. Call yourself a Socialist! You're more of an embalmed old Tory than ever Major Roper is. The stairs! The stairs! The size of the rooms! Houses like these want three servants at least. The horrid murky basement—'

'Oh, come, dear! The basements are only semi-basements and quite light.'

'Mine isn't. Possibly it's due to the enormous trees that you won't have cut. And it's damp. How the Warmans live down there without committing suicide I don't know. Perhaps they will shortly. Using my gas and wasting a lot of it all night. People use so much more than is necessary on these occasions. Don't think I'm ungenerous, but I should like to think there was someone there to turn it off when the job was done. Mrs.

Warman's always in the depths of despair, saying she "can't cope". Don't your Pelly and Capes say they can't cope?'

'No, I tell them to get in all the help they want.'

'Well, I'm not as rich as you are, and *I* have to do the helping —with some help, but not much, from Bronwen sitting there.'

'I help a lot,' said Bronwen. 'Heaps. Gosh, what a lie.'

'No, you don't, and the long and the short of it, Mr. Marcus, is, I can't cope either. Not so young as I was. Do you know I'm sixty-three? Almost seventy'

'Well, all I can say is you look splendid for sixty-three.'

'Never mind what I look like. I know I look splendid. All the same I sometimes feel ninety-three. What I'd like is a nice little modern flat which Bronwen and I could work ourselves—'

'I'm not going unless Uncle Mark comes too,' said Bronwen. 'It'd be ghastly, not living next door to Uncle Mark. Absolutely poisonous.'

'You keep quiet, young woman. The only thing I'd really miss, Mark, is the copper beech. Your Trees Superintendent says it's the finest of its kind in Keys.'

'Afraid you can't take it with you, my dear.'

'No, alas. But, Mark, we'll have to go sooner or later. The whole neighbourhood is sinking fast. There's not a house except these two that isn't converted into one smelly flat on each floor; or, worse still, in multiple occupation. The whole place'll soon be a slum. If it's not a slum now, it's certainly a twilight area. I heard someone call it the rotting heart of Keys.'

'Rotting? These are the most magnificently built houses in Keys, and you can gamble that with our chronic housing famine no one'll disturb them for fifty or a hundred years.'

Belle sighed. 'Well, here we are, I suppose, and here we stay. Till the end.'

'I'm certainly not going from my house. I was born in it, I've always lived in it, and I'm quite happy in it now.'

'Good lord! *Men!*' Belle deplored. '*Men*, Bronwen!'

One thing Mark learned as she talked: that he didn't want Belle to go; that he didn't want to be alone in this house without her on the other side of the wall. Strange how much of the frightened and deceitful child lived in him still. In his bed that night, remembering her talk, he perceived suddenly, and with a sharp pity, that Belle had become ashamed before her friends of the street in which she lived. So real was this pity, and yet so strong his desire to keep her near, that in the next weeks he had the whole exterior of her house restored and repainted at a vicious cost, and now the high white cube containing their two homes was the one bright block in a weather-beaten, grey, and mouldering street, so that, more than ever, passers-by pointed it out as 'our famous Mayor's house'. The interior he fitted with every new labour-saving machine. He suggested she should make a maisonette of the lower floors and shut up the higher for good, and to a certain extent this was what she did.

The idea came to him at times that he might make a flat for Belle and Bronwen on *his* upper floors, but no—he didn't like to think of Belle and Bronwen living, all unaware, in this house and looking down from high back windows at the garden.

So they stayed where they were, and Mark was left thinking, 'Maybe they'll have to go in time, but I—I must go on living here till death, on guard.'

Till death. Yes, but what then? With his iron health—never once ill in sixty years—he might live another twenty or even thirty years. What then? Surely no new owner or tenant would make more than a shallow flower-bed under the broad-branched ailanthus tree. He heard again Mr. Luddermore speaking. 'Grass won't grow properly—much less flah'rs—under that there tree. You might tinker a bit with the soil, shoving in leaf-mould or stable muck or something, and see if you could induce some begonias or phlox or nasturtiums to come up—and some medder saffron perhaps in the autumn—but I can't see any of 'em coming to much; no, I can't, really; not meself.'

So probably would any good gardener tell any tenant, and no tenant could fell the tree unless the Council rescinded its preservation order; which was more than unlikely since so large and princely a tree 'contributed (in the Council's language) to the amenity of the neighbourhood'. Then surely the future was safe enough for as long as mattered.

Like himself the fine old tree stood on guard too, a veteran accomplice, large, powerful, complacent, and longer-lived than he.

Often he thought this, standing alone in his study and looking out at it. And he would come away from the window unperturbed about the future—on this earth at least. Though not without thinking, perhaps, how terrible was the adjustment whereby all guilt found comfortable accommodation at last in a back room of one's mind and there lodged, worrying about its fruits no more.

But what came about, and quickly, was something he had never foreseen.

17. A Labour Council is Progressive

All in the Chamber, aldermen and borough officers on the dais, councillors in their seats, pressmen at their table, public in the horseshoe gallery above, rose in respect as the Mayor's Sergeant, mace on shoulder, led in the Town Clerk and Mayor. Town Clerk and Mayor diverged to their central seats, the Sergeant laid the mace on its bracket beneath them, the Mayor bowed to the aldermen on his right and his left and then to the whole Chamber in front of him. The bows having been reverently returned, the whole Chamber sank to its seats. The Council was in session.

The horseshoe gallery, sloping like a dress circle above the councillors' stalls, held an unusually large sprinkle of public spectators this evening. It was as though a rumour had swept over certain parts of Keys that a disturbing matter would be discussed in Council before the night was over.

The Mayor in his high place knew what was coming. There had been pre-Council meetings of the Labour Group to discuss it. There had been the legal expositions from the Town Clerk's Department. And now, as Mayor, neither pleading nor voting, a mere pilot on a bridge, he must preside over its discussion by the Council—with death in his heart.

No one must detect the terror in his heart, and his voice rang out clearly enough as he read the apologies and announcements. True it trembled once, but he coughed to cover the weakness, and nobody noticed it.

Take matters in their order with apparent ease; first things first; following the agenda before coming to the dread business. 'The Report of the Entertainments Committee. Councillor Miss Farman.'

(Entertainments forsooth! A grim unimaginable entertainment for Keys in the coming days.)

Councillor Miss Farman, rising, begged to move that the report be received and adopted.

The Mayor, in the same unsuspect voice, clear, controlled, put the report, paragraph by paragraph, from first to last: 'Paragraph five. Section a . . . b . . . and c. Recommendation d.' No one queried or debated anything. 'I put the report of the Entertainments Committee. Those in favour? Against?'

Carried.

And so to the Report of the Civil Defence Committee, queried by none and as quickly despatched.

But now—no tremor in his voice—'The Report of the Planning Committee. Mr. Councillor Lammas.'

Arthur, as Chairman of the Committee, rose and formally, not lifting his face from his agenda paper, and hardly troubling to make his voice audible, moved the adoption.

'Paragraph one.' No halting here; it was but a single-line paragraph reporting the election of a vice-chairman.

'Paragraph two. Delegated Applications under Town Planning Acts.' No disputation.

Nor at paragraph three. 'Delegated Applications under London Building Acts.'

'Paragraph four. Seven Brides Estate Redevelopment Scheme.'

This was the paragraph that, unknown to all in the room, waited like a time-bomb beneath the life of the Mayor. Waited for the Council to release all the bomb's safety devices and start it ticking. 'Paragraph' indeed, when it filled five whole pages of the agenda, each page divided and subdivided into sections! Arthur Lammas spoke instantly. 'I feel, Mr. Mayor, that the Council will expect me to enlarge somewhat on this very important paragraph.' Councillors lifted their eyes from the paragraph and looked at him. Grimacings about the lips of some registered, 'Yes, to be sure.' Arthur stood there with spectacles on his brief nose and sheets of notes in his hand. This was quite unlike his usual manner when about to address the Council. Usually his round face was free of spectacles and stared truculently at the party opposite, which he was probably attacking. His hand would hold a few notes but most of his words would be impromptu and brisk, not to say brusque, not to say shockingly impolite. Today the unfamiliar spectacles and the copious notes beneath them suggested serious business in hand.

He began, 'It will probably be agreed by all, Mr. Mayor, even by the party opposite, that many streets in that part of our borough which used to be the Seven Brides Estate and is still so called are obsolescent in their lay-out and housing—'

Here came one or two murmurs of dissent, and a whisper from a Tory, 'Obsolescent yourself,' which won a few titters around it, but in the main a pregnant silence greeted the word and suggested that most thought it applicable to Seven Brides.

'Take, for instance,' continued Arthur, unusually tolerant and temperate, 'the Mornington Gardens area; its whole lay-out belongs to an age far behind us now. With its huge, old-fashioned, large-roomed houses it entirely fails to make optimum use of its building land—'

Many eyes swung to the Mayor, a resident in the Gardens, who provided a smile for them; to the Mayoress also, in her unofficial chair by the wall, who smiled too, but without effort.

Meantime Councillor Lammas was saying, 'All too many of the houses are in bad repair, and even we of the Labour Party, who have no great love for landlords, feel a sympathy for those who would have to spend outrageous sums on reconditioning and then get a totally uneconomic return on their outlay. I suggest that it is impossible to walk the length of Mornington Gardens and to glance down its side-roads, which are little but side elevations and listing garden walls, without thinking that here is an area ripe for redevelopment and, in some places, overripe. Of course we know that one or two distinguished persons still live in Mornington Gardens (laughter) but we in this Council know very well that they are people of great public spirit who have the interests of our borough at heart ('Hear, hears', and sidelong, humorous glances at the Mayoress). We know they will accept what is best for Keys. I have little doubt that the official density of this area has long been exceeded,

thanks to multiple occupation everywhere, and we of the Labour
Party, while accepting this need for a higher density, are determined to see that people are housed in healthy modern conditions. The population of our country is increasing at a mean
rate of nearly half a million a year, and this isn't the whole
story. In these days of full employment and high wages—'

'Thanks to Conservative government,' put in a Tory, and
for once Arthur was at a loss for a rude reply, so he just muttered, with a dismissive gesture of his unoccupied hand, 'Oh,
get yourself lost,' and travelled on.

'—days of high wages people marry earlier and the demand
for homes increases even more rapidly than the population.
Well, probably no part of our country feels this pressure of
population more than boroughs like ours on the periphery of
the metropolitan conurbation—'

'*Phew!*' whistled a humorist, as if in wonder at the unexpected appearance of these last magnifico words.

'—metropolitan conurbation,' Arthur pursued, after looking
up from his notes at the Phew but not feeling competent as yet
to deal faithfully with interruptions limited to phews, 'and it
seems plain to us that the best thing to do will be to clear this
area, where the houses are more than a hundred years old and
at the end of their useful life—'

'Nonsense!' came a woman's voice from the gallery, and
'Rats!' from a man's.

'—and then we can use the land to better purpose. In the
Seven Brides Estate we could increase the density by building
good terraced two-storey or three-storey houses—dwellings of
the size that is in greatest demand—and perhaps here and there
a tower block of flats—a mixed development, you see, of houses,
flats and maisonettes, bearing in mind that the cost of land and
building diminishes as density increases. With good modern
designing it should be possible to achieve densities of well above
a hundred p.p.a.--'

'What's that?' came from a lounging Tory, new to the Council after a by-election and therefore ignorant of its esoteric
phrasings.

'A hundred persons per acre, sir, if we build the sort of houses
pre-eminently required by families with children. Now it's not

to be denied that this proposed redevelopment of Seven Brides is a great undertaking but, as you will see from the report, we are thinking of it as an undertaking where private enterprise may well come into partnership with the local authority. You will see further that a private development company with large financial backing, the Two Centuries Property Company, is prepared to co-operate with us and has submitted designs for a comprehensive development of the area. These designs my committee has studied with care, ably advised by our officers, and we have decided to commend them to the Council. The Council will have to participate in the scheme because its powers of issuing C.P.O.s—'

'C-P-whose?' begged the ignorant and now despairing councillor.

'Compulsory purchase orders, sir. These powers may have to be exercised here and there, but it is not thought that such a sledge-hammer procedure will have to be largely resorted to. We think that most residents will accept our proposals, well knowing that as long as Labour controls this Council'—here he looked up from his notes with a mischievous smile—'which will be for a long time yet, we shall insist on any developers making preparation to re-house all evicted families who may want to return to the area. And, for once in a way, I feel disposed to add that in the extremely unlikely event of the party opposite regaining control of the borough (laughter) they would do no less.'

'Very handsome,' conceded a Tory voice.

'Thank you, sir.' Arthur bowed to the voice. 'But whether the Tories would go as far in another respect as we most certainly shall, I doubt. *We* are determined that a substantial number of these houses and flats shall be for *letting*'—he threw the word fiercely into the voice's smiling face—'*and* letting at rentals within the means of our lower-income groups. Now, Mr. Mayor, this large redevelopment may take as long as five or six years, so the only thing to do will be to set about it by a process of phasing. Phase One should clearly be the Mornington Gardens area where work can be begun immediately.'

'What in this context does "immediately" mean?' demanded a scholarly and precise Tory.

'It means soon—within the next few months.'

'It never did when I was at school,' was the scholar's only comment.

Immediately. The Mayor with his pencil was drawing squares and rectangles on the blank paper before him and shading them in with diagonals. He did not know, but perhaps the squares and rectangles represented the tower blocks or the terraced houses that would arise along Mornington Gardens. Within the next few months. How deep would the foundations go for a three-storey house or, worse, for a tower block? A few months and then what? An arrest. A headlined sensation read the country over. A story to charge with excitement every heart in Fleet Street. A few more months and then . . . a trial, watched by the world. A few more weeks, and . . . ? He shaded in another square. He had tried to make *some* amends for a year and more, but apparently God was not prepared to withhold the full punishment.

'Evidently you cannot cheapen with God. Cannot offer fifteen shillings if your debt and your duty are a pound. A few months of grace or a few years, and he forecloses. Or he chooses to do so in some cases. In mine. But if this is God, his way is stern. He is not a man that he should forgo the uttermost farthing. Nor suave and delicate as a man might be. What man, with mercy in his heart, would use my friends to undo me? And yet little Bronwen was used in the street to tell my enemy all about me and to charge his guns for him. And here is Arthur speaking on behalf of himself, myself, and my party in more statesmanlike fashion than ever before—splendidly unaware that he is bringing down judgment upon me. If this is the way God's wisdom and mercy work, their attack is terrible indeed. Does he strip a man to the utmost that he may suffer all and be saved?

'But go on with it, Arthur, go on.'

'In the Mornington Gardens area, thanks to its outmoded site-planning, the clearing costs will be less heavy than anywhere else, and if the Council accepts the Two Centuries scheme, there is no reason why we shouldn't start this first phase in a few months' time. Mr. Mayor . . .' A pause, a dropping of his notes, a drawing off and folding up of his spectacles showed that his peroration was at hand. 'I submit that this great scheme offers us a magnificent opportunity to transform an area of uneconomic lay-out into a splendid piece of modern planning. The compelling need to house more people has presented us with a challenge to produce in Keys a brand-new urban unit as good to look upon as it will be good to live in, and a matter of pride to our borough.'

Soft 'hear, hears' came generously from all parts of the Chamber. So well distributed were these plaudits for an able speech that it looked at first as if approval for the scheme would be universal. No sign on the Mayor's face that he was pleased or displeased by this widespread approval.

But endorsement was not to be universal. Nor did the objectors rise from one side of the Chamber only. Major Roper, rising first, probably because he felt it his duty as Leader of the Opposition to say something in opposition, asked, 'Am I really to understand, Mr. Mayor, that *all* the properties in Mornington Gardens and its neighbouring roads are to be destroyed—I beg pardon, "demolished"?'

Arthur, ready now to deal with opponents in his more customary style, and especially with the Major, retorted, 'I do not see what other meaning my words could have conveyed to the councillor. It would be difficult to build three-storey houses or tower blocks on top of houses already standing. The answer is Yes. . . . Is that okay, Squire?'

Major Roper smiled. 'I thank the councillor for his courteous reply.' Bowing two inches, he resumed his seat, still smiling.

His good humour was certainly not lessened when a Labour councillor, rising far away from the Major's seat—and even farther away politically than geographically—showed that he was ready to defy his party rule and actually *speak* against the party line. 'As a resident in this area so gaily sentenced to total destruction,' he began, 'I must say that the news of this scheme has come as a shock to us all—'

Interruptions of 'No, no' from the floor, and a cry of '*Yes, yes!*' from one strong male voice in the gallery. The Mayor looked up at the voice, wondering whether it was his duty to rebuke a brawler, even though his heart was with him; even though the man's voice had been like a sop of comfort thrown to him in his pit.

'Well, let me say,' the councillor amended, 'as a shock to all except those who will continue to live in peace and comfort outside this doomed area. Where, please, in the plan is there anything specific about how, where, or when some hundreds of evicted families are to be re-housed? I submit we have had a pious opinion only, and a pious opinion is balm to no one. It's a roof over nobody's head.'

Whereupon another Tory jumped up quickly to extend a crutch even to a Socialist if he was struggling on the right road. 'For the first time,' he said, 'and I strongly suspect the last, Mr. Mayor, I am in agreement with my good friend opposite. Councillor Lammas has described these properties as obsolete when in my view there's not one of them that with reasonable care could not stand for another fifty years.' ('Hear, hears' from the gallery, including one '*Hear, HEAR!*') 'Builders a hundred years ago knew how to build properly and troubled to do so—'

'And they still would,' interposed Arthur, 'if their capitalist employers would let them. I am a builder myself.'

'*And* a capitalist employer,' the Tory quickly pointed out.

'Perhaps, but not a profiteering Tory one.'

'I take no note of that piece of abuse. It merits no answer,' said the Tory, having no answer. 'To proceed on a level of reason rather than invective, I submit that it's astonishing, even criminal, to propose the demolition of sound homes at a time when, as Mr. Lammas has just told us, in one of his cooler moments, there is a pressing need for more and more homes.'

Nothing on the face of the Mayor to show that his heart had leapt with a desperate hope. But not a hope that reason would support. It sank even as it began to rise.

The Tory was still speaking. 'I repeat, it seems to me almost criminal, on our part in Keys, to call upon the country's over-strained building resources for the replacing of good solid homes when there are slums all over London in desperate need of being cleared and redeveloped.'

A subdued and yet emphatic 'Hear, *hear!*' from the brawler in the gallery—subdued because he'd seen last time that lift of the Mayor's eye.

Several members now rose together, and the Mayor gave the word to a Labour member; who said, with an anxious loyalty to his party line, 'While supporting this scheme as one of the most impressive and imaginative ever laid before the Council, I would like to go on record as emphasizing strongly something our Leader said. I do not feel that the plans outlined here show a sufficient sense of the crying need for houses or flats capable of being let at reasonable rents to working-class people. This is the need of the hour. I for one shall be only too glad to see these hopeless old houses levelled to the ground and small attractive homes for the workers rising in their place—and this with all respect to a certain great and good man who continues to live in one of them.'

Scattered laughs.

Joke on. Argue on. The only way out is death. The night before they begin digging foundations in the garden of my late home your Mayor dies. Dies and leaves an insoluble story to explode upon the world. A death if possible—since he has the skills—which will attract an open verdict. Or Misadventure. Black suspicion may be left behind, certainly, but no sure knowledge of what really happened; no proof of a murder. An insoluble mystery. The loyal imaginations of Belle and Bronwen and Jasper will do their best for me, but whether or not this death 'obscures the phenomena', the simple fact is that I could never face Jasper once the phenomena are uncovered. Never. Nor Bronwen. Nor Arthur. . . .

Since a mayor does not plead or vote at a Council meeting, but presides only, Councillor Dolmen, vested in scarlet and gold, seated on the room's highest throne, and sometimes lifting his golden quizzing glass to his eye, was feeling more like a collarless prisoner in a humble dock who does not speak, though counsel in front of him, not unhappy in their expert play, argue for the death sentence or for a free discharge.

Argue on.

'And further to what the councillor has just said'—this was another Tory, suddenly inspired, enthusiastic about his inspiration, indifferent to the fact that he was linking arms with a Labour man, and indifferent to the rising of all the same members again—in a word, getting in first—'I invite the Council to lift this business out of paper paragraphs and into human terms. May I suggest that the human disturbance we are so blithely considering will be little less than a human disaster.

For example: quite apart from the fact that many of the inhabitants of this area are elderly people who love their old homes and wish to end their lives in them, there is the other fact that for some of them their houses, just because they are so large and unworkable, constitute a large part, if not all, of their livelihood. Many are divided, as we know, into tenanted rooms or sublet flatlets catering—and here is another human consideration—for an honourable class of persons whom we are glad to have among us: students, widows, widowers, old-age pensioners, young working girls living alone or together. All these are people who deserve to be considered. I beg you to consider them.'

Such a general murmur of sympathy greeted this that for a moment the Mayor thought, 'Perhaps one may hope . . . perhaps . . .' but no; his head shook, and none in the Chamber observed that he passed a hand over his brow and behind his head, which had bowed a little.

Shamus O'Donoghue had been among the several who had twice risen. It was rare for him to speak in council but he seemed to have been visited by an idea which he was loth to leave unexpressed. He stood again, swinging his agenda paper between two ringed fingers, and before a notable waistcoat. The Mayor's eye, attracted by a gently swaying paper, signalled to him to proceed, and in his high voice with its languid tones he ventured, 'One point seems to me to have been overlooked so far. The trees. The really splendid old trees that stand in the gardens of these old homes. I am a great lover of trees—'

'Go *on*!' murmured a second humorist, affecting incredulity.

'—and I would like to know what is going to happen to them. I understand that most of those visible to the roads are scheduled trees. Are we now to accept the cancellation of many preservation orders and the felling of many trees?'

The Mayor's eyes, as in duty bound, swung to Councillor Lammas for his answer, though behind his eyes there was little hope. And Arthur replied, 'I take it that the fate of some of the trees is uncertain. The widening of Mornington Gardens and the setting back of the houses must necessarily involve the loss of some trees. If they have to go it will be the price we must pay for something even better and more necessary. Part of the attraction of the Two Centuries scheme is that in this area the old gardens lying back-to-back will enable new houses to be set well away from the busy road and have attractive gardens in front as well as behind. But I can assure the councillor that we will watch the matter carefully.'

'Thank you,' said Shamus, bowing and patently pleased that his little speech had hit a mark.

But meanwhile the Mayor, still doodling with his pencil, had drawn a new square and shaded it in. It represented the ground plan of a new house set back from the road, and it overlaid the site of his Tree of Heaven. The only asterisk he could draw on the paper to indicate a tree represented the tall black poplar, beyond the Tree of Heaven – and the neighbouring grave. He drew it, and then shaded in more of the square, while he felt as if he were shading his life away.

A lay reader. And a mayor. A preacher in many parts. Called by one excitable paper 'London's most famous mayor'. How the world would laugh at the trickery. But it had been no trickery; it had been an attempt to do a little good, if not enough; and he would go on attempting this to the end, whatever the end might be. Partly because he had believed in it, and still believed in it, and partly in the hope that God might relent.

After Shamus's contribution and its answer, the debate was seen to be dead of inanition, since the Council as a whole favoured a new and stirring scheme. It remained only for Arthur to give the final reply. More conciliatory than usual because some of the dissatisfied had risen from his own benches, he said in sympathetic, indeed gentlemanly, tones, 'Mr. Mayor, we have heard with interest the queries and criticisms of members, and I assure the Council that my committee will give consideration to all of them. But I do want to assert emphatically that the people in Seven Brides need not be alarmed or despondent. I have already stated that everything will be done to ensure that those who want to go on living there will be enabled to do so. And I like to think that, in the end, they will find themselves better housed than they are now and will wonder why they were ever afraid—'

'Sez you!' dropped from the gallery.

Arthur took no notice. 'I therefore hope that the Council

will accept the recommendation—' whipping on his spectacles, he looked at his agenda and read out, 'that the Council do agree to be associated with the Seven Brides Redevelopment Scheme, as outlined by the Two Centuries Property Company Limited, subject to their being satisfied as to the financial liabilities arising therefrom, and to such further study with the developers as may be thought desirable.' He removed the spectacles and pocketed them. 'An acceptance of this recommendation, you see, will not amount to a final decision. There is still time for would-be opponents to muster their forces and gather their ammunition. Still time,' he concluded with a smile.

'And still hope,' thought the Mayor. 'Still some hope, perhaps.'

The Planning Chairman having said his last, there was nothing now but for the Mayor to put the whole report. In a firm unbreaking voice, which must belong, he thought, to some part of him that had lost contact with his heart, he said, 'I put the report of the Planning Committee for adoption. Those in favour?'

All the right hands in the Council, except five, went up.

'Against?'

Not a hand.

'I declare the report adopted.'

'Shame!' from the strong voice in the gallery, but the Mayor was already saying, 'The Report of the Establishment Committee. Mr. Councillor Locke.'

18. Dialogue with Belle

'What do we do now?' demanded Belle. 'And where do we go from here?'

'Never was cliché more to the point. Where indeed do we go from here?'

Belle and he were sitting at the end of his long dining table and sipping whiskies that same evening after the Council. He had said, 'Come into the dining-room, Belle,' because tonight more than any night he didn't want her seated in the study. She was all too apt to sit happily in Angelo's chair.

'Yes,' she proceeded, 'where, when, and how? It's the first time I've been thrown out into the street.' She was full of fun tonight. 'Not but what I'm quite happy about it. I'm merely excited about where I'm going.'

'*I'm* not happy about it. You've only lived a dozen years in your home. I've lived in this house since the first day of my life. This was Lorelei's and my home.' He was about to add 'Lorelei died here', but found he could not trade that sacred fact in order to buy cover for his sins. Even though nearly drowning in a despair he would not use Lorelei as a life-buoy. 'I've not the least desire to be dragged up by the roots.' A cheap stock metaphor: roots. And one that for the secret reason could shiver his heart as it left his lips.

'Well, shall you resist it?'

'There's no resisting it, my dear. A compulsory purchase

order enforced on the Mayor would be a pretty spectacle. Perhaps I should never have become Mayor.'

'But do you mean you can't resist? Do you mean they can just pinch your property and order you to get out?'

'That's exactly what I mean.'

'How utterly base. I won't be Mayoress any more.'

'One can appeal, of course, and some will. I can't. How can I appeal against my own party?'

'But it's not settled. They said something about further study. And opposition.'

'There'll be plenty of opposition, but it was very clear to me what the Council will do. It'll make a few concessions and pass the final acceptance in a month or two.'

'Month or two!' Belle let loose a little shriek. 'I can't get out in a month or two. Suppose there's nothing suitable anywhere for you and I?'

'There can never be anything suitable "for I". "For *me*", dear. "For you and *me*."'

'Oh, don't start worrying me with your beastly grammar when I've something proper to worry about. It'll take me ages to find the place I want. *I* shall have to live in it, not the Borough Council.'

'There'll be another month or so before the demolition begins. But you heard them say Phase One was us. Mornington Gardens.' (Why, he thought, does a man with a private alarm want to speak alarm to others?)

'And where are you and Bronwen and me going when they start?'

Contrite, he resolved to comfort her with an opposite of alarm. 'Well, with building land at its present inflated price I shall expect to get a fantastic sum for this double property, and there are delightful modern flats about if you'll pay enough. I'm thinking of two nice little luxury flats, one for you and Bronwen, and one for Jasper and me. The one for me may be far from here.'

'Oh, but *no*!' she cried. 'Where?'

'Somewhere in London, perhaps, nearer the centre of things.'

'But you're Mayor. You can't leave Keys. You can't.'

'I've only ten more months of my three-years sentence to

serve.' (But would he finish his year? What happened when a mayor was taken away by the police? Did he return to his throne if remanded on bail? Bail? There was no bail on a murder charge. Oh God above. . . . But let there be a parade of joking for Belle's sake.) 'I shall have to serve the remainder of my sentence. Three whole stretch. Unfortunately a mayor gets no remission for good behaviour.'

'What do you mean? What are you talking about? They want you for a fourth year. Arthur said so.'

'He said that before he ordered me out of my home.'

'Don't talk nonsense, Mark. You'll never leave Keys. It's not in you to leave it. Besides, you'd break Bronwen's heart. She's crazy about you.' (It's something else that'll break her heart, he thought, and the thought came near to breaking his own heart.)

He kept silence, and Belle continued, 'It's only when one knows one has to go that one realizes all one will miss. There's my copper beech and my garden, which is *too* lovely just now. They'll dig up all my garden, I suppose. And then there's my new friend, the pigeon.'

'The pigeon?'

'Yes, he now sits somewhere on the gutters above my bedroom and at six or so every morning broadcasts a commentary on the scene in the garden. Or perhaps it's a "Lift up your Hearts" talk, like that bishop's of somewhere. I've seen him: he's as sleek and fat as any bishop and I'm greatly attached to him. Unless it's his brother. I can't have a garden at a flat, but we might persuade my episcopal pigeon to come too. Is it really certain we'll have to go?'

He had no doubt himself the answer was yes; still, let the certainty approach her gently. No need to destroy too soon this happy, laughing mood. So with a lift of the shoulders, shrugging, he said only, 'Who knows? Strange things can always happen. We can only wait and see.'

It was not yet half-past nine when Belle left, and as this was one of June's last days, the evening was full of light, for the sun was barely gone. Beaten punch-drunk by despair, he felt able to do nothing but take to his bed and rest there, thoughtless as a log, so he climbed to his high bedroom, and when the door was shut, remembering Belle's talk, he looked out at her garden and his. And it seemed to him that their contrast matched well enough the difference between her attitude to the day's news and his. Her garden was gaily celebrating the brightest hours of its year. In the large central bed were roses of every colour, full-blown but glorious in their last brave flamboyance before they dropped. Another bed displayed proudly its dahlias of every colour. Elsewhere, in beds for smaller flowers, under the wall, were pinks and African marigolds, the violet alyssum and the blue lobelia. As for his garden, why, Luddermore, sick, had not appeared for weeks, and he himself had felt less willing to work or mow in that garden than anywhere else on earth. So the grasses stood high and feathered with seeds; while thistles, sorrel, and strange tall weeds had somehow gate-crashed into their company and stood boldly among them. Above the rioting grasses the un-lopped trees were heavy with leaf and darkening with the year. His open-work iron steps leading down into high grasses looked like a derelict stairway from a house long empty and dead.

Yes, indeed, the two gardens pictured the difference between Belle's life at this hour and his; her garden was lively with varied blooms, all of them examples of nature's munificence and man's good handiwork; his, on the other side of the wall, looked to have gone rioting back to the wild.

19. Dialogue with the Unseen

'Not for my sake who deserve nothing, but for the others—save me, save me, if you can, even yet. The others. Let me not think of myself. Let me ask the impossible, but not for me, not for me. There is Jasper. Jasper at school, at Cambridge, and all through his life. If you have mercy, think of him. And Bronwen and Belle. Surely it will be too cruel a punishment for all these who have done nothing. You are not cruel. It was my fault, I know. But . . .

'I see what you are doing. Even if I have been struggling to make some recompense I have perhaps come to live with my memories too easily, and you are driving me back till I see something. But I do see it now, I do: *he was your son too.* Every bit as much as I am, with all his sins. I see. I suppose this thing was even more terrible in me whose whole trade belongs to life, doing battle with death. You want me to realize this. You want to drive me farther into penitence. But I *am* penitent, only I don't know what to do about it, or where to turn.'

In his study facing the haunted chair, in his spacious consulting room when the upholstered chairs were empty till the next patient came, in the Surgeons' Room of a hospital as he was getting gowned and capped and masked, most of all in his bed before the sleeping pills worked their mercy, this dialogue went on. At such times everyone else in his life faded from consciousness and he sat, or paced, or lay with this one Listener in his mind. If the Listener was there. If he was really there.

'He was your son too and you are forcing me to remember this. I see. I have farther to go. I thought you had spoken to me in old Craikie's sermon, I don't know why but it seemed like a message. Was that your first step? Since then I have liked to feel that you were guiding me, and I was almost happy, doing the things you seemed to suggest. Was I too self-satisfied in this? But listen: I felt cheated. I felt so miserably caught and cheated. For years after Lorelei's death I went with no women. Perhaps this was no credit to me because I didn't want any other than Lorelei, I couldn't bear the thought of anyone but her. And in the later years it has been only once or twice when I felt driven beyond my powers of resistance. It was only twice with Desiderata, and there was a year between. And I did not kill her. Be good to her, oh God, wherever she is, if she still is—anywhere. I did put her out into the street because I was a coward, I know, I know. But was not her death in my arms a sterner punishment than I deserved? I couldn't, couldn't, confess how she died. Then *he* came. Driving me mad.

'And oh God, listen, listen again. The only result of having tried to serve you in your church will be to make things worse, far worse, for me. The sensation and the shame will be all the greater because I have served and preached in your church. And so here I feel cheated again. Once again. All things have turned against me.

'Are you still insisting that all I can't confess must be uncovered to the world? In spite of all? In spite of all? Is that what you want—but oh, hold your hand, oh God, if not for my sake, then for *theirs*. Give me out of their sight the pains that I deserve but stop this for them. Only something like a miracle can stop it now, but what are miracles to you?'

A dialogue with only one speaking. The other silent. Present perhaps, but only perhaps and the days speeding by—to what issue? *Was* he answering? In his own way? Things happened but were they to do with him, or was this a vain imagining, and they but hopeless hopes? A hope sprang when angry tenants and leaseholders in the Seven Brides Estate, at a crowded meeting in his own Town Hall, formed an association 'to fight this monstrous and ill-conceived plan every inch of the way'.

The large Assembly Hall was packed to the walls for this meeting, and the two members of his own Labour Party who had criticized the plan in council now spoke fervently against it. One pleaded for its abandonment; the other, who had called it 'impressive and imaginative' in council, now pleaded for its postponement till far greater study had been given it. 'As for the strong old houses in Mornington Gardens,' he said, 'they could be left for years yet. They could even outlast the lives of many of us.' He was a man much of an age with Mark. Both parties were split about the plan, though only to the extent of losing splinters at their edges; after the two Labour members two Tories spoke to this noisy and excited gathering. One of them, enlarging on Shamus's query, asked about the 'enchanting old trees' in the Mornington Gardens area.

'Practically all these trees have p.o.'s on them,' he said, which jollied up the meeting not a little, evoking protracted laughter, though he had intended no joke. 'Preservation orders,' he explained with an apologetic smile.

The other Tory produced an argument that must have pleased the leaseholders but shaken the Labour councillors who had not come to the Town Hall to hear this manner of talk. He appealed for delay and reconsideration on the score that the proposed compensation to dispossessed landlords of half the gross value of their houses was grossly inadequate. 'As we all know,' he said, 'many of the houses in Seven Brides have rooms and floors sublet and so produce for their owners dividends in rents that have no relation now to the annual gross value. For example I could tell you of a house with a half-gross-value of two hundred and thirty pounds and a reputed income of nearly two thousand.'

The two Labour councillors quaked at this apparent defence of multiple occupation and monstrous famine-rents, but they did not spoil the meeting by expounding their shock. One, however, felt the need to come up at once with something that sounded more like Socialism, and he rose to say, 'What angers me is that the Council seems to think that if they don't bulldoze this plan through quickly, the Two Centuries Property Company will withdraw, taking their money with them. Well, let 'em, I say! [Loud applause.] The Council is elected to serve the people of Keys, not millionaire financiers and property specu-lators from the City of London.' This raised fine cheers, but whether the Tories were associated with the sentiment was doubtful. Their voices did not ring among the others.

Since one must hope, Mark dared to wonder, could any of this mean that the silent Listener, having brought him to his senses by a mortal fright, would after all show mercy?

'Or is it that your love is fire and you know that the only way for me to save my soul is to lose the whole world?' As he asked this, seated at his desk in his consulting room while waiting for a distinguished patient, he remembered at once the great dean's prayer, which he had never been able to utter, and could not utter now, but only recall. 'Batter my heart, three-personed God ... o'erthrow me, and bend your force to break, blow, burn and make me new.' No, he still could not say all of this; not if it meant bowing before God's free hand; all he could say was, Burn me as sternly as you feel you must, but not by the fire of exposure which must burn so many others too. Two children in their schools. And those to whom I tried in honesty to preach you. Good simple seekers after you. Must all these be battered and burned too? The preacher in whose words they found help, the mayor whom all honoured, a murderer with a victim buried in his garden! How the world will condemn and execrate and scoff. But it will not know the story. You will know that I wasn't quite the impostor I seemed. Punish me fully, but not by damaging the faith of many and cruelly damaging again poor old Craikie's church which I did try to help. What am I to do? What *can* I do? I shall go on helping Craikie in the hope that you will help me; if not ...' But here he could only shake his head at his empty room. 'I shall go on doing my operations as perfectly as possible so as to be of help to others and my council work—oh, if only you would let me go on like this! Help me to be more and more selfless—but not to the extent of con-fessing all. Lorelei, if you are anywhere, pray for me.' Suddenly he had turned from the great imagined Presence to one who was more remote than any, a pale wraith who might or might not be. 'If you are anywhere, my dearest, pray to him for Jasper and me. Forgive me the dreadful things I did, but some of it, much of it, was done for our Jasper's sake. I love you still, my dear. . . .'

He rose from the wide consultant's desk and by inveterate habit, since in worry or pain he walked always towards the light, he went to the window and stood looking out at Queen Anne Street. But it was little that he saw of Queen Anne Street, or the corner of Harley Street opposite, because he was seeing, or imagining, the shadowy, unfeatured Shape, creator of a million worlds, lord of all the stars, with whom he was trying to compromise, to negotiate a deal.

'I shall go on till the end trying to do the things you would wish, but if you . . . if you make the worst happen and it's clear that all will be discovered, then I shall have to do what they say is mortal sin. I shall have to die before the truth is known. It's the only way I can leave behind me a mystery which can never be solved, whatever suspicion may say. But wait: Luddermore. Old Luddermore and his son, who dug the pit together and know it was I who replaced the soil and sowed the grass. Old Luddermore is sick—help me not to wish he may die of it—no, give him back his health at—at whatever cost to me. But let me die when the hour comes, even if it is mortal sin. Surely you will allow, if only for Jasper's and the others' sake, this small—'

'Sir Oliver Fenton, sir.'

'Oh, thank you, Muriel. Yes, bring him in.'

And he went to his large swivel chair behind the great desk to welcome with smiles his famous patient.

Through the days and weeks he pursued this dialogue with his silent and perhaps unsubstantial Listener. He could not desist from it because his mind was never for long away from the threat of a catastrophe far darker than death. And the answers? Sometimes a verse from the Bible read in church seemed for the moment like a word addressed to him, but his reason would not allow him to hold this comfort long. Sometimes when he prayed in the morning for power to go on loving others and doing unflawed work in his theatres despite the weight of alarm on his heart, he did feel, or imagined he felt, an influx of power. Could this mean that an unseen and silent Visitant was hearing him and would indeed show mercy? At other times the answers seemed more like No, and No again. His greatest hope, the Tenants and Leaseholders Association, lost its first rapture, and its supporters fell away. The two Tories who'd spoken at the inaugural meeting defected quietly; they couldn't digest the tough and stodgy Socialism of some of the Left-wing members; likewise the two Labour councillors tacitly disappeared, not relishing their association with landlords who were thriving on the multiple occupation of many-roomed Victorian homes. The officers quarrelled among themselves, and some, deserting, formed a rival organization, called 'Save Our Homes Campaign'. For a little, desperate for hope, Mark dredged up some from this, but quickly his saner parts told him that when the opponents of a plan split hither and thither, it was the proponents who won.

Weary after eight hours of work Mark sat in his study chair and picked up that day's *Keys and Hadleigh News* to read it for the first time. At once the two chief headlines, one beneath the other, hit him like two fist-blows on the heart. 'Shock Decision for Council. Planning Committee says Go Ahead Immediately with Two Centuries Plan.'

As mayor he was an *ex-officio* member of all committees but not expected to attend their meetings, so he'd had no part in the Planning Committee's debate and decision of two days before. He read of them now, while his mouth squared with terror newly inflamed, his jaw bit over his lip, and his heart hammered like some engine missing control.

'Emergency meetings of the Seven Brides Tenants Association and the Save Our Homes Campaign will be held this week, following the shock decision of the Keys Council's Planning Committee to go ahead immediately with the Redevelopment Plan put before the Council four months ago. The Committee's report, to be considered by the Council tomorrow, runs as follows—'

'To be considered'—a cautious synonym for 'to be passed'. Oh, well. . . . This then is death.

'—runs as follows: "On 20th June the Council agreed to be

associated with the scheme prepared by the Two Centuries Property Company, Ltd., for the redevelopment of the Seven Brides Estate. Such agreement was conditional upon the Council being satisfied as to the viability of the scheme both financially and from the point of view of town planning and of the re-housing of present owners and occupiers. It appears to us that the scheme can be financially successful. We are advised by the District Valuer, the Quantity Surveyors, and the Borough Treasurer that the figures supplied by the developers, both as to capital cost and financial return, appear to be reasonable in the light of information available. As regards the rehousing of occupiers we have emphasized to the developers that steps must be taken to secure the rehousing of all families who wish to live in the area. Much consideration has been given to the criticisms of tenants' associations, and we are glad to report that our dis-cussions with the developers have resulted in a substantial in-crease in the number of dwellings to be made available to middle- and lower-income groups—'

More and more of it in the heavy, formal, inhuman language. He read no more beyond sweeping his eye down the page to see if a date was given for the scheme's commencement, and the eye caught amid the verbiage, 'Phase One, it is anticipated, will begin early in the new year.'

And Phase One was Mornington Gardens.

Which would seem to mean, since it was October now, that he had less than six months to live.

He let the paper drop to the floor at his side; and in the same instant decided to let his dialogue with that Other drop too. Why go on with it? Plain enough that the Illimitable was not disposed to chaffer or abate a price; his costs stood. With the arm that had dropped the paper still hanging at his side he looked up at the walls of the room. A few months, and they would be lying as so much rubble on the ground, and the place where he was sitting now, five feet above ground-level, would be but open air continuous with ultimate horizons. Soon the whole house, which in its hundred years had witnessed so much of evil and good, would lie as rubble on the ground or be journey-ing away as debris and dust with all its memories, Heaven knew where and to what final use, in the contractors' tipping lorries. Next, without a doubt, men would be felling the Tree of Heaven. New houses set back so as to leave parking space in front, as the Council always demanded now, must involve its death. The digging of foundations or the grubbing up of the tree's roots, or both, must grub out the truth. Very well. He would be dead before the first pick broke the soil or the first saw cut the tree. In months. Strange idea. Strange feeling. That clock on the mantel was ticking his last hours away.

From now he must begin looking his last on all things. Looking his last on Jasper. Was it cowardly to abandon Jasper, a boy of fifteen, because he could not face him after exposure? Very well: he was cowardly. He would provide abundantly for him; Belle would take him in; and in time he and Bronwen would again be happy children together, whatever their thoughts of him. Strange, unexpected end to a successful life. Looking his last on Bronwen. And Belle, his sister and friend of sixty years. Arthur. Colleagues. Servants. All.

What would he do in these last few months? He was not conscious of any bitterness against God; only that he had broken off the argument since his appeal had clearly been disallowed. He would go on trying to be unselfish, and to serve well as mayor, reader and surgeon till the end, not without a small wonder whether such behaviour might not mitigate the penalty for mortal sin. This unspoken wonder was all that remained of the argument.

He got up and went to the window to take a first of these last looks at one tree and at a site beneath it. The rusting of the sycamore's foliage, and a drifting downwards to the grass of the restless black poplar's few disheartened leaves, told him that it was more than two years since he had filled up that grave. Surprisingly, as he stood there thinking this, and tired out by these extremes of hopelessness, there came at first no more than a yawn. But then, patting his mouth to contain the yawn, he found himself opening a brief and bitter dialogue, after a hopeless laugh, with another voiceless person. Invisible too, but out there and not far away. 'So, my dear Angelo, you win. I thought I'd put an end for ever to your blackmailing and the likelihood of your vengeance, but it seems you are going to appear again.

And, as it's two years since we parted, Angelo, will it be your little grinning skull that has the last laugh?' With a helpless, shrugging acceptance he concluded, 'Very well. Let be. "*Va bene*," as you used to say. "*Va bene, signor dottore*, I go to the police." Ah well, poor Yorick, so be it. Go.'

And he turned back into the room.

20. Before the End

But in the middle of the night, lying awake with the world silent around him, he suddenly—startled into hope—spoke aloud in his dark room. 'Oh no, Angelo. Oh no, you do not go to the police, you go after all to some hidden brushwood somewhere or over a bridge into some deep water far away or into some bombed ruin which is still to be found. Surely, surely, I can dig five feet deep in the depths of a long winter night and, finding you, fill up your grave before it is daylight again. Surely you are but bones now and I can hide you till I carry you far away—a hundred miles from Keys. Why, oh why, didn't I think of this before? It will be difficult, digging all through the night, but a better way than death. Am I going to be able to live after all?'

Not without a horror of this nocturnal business, not without stabbing doubts of its possibility and heart-sinking realizations of its risks, he contrived to make of it a temporary balm so that he dropped again into a stormy sleep.

All the next days this idea was with him, but night followed night and he did nothing; he could not start, and the time for action narrowed.

He had to be out of this house by January or February. For in a desperate deceit he, as Mayor, had suggested to the Council that his two houses should be the first to come down because he could better afford than others to buy new homes. This could only advance by a few weeks the diggings on his plots but it looked noble and might throw some dust in the eyes of the world, for what man would promptly offer his estate to housebreakers and builders if he knew himself responsible for a strange discovery in the garden? It would be one more small way of 'obscuring the phenomena', he had thought, because he himself would be out of reach when the discovery was made.

But now it looked as if with this supreme deceit he had been far too clever, only twisting a noose for him in which to hang. It had limited his time of action to weeks, and these the hardest winter weeks. Frost. November and December frosts. The ground iron hard. The work noisy and Belle—or Bronwen—awakened by it and looking from their windows through the openwork of winter-naked trees. A passer-by—a policeman perhaps—surprised by sound of pick and spade at midnight looks over the garden wall. And if it was not bones by now, what was it? What was it? How dare one approach and touch it? And all must be done in a night or the explanation to Belle and Bronwen, to Pelly and Capes, to Luddermore now active again, would be too difficult—incredible even from an elderly, heavy man who'd always said his surgeon's hands must be protected from rough garden work.

Well, the frosts set in. A hard winter at hand, people said; and hard and chilled it was. Hoar frost lay like snow on roofs. roads and gardens, and on the tops of parked cars. There were brief thaws on some days, but one could not dig in the daylight, and with the sinking of the sun the cold bound the earth again. Surely these stern frosts had come strangely early. Was it that God, resolved on his punishment, was shutting that grave tight? The terrible difficulty of the task, the terrifying risks in it, a sick recoil from this last indecency, all the old hungry desire for amendment—these and a dozen other doubts and fears soon piled up a barrier round that grave so that he could not approach it. Demoralization, after months of anguish, disabled heart and will so that he said again and again, 'I cannot dig, I cannot, I cannot.'

It was as if God had not only frozen that grave for probate but also inhibited the use of his hand.

*　　　*　　　*

Shaking a hopeless head, he said, 'I cannot dig. I just cannot.' Then only the other choice remained: death before the discovery. 'I planted him too deep. And in my own garden. All too clever once again. Too clever.'

Very well. There it was. But one must make a pretence of expecting to continue in life, and one had an ever-mounting death-bed desire to do good things for all before the end—to bring home presents as surprises for the family, to be frequent in gifts to Craikie for his church, to send wine to those whom parishioners reported sick and flowers to those in hospital—so Mark in January of the next year, urged on by Bronwen, bought two small 'luxury' flats which faced one another across a stairhead in a newly built block overlooking the Keys Memorial Park. He concluded the purchase early in January so that Jasper and Bronwen could dash about the two empty flats as happy owners before Jasper went back to school.

Since he went back to school a few days before Bronwen, she insisted on being driven to Benfield with him. Mark was going to drive him there. Not in the old Rolls, which had gone to its knacker's yard at last, but in a glistening new Mark 2 Jaguar, which was the pride of Jasper's eyes. Unlike the Rolls with its suit of solemn black the 'Jag' was silver-grey without and red-upholstered within. It had a bench seat in front, at Bronwen's bidding, so that she and Jasper could both sit there while Uncle Mark drove. The buying of this bright and moderately expensive car had been yet another way of suggesting to the world that there was no thought of death in Mark's mind; that death, if it came, was an accident.

There was a reason stronger than ever today why he should want to be Jasper's driver to school and to be with him till his last free moment. Three months had gone since the Council accepted the Two Centuries plan, and it was more than probable that before another three had gone, and Jasper was home again, the demolition would be over, the builders about to dig, and the time have come to die. If so, then 'look thy last' on Jasper. Difficult to hold his thought, but there it was, an incredible choking thing in mind and heart. A blinding thing. How hide it in a cloak of merriment?

'Get in, Jasper, old boy. Everything aboard? That silly and

215

unnecessary tuck box? Get in then. Oh but, Miss Bronwen, your pardon. Ladies first, Jasper.'

'Gosh, isn't it rather fab?' said Bronwen, clambering on to the bench seat so as to be next to darling Uncle Mark, the driver. 'I wish I was going to a boarding school.'

'She must be mad,' said Jasper, getting in next to her.

'Instead of a rotten old girls' high school,' continued Bronwen, settling herself comfortably. 'Still, can't be helped. There it is. Who'd be a woman?'

'But, Marcus, they'll hamper you, won't they?' asked Belle from the pavement. The four of them had been having a farewell luncheon in Mark's house. 'Is it safe with them there? Don't have an accident, please. With all three of you killed I should be alone. I think, on the whole, I should miss you all.'

'No difficulty, Belle dear. They're just a couple of skinny kids.'

'*I'm* not skinny,' Bronwen objected. 'I've got bosoms.' These were recent, and she was proud of them.

'Well, don't forget, children. And don't talk to the man at the wheel.'

'Oh, hell! I feel I'm going to talk a lot,' said Bronwen.

'They'll be all right with me, Belle. Say good-bye to your Auntie Belle, Jasper.'

'Oh yes, Auntie. 'Bye.'

'Good-bye, darling Jasper. Have a good term.'

'If there is such a thing,' said Jasper.

'And say good-bye to Mrs. Pelly.' For Mrs. Pelly was now on the pavement, having come up from the kitchen with a post-luncheon dishcloth in her hand.

'Good-bye, Pelly.'

'Good-bye, Master Jasper.'

Bronwen said, 'Good-bye, Muzz' and ''Bye, Pelly,' though she would be back in town that evening.

'Are we ready?' asked Mark.

'Yes, all aboard and the cargo well and truly laid,' replied Jasper, who, like his father, was masking with merriment his sad recoil from an inexorable fate. It was a sadness less wholly heart-sinking than Mark's, but sufficiently heavy on a boy's heart.

'Good.' Mark switched on the ignition. 'Well, Jasper, look your last on 21 Mornington Gardens. The odds are she'll be down when you come back. A poor ghostly memory and no more.'

'Oh lord, yes. I'd absolutely forgotten that. Ta-ta, Number Twenty-One.' He waved his hand to the house but didn't look at it a second time.

'She's not been a bad old friend,' said Mark, a little disappointed by this casual good-bye. 'She's given you quite a good time for fifteen years. Well, never mind. Let's go.'

' 'Bye, Auntie. 'Bye, Pelly.'

' 'Bye, Muzz,' called Bronwen again; and Jasper with another wave, said, 'Yes, 'Bye, Mrs. Mayoress. 'Bye, Pelly. Be good girls, both of you.'

And so off and round the corner into Menworthy Rise. Not fast, because Mark wanted to suggest, as they passed the garden wall, 'Better say good-bye to the Tree of Heaven. She's probably coming down too.' And there it stood, a tree bared of all leaf and with outstretched skeleton fingers turning upward in a hopeless begging towards the winter sky; all its long arms transformed into the bones of witches. Behind its black skeleton shape, and beneath the clean blue January sky, a mauve light lay caught among the emptiness of these far-reaching back-garden trees. Doomed, most of them, it was doubtful if many would put forth one green leaf again.

'Oh, but they couldn't be such clods as to pull that down, could they?' Jasper protested, glancing up at the ailanthus.

'I imagine they're certain to.'

'The unspeakable oaves!' This was all he said by way of farewell to the tree, for his thoughts were really elsewhere. 'I tell you what, Daddy. When you deliver me at the gates of the reformatory, don't drive off at once but talk to me for a bit through the car window. I want the chaps to see the Jag.'

'Some of their fathers have probably got much finer cars.'

'Some, perhaps, but I doubt if any of their buses are quite as young and beautiful as Olivia. You must admit she's quite a girl.' Olivia was Jasper's name for the car. He had wanted at first to call it Alphonse, but Bronwen had insisted 'All cars are she's like ships,' forgetting that the old Rolls, Percy, had been a gentleman, and this had led them on to a further argument

217

as to whether male or female jaguar was the fiercer animal. Jasper, proud of his sex, declared that of course it was the male, but when Bronwen admitted, 'The female jaguar may be a little smaller, but that doesn't stop her being the fiercest,' Jasper accepted this composition of the dispute and, observing with inhuman relish, 'Well, whether male or female, a jaguar is one hell of a man-eater,' was content to give a lady's name to this new member of the family and a creature so beautiful. 'A jaguar's just about the most ferocious animal in the world,' he explained to Bronwen with appreciation, thus concluding the argument with a point that would be satisfying to both.

The Jaguar went out of London by the Great West Road, and when it was clear of the major traffic, and open fields appeared on either side, Jasper began to urge his father, 'Make her go at her fiercest speed. Go on, Daddy. Get her up to a hundred. She'll do it, I know. Olivia's as fast a little girl as they make them.'

'Now behave yourself, Jasper.' Mark was acting a like jollity though his heart could barely contain the love he was feeling for this fresh youthful creature, brim-charged with the energies, vivacities, and absurdities of fifteen, who was his son, sprung from him and from Lorelei. Might he not be driving towards a last sight of him? Who wanted to drive quickly? 'I'm certainly not going at a hundred or even seventy. Your Auntie Belle said we were not to have an accident. She's quite fond of Bronwen and would miss her.'

'Well, I hope you'd miss me too,' said Jasper.

'My dear boy, I shouldn't be there. Your plan, as I understand it, is that we should all perish together.'

'Would you miss Jasper as much as Muzz would miss me?' asked Bronwen, introducing a nice point which interested her more than this question of a crash and some slaughter.

'I dare say I should miss him a little.'

'Don't you miss him when he's away at school?'

'Now and then, perhaps.'

'Well, look, Daddy, I'll willingly stay at home if you feel like that. I'll sacrifice myself and give up school for your sake.'

'No, it's for parents to do all the self-sacrificing. That's what they're for, and not much else.'

'But look: what about a private tutor? Say for a couple of hours each morning. That'd do. I'd learn twice as much.'

Difficult for Mark in such an hour to sustain the family facetiousness, and he could say only, 'No, it'll be good for you to have Benfield behind you when you go up to Cambridge.' (When I shall not be there. When I shall be *what* in your mind?) 'And in the shockingly unfair arrangements of society at present, it could be of some help to you all through life.'

'Cambridge is going to win the Boat Race,' Bronwen informed them, having heard that loved name. 'Oh, I'm so glad I'm Cambridge. I was Oxford till Muzz said you were Cambridge, when I promptly changed over.'

'Turncoat,' Jasper scoffed, and quoted, '"Oxford upstairs eating all the cake, Cambridge downstairs, got a stomach ache."'

'Really, Jasper,' Mark rebuked. 'I thought you got over all that sort of thing at your prep school.'

'No, he's still astonishingly immature,' said Bronwen, who had learned from Jasper that pleasure was to be found in the display of impressive adult words. 'And, at any rate, he's Cambridge really,' she added, so that Mark should not worry.

'I'm relieved,' said Mark.

Bronwen began to sing. Often in the holidays, when he had a free day, Mark had driven the two children to a riding school near Guildford, where he had put them on ponies and himself on a big grey, after which they had turned south and ridden all day through the bosky and sun-dappled, fern-fringed glades of the Lower Greensand Hills. They would emerge from the bracken or the trees on to those fine open promontories, Holmbury Hill, Ersley Head, and Leith Hill, and there, astride their horses, they would look across the far-spread tilth and islanded woods of a silent and dreaming Weald towards a long shadowy roll under the sky, which was the South Downs. In the car, driving down to these 'special treats', the three of them had established, for it was a long way and they had started early in the morning, a custom of singing in hilarious unison a series of comic songs. They were songs that Mark had taught them. One (for their moral instruction) was 'I'm a man that's done wrong to my parents.'

I once wronged my father and mother,
  Till they turned me out from their door
To beg, starve or die, in the gutter to lie,
  And ne'er enter their portals no more.

I'm a man that's done wrong to my parents,
  And daily I wanders about
To earn a small mite, for my lodging at night,
  Gawd 'elp me, for now I'm cast out.

Another was a brutal ditty from his childhood in which each
verse told of a man who'd fallen from the top of St. Paul's
Cathedral, or walked absent-mindedly under a brewer's dray,
or otherwise died unexpectedly, and the choruses ran, 'I don't
suppose he'll do it again for months and months and months.
In all the time I've known him he's only done it once, And I
don't suppose he'll do it again for munce and munce and
munce.'

In loyalty to this memory, and in her present boisterous
spirits, Bronwen started a song up now. The January day was
clean and lucent and bright, a pale but lively sun was on the
fields, and on the cheeks of the hills, and she felt like singing.
The others, though less untroubled than she, could not break
an honourable custom, so they joined in, and the silver-grey
car drove on through the pleasant winter landscape with the
three inside it singing, 'In all the time I've known him he's only
done it once, And I don't suppose he'll do it again for munce
and munce and munce,' Jasper loudly, Mark gently.

But all too soon they were among the flat fields and slanted
hills that meant the approaches to Benfield; and Jasper went
quiet; Mark too, who had slowed the car's speed, compelled
to do so by the hardly bearable pain. The last of Jasper? In
minutes now? But one could not stop; one could do nothing
but drive on. Drive on ... and there now was the towered red
pile of the school in its spacious green playing fields. Cars stood
in line ahead at the school's main entrance and parents and
boys were walking up its steps and under the great arched
doorway.

'Well, there's the old place,' said Jasper. 'Isn't it pretty?

'Same old windows. Same old stink. I can smell it from here. Why don't they pull that down instead of our nice house? Won't we turn round and go home again?'

'You must try to be happy there,' said Mark. 'It's everybody's experience that things get better and better as you get older and older and higher up the school.'

'Oh, I'm not saying that the place is undiluted hell. Not at all. It's just that I prefer Twenty-one Mornington Gardens.'

'Well, you've *had* that,' Bronwen reminded him.

'I know. It's already but a ghostly memory.' Often he reproduced his father's words exactly.

'But you'll have a marvellous flat to come back to, Jassy.' Though only fourteen Bronwen was already able to change from a nonsensical and ruthless child into a soft feminine creature, ready to console and minister. 'It'll be Easter then, and we'll have most awful fun. Won't we, Uncle Mark?'

'We will.'

'Perhaps we could go riding again. The woods are an absolute knock-out in the spring. Will you take us riding again, Uncle?'

'I might.'

'Okay,' said Jasper, pocketing this present heavy account and settling for the hopes of spring. 'Drive the tumbril in. Are you coming to see Old Fish-face, Dad?'

'Old Fish-face being . . . ?'

'It's what the chaps now call the Head.'

'Certainly I'm not coming in to see Old Fish-face,' said Mark, thinking that of all possible nicknames 'Old Fish-face' was the least suitable for the young, friendly, smiling headmaster in the neat grey suit.

'Oh, let's go in and see him,' Bronwen begged. 'I want to know what he's like. I bet he's ten times nicer than our Miss Seymour. She's the outside sticky limit.'

'No one's going in to see anyone,' said Mark firmly. And he stopped the car before the doors.

A porter in a green apron came down the steps. 'You have the young gentleman's luggage with you, sir?'

'Yes, a trunk and a tuck box and a few sundries. In the boot.'

'"Young gentleman",' whispered Bronwen, entertained by this description of Jasper.

'I'll get out and open up the boot,' said Jasper sorrowfully in part, but also pleased that passing boys should see whose Jaguar this was.

'That's right, old boy. You go and help.'

The porter, having the great skills of his profession, carried trunk, tuck box, overcoat, hockey stick and football boots, all with two hands only, into the school.

Jasper returned to the car.

'Perhaps I'll walk with him a little way,' said Mark and, struggling past Bronwen's knees, got out of the car to stand on the drive with Jasper.

'No, you needn't trouble, Daddy. I know my way all right.'

'Very well. . . .' Mark put out his hand for the good-bye. He was thinking of that first time when Jasper, forlorn in a first parting, had kissed him in the empty street almost passionately, tears in his eyes. Mark had guessed then that this would be the last kiss from Jasper, ending a childish epoch. There could be no such thing now with Jasper fifteen. And tall schoolfellows passing by.

'Good-bye, Jasper, old boy. Soon be holidays again.'

'Yes, I know. Good-bye, Dad. Good-bye, old Bronwen.'

' 'Bye, Jassy. All the best. Nice flat to come back to.'

With a firm shake of their hands father and son parted, and Jasper went up the steps to disappear through that arch into the school's dusky maw. And that, thought Mark, was that. That was his poor famished parting with Jasper. How make more of it, with Bronwen watching and waiting? A single sigh and he returned to his driving seat. But he could not immediately start up the engine and drive away. He just sat there, staring through the windscreen. That boy, still so like Lorelei, even at fifteen. Ever see him again? His left hand rested on his knee, sometimes drumming there with its fingers. Bronwen, detecting the sadness at once, and having now so much of the woman in her, laid her hand on the top of his to comfort him.

But soon there must be a leave-taking of Bronwen too. Oh, well . . . let in the clutch at last and drive home.

They moved to the new flats in February, not without sadness

222

since no one leaves an old home without the lingering backward look. And now their two tall homes stood empty, condemned, and moribund. Soon the whole of Mornington Gardens, all its households gone, was one long grey and lifeless road, only the weeds alive and free to flourish extravagantly. As always, the work of demolition was postponed and postponed, so that the grass and the weeds, invaded by half the wasteland plants of London, rose higher and higher in the deserted gardens. In one garden they stood high and thick above an unsuspected grave.

Away from her old unmanageable home, Belle rejoiced in her modern flat with its floors of hardwood blocks or thermo-plastic tiles, its built-in cupboards and stainless steel sink, its electric cooker and washing-machine, and its serving-hatch to the meals room.

Mark, getting ready to die, drew consolation from her pleasure and Bronwen's excited delight. He pretended to a similar pleasure in his own new home. But often when alone, he quietly went from it, shut the door, and walked the half-mile to Mornington Gardens. There, walking at a slow pace, he looked up at the two old homes whose familiar windows were now grey with murk and dust, and as sightless as dead men's eyes. Their stucco dressings had begun to flake and fall. Mischief-laden stones had shattered the windows of Bronwen's and Jasper's bedrooms, these higher panes being the popular target-area for local sportsmen.

Sadly he turned the corner into Menworthy Rise and looked over the garden wall at the brushwood wilderness within. Some of the trees were losing their bareness. Belle's great copper beech was putting forth a purple haze as its buds broke. A sprinkle of green buds appeared on the sycamore, but the ash and the ailanthus were still monotones of dark cindery grey, their branches pencilled against a pale-paper sky. The earth under the weeds looked soft and rich again. Surely he could have dug while the earth was still soft. Or could he? Would not the risks have been far too great even then? Anyway, not now. His chance, if ever it had existed, was gone; the garden was his no more; it belonged to the weeds. Already among the weeds the purple deadnettle was branching upward, and tough-rooted dandelions were stubbornly holding their own with the lank and huddling grasses. Perhaps because the fine forest trees had now been deserted by men, and the gardens were going back to the waste, a chaffinch somewhere was sounding ever and again its glad defiant call.

21. The Demolition

An early April day and the boards were up. At last. In one of his covert walks through a warm spring evening, back to the old homes, Mark saw them. Two great blue boards on poles, one in front of the twin houses, the other above the garden wall in Menworthy Rise.

DEMOLITION
BEARDMORE LTD
Isl. 70992

Nothing as yet was happening behind those blue boards, but they ravaged and wasted his sleep that night. He tossed from side to side, impatient for the following evening when Arthur would come to the flat on party business and could be probed with apparently casual questions. Had not Arthur been a foreman builder?

Next evening Arthur's massive shape was set comfortably in an easy-chair before him—not Angelo's chair because Mark had bought new and smaller furniture for his new and smaller study in this flat, and that haunted chair, that dead man's fauteuil, had gone travelling away to a warehouse from which it would one day find its place in some cheaper home whose people would see nothing strange about it—or within it.

In a light and easy manner Mark said, 'By the way, Arthur,

I see the demolition boys are in at 21 and 23 Mornington, or at least they've put their boards up. How long will it take them to pull that little lot down?'

'Depends who the contractors are,' said Arthur, pleased to be an expert whom laymen consulted. 'We're only a small firm but we generally put our demolition work out with Cole's Demolition and Excavation, Ltd. A good crowd in Isleworth.'

'*Excavation?* What excavation?'

'Oh, that's just their name. I don't see what excavation would be wanted with your houses. The basements perhaps.'

'But what about the foundations for the new houses?'

'That's the builders' pigeon. Who's doing the demolishing? Did you notice?'

'Yes, I think I did. . . . "Beardwood" . . . ? "Beardmore" . . . ?'

"Oh, Beardmore's; they're another good Isleworth crowd. It's a big and thickly built block, yours. I'd say they'd have it down in five weeks . . . six . . . ?"

'What about—what about the trees? I'm told the ash and the ailanthus'll have to be thrown.'

'The developers'll hand that over to some Tree Felling and Land Clearing Contractors.'

'Land Clearing? Clearing what?'

'All the underbrush. There's generally a forest of weeds about seven feet high.'

'But the roots? Do they clear the roots?'

'Roots? I don't know for sure. I think they grub up the tap-root of a tree. Not much more.'

'But the roots that branch away from the tap-root?'

'I guess they axe them away at their base and leave 'em there. "Axed at source", so to speak, ha, ha, ha, like some of your best dividends, dear boy.'

Axed at source. So far, good. But five weeks. Five weeks would be soon after the Borough election in May. If the Labour Party retained control of the Council, as was almost certain, they might just have time, a couple of weeks later, to re-elect him as Mayor before the builders began to dig.

Arthur went on talking of such party matters while Mark was wondering what sort of death could be contrived which a

226

coroner would interpret as Misadventure. Within the next five weeks . . . or six.

But as before, as always, or so it seemed, the boards stood there for days, staring out into the silence of dead streets, and the work of demolition did not begin. Jasper came home again for Easter, and he was gone again for his summer term, before there was any movement of men behind those boards. This time, Bronwen being at school, and Mark unable to bear that sad ride to Benfield, he said his good-bye on the platform at Waterloo, and watched the long train curve away with Jasper waving. For some time after it was out of sight he stood looking the way it had gone. The last time? The last view? An end . . . ?

Wearied at length by fruitless visits to the silent condemned houses, he did not walk back to them, or drive past them, for some days. Then one afternoon, when he had no operation list and could come home after his consultations in Queen Anne Street, he drove slowly up Menworthy Rise to see if the dismantling had begun—and he saw that nearly all the south wall of his house was down. So quick? From roof to basement the fragmented rooms gaped at the open air. They were like the exposed rooms of Bronwen's doll's-house. There, exposed to sun and weather and the eyes of all wayfarers, was the large guest chamber to which Desiderata had first come; its big cupboard and its wash-basin were still up there on either side of the mantel but there was little approach to them because the floor-boards were gone from the joists, and the joists were gone too. On the wallpaper over the mantel was a square darker patch where the picture of the Piazza del Campidoglio had hung. The wallpaper drooped in dog-ears beside it. Above was his own bedroom—or rather two broken walls of it—where she had died beneath him, and he had dressed her body for the street.

Standing against the sky where the roof was off, balanced on a broken wall with a sheer brick face (and eternity) below him, was a grinning negro dutifully hacking away from under him, as it appeared, his stance in this world. It looked as if, did he sway, he would have only the sky to hang on to. But he grinned up there, swinging his mattock.

Mark stopped the car where he always used to stop it, under

227

the spread of the Tree of Heaven. Getting out, he looked over the garden wall. Hills and valleys of brick rubble covered much of the garden, and the dust from the falling brickwork clouded and drifted about the air. This powdery dust, he noticed, lay nearly an inch thick on the pavement so that he disturbed it as he walked. Quickly too this dust of his home dried on his lips and his palate as he watched. In the midst of the garden a piled bonfire of splintered and useless wood—floor-boards, skirtings, dadoes, overmantels—crackled and roared and flamed high. It made an honourable pyre only a yard or so from Angelo's grave, its blue smoke slanting doubtfully towards heaven. The strong scent of burning wood built old Christmas days for him, with Belle and the children about the fire and the Yule log and its kindling wood, well ablaze, filling the room with a resinous fragrance like incense in a church.

Walking round to the front of the house, he was halted by a new notice nailed beneath the 'Demolition' board. WARNING, it said in big red letters. 'The police have been instructed to prosecute any persons trespassing or removing materials from this site.' An even harsher notice was roughly chalked on an improvised board nailed to the garden gate: NO ENTRY. KEEP OUT. AND THAT GOES FOR YOU.

He instantly trespassed. He instantly entered. He walked by the tradesmen's narrow entry at the side of the house into the garden. Here a little red-faced man in gum boots, jeans and a torn brown cardigan, presumably the foreman, was shouting angrily and bossily at another negro labourer, who stood on a dizzy brink of the drawing-room wall with a sledge-hammer resting at his side like a walking-stick. The foreman heard steps and turned an astonished face towards a trespasser. Truculence sat on his dust-coated underlip and gleamed in his small eyes under the white-dusted eyebrows.

''Ere! What the hell, guv? What do you want?'

'Just to see what's going on.'

'Blast it, can't you read?'

'I can read. Yes.'

'Well, ain't there a notice up saying trespassers'll be prosecuted?'

'There is.'

'And didn't you see another one saying "Keep out"?'

'I did. In chalk. On the gate-post.'

'Okay then: what the hell?'

Mark declined to explain what-the-hell. Because the man was truculent and aggressive, especially with the negroes, he had a mind to humble him. He said nothing but continued looking up at the house, as if uninterested in the man's questions.

'You read them notices?'

'I read them.'

'Well, would you mind 'opping it, guv? There's no admittance 'ere except on business.'

'So I see.'

'Well then, would you blasted well—'

'Look, young man: the Borough Council happens to be the Development Authority for this work, and I am its Mayor.'

'Eh?' The man looked almost as shattered as the rooms above him; he gaped as they did. He looked as unseated as any of the walls and in the same danger of a tumble. 'Mayor? Go on! Mayor?'

'Yes, and what is more strange, this house used to be mine. So too was the house next—'

But, as he spoke, the whole side-wall of Jasper's high bedroom tilted, leaned over, became horizontal, disclosing a white labourer at work there, and with a roar avalanched down to the strewn ground, sending up a cloud of dust like the smoke of an explosion. Jasper's wallpaper and comic pictures pasted on it were now exposed to the world. The dust slowly settled, some on Mark's closed lips which he brushed with his handkerchief.

'So too was the house next door, or rather the other half of this block.'

'Go on! I never! ... Oh, well, sir, 'ow was I to know any of that? But you see, guv, these 'ere walls are a bleedin'—are a bit dangerous when they come tumbling down, so we don't care for strangers walking about. Half a brick wall on your head could be painful. Especially if them Victorians built it about five bricks thick. See what I mean?'

'I see well what you mean. Your warning notices are perfectly in order, but they might be more courteously expressed. I may suggest as much to your employers. As Mayor, I don't like my citizens treated impolitely.'

'No one wants to be impolite to no one, guv'nor.'

'I'm not so sure of that. Some crude people obviously enjoy it. But there's no point in hurting people. Those poor coloured gentlemen up there, for instance.' At any time he would have felt driven to say this but never with more assurance of its truth than now on the eve of death and of being done with the world.

The man looked sullen and did not answer, so Mark turned to something else. 'How long is this job going to take?'

'I'd say a tidy time. Look at the thickness of them walls. The Victorians built to last. They didn't reckon on us coming and pulling them down after only a 'undred years or so.'

'What happens to all these mountains of rubble? You clear them away, I suppose?'

'That's right. There's rather too much for a rock-garden.' He was becoming more cheerful. 'We might roll some of it in.'

'What's that?' A small piercing stab of hope. 'Roll it in?'

'Yepp. Depends on what the site's being used for. Might roll it in to make a hard core for a ground-floor.'

'The site's going to be used for smallish houses.'

'Then it depends where they're putting the 'ouses. We must leave the folks a bit of garden. They say builders are bad gardeners, but I reckon we demolition boys are a dam-sight worse.'

Mark nodded. 'Well, I'll allow you've made a fair old mess of my garden.'

'Sorry, sir.'

And with this dim jesting, and a couple of unfinished smiles, they parted, the incipient quarrel forgone.

It was days before Mark came by the house again at an hour when men would be at work. But at last, on one of his easier days, he came slowly in his car up Menworthy Rise at about two in the afternoon—and now there were no houses there. Or he could see no hint of them beyond the untouched garden wall. Only the trees were in place with nothing but the open air behind them. Down! Was this then the hour to die? Come upon him days before he expected it? He stopped the car—and observed an excitement in the Rise. There were voices and heads of men in the garden. Pedestrians, standing on the opposite pavement, were staring towards the garden. A long green lorry, with two youths fussing around it, waited on the exact place where his own car usually stood. Tools rested against the brick wall: spades, shovels, and an axe with a long curving haft like an executioner's.

Spades?

Had the men found it?

It was then that, looking upward as the eyes of some watchers did, he saw a man among the higher branches of his Tree of Heaven. He was sitting within the sharp angle of bole and stout branch, astride the branch. A power-saw moaned in his hand as it cut through the base of this long out-flung limb. Blue smoke rose from the saw's petrol engine, and the sawdust sprayed outward like water from a can's rose or spluttered like sparks from a dry-wood fire. From a strong joint above and behind the man a rope hung down so that he could get a noose on the neck of the branch before it fell. It hung like the waiting rope of a gallows.

However, these things at least told Mark that the watchers' interest was directed at the throwing of a great tree, and probably at this alone. Glancing again at the long green lorry, he saw on its side, 'Crown Tree Fellers; Harrow', and noticed for the first time the red danger flags hanging from its cab and its tail-board. A flow of relief eased through his veins.

Though why those spades against the wall?

Moving his car to park it round the corner, he saw that between the lorry and the wall, long leafy branches of the tree lay on the pavement—just where Desiderata had lain—and that the two young men were chopping them into portable lengths for loading on the lorry. To help them the man in the tree was casting the smaller branches out on to the pavement rather than down into the garden. When his power-saw was almost through the big stout branch on which he sat, he got hold of the rope belayed above and noosed it round the branch's end. Immediately one of the boys, never more happy in a task, ran on to the crown of the road and lifted a warning palm like a policeman's to stop any cars behind and—in his joy—to wave Mark's on. Mark did not at first obey.

The man in the tree lowered the sawn branch as far as the garden wall, and here the other boy caught it and, drawing it outward, deposited it carefully, almost gently, on the pavement by the wall. Where Mark had once gently laid a woman, cast out from his home.

To watch this he was keeping the car still, and now a good-looking, well-dressed young man, with fair curly hair and pleasant eyes, came to his window and said, 'I should move a little farther away, sir, really. Just a little. We are never quite sure how these long branches may fall.'

It was said so courteously that Mark answered at once, 'Of course I will. Thank you for telling me.' But wondering who and what this young man could be, for he was no more than twenty-one or twenty-two, and his voice suggested, more than anything else, a graduate just down from the university, he asked, 'You're not telling me you're the foreman, are you? You're much too young.'

'Oh no, sir. I'm just a learner. I'm what you might call, I suppose, the son of the firm. Actually, I'm only just down from Cambridge.'

'I rather guessed that. Well, you followed *me* down, but after forty years interval. This was my garden that you're messing about in, and that was my best-loved tree. May I be allowed to come in and watch it die?'

'Why, certainly, sir. *Your* garden? Are you then the Mayor?'

'At the moment, yes. But I may be uprooted and thrown into the street after the elections in May, rather like those logs of yours. But how did you know this?'

'Someone told my father. I think it was your Superintendent of Trees. He said to the old man—to my father—"Just you do a good and humane job on that tree because it was the Mayor's and he loves it." We're not a local firm of course—we come from Harrow—but we knew all about you from other sources —the papers and all.'

The papers and all. What would this attractive boy be reading in the papers soon? Tomorrow perhaps. And this was a young stranger's respect and even admiration which one would like to have held, since one was ever a fool.

'Very flattering. To be known even in Harrow! How long's this job going to take you?'

'Well, when we've got all the branches lopped off, we generally say one and a half to two minutes for every inch of the bole's diameter, if it's a big tree like this.' As a learner, he was proud of his new knowledge. 'That looks like another half-hour, doesn't it?'

'Only another half-hour. Then, if I may, I'll stay and see the end.'

'Of course you may, sir. It may take a shade longer because this isn't the best time for felling—with the leaves on the branches and the sap in the tree.'

'You mean you're killing my tree while it's alive and conscious?'

The boy laughed. 'Afraid so, sir. Something like that.'

'Sheer murder. One of the grandest trees in all our borough. After the limbs are amputated, you throw the torso into the garden? Is that it?'

'Not quite, sir. In a narrow garden like this, we'll have to saw through the bole again and again till there's only about fifteen feet standing.'

'And it's the fifteen feet that falls?'

'That's about it, sir.'

'In what direction?'

'Across the garden. Not near this wall in case it falls crooked and damages it. Besides, we shall pull on it with a rope so the boys'll need room to move.'

'I must certainly stay and see this . . . with your permission.'

'Certainly, sir. Delighted to have you.'

Taking the car round into Mornington Gardens, he saw a board propped against the old Victorian lamp-post at the corner. DANGER. TREE FELLING IN PROGRESS. YOU HAVE BEEN WARNED. A sudden terror greeted him as he entered the garden for he now saw what had been hidden by wall and ash tree: a huge 'Caterpillar Traxcavator' with a long iron neck and a wide-grinning sharp-toothed maw, like some giant armoured reptile from the Mesozoic age, gouging up rubble and emptying it into a square hollow that had been Pelly and Capes's basement. Taking no notice of the tree-fellers, it waddled and swayed over rubble-mounds like a tank at war. Some comfort succeeded the terror as he saw that it had already mouthed up rubble from the rest of the garden, and the long scrape of its pointed teeth had not gone deep. But ... was the moment getting nearer?

The young man now asked the traxcavator's driver to stop as the tree would soon fall, which the man was well pleased to do so that he could sit in his cab and watch. Mark was thus able to stand on a low mound of detritus, which, as he could recognize from fragments, had been part of his study, and watch too.

He watched the man in the tree saw through the main bole at four- or five-foot intervals and lower the sawn logs to the ground till at last only the naked, decapitated fifteen-foot was standing—a rough-barked obelisk or phallic symbol rising from the ruins of a home. The man came down from the tree, and the youths, called in from the road, tossed the heavy logs over the wall towards the lorry. And now all was ready for throwing the last of the tree.

First the youths with their felling axes trimmed away a root-buttress from the base; then with bow saws they cut a V-shaped 'mouth' in the base on the side the tree must fall. Next they sawed on the opposite side from this mouth at a point a little above it; as they sawed they put in wedges behind the saw. The trunk strained and creaked; it leaned an inch. Since it seemed ready to come, they ran to the rope which was attached near the top of the fifteen-foot pillar and standing there, just beyond Angelo's grave, waited their moment to pull. A wordless signal from the man, and they strained on the rope in tug-of-war fashion. The high stump of a once-splendid tree creaked again, stammered a guttural protest, and, with a loud, angry, cracking report fell mightily towards Angelo's grave.

The pleasant young man turned towards Mark with a smile. 'There you are, sir,' he said, proud of good workmanship.

Mark gave him an answering smile. 'Good. As a surgeon

I recognize a nice piece of surgery. What now? What do you do now?'

And as he said 'What now?' the hand of terror closed round his heart again. What now? What would they do with that stump rising a foot or more above the ground? It must be cleared away before the builders came to dig foundations. And the far-stretching roots. What would they do about them? See. One youth from the pavement was handing the spades and picks over the wall to the other on the garden side. To dig down and grub out the stump? How wide would they dig? Would they grub up some of the long roots? What had Arthur said? 'I guess they grub out the tap-root and only axe away the branching roots and leave them.'

But if not? If he was wrong? If these men had instructions, or if it was their custom, to dig out the main roots, was he about to witness the . . . the Uncovering? Should he run at once from this place? Was he already too late with his death? What could happen now—what would they say—if they came upon —*it*?

He could not speak. He could not even mumble again to the young man, 'What now?' God forbid that he should remind them that the travelling roots of a Tree of Heaven travelled far. Nor could he move. He must stay there and see. Did the worst happen, he must—the moment must give him words and deeds.

The youths began to dig a crater round the stump. They dug deep. Two foot and more. When their pit was nearly three feet deep, they stopped, threw aside their spades, and stretched out hands for axes. He did not move to look closer but had little doubt that they were axing away the branching roots.

Oh, God be praised: they were now using both axes and saws and soon they came erect and blew out long breaths like men who had laboured hard. They laboured again and came erect again, one wiping sweat from his forehead. More such work and then with a pole, with spades, with mattocks, with their hands, the three of them, the two youths and the man, levered out a truncated and limbless butt and rolled it away towards the garden's gate. Much tumbling soil and coarse rootage had come up with it, but nothing else. It was too far from anything else. Leaving the butt, the young men—to Mark's racking relief

—shovelled back the up-thrown spoil into the large rough hole and levelled it off neatly.

'There you are, sir,' said the son of the firm again. 'A slight depression, perhaps, but you'd hardly guess there'd once been a great seventy-foot tree there, would you?'

'No. Is that all you do?'

'That's all *we* do, sir, apart from getting the logs and the cord-wood away.'

'But surely there are long roots you haven't touched?' Safe to put this question now.

'Oh, it's up to the builders to do whatever they fancy with them, sir. We can't go chasing roots all over the garden.'

'I see. Well, thank you very much for an interesting and instructive entertainment. But I grieve for my poor tree which had years and years to live.'

With that courtesy to all on which he prided himself he nodded to each of them in turn as he said, 'Thank you' and 'Thank you', before walking away.

22. The Last Deceit but One

The Council assembles. Assembles for its Statutory Meeting after the borough elections. In their strength the parties are identical with those that assembled three years before to elect Mark as a Labour mayor. With but two exceptions the councillors are the same; the only differences in the councillors are the memories they have brought into the Chamber of increased or lessened majorities. After chattering in groups and then glancing at the clock they go to the same seats as they've occupied for the last three years. Soon all are seated, and only the aldermanic bench on the dais and the Mayor's throne are empty.

The scene is almost a replica of that three years ago. Bronwen is in the front row of the public gallery with the faithful Pelly and Capes—at her instigation—on her either side. Only Jasper is not there, being far away in Benfield school.

A minute to the half-hour, and silence stills the room—the silence of people waiting. The doors open and, as the robed aldermen proceed to their places, the Chamber rises to greet them. All remain standing for the Mayor's procession. Mace-bearer and Town Clerk bring him in. The Mayor? But the mayor they bring in is not Mark. It is the Deputy Mayor, Councillor Strood. In this gap between the old council and a new Mark is still mayor until a new mayor is elected at this Statutory Meeting; then how comes it that he is sitting, in ordinary civilian suit, unrobed, by the side of Belle against the wall?

It is because he is not officially in the Chamber at all. If officially in the room he must preside, but he cannot preside over his own election. He cannot sit as judge in his own cause. So, by a fiction, not sitting in a councillor's seat, he is technically absent and invisible except as a memory. Nevertheless as Mayor and Mayor-designate, he can look up at the throne and know that he will be occupying it in less than a half-hour.

And he knows that never in this Chamber's history, and certainly never on that throne, has a mind held such thoughts as his now. Soon they will robe him in scarlet and lace and gold chain, and he will know, as they are robing him, that probably no man in history has been vested by his friends in a falsity so total, so unimagined, so bewildering. Only this very evening, one hour before the Council assembled, he has taken a quiet walk to his devastated garden, and by a last irony of God, seen the builders' site-hut or office already erected there. Furtively, like a trespasser, he has walked in the evening quiet of dead houses and emptied streets, across the waste of his own garden to that hut and tried its door. Locked. But through its window, on a sloping desk-top beneath the window, he has seen the builders' plans. The foundation plans. This suggests that they may start digging tomorrow—or if not tomorrow, a Friday, then on the first day of next week. Thus his part in this present crowded scene, and in the picturesque installation to come, is surely his last great deceit in the world of men. One goes on with it all as if one were free of the smallest fear. Within hours of exposure?

Or the last deceit but one. The final deceit will be the staging of a death that can never with certainty be pronounced a suicide. 'I shall record that the cause of death was unexplainable.' 'I shall record a verdict of Misadventure.' He has decided, after hours of thought, wandering about rooms, sitting or standing like a statue, lying in a sleepless bed, what the stratagem shall be. Might it have to be performed tomorrow?

Meanwhile no one in the Chamber, no councillor, alderman, or borough officer, neither Clerk nor Deputy Mayor, neither the people in the gallery nor Belle at his side, can know or imagine these thoughts.

The Deputy Mayor is speaking. 'Our first business, as you

know, is to elect a mayor for the ensuing year. May I have a nomination or nominations, please?'

Councillor Lammas. He rises, big and square as a bull, one finger in a waistcoat pocket which throws back his jacket and exposes an unbuttoned purple cardigan, little suited to this stately occasion. In tones that suggest there's nothing remarkable in nominating a mayor for a fourth term he begins, 'I would like to nominate Councillor Dolmen—'

'Go on! Not really?' interrupts one of the Tory wags, Councillor Mant, an elderly man with a very long nose and a wide mouth beneath it, well adapted to a wide grin. The Tories, aware of what is foreordained and powerless to do anything about it, are in a mood to treat it with good humour. Their laughter applauds this interruption.

Councillor Lammas, never quite ready in his first few minutes to deal powerfully (if crudely and like a steam-roller) with witty interrupters, merely looks at the wag and proceeds, 'Councillor Dolmen, as you all know, has been our Mayor for three years—'

'Yes, we'd observed that.' A second Tory, anxious to be witty like Councillor Mant.

And 'Yes, yes; we've certainly noticed that, ha, ha,' from Mr. Evans the Echo.

Arthur, still not equipped with his really pulverizing disciplines for such as were using their rapiers to scratch him, can manage only, 'Mr. Deputy Mayor, may I ask the protection of the Chair so that I can continue my remarks without interruptions from the defeated and discredited party opposite?'

The Deputy Mayor, a small and neatly shaped little man with a trimmed moustache and goatee beard surmounted by lively eyes, responds to this with a tight little smile and one sharp little knock of his gavel on his desk. Whether this knock implies a rebuke to the interrupter or a genial reprimand to everybody, no one can be sure. The interrupter himself, Councillor Haynes, a grey, wan but would-be humorous man, with grey hairs on the brink of his nose, only grins, while Arthur, choosing the former and happier alternative, proceeds, 'Thank you, Mr. Deputy Mayor. Under your protection, and in such conditions only, I will continue. Mark Dolmen has now served the borough as councillor for more than twenty years and as mayor for three, and I defy the gentlemen opposite to deny that he has not only conducted our meetings in this Chamber with fairness and courtesy to all, but that outside these walls too, he has never spared himself in labouring for the good of the borough. And not as mayor only: it will be within your knowledge, sir, that long before, as well as during, his mayoralties, he has worked for the welfare of our people in numberless ways—as chairman of the Council of Social Service, as our representative on the Children's Committee, on the Greater London Playing Fields Association and on the Keys Old People's Homes—continuous and devoted work, you perceive, for our people at all periods of their lives—'

'Yes, I agree with that.' Softly Councillor Evans has again given voice. 'I accept that.'

'Only recently, Mr. Deputy Mayor, he gave us a remarkable example of his readiness to sacrifice himself for the good of us all when he allowed his life-long home to be demolished before all the others in Mornington Gardens because he knew he could find another home more easily than his poorer neighbours.'

This draws murmurs of approval from every corner of the Chamber.

'Then there has been, from first to last, his interest in the borough's cultural life; his sure support at all times for our musical, literary, and artistic societies. And let me remind you that this public-spirited work has not been done without a considerable financial cost to himself—but I will not expand on this because Mark is a modest man and would not wish me to do so. I shall mention in a whisper only, trusting he will not hear—since officially he is nowhere in the room—that he has made many charitable benefactions to Keys, of which, maybe, you have never heard, because he is not a man to let his right hand know what his left is doing.'

'True enough, yes.' Evans from the distance. 'Yes, I agree with that.'

As they speak, the subject of this eulogy, his mind so dulled and numbed as to be almost empty of feeling, sits thinking, 'Only I know that this is probably an obituary. Composed a few hours or a few days too soon. And a most inappropriate one that will need some difficult reconstruction. But go on, Arthur. Pile on the praises—for the last time. . . .'

And Arthur goes on, 'I'm well aware that it's not the custom of the party opposite to elect a mayor for a third and a fourth term but we on this side of the Chamber are proud of our first mayor and well content to keep him—'

But here Councillor Willet, one of the newer members, having a mind to get away from adulation and back to some fun, murmurs loud enough for all to hear, 'Perhaps you've no one else.'

Councillor Lammas is much readier now to deal with him. He looks at the grinning interrupter, and while still fixing him with his eyes, says, 'We have plenty of others, cock, and don't you doubt it. I'd make quite a good mayor myself, and so would any of these chaps sitting by me, but we all know a better man than ourselves when we see one. I could give you a list of chaps who'd make mayors as good as, and probably much better than, any your party can provide, my old beauty.'

Instantly the tall heavy figure of Major Roper, leader of the Tories, is standing like an outraged father among his children. 'On a point of order, Mr. Mayor—or, dammit, Mr. *Deputy* Mayor! A point of order!'

The Deputy Mayor turns his eyes towards him. A signal to speak.

'Is it in order for the Councillor to refer to my friend, Mr. Councillor Willet, as an old beauty?'

The Deputy Mayor taps his gavel to silence laughter but does not disperse his own smile. He submits, 'I cannot think that the Councillor's remark was meant to be taken seriously. Councillor Willett is obviously not old'—a pause—'nor is he exactly—'

A roar of laughter drowns the rest, the loudest contribution coming from Councillor Willet.

The gavel taps again, and the Deputy Mayor, pleased with his little joke's success, recommends, 'Let us then consider that the words, since they are both manifestly absurd, were really spoken in affection.'

To which Arthur, not averse from sharing in the fun, subjoins, 'Well, I'm not so sure about the affection, Mr. Deputy Mayor,

241

but I am certainly willing to withdraw the words "old" and "beautiful" since you from your high place and your fine observation-point have pronounced them absurd. We were, I think, discussing the election of a mayor, and about that I have nothing more to say. I propose we elect Councillor Dolmen and, in view of his services in the past, I hope we elect him unanimously.'

Rising from Arthur's side, Councillor Brest, second-in-command of the Labour group, says only, 'There is little need for me to do more than formally second this nomination. There is, I am sure, no question among any of us that Councillor Dolmen is a man of sterling character. The single point I would wish to make by way of elaborating all that Mr. Lammas has said is to tell the Council what may surprise even some of its oldest members, namely that the number of official engagements, in Keys and outside it, which our Mayor did not hesitate to attend as our representative during his last year of office, easily exceeded three hundred. Nothing, surely, can better illustrate that strict unfailing conscientiousness of Councillor Dolmen to which my colleague has just paid tribute. I am more than happy to second.'

Now Major Roper is on his feet again. A smile moves under his small beaked nose and crisp grey military moustache. He stands in silence for a few seconds with his baggy suit hanging limply around him.

'Mr. Deputy Mayor . . .' He has begun with a slow heavy enunciation that might portend anything. 'We on our side of the Chamber, as you know, do not endorse, unless an emergency should warrant it, this new-fangled trick of re-electing a Mayor for a third or even a fourth term. Councillor Dolmen bats on this particular pitch quite well—I would even admit that he bats with distinction and grace—but if only for the sake of variety we would like to see someone else occasionally at the wicket—'

'Hear, hear. Yes, that's what I feel.' Evans the Echo.

'May I say, with all respect, that I should quite like to see Mr. Lammas himself on the mayoral throne. He—since we are being a little personal this evening—would obviously fill it very comfortably, and it might at least keep him quiet, so that we should be preserved from his more unparliamentary observations.

Councillor Lammas made mention of Mr. Willet's age and beauty, and you, sir, passed the remark as acceptable, so I feel justified in suggesting—but with truth for a change—that Councillor Dolmen has certainly been for all these years—I nearly said "for as long as we can remember"—a most handsome, imposing and impressive mayor to look at—'

'Yes. Oh, yes.' (Mr. Evans.) 'Agreed.'

'—but the best of us can weary of staring at the same fine flower for ever and ever. Even the poorest gardeners occasionally change the perennials in their herbaceous border. Having said this much, I am happy to announce that we on our side will not oppose this re-election or nominate anyone else. On the contrary we have decided to vote for him so that his election can be unanimous—'

'Hear, hear.' Mr. Evans enthusiastically supporting his leader.

'—unanimous, always supposing the Liberal Party in the Chamber will cast its vote with us. This we shall do as an acknowledgement that, while we differ profoundly in politics from—from our now permanent mayor—we are sensible of the fairness, the courtesy and indeed the charm with which he has conducted our meetings here, and the undoubted distinction which he has lent to our borough in mayoral duties farther afield—a distinction which he will presumably continue to lend them for the next three years. Thereafter, no doubt, a new election and a happy change in the borough's control will allow him an honourable and well-earned rest. I endorse all that Councillor Lammas said about his social and charitable activities. They have nothing to do with his politics, thank God. I will go farther, Mr. Mayor—Mr. Deputy Mayor, dammit— and admit with Councillor Lammas that our Mayor-designate has all the virtues except one. There is nothing wrong with him except, alas, his politics; and it seems to all of us over here a pity that a good man should go so wrong on that score. Fortunately a mayor, in a sense, can have no politics, so we shall be able to enjoy his presidency without reservations. With pleasure, Mr. Deputy Mayor, and as a tribute of gratitude for work well done, we are all decided to support this nomination.'

'Hear, hear's' from everywhere, carrying an extra one or

two from Councillor Evans. The more the voices, the more the echoes.

No need for any further speeches, or so the Council thinks, for the Liberal Party is always apt to be forgotten. But this resolute party, embodied in the person of George Colls, thinks differently. It—or he—rises amid a rumble of mock cheers and amused murmuring, so jovial is everyone this evening. He declares that 'the Liberal Party in the Council' fully agrees with all its opponents as to the admirable qualities of Councillor Dolmen and 'like the two other parties its vote will be unanimous'.

He resumes his seat to friendly if satirical cheers, and a muted 'Good, good,' from the echo.

The Deputy Mayor, after glancing round for other speakers and finding none, puts the nomination to the vote. Every right arm in the Chamber rises, some from the Labour benches shooting enthusiastically high, and the Town Clerk, hardly troubling to count them all, turns and speaks to the Deputy Mayor; who then says, 'There being no dissentients, I declare Councillor Dolmen duly elected Mayor of the Borough for the ensuing year.'

'Probably all ensuing years,' mutters one of the humorists.

So Mark for a fourth time, but thinking his thoughts of death within hours or days, goes from the Chamber with Deputy Mayor and Town Clerk. He leaves that fictitious chair by the wall—fictitious in two senses, one of which is beyond imagining by all who watch him. A few moments, and Mace-bearer and Town Clerk bring him back vested in the full regalia of scarlet and fur, lace jabot, gold chain, and the whitest of white gloves.

The last deceit but one. On the throne he makes his declaration of 'acceptance of office', signs it, and takes the Chair. Seated there, he delivers his speech of thanks in phrases well turned and sharpened and polished in his room and his bed last night. The graceful speech—his last?—even comprises more than one laughter-stirring jest to match the mood of the evening.

One must sustain the deceits to the end.

The meeting over, Bronwen waits on the stylobate steps of the Town Hall to be taken home with Mayor and Mayoress in the big chauffeur-driven, arms-bearing, mayoral car—a dignity which always delights her. When at last Mark emerges from the great doors she puts a congratulatory hand into his and asks, dragging him merrily towards the regal car, 'Isn't it rather terrific to have all those lovely things said about you? By everybody and in front of everybody? I was thinking all the time, Nobody'll ever really love *me* like that. Lucky old you.'

23. The Bridge

Monday. With a dumb, blind terror he drove towards his work in town along Menworthy Rise. Unable to keep away. And yes: the builders' hut was open; men were moving in the garden. He stopped the car, got out, and looked over the wall. The men were marking out with tapes the foundations, and one line— the sight of it was like a bullet that meant death—ran taut over the grave. So they would soon be digging there. Not today, oh God, or my plan must fail! Death will come too late. Give me till tonight. At least till tonight.

But that taut line was his order to die.

He got back into the car and sat driving it skilfully through the morning's traffic, while the one astounding thought went with him: in a dozen hours he would be dead. All the way through the West London traffic towards Queen Anne Street, he was thinking, 'Tonight. It must be tonight. Oh, they must not make the discovery today, or the police will be at my door before night and then, even though they will not arrest at first, I shall be unable to stage my act; I can still die but only in some way that will leave the coroner his answer. He will state simply, "I shall record that he died in such-and-such a way, and that he did kill himself."'

And there would be no doubts left in which Belle and Bronwen and Jasper could seek their refuge.

Tonight. Say eight hours from now and six o'clock. Capes

would not be in the flat because, half suspecting he'd act to-night, he had told her he would dine at a restaurant and she need not come. This would allow him to begin early, in an empty flat, and have the evening and a long night to make death certain.

His final plan had been with him for weeks now. When the two families moved into the new flats he had joked with Jasper that even though they were centrally heated he must have his old anthracite stove in his study 'because it was a friend of long years and almost one of the family'. He and Jasper had even given it an affectionate name. It was 'Bardolph' because its 'zeal burnt in its nose' and its face was 'like Lucifer's kitchen'. (Jasper had been 'doing' Shakespeare's *Henry IV* at the time of this naming.) Still 'honest and faithful' like Bardolph, it now stood in his new study, which was so much smaller than the lofty Victorian room in Mornington Gardens. Fortunately there had been cold days of late, and he'd had fair justification for saying that, now the central heating was 'off', he'd like to see the old familiar glow burning quietly in the friendly old stove. And there he'd had it burning for some days, ready—as a faithful friend—for its duty tonight. The stove was indeed old, and it would be easy to disjoin and displace its flue pipe so that fumes escaped into the room. Having no smell, they could flow into a room unperceived, so that no one seated in the study 'need have noticed them'. Unnoticed, if the person had fallen asleep in a cosy chair, they could saturate his blood with oxide of carbon, and he could be suffocated and dead in as few as four hours. And for him tonight there could be twelve hours at least before anyone found him. So then. He would sit com-fortably and cross-legged in his easy-chair, and the evening paper would have dropped from his knees to the floor while his hands had fallen to his side. The angle-poise lamp would be directed to where the paper had been and be burning in the bright light of morning. So also the hanging light from the ceiling. On his desk would be closed letters to friends and patients, making plans for this week, next week, or later. (He had thought of a merry letter to Jasper speaking of plans for the summer holidays—but no, he would not drag Jasper into this.) It would all be painless enough: drowsiness, numbness, some heavy oppression but no sickness if he did not move, and the fainting at last, with the coal gas, heavier than air, mounting from the floor like an invisible tide and drowning him.

What man in the world could say with confidence that this had not been an accident?

In his will, made long ago, there was provision for gifts to club servants, to his secretary, to hospitals, to those charitable associations on which he had served—but not to Pelly and Capes. This worried him, as he drove, and he resolved on a letter to Belle, attached to the will but dated months ago and written on old discarded note-paper. In it he would say, 'This is not worth a codicil and witnesses, I just want you to give a hundred pounds each to Pelly and Capes with my love and thanks for their long friendship.'

So Mark was thinking as his grey car glided with the rest of a long serpent, town-bound, out of the Great West Road into Chiswick High Road. Soon the High Road ran straight for a full mile and he could see an endless stream of cars which probably stretched for another three and four miles to Kensington, Knightsbridge and Piccadilly. Behind him no doubt was another mile-long trail of city-bound cars. And in all this winding trail he alone sat driving with a master's careless ease, and with the thought that tomorrow he would be nothing. Mayor of Keys, surgeon of good repute, preacher of some local fame, lover of Jasper and Bronwen—and tomorrow: nothing.

But would one perhaps find Lorelei again? If such things happened, would this one be granted him after a mortal sin? Or denied him as punishment? Would he perhaps see his dear old father again—the bad old man—who, he was certain, would understand, forgive, and welcome him. 'Marco Polo. . . .' Or were all these things, whether peace and love at the last or punishment, an illusion of poor longing fools?

Here he was at the corner of Kensington Church Street, and he swung into it so as to come at the Bayswater Road and thence to his own Queen Anne Street. The next few hours must be a last round of kindly duties and careful deceits. Only a few brief hours. He had but one operation at two o'clock, and by the early afternoon he could be back at Keys and learn how widely the builders had dug. Oh, let them not reach the place today. Give him a day and a night. A race was begun between death and discovery. Death must win.

This last round he performed with a skill no actor could have surpassed. The need provided the skill.

In his consulting room he advised his patients one after another with uncurtailed thoroughness and much gentle encouragement; not seldom, if suitable, with jokes and laughter. Shaking hands with them as they went out, he sometimes laid an encouraging palm on their shoulders. A final hour he gave to his secretary, Muriel Lynns, dictating letters that made appointments in the future. For days past he had been secretly diminishing his supply of embossed note-paper and payment-request sheets so that he could say to her today, 'You'd better order some more paper, dear, and, while you are about it, some more of these polite requests for payment. It's only by these that I can live.'

At one o'clock he drove to his club so as to be seen lunching there in good spirits. He ate a fair meal with more appetite than he had expected. He had supposed he'd have to force food down as part of the deceit, but in fact he felt hungry. Did this make more credible the stories of condemned men eating a good breakfast on the morning of their execution? All through the meal, sitting at the long centre table, he talked amusingly with members beside him or opposite him. Opposite him was Pete Linden, the Q.C., whom he had liked for years, and he persuaded him to take a cognac with him as they drank their coffee. Nothing unusual in this, and·Pete could not know that Mark was pleased to be standing him a good-bye drink.

To his surprise, but to his satisfaction, he suddenly saw at a private table, sitting as a guest of Bill Ardrey, professor of forensic medicine, none other than McLaurie, the coroner. There he sat, looking as long and cadaverous as ever, and as well dressed as ever, and conceding his host an infrequent smile or even an audible laugh, so far as he ever allowed himself this primitive practice. Profitable coincidence! He made a point of encountering McLaurie in the Morning Room. Who could believe that a man seen chatting and laughing with his local coroner was about to die by his own hand? Going down the steps of the club, he paused at the hall-porter's office and arranged with him for the reservation of a dining table for two on the Monday of next week; then went from him with an up-raised hand and a friendly 'Good day, Alfred.' The friendliness was sincere.

In the hospital he performed the operation with never more studied care. An easy one, there was no doubt of its success, and it was good to save a life on his last day.

So finished the last round. He drove the car slowly, through a golden afternoon, back to Keys; slowly because it was a drive towards death. Should he return by Menworthy Rise and see what the men were doing there now? No, because there was one thing he must do first. It was something he wanted to do well, and he didn't want to be distracted in it by the memory of builders digging near the place. He must gamble on them not getting near the place yet, and be able to give this Last Thing all his heart. After it he would go to the garden wall in Menworthy Rise.

This Last Thing was a last word to his silent, uncertain, experimental God. He drove the car to an indefinite station a little way beyond the gates of Craikie's church and left it there. Entry into the church was easy now because Mark himself had persuaded Craikie to leave it open on weekdays, promising, if anything should be stolen, to restore it. He pushed open the swinging west door and went into the wide enclosed silence. Three o'clock on a bright afternoon; the sun's rays slanted down through the coloured mosaics of the south windows, and the dust-motes floated and danced in them, transfigured as if in streams of many-hued vapour. But in its north aisles the church was twilit and cold, like some shadowed place into which one came suddenly, out of the sun. It smelt of its floating but un-transfigured dust.

He knelt in the last pew of all, the pew farthest back from that front place where he had so often sat in state as Mayor.

Was there a Listener for him here? He could only trust. 'They say it is a mortal sin, but is it always so, oh God? Even if it is, forgive it if you can. I see there is cowardice in it, and that it would be brave to admit all and take all, but how can I?

I cannot. I cannot. I have got myself into such a pit, oh God, that there's nothing to do but die. No other way. If I confess to casting her out into the street and to a premeditated murder, how can I look into Jasper's eyes? Or Bronwen's? Or Belle's? And what of the Council, the hospitals, this church—'

But stop! Had the door opened behind him? Was there someone standing there? A few feet behind him? Keep your face in your hands that no one may know who you are. Yes. A soft step. And a breathing heard easily in this silence. Someone waiting. He could feel eyes staring at his back. He guessed they identified him. Had something been found and he been traced here? Was all over? A halt, almost a long halt, and the steps turned away, even more softly: the church's swinging door whined. It swung to a close, and now there was no step or breath any more. He was alone in the church again.

Who? Who could have come like that, and slipped away like that, on recognizing him?

But leave it. Think only of the One in front; not of this stranger behind.

'They were terrible things that I did, oh my God, mad inconceivable things, but they seemed forced on me. By cowardice, I know—but what else was possible? Those steps which took Desiderata into the street were a coward's steps —but not cowardly only; they were not for my sake only, but for the boy's. If you could think on this and forgive them ... Oh God, forgive. . . . All the rest has followed from those first dreadful steps, but each time confession became more and more impossible; far beyond any powers of mine. . . .

'And now I must take this last step. I have to die because only so can the truth remain obscured; but could you not, oh God, accept this dying, not only as a coward's act, but as my sentence on myself and an attempt to save the others from a little of the punishment? The children are young, and have done nothing. Spare them as far as may be. I do not see how you can protect them from great pain, but with you all things are possible. There are those to whom I have tried to preach—I meant this as some small reparation—is it possible to protect them too? I do not see how; I am lost; but with you ... something may be possible. . . .'

No answer in the silent church; no clear sound of one in his thoughts. Trust only.

'Forgive me, oh God, for what I am about to do now. Spare, spare the others if you can, even if I am to be spared nothing. . . .'

He rose from his knees, nearly hopeless, but not wholly so; still desperately hoping. He took a last look at the chancel where he'd dared to officiate, and at the pulpit from which he had dared to preach. He remembered the words with which Craikie in that pulpit had ended his 'message of the wilderness' sermon: 'There is no happiness without love, try as you may to find it. And equally no love without happiness. The two march as equal partners, I think, side by side.' He remembered how he himself had once repeated those words to the people because they seemed simple and true. And he thought now, 'If only this death could be lifted from me, I'd try to live like that. I *have* tried a little, but it seems there's to be no more of it.'

He knelt down yet again and prayed for Craikie and this church. 'Save them all you can and help them after I have gone. How you can save and help them both I don't know, but with you all things are possible.' A beautiful, loved sentence, remembered from his reading of the lessons, came into mind, and he uttered it, for what it might be worth, if anything, to him now. 'When we pray towards this place, hear thou in heaven thy dwelling place, and when thou hearest, forgive.'

A shrug, a sigh, even a melancholy smile, and he came out of the church into the sunlight again.

And so to the last look at the garden. He drove very slowly, saying or thinking farewell to every familiar building or street.

In Mornington Gardens he stopped the car a hundred yards from Menworthy Rise. Several houses beyond his and Belle's were now demolished so that a great expanse of unfamiliar sky stretched down from the zenith to the undisturbed piers of the houses' front gates. Heart pulsing falsely, breath shortening, he walked towards the Rise, and all the way he was telling himself, 'I don't know. . . . I don't know yet. . . .' As he turned the corner of the Rise he was praying again, if 'Oh God . . . *God!*' was a prayer.

And so to the garden wall.

Here a temporary relief: they had dug as yet only a trench

parallel with the wall. Except at one or two points this trench was strangely shallow, but at these points it was all of five feet deep. Five feet. Possibly more. This stopped the heart.

No men were digging now. The ravaged and littered garden lay empty. But the sunlight poured into the site-hut, and he saw the men within it seated on sacks, boxes, and a bench, with mugs of tea in their hands. He saw also the sloping desk-top with the prints and drawings spread untidily over it, and thereupon an idea pounced out at him: perhaps one of those prints would show how deep—how deep—the foundations would go.

This thought sent him strolling through the open garden gate towards the hut, displaying casualness but actually with two fears shaking him, the one a fear of what he would learn, the other the old fear that had been his since childhood but was surely meaningless now: the fear of being an unwelcome nuisance and disliked.

Standing within the hut was as magnificent a figure as he had ever seen, a man of six foot five at least, with fine shoulders, strong features, and a bush of white hair more suited to an elderly professor than to a middle-aged builder in dusty blue dungarees. His handsome face had the clean pinkish tint often seen under hair prematurely white. Obviously this was the fore-man; inconceivable that any of these rougher men seated on sacks and boxes, or loafing against the wall, could give orders to such distinction. That feathery nimbus of white hair would have made him an outstanding foreman in any multitude.

They all looked with wonderment at this appearance in their doorway of a large city-dressed gentleman with a hanging gold eyeglass on his breast. They even looked at the appearance guiltily—perhaps because of their inertia at three o'clock in the afternoon and their mugs of tea. So Mark quickly provided his most uncensorious smile. 'No, don't get up. Don't let me spoil the party. I just happen to be the Mayor of Keys, and my Council is interested in what you are building here. But get on with your tea. I'm sure you've earned it.' He turned towards the white hair. 'You're the foreman, of course.'

'That's right, sir. Tim Wellbright. I—er—' Most inappro-priately and somewhat disappointingly this splendid foreman was obviously feeling as guilty as the others about those tea-mugs. Such height, such hair, should never feel ashamed. Nor, one felt, should they admit so easily to an undistinguished name like Tim. 'I—yuss—I've let the lads knock off for a quick cup because they missed their break earlier, see? They simply 'ad to complete a concreting job as far as the next joint, you see.'

That 'see' and the dropped aspirate were another disappointment coming from such facial splendour, though they came well enough from the dusty and worn dungarees. Mark didn't 'see', but to put them all at their ease he hastened on, 'It's a four-storey block you're building on this site, isn't it?'

'That's right, sir. On this 'ere corner site, yes.'

'I see you've started to dig. Is it for the foundations?'

'That's right, sir. Here's the engineer's drawing for the founds.' He pointed to a sheet spread out on the desk. 'Would you care to see it?'

The moment of terror. The moment of truth. 'Why, yes, that'd be interesting. I don't suppose I shall understand it.' He raised the quizzing glass to scan it, and after a while shook an uncomprehending head over these rectangles, these figures and dots and symbols, these captions such as 'Foundations to Columns 1 and 4', 'Bases to Columns 8 and 9.'

'No, I'm lost,' he said. 'Can't make head or tail of it.'

'It's the specialist drawing provided by the Reinforced Concrete Company, sir, from Muswell 'Ill.'

'So it may be. But it tells me nothing. Columns? You're not building a church, are you?'

'No, sir. It's like this 'ere, sir.' He took a pencil, and Mark learned once again, perhaps for the last time in his life, how needless it was to be nervous about worrying a specialist for information. No man in the world who didn't rejoice in being the expert for a while and your superior because of his technical knowledge. This specialist scratched with the pencil through his mane of white hair; then laid the point of the pencil on the drawing. 'This 'ere's to be a building where the loads are transmitted to the foundations through a framework of reinforced concrete, see?'

'No.'

'Well . . . like this 'ere . . . the 'ole building is really supported on columns; it's a framework of reinforced concrete with only screen walls between the columns.'

'Screen walls?'

'That's right. Walls that enclose the floor-space but don't support no load. 'Ere's the ground-plan.' With the pencil he drew a large square on the back of the print and at its corners, and at intervals along its outline, shaded in small squares. 'Them small squares are the columns, you see, and all the rest is just wall. Just plain wall.'

'Oh, I see. Yes, I see.' Almost unbearable the surge of hope. His eyes swung to the line of the square which must represent the back wall of the block. 'Is this the wall that goes across the garden?'

'That's right, sir.'

'And these squares are the columns?'

'That's right, sir.'

Not one of the columns was near the place. Oh, God, oh God, could it be? He hardly dared question again. 'I suppose . . . I suppose the intervening walls don't need foundations as deep as the columns. How deep?'

'Practically nothing, sir.'

'Yes, but how deep? I had a bet with a friend and he said foundations might go ten feet down. I said no more than three.'

''E didn't know what 'e was talking about, sir. There's generally a good bottom three foot down or less if it's undisturbed soil. Different over there where there's bin a basement. Got to go down to the old foundations there.'

The basement had no interest for Mark. 'Yes, but what . . . what are the foundations for this screen wall that crosses the garden?'

'Practically nothing at all, sir. Twelve inches, don't it say? Plenty for the span between the columns.'

Twelve inches! Only twelve inches?

'Twelve inches? Twelve inches only? Do you really mean that?'

The handsome man, smiling, jerked a thumb towards the specialist drawing. 'There it is, sir. That's what it says, don't it?'

'Well . . . I'd never have believed it. . . .' And this was all he

255

could utter, though it meant life instead of death. So incredible was it that he had to seek some flaw in it. 'But . . . look: if you come to a part where a flower-bed, or something has been dug —or perhaps someone has dug a deep hole—some child for fun —wouldn't you have to . . . to go deeper?'

'Oh, no.' The man said it cheerfully. 'If we find we're crossing a soft bit like that, we just bridge it.'

'*Bridge* it?'

'That's right, sir. Strengthen the concrete at that point and just bridge it.'

Mark stared, and because he could not speak for stupefying relief, the man explained further. 'Reinforce the concrete enough, and it'll take care of anything like that.'

'I see. . . . Yes, of course. . . .'

And this man before him, tapping the drawing with his pencil's chewed top, didn't know that his visitor in the fine city clothes was charged with such an ecstasy of relief as seemed to have completed a circle and become pain. 'Oh, God . . . God . . . have I to thank *you*?'

His urgent need now was to be out of the garden and alone. And yet, even with this seizure at his heart, he was able to enact for the men a smile and a parade of carelessness. 'Well, that's all most interesting. I seem to have won my bet.'

'I'd say you 'ave, sir. 'Ow much was your bet?'

'Not a large sum.' Mark evaded the question with a smile. 'I must be going now. Thank you all very much.'

'That's nothing, sir. Don't mention it. You said you was the Mayor, didn't you, sir?'

'That's right.' The Mayor, shaken, had fallen into the foreman's language.

'Well, I'll tell the guv'nor you come along. He'll be interested.'

'Not as interested as I have been, I'm sure. I do thank you all so much. Good-bye.'

'Bye-bye, sir.'

'Good-bye, sir.'

And a muffled voice adding, 'Ta, ta, guv'. Thank you for calling.'

Out into the street to be alone.

Home. Home to borough, family and good name.

As when one has lost something of value and then suddenly found it again, and all the torments of loss seem a price well paid for this joy in recovery, so it was now.

'Let him rest.' The voice of Chance—or of God? Had there really been a Listener to those dialogues with the Unknown? Had the Listener heard him, and after letting him be punished to the very lips of death, set him free? Who could know? Perhaps.

Anyhow the secret rests. The new Brides area has shut over it a monument of concrete, steel and brick.

'Oh God, I thank you *if . . . if . . .*'

Back to the car. The secret rests. Back to Jasper who may now keep his love for his father. To Bronwen who can still believe in her 'darling Uncle Mark'. And—yes—back to Pelly and Capes. To the borough who are already proposing to have his portrait painted—'First Labour Mayor'—and hung with others in the Assembly Hall; who have already decided that the tower block at the end of the old Mornington Gardens shall be called 'Dolmen Tower'. Back to his hospitals where he must try to do better work than ever, always making amends. Back to poor Craikie and his church which (whether or not God has been in this) he will serve now with a new humble gratitude, and not without a prayer at times for the dust beneath a screen wall. He must try to be worthy of what, possibly, has been done for him.

But who can ever know?

Such were his thoughts as he turned homeward that day— that shining, bewildering day when, as he would think in after years, the doors of a prison were flung wide to the sunlight within hours of Justice requiring death. He turned into his block of luxury flats, and when the lift deposited him on his third landing he saw, to his surprise, the door of Belle's flat, opposite his, wide open. And as he felt for his key, she came running out to him. His sister. Belle. Given back to him.

'Is that you, Marcus? I didn't know you were coming back this evening. You told Capes you were dining in town.'

'So I did, but things happened.'

'Where are you going to have dinner? Can't have dinner without Capes.'

'There are places in Keys.'

'Stuff and nonsense. You'll have dinner with us. Certainly you will.'

Bronwen rushing out from the living-room at the sound of voices. 'Is that my beloved uncle?'

'It's your beloved uncle,' Belle agreed, 'and he's just said he'd like to come to dinner with us—which is nice of him.'

'Oh, whacko. How gorgeous. He can help me with my filthy French.' Running forth, she put her hand in his after her fashion to lead him into her home. 'Can you come now? Yes, *do*.'

'Not immediately, my darling. In an hour's time, say. Keep the filthy French till then. I shall love to do it for you, though it'll be a most immoral proceeding.'

'Oh, never mind that. That doesn't matter. You'll do it in half no-time, and perhaps I'll admit to having had a wee bit of help.'

Belle laid a hand on his arm just below the shoulder. 'Come as soon as you can, my dear. We'll have it all nice for you.'

He nodded, with a smile.

Mark was never to know this, but the step behind him in the church had been Belle's. She had come for no other purpose than—after removing withered blooms from the altar—to kneel and pray for him as a sister should, so disquieted had she been of late by the long sadness which she detected in his face and bearing. She had been praying for him, during weeks past, at her bedside, and now she had the thought of bringing a lone prayer into the temple. But there he was—kneeling in the last pew of all, within feet of her, his face deep in his hands. What sister would fail to recognize a brother's clothes? Doubtless he was praying there because of the hidden pain. Not to disturb him, she crept out again, whispering her prayer, and when back at the flat, left her door open in order to hear him if he returned, as was likely, now that he was back in Keys. Hearing him, hurrying out to him, she was astonished, rejoiced, even as she spoke commonplaces about a dinner, to perceive a new, quite different look in his face, a serenity, a sad smile that was almost an exultation. Her eye suspected at once that things had happened to lay the mysterious sorrow to rest. Had her prayer then been answered, even though it had not been said in the church but only offered in the street? 'Oh God, help him,' was all she had managed to say, but again and again, 'Help him.' And no doubt, she thought, poor old Craikie's been saying prayers too. And now, look. 'Oh, let him be happy now with me and Bron. My poor dear Marcus with his secrets! What, oh what, has it all been about?'

Mark, for his part, had wandered into his empty flat and into his study where his stove burned with a friendly glow and need not be disturbed. Summer was here now, and he could let the fire die. Walking inevitably to the window, he stood there gazing out, not at an old garden laid waste, but at the formal trees and coloured flower-beds of the Keys Memorial Park, and the young summer asleep on the grass.

The small Borough of Keys is no more. It is merged now into the Greater London Borough of Hadleigh and Grayes, which has a population of a quarter of a million. Two years before the merger Mark at his own request ceased to be Mayor of Keys. He lapsed back into a local surgeon of considerable reputation but one who had never quite made the topmost heights of his profession. And his days went by. (How do we live with some of our memories? But we do.) Always a prominent figure in those streets which used to be the Borough of Keys, he was liked and admired by nearly all, though sometimes they might smile at his portly and familiar figure when it passed by with red carnation in button-hole, gold quizzer dangling, and perhaps his rolled umbrella on his shoulder like a gun. Often, with the gun still in position, he would feel moved to stop and share a moment's fun with children playing in the street. Usually they appreciated this attention and paid him with happy sauce and laughter. Hardly a grown man in the High Street with whom he had not shared talk and a joke during his many years as Mayor, and such a one he might greet with a jocular salute by lifting the umbrella above his head like a flag or lowering its outstretched point towards the pavement like a sword. In the view of most he was a kindly old gentleman who went about doing good in many walks of life, and if anything could be held against him, it was only a reputation for amiable eccentricities.